TARGET OF A LIFETIME

Fluckey moved in, maneuvering through escorts at very close range. Then he saw something in the darkness, the target of a lifetime:

> *Ye Gods, a flat top! This was the large pip about 300 yards to port and just ahead of the very large tanker in the starboard column. Range 4900 yards. Went ahead to close for a good shot.*

2328   *Working for an overlap. Undoubtedly the prettiest target I've ever seen.*

2331   *We have a perfect overlap of the tanker and the flat top.*

2332   *Commenced firing all bow tubes. Point of aim bow of tanker. Range 1820 yards. Torpedoes away. As soon as all fish fired went ahead emergency with full right rudder.*

2333   *Dived. Rigged for depth charge, going deep.*

2334-5   *Two hits in tanker. Three hits in carrier.*

2337   *Breaking up noises, heavy underwater explosions. One ship sank. Random depth charges started. Second ship sank.*

IN ONE FAMOUS SALVO—NOBODY HAD EVER DONE IT BEFORE—FLUCKEY HAD SUNK TWO SHIPS, UNYO, 20,000 TONS, THE CARRIER, AND AZUSA, 11,000 TONS, THE TANKER.

THE BANTAM WAR BOOK SERIES

This is a series of books about a world on fire.

These carefully chosen volumes cover the full dramatic sweep of World War II. Many are eyewitness accounts by the men who fought in this global conflict in which the future of the civilized world hung in balance. Fighter pilots, tank commanders and infantry commanders, among others, recount exploits of individual courage in the midst of the large-scale terrors of war. They present portraits of brave men and true stories of gallantry and cowardice in action, moving sagas of survival and tragedies of untimely death. Some of the stories are told from the enemy viewpoint to give the reader an immediate sense of the incredible life and death struggle of both sides of the battle.

Through these books we begin to discover what it was like to be there, a participant in an epic war for freedom.

Each of the books in the Bantam War Book series contains a dramatic color painting and illustrations specially commissioned for each title to give the reader a deeper understanding of the roles played by the men and machines of World War II.

COMBAT PATROL

ABRIDGED FROM SILENT VICTORY

by CLAY BLAIR, JR.

RL 10, IL 9-up

COMBAT PATROL
A Bantam Book | December 1978

Maps by Alan McKnight.
Drawings by Robert Blanchard.

The excerpts from Submarine! by Commander Edward L. Beach, U.S.N., are reprinted by permission of the publishers, Holt, Rinehart and Winston, Publishers.

The excerpts from the article "Unlucky in June: Hiyo Meets Trigger," by Commander Edward L. Beach, U.S.N., are reprinted by permission from Proceedings; copyright © 1957 U.S. Naval Institute.

The excerpts from War Fish by George Grider and Lydel Sims (copyright © 1958 by George Grider and Lydel Sims) are reprinted by permission of Little, Brown and Co.

The excerpts from The Codebreakers by David Kahn (copyright © 1967 by David Kahn) are reprinted by permission of Macmillan Publishing Co., Inc.

The excerpts from Sink 'Em All by Charles A. Lockwood are reprinted by permission of Mrs. Charles A. Lockwood.

The excerpts from Wake of the Wahoo by Forest J. Sterling (copyright © 1960 by the author) are reprinted with the permission of the publisher, Chilton Book Company, Radnor, Pa.

ISBN 0–553–12279–7

Published simultaneously in the United States and Canada

Bantam Books are published by Bantam Books, Inc. Its trademark, consisting of the words "Bantam Books" and the portrayal of a bantam, is Registered in U.S. Patent and Trademark Office and in other countries. Marca Registrada. Bantam Books, Inc., 666 Fifth Avenue, New York, New York 10019.

PRINTED IN THE UNITED STATES OF AMERICA

To the 3,506 U.S. submarines
still on patrol. Sail in peace.

Fleet submarine

In 1975, I published an exhaustive account of the U.S. submarine war against Japan: *Silent Victory*. What follows here are substantial excerpts of that volume, focusing on unusual or outstanding combat patrols and personalities, together with an occasional summary of results and progress.

CONTENTS

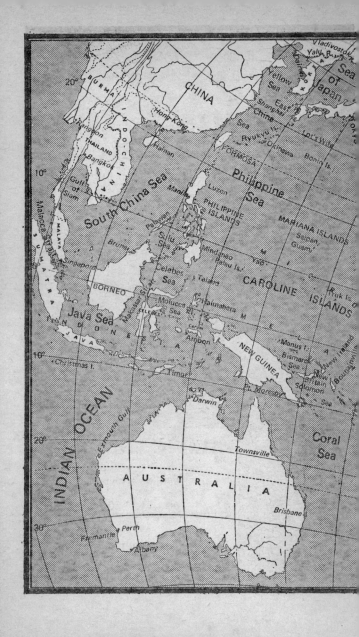

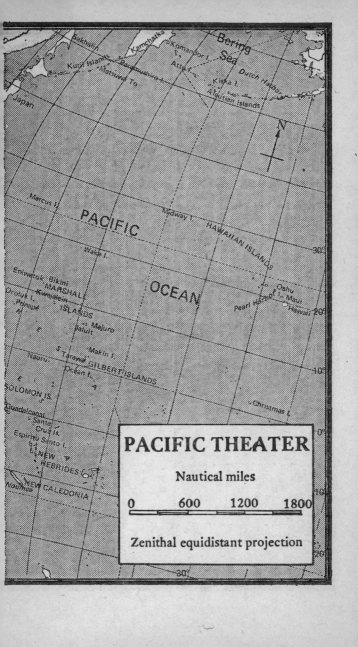

FOREWORD

During the naval conflict in the Pacific between the United States and Japan, 1941–1945, there was a little-known war-within-a-war: the U.S. submarine offensive against Japanese merchant shipping and naval forces. A mere handful of submariners, taking a small force of boats on 1,600-odd war patrols, sank more than 1,000 Japanese merchant ships and a significant portion of the Japanese navy, including one battleship, eight aircraft carriers, three heavy cruisers, and eight light cruisers.

A strong merchant marine was vital to the economy and warmaking potential of the island nation of Japan. Its ships imported oil, iron ore, coal, bauxite, rubber, and foodstuffs; they exported arms, ammunition, aircraft, and soldiers to reinforce captured possessions. When submarines succeeded in stopping this commerce, Japan was doomed.

After the United States recaptured Guam and Saipan in the summer of 1944, U.S. submarines basing from those two islands imposed a virtual blockade against Japan. Few ships entered or left Japanese waters without being attacked by submarine; most that attempted it were sunk. Japan ran out of oil for her navy; gasoline for her aircraft, trucks, and automobiles; steel, aluminum, and other metal for her industry; and food for her teeming population. After the war, when the full impact of the submarine blockade became known, many experts concluded that the invasions of the Palaus, the Philippines, Iwo Jima, and Okinawa, and the dropping of fire bombs and atomic bombs on Japanese cities, were unnecessary. They reasoned that despite the fanatical desire of some Japanese to hang on and fight to the last man, the subma-

rine blockade alone would have ultimately defeated that
suicidal impulse.

In the prosecution of the undersea war, the U.S. submarine force took a secret weapon into battle: from
1941 to 1945 U.S. Navy codebreakers "read the Japanese mail" with comparative ease. Because codebreakers
supplied the submarine force with precise information on
the sailing dates, course, speed, and routing of most
Japanese convoys and naval formations, U.S. submarine
force commanders could direct their boats to the proper
intercept positions to lie in wait for the oncoming enemy
forces. Although no precise accounting has ever been
made, the codebreakers assisted, directly or indirectly, in
the sinking of perhaps half of all Japanese vessels destroyed by U.S. submarines. The Japanese were unaware
of this weapon.

Even so, it was no easy victory. Before the attack on
Pearl Harbor, the United States had sworn in various
international treaties never to engage in "unrestricted
submarine warfare," that is, submarine surprise attacks
against merchant vessels. During peacetime years, U.S.
submariners who hoped to become part of the U.S. battle fleet mostly concentrated their training on tactics
aimed at sinking important enemy men-of-war–carriers,
battleships, cruisers—and their boats, known as fleet submarines, were designed with this goal in mind. After
December 7, 1941, however, the United States abandoned its high-minded moral position and ordered unrestricted submarine warfare against Japan. By an accident
of history, the fleet submarine proved to be the ideal
weapon for war against the Japanese merchant marine.
However, the shift in missions caught the submarine force
flat-footed. It required new strategy and tactics. Many
months went by before the submarine force got the hang
of this new role.

There were other problems. Peacetime exercises, most
of them unrealistic and artificial, had led submariners to
believe that aircraft, sonar gear, and powerful depth
charges made the submarine highly vulnerable to enemy
counterattack. This belief in turn had led to extreme caution in the submarine force. The best way to survive, the
peacetime submarine commanders believed, was to make
an attack from deep submergence, using sonar apparatus.

The daylight periscope attack, the night periscope attack, and the night surface attack were considered hazardous, and for a submarine to operate on the surface within 500 miles of an enemy air base was considered fatal. Too many months went by before submariners discovered these preconceptions to be wide of the mark.

The cautious peacetime training led to serious personnel problems in wartime. In peacetime bold, reckless, innovative skippers who were "caught" in war game maneuvers were reprimanded, and older, conservative, "by-the-book" officers, who were strict disciplinarians and conscientious with paperwork, rose to command. When war came, too many of these older men failed as skippers. During the first year and a half of the war, dozens had to be relieved for "lack of aggressiveness" (a disaster, both professionally and emotionally, for the men involved) and replaced by brash devil-may-care younger officers, some of whom would never have attained command in peacetime. This general changeover took months to accomplish, and many valuable opportunities were lost before it became effective.

The failure in leadership extended to the highest levels of the submarine force. When the war began, the forces were commanded by officers who had risen to the top by the safest and most cautious routes, who did not understand the potential of the submarine. They placed a premium on caution; bring the boat back. Yielding to higher authority, they allowed their forces to be fragmented and employed in marginal, fruitless diversions. At least a year and a half went by before these command problems were ironed out and men with a good grasp of how submarines could be most profitably employed took over the top jobs.

The product of codebreaking turned out to be a two-edged sword. On the one hand, it provided marvelous intelligence on enemy naval and merchant marine movements. On the other hand, its secret nature and glamour led submarine force commanders to divert far too many boats from the war against merchant shipping to pursue the dramatic "big kill" that would look good in the dispatches—Japanese battleships, carriers, and cruisers. Countless times, U.S. submarine captains were vectored to such targets only to find that, because of navigational

errors on the part of the Japanese or themselves, these
high-speed prizes passed just beyond attack range and
could not be overtaken. Months went by before it dawned
on the force commanders that a Japanese tanker—easier
to find and sink—was as valuable to the overall war effort as a light cruiser.

Last—but by no means least—the submarine force
was hobbled by defective torpedoes. Developed in peacetime but never realistically tested against targets, the U.S.
submarine torpedo was believed to be one of the most
lethal weapons in the history of naval warfare. It had
two exploders, a regular one that detonated it on contact
with the side of an enemy ship and a very secret "magnetic exploder" that would detonate it beneath the keel
of a ship without contact. After the war began, submariners discovered the hard way that the torpedo did not
run steadily at the depth set into its controls and often
went much deeper than designed, too deep for the magnetic
exploder to work. When this was corrected, they discovered that the magnetic exploder itself was defective under
certain circumstances, often detonating before the torpedo reached the target. And when the magnetic exploder
was deactivated, the contact exploder was found to be
faulty. Each of these flaws tended to conceal the others,
and it was not until September 1943, twenty-one months
after the attack on Pearl Harbor, that all the torpedo defects were corrected.

Had it not been for these command weaknesses, mis-
conceptions, and technical defects, the naval war in the
Pacific might have taken a far different course. Intelligently
employed, with a workable torpedo, submarines might
have entirely prevented the Japanese invasion of the Philippines and the Netherland East Indies. Skippers em-
boldened by swift and certain torpedo success, instead of
puzzled and dismayed by obvious torpedo failure, might
have inflicted crippling damage on the Japanese navy
much earlier. The war in the Pacific might have been
shortened by many, many months.

Clay Blair, Jr.
Malibu, California
1977

1

A PIONEERING BLOW

On the morning of December 7, 1941, there were a total of twenty-one submarines assigned to the U.S. Pacific Fleet in Pearl Harbor. They were commanded by Rear Admiral Thomas Withers. Six were older models, but the other fifteen were new—some still in shakedown status. Only four were actually berthed in Pearl Harbor when the Japanese attacked. The others were out on simulated war patrols at Midway and Wake Islands or in Hawaiian waters on training exercises, or en route to and from California. All twenty-one Pearl Harbor-based submarines survived the Japanese attack without any damage. Within a very few days, Admiral Withers ordered seven of the boats to conduct war patrols against the Japanese—three to the far distant Japanese home islands.

The first of the latter to leave Pearl Harbor was *Gudgeon*, commanded by Elton Watters ("Joe") Grenfell. Joe Grenfell represented the first offensive strike against Imperial Japan by the U.S. Navy in World War II. In terms of his background and training, he was typical of the average fleet boat skipper in December 1941. Thirty-eight years old, a lieutenant commander wearing two and a half stripes on his sleeve, he received 25 percent extra pay for serving in submarines. (Naval aviators earned 50 percent extra pay, and later in the war submariners also made 50 percent extra.)

Grenfell had graduated from the Naval Academy in 1926. During peacetime, selection to command of submarines (and other vessels) was usually made by "class year"; at a certain period, all members of a certain Naval

I

Academy class would (in the ordinary course of events) become eligible for command of an S-boat or a fleet boat, depending on seniority, and those qualified would move up to command more or less as a group. Of course, there were overlaps; it was not possible to work it as smoothly as the Bureau of Personnel might have wanted. In the year or so before the war, the classes of 1925, 1926, and 1927 had become eligible for command of fleet boats and moved up accordingly.

After a mandatory two-year service in surface ships, he had volunteered for the six-month Submarine School at New London in 1928. After an extra-long tour on *R–4*, he had attended postgraduate school, obtaining a master's degree in Mechanical Engineering, then served two years on *Pickerel* during her commissioning (formal acceptance as a fleet unit), shakedown cruise (a 4,000-mile trip to the Amazon River), and exercises with the fleet in 1938 and 1939. After a shore tour in Washington (Bureau of Ships), he had assumed command of *Gudgeon*, placing her in commission in April 1941.

As skipper of *Gudgeon*, Grenfell commanded a normal complement of four other Naval Academy graduates and fifty-five enlisted men—in all, a crew of about sixty. (In addition, on this cruise Grenfell carried two reserve officers for indoctrination purposes.) The second or executive officer was Hyland Benton ("Hap") Lyon, class of 1931. Usually the exec of a fleet boat was fully qualified for command, in case something happened to the skipper. As on surface ships, the exec played an important role in administration, being in charge of most paperwork, ordinary discipline, navigation, morale, and a hundred other day-to-day details. During attacks, he served as assistant approach officer. A good exec enabled his skipper to remain aloof from routine problems so that he could concentrate on the objective of the mission.

The other three regular officers on *Gudgeon* were Robert Edson ("Dusty") Dornin, class of 1935, Richard Marvin ("Dixie") Farrell, class of 1935, and Sigmund Albert Bobczynski, class of 1939. Dusty Dornin, a famous football player at Annapolis (many had entered the submarine service), was the fire control officer—the main torpedo data computer (TDC) operator. *Gudgeon* had not yet been in commission five months, but already Dornin, an extraordinarily able officer, had proved himself one of the best TDC operators in the submarine force. In practice, *Gudgeon* had "sunk" thirty-two out of thirty-three targets—a record. Dixie Farrell was the engineer and diving officer. Young Bobczynski, two and a half years out of the Academy, fresh from Submarine School, was "George"—the low man on the wardroom totem pole who took care of the commissary and other minor duties.

The fifty-five enlisted men, including half a dozen chief petty officers, were mostly experts, with long submarine experience. The chiefs on many submarines were quite old and conservative. Reported one submarine skipper, "The average age of my chiefs was up in the fifties, and I even retired my chief electrician during wartime at age sixty-five. I can assure you that at least half these chiefs had no other thought than that the war would soon be over and they would return home safely. They were extremely cautious and only interested in the most cautious operation of the submarine with the utmost safety." First and foremost among them was the senior chief, who was called "chief of the boat." An important man (comparable to an army top sergeant), the chief of the boat generally held sway over all enlisted men and dealt with many of their administrative problems. During battle stations, he usually stood watch at the diving vents. In addition to the chief of the boat, there was one yeoman (male secretary), one pharmacist's mate (inevitably "Doc"), and two black or Filipino stewards. The rest of the crew were torpedomen, machinists, electricians, quartermasters (who helped with navigation and kept the logbooks), cooks, gunner's mates, and seamen and firemen just starting out.

Most hands except Grenfell stood watches—four hours on, eight hours off. The off-watch officers usually had many duties to perform. They slept in staterooms in the forward battery compartment (usually two men to a stateroom). The chiefs slept in a more private space (in the aft end of the forward battery compartment) than the other enlisted men, who slept in a crowded bunk space in the after battery compartment or in bunks rigged over the torpedo storage spaces in the forward and after torpedo rooms. When off watch, the enlisted men worked on machinery or "routined" torpedoes. They sometimes gathered in the crew's mess and passed a few free hours playing poker, cribbage, or acey-deucey or listening to the radio. In keeping with navy tradition, all hands drank gallons of weak coffee and ate hearty, wholesome meals, but, to a man, the whole crew worked very hard indeed.

Withers had told Grenfell to proceed with extreme caution; there might be Japanese submarines all along his route. No one knew what surprises the Japanese might produce. They might have radar or an antisubmarine weapon unknown to the U.S. Navy. The skippers were told that when they were within 500 miles of an enemy air base they were to remain submerged in daytime. At night, they were to run on one engine to conserve fuel. They were to husband their torpedoes, using only one or two against a merchant ship. There was a critical shortage of submarine torpedoes at Pearl Harbor and no sign that the production facilities would soon catch up. "We can't shoot ourselves out of torpedoes," Withers had said.

All submarines had orders to maintain strict radio silence. If Withers had information or orders for his boats, he sent them messages over the nightly Fox schedules originating from Pearl Harbor. The submarine radio operators "guarded" (i.e., monitored) these broadcasts, watching for their own coded call sign. When it appeared in the long string of messages, they would copy it. The message would then be decoded by the communications officer or by other officers designated for this task. All messages were repeated three times. Very important messages were repeated on successive nights. Messages containing information derived from Japanese codebreaking began with the word "Ultra" for Ultra Secret. Only the captain was authorized to decode these messages. Messages were numbered serially. If an operator missed a message because he was submerged when it was transmitted or for other reasons, he had orders to "open up" (i.e., break radio silence) at the earliest opportunity and request that it be repeated.

It took Grenfell about twenty days to reach the vicinity of Japan. It was a slow, tedious, monotonous voyage, carried out cautiously, as Withers had ordered. One officer came down with pneumonia and kept to his bunk for twenty days, until he was pronounced fit. Eight hundred

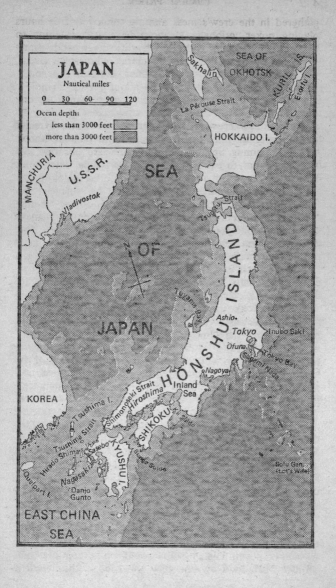

JAPAN

Nautical miles

```
0    30    60    90    120
```

Ocean depth:
 less than 3000 feet
 more than 3000 feet

MANCHURIA

U.S.S.R.

SEA OF OKHOTSK

Sakhalin

KURIL IS.

Erotfui

La Pérouse Strait

HOKKAIDO I.

Vladivostok

SEA

OF

Strait

Tsugaru

HONSHU ISLAND

JAPAN

Tuzama Bay

Ashio

Tokyo

Inubo Saki

Ofuna

Tokyo Bay

Demi Nida

KOREA

Nagoya

Tsushima I.

Shimonoseki Strait

Hiroshima

HONSHU

Inland

Sea

SHIKOKU

Tsushima Strait

Hirado Shima

Sasebo

KYUSHU

Bungo Suido

Nagasaki

Danjo Gunto

Queipart I.

EAST CHINA

SEA

Bofu Gan.
(Lot's Wife)

miles off the coast of Japan, running submerged, Grenfell saw a few fishing boats. At about 10 A.M. on December 31, he picked up his first real target: the mast tops of what looked like a freighter. Remaining submerged, Grenfell tried to overtake for twenty-five minutes but could not get closer than 14,000 yards—about 7 nautical miles. (A nautical mile is about 800 feet longer than a statute mile.)

Grenfell now proceeded with even more extreme caution. During daytime, he remained submerged at about 100 feet, coming up for periodic periscope observations but careful not to expose too much periscope. His sonar men listened carefully for the noise of other ships, especially enemy submarines. After dark, he surfaced to charge batteries. Four lookouts and the officer of the deck kept watch for enemy antisubmarine patrol planes. (They saw none.) Inside the hull, tension ran high. The experience was new and terrifying. "For the first time," recalled Grenfell later, "you realized that you could get killed. We were out there, all alone. Even a serious operational casualty, such as a battery fire, could land us in the hands of the Japanese."

There was another matter, somewhat delicate. In effect, Grenfell was breaking the London Submarine Agreement. Neither the United States nor Japan had publicly abrogated the rules of international warfare. If caught, Grenfell conceivably could be hanged as a pirate. To help him out in such an eventuality, he carried a paper signed by Withers, ordering him to wage unrestricted submarine warfare against Japan.

On January 2, after a voyage of twenty-one and a half days, Grenfell arrived on patrol station off Bungo Suido, the southern entrance to Japan's Inland Sea. He was astonished to find navigational beacons ashore burning brightly and sampans cruising with running lights. On the afternoon of January 4 he sighted a small coastal freighter, closed to 2,600 yards, and fired two torpedoes. Both missed. "It had been the almost perfect approach," Grenfell recalled later. "Dusty Dornin almost wept."

It had long been clear to Joe Grenfell and Dusty Dornin that even with the help of the TDC the firing of torpedoes at an enemy ship would be a complex and difficult business. Now that they had tried it, they knew it for certain. Once the enemy had been sighted, it was not easy to maneuver into proper position with *Gudgeon's* slow submerged speed. The enemy's range, speed, and "angle on the bow" (the relative bearing of the submarine to the enemy) all had to be estimated from quick periscope observations, during which time the skipper was also sweeping around the horizon, keeping an eye on enemy escorts and a sharp watch for aircraft. To obtain a fairly accurate range estimate, it was necessary to guess accurately the height of the mast of the target vessel, then extrapolate from the horizontal lines in the periscope cross hairs, using a slide rule or a device built in the periscope called a stadimeter.

In peacetime they had trained with high-speed fleet units, such as destroyers, with known masthead heights. Setting up on a slow-moving shallow-draft merchant ship whose masthead height could only be guessed at was a wholly different ball game. Where there were two or more ships involved, or ships were zigzagging, it was even more difficult. The skipper had to keep in his head at all times a picture of what was happening on the surface. The approach party had to guess the zigzag pattern, estimating when the zigs and zags would occur so the submarine did not set up in one place and then find itself far out in left field.

Then there was the question of torpedo "spreads"— how to space the firing of torpedoes to obtain hits. Under ideal circumstances, peacetime exercises had shown, it was best to fire three torpedoes: one forward of the bow, one at the middle of the target (MOT), and one astern. This spread compensated for errors in speed estimates or changes in target speed. If the target was moving faster than estimated, the torpedo fired forward of the bow would actually hit in the forward end of the ship, the MOT torpedo in the stern, with the torpedo aimed at the stern missing. If the target was moving slower than estimated, the one aimed forward of the bow would miss ahead, the MOT would hit in the bow, and the stern shot about the middle of the target. In sum: in a spread of three torpedoes, two would probably hit.

However, the orders from Withers had been not to fire three-torpedo spreads at merchant ships; one or two should suffice, he said. Grenfell and Dornin had to revise spread techniques, aiming torpedoes to hit. This, in turn, meant that the man on the periscope had to estimate with a high degree of accuracy not only the speed and range of the target but also its length.

All these observations, estimates, and calculations had to be carried out with efficiency and coolness under great stress. During the approach, the skipper had also to be thinking of his move immediately after firing, should an escort ship charge down the bubbles and vapor of the torpedo track. The diving officer in the control room had to maintain the boat in precise trim at periscope depth. An error could take the boat too deep to raise the periscope or bring it up so shallow that the periscope shears were exposed.

Although Grenfell had been positioned on what was thought to be the busiest sea lane in Japanese waters, five long days passed before he spotted another target. It was night, and *Gudgeon* was on the surface, charging batteries. Grenfell decided to remain there and make a night surface attack. From 2,500 yards, he fired three torpedoes. On the bridge, Grenfell felt the shock of an explosion. The sonarman reported a hit. Grenfell and Dornin were certain they had sunk a freighter of 5,000 tons.

Meanwhile, U.S. Navy codebreakers who had "lost" the Japanese code prior to Pearl Harbor, now regained it. They gave high priority to Japanese submarine traffic. This proved to be easier than it seemed at first glance. Japanese submariners were irresponsibly chatty, communicating almost daily to their commanders or home base, in a code that was not difficult to break. They were ordered about by the Japanese submarine commanders, with specific departure and arrival dates, speed of advance, tracks, and "noon positions" to be adhered to. Departing from an assigned area, the submarines often—and stupidly —lobbed a few shells from their deck guns into islands, positively revealing their positions.

A case in point was the three Japanese submarines patrolling off the west coast of the United States. On departure, they fired a few shells into a refinery near Los Angeles. On the night of January 25, the three submarines passed Midway Island, where they paused to fire a few shells. Alerted by this bon voyage gesture, the code-breakers plotted their great circle course from Midway to Kwajalein and determined their speed of advance, based on previous observation. It became clear that Joe Grenfell in *Gudgeon*, returning from Japan, was almost in their path. Soon a coded dispatch was on its way to Grenfell, ordering him to lie in wait for the Japanese submarines.

On January 27, Grenfell remained submerged exactly on the projected point of interception. At 9 A.M., Grenfell's exec, Hap Lyon, was manning the periscope. Sure enough, right on schedule, he spotted a Japanese submarine. "It was coming along, fat, dumb, and happy," Grenfell said later. "The boat was not even zigzagging. The men were lounging on the upper deck, sunbathing and smoking."

Grenfell went to battle stations and fired three torpedoes from the bow tubes. Upon the exit of this great weight forward, the diving officer momentarily lost control. He overcorrected and *Gudgeon* nosed down, dunking her periscope, leaving Grenfell blind. However, at eighty-one seconds, Grenfell thought he heard a dull explosion. When *Gudgeon* got back to periscope depth, there was no submarine in sight and no propeller sounds on sonar.

Had they hit it? Dusty Dornin and Dixie Farrell were doubtful. "I don't think the torpedoes exploded," Dornin said later. "What I think happened was they either saw the torpedo wakes or the torpedoes dudded against the side and they panicked and dived with the hatches open and flooded the boat." Grenfell did not report the submarine as sunk, merely "damaged."

The codebreakers knew otherwise. After that morning one of the three Japanese submarines, *I-173*, no longer came on the air to chat. It disappeared from radio traffic forever, proof that it was sunk.

I-173 was the first major Japanese man-of-war sunk in World War II (two midget subs had been sunk during the Pearl Harbor attack) and the first vessel to go down as a direct result of radio intelligence. For the remainder of the war, the codebreakers achieved a high degree of success in tracking the movements of Japanese submarines. The intelligence thus gained enabled naval commanders to route their forces around Japanese submarines and to make many kills. For this reason and others, the

Japanese submarine

Japanese submarine force was almost completely ineffectual.

One by one, the first seven boats returned from patrol to Pearl Harbor. In accordance with procedures developed by Withers in peacetime, the regular crews turned the boats over on docking to relief crews, who would make the necessary repairs while the regular crews rested. In the interim, Withers had rented the plush Royal Hawaiian Hotel on Waikiki Beach for a rest camp. Each crew rested two weeks.

On return from patrol, each skipper was required to turn in a patrol report containing a day-by-day log, recounting the highlights of the patrol and including special sections for detailed analyses of torpedo attacks, ship and aircraft contacts, matériel failures, and other data. These reports were forwarded in turn to the division commanders, the squadron commander, and Withers. The division and squadron commanders and Withers attached comments to the reports—called "endorsements," whether approving or condemning—summarizing the patrol and its results, with judgments about the way the patrol was conducted, particularly the attacks against enemy ships. The reports, together with the endorsements, were then reproduced and distributed to boats preparing for patrol, to higher headquarters, and to Washington. These endorsements became the principal policy-making documents for the submarine force.

The endorsements also contained a section dealing with damage inflicted on the enemy: ships sunk, ships damaged. These scores were arrived at after detailed personal interviews with the skipper and his senior officers and consultations with the codebreakers, who frequently had information from attacked Japanese vessels that reported the results by radio. But with all of this, the system was imperfect. Submarine skippers had a tendency to exaggerate the size or tonnage of the target and to claim sinkings that had not really occurred. After the war, when Japanese records could be consulted in detail, it was discovered that the submarine force had "confirmed" sinkings double the actuality. These first seven war patrols were typical. Seven sinkings in total were credited when in fact only four had occurred.

The first endorsements handed down by Withers and his staff came as an unpleasant surprise to many submariners, including Joe Grenfell. In some instances, they amounted to a complete reversal of peacetime training. Although Withers had instructed him to proceed at one-engine speed and submerge when within 500 miles of enemy airbases, he carped about the extreme length of time it took to reach station and return. "With efficient lookouts," Withers wrote in the endorsements to Joe Grenfell's report, "more surface cruising could have been done, reducing the terrific overhead in time, a great part of which should have been spent on station." Withers also criticized Grenfell for remaining submerged each day until 9 P.M., stating that *Gudgeon* should have surfaced immediately after dark. Grenfell was also rapped for being profligate with torpedoes. Grenfell had fired two torpedoes at the small freighter on January 4; Withers thought one would have been sufficient. On the January 9 attack on the 5,000-ton freighter, Grenfell had fired three torpedoes. This was "excessive," Withers wrote. "Until the supply of torpedoes is augmented, it is essential to conserve torpedoes for more appropriate targets."

Nonetheless, Withers awarded Joe Grenfell the Navy Cross for this pioneering war patrol. He was credited with sinking the submarine and a freighter. When Japanese records were consulted after the war, the freighter was disallowed. It had not sunk. But this is unimportant. What was important was that *Gudgeon*'s handful of valiant officers and men had struck a pioneering blow against the Japanese maritime forces. A mounting crescendo of blows would follow. It would take time, much time, before these blows would have a telling effect on the Japanese war effort, but in the end, they would prove decisive. Now, at least, the process had begun.

2

A DISMAL STORY

Eight hours after the attack on Pearl Harbor, the Japanese struck the Philippine Islands, the first step in a well-coordinated plan to conquer all of the Far East. By this time, the surface units of Admiral Thomas C. Hart's small Asiatic Fleet had withdrawn to southern waters for safety. The primary naval force remaining for the defense of the Philippines was a flotilla of twenty-nine submarines, commanded by Captain John Wilkes. Six of these were World War I vintage "S" boats, but the other twenty-three were modern fleet boats. One of the latter, *Sealion*, was lost in an early bombing attack; another, *Seadragon*, damaged in the same attack, was patched up and hastily sent south to Java for extended repairs. The remaining twenty-seven submarines were soon sent on war patrol, some to distant enemy bases, some on defensive patrols in Philippine waters.

The mission of the Manila-based submarine force was clearly defined: defend the Philippine Islands against the Japanese invasion that was certain to come. For a variety of reasons, including ineptness in the high command echelons, faint-heartedness on the part of too many sub skippers and torpedo malfunctions, the submarine force failed in its duty. The story is one of the most dismal in Naval annals.

By December 11, twenty-two of the surviving twenty-seven submarines had gone to sea. Since it seemed most likely that a Philippine invasion force would approach from Japanese bases to the west or northwest of Luzon —Formosa, the Pescadores, Indochina, or Hainan—thirteen boats were sent to western areas. Since Palau, lying to the eastward of Luzon, was also believed to be a heavily fortified Japanese base, five boats were sent to areas off the east coast of Luzon. The remaining four were stationed along the southern approaches to Luzon.

The five boats going eastward were *Seawolf, Sculpin, Skipjack, Tarpon,* and *S-39.* The four fleet boats went through San Bernardino Strait, then dispersed; *S-39* remained in or near the strait. All five ran into foul December weather on the east side of Luzon.

Tarpon, commanded by Lewis Wallace, was twice "pooped" (swamped by huge waves). She rolled violently and took heavy water down the conning tower hatch. The water rushed into the pump room, a compartment below the control room. Before Wallace got control of the boat, water was waist deep in the pump room and two feet deep in the control room. A great deal of the machinery was flooded out. After Wallace got the damage repaired, he sighted one fair-size Japanese ship sailing alone. He made a sonar approach. It was botched when a torpedoman, distracted by a leak, accidentally fired a torpedo.

Seawolf, commanded by Frederick Burdette Warder, thrashed around in heavy seas and then proceeded northward along the east coast of Luzon to Aparri, where the Japanese landed a small invasion force on December 10. Freddy Warder was a courageous and prepossessing officer, a salty-tongued fighter who was worshiped by his officers and crew. In the immediate prewar days, Warder had stood toe to toe with Admiral Hart in a dispute over one of his enlisted men, wrongly accused in a barroom scuffle. Warder had risked being relieved of command in order to right this wrong, and in the face of Warder's adamant stand Admiral Hart had backed down.

Arriving at Aparri, Warder found a destroyer guarding the mouth of the harbor. Warder eased *Seawolf* around the destroyer—which to his surprise was pinging—and proceeded boldly into the harbor. In brief and careful periscope observations, Warder found a Japanese seaplane tender at anchor. He set up and, from a range of 3,800 yards, fired four bow tubes—two torpedoes set to run at 40 feet, two set to run at 30 feet, so the torpedoes would pass under the keel and actuate the magnetic exploder.

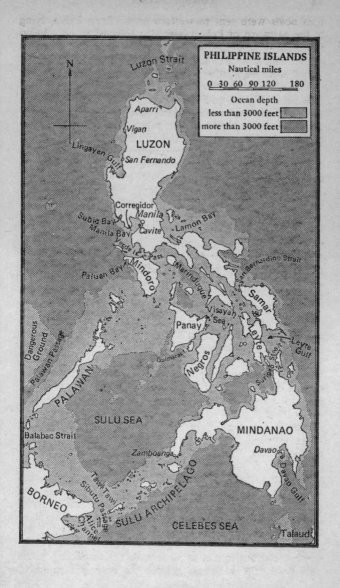

PHILIPPINE ISLANDS

Nautical miles

0 30 60 90 120   180

Ocean depth
less than 3000 feet
more than 3000 feet

N

Luzon Strait

Aparri

Vigan

LUZON

Lingayen Gulf

San Fernando

Corregidor

Manila

Subic Bay

Manila Bay

Cavite

Verde Is. Pass

Lamon Bay

Paluan Bay

Mindoro

Marinduque

San Bernardino Strait

Samar

Visayan Sea

Panay

Leyte

Leyte Gulf

Guimaras

Surigao Strait

Negros

Dangerous Ground

Palawan Passage

PALAWAN

SULU SEA

MINDANAO

Balabac Strait

Zamboanga

Davao

Davao Gulf

BORNEO

Tawi Tawi

Sibutu Passage

Alice Channel

SULU ARCHIPELAGO

CELEBES SEA

Talaud

Warder waited. There was no explosion. He had missed a fat target at anchor! Turning to run out of the harbor, Warder set up his four stern tubes, firing from a range of 4,500 yards. Watching through the periscope, Warder saw a plume of water near the waterline of the ship, but there was no explosion, no flame or smoke. If the torpedo hit, the exploder must have failed. Warder was furious. He had penetrated a harbor, fired eight precious torpedoes, achieved zero results. Following this, Warder received orders to round the northern tip of Luzon and proceed down the west coast of Luzon to Manila.

Sculpin, commanded by Lucius Henry Chappell, patrolled off Lamon Bay. The weather was foul, the visibility abysmal. When *Seawolf* was shifted from Aparri, *Sculpin* was directed to take her place. On December 21, Chappell headed northward, leaving Lamon Bay unguarded. Three days later, a large Japanese landing force from Palau steamed into Lamon Bay and put troops ashore. Chappell spotted a ship coming out of Aparri but was unable to get into position to fire. After *Tarpon* was swamped, Chappell requested permission to return south near Lamon Bay. He ran into such foul weather he was unable to attack Japanese shipping going in and out of the bay.

Skipjack, commanded by Charles Lawrence ("Larry") Freeman, proceeded eastward toward the Palaus. During the day, Freeman, following peacetime drills, ran submerged at 120 to 150 feet, maintaining a sonar watch. If the sonarman heard anything, Freeman came up to periscope depth for a look. On Christmas Day, Freeman's sonar picked up fast, heavy propeller beats, indicating a big ship. Freeman surfaced and ran in to 12,000 yards, where he saw his quarry was an aircraft carrier and a destroyer! This—the first time in the war that a U.S. submarine encountered a Japanese carrier—was for a submarine skipper a truly momentous occasion, as it would continue to be throughout the war.

Freeman submerged and began his approach by sonar from a depth of 100 feet. When the sonarman reported a range of 2,200 yards, Freeman fired three of his four bow tubes. (The fourth was out of commission.) After firing, Freeman went deep—to 230 feet—passing up an opportunity for a stern shot. All three torpedoes missed. In the postmortem on the attack, the sonar operator decided he had made a mistake on the range. It was not 2,200 yards but more like 3,000 or 3,500 yards. Freeman noted in his log, "It was not a very Merry Christmas after that."

The five boats going to the east of Luzon thus achieved zero results. Freeman missed an aircraft carrier, Warder missed a seaplane tender at anchor, Chappell missed the landings at Lamon Bay, Wallace almost lost *Tarpon* in heavy seas, and *S-39*, patrolling San Bernardino Strait, found no targets worthy of attack.

The four boats deployed to the south of Luzon were *Shark*, *S-37*, *S-38*, and *S-40*. *Shark*, commanded by Louis Shane, Jr., went down to the island of Marinduque and anchored in Santa Cruz Harbor. Shane induced the mayor to extinguish the navigation lights but did little else. After ten days of idleness, he was ordered to return to Manila. *S-37*, *S-38*, and *S-40* patrolled Verde Island Passage. On December 12, Wreford Goss ("Moon") Chapple, the much loved but not exceptionally bright officer commanding *S-38*, fired one torpedo at what he believed to be a Japanese ship off the northwest tip of Mindoro and claimed a sinking. However, no Japanese ships were in the area at that time. If Moon did, in fact, sink a ship, it must have been friendly.

On paper, the deployment of the thirteen fleet boats to the west appeared to be a classic solution to the problem confronting Admiral Hart and John Wilkes. Half the boats—seven—were sent to distant points from which the Japanese might launch invasion forces. Two went to the Formosa-Pescadores area, one to the Hong Kong area, one to Hainan Island, and three to the Camranh Bay area in Southeast Indochina. Their missions were to warn of departing Japanese forces and attack these and merchant ships when possible.

The two boats sent to the Formosa area were *Sturgeon* and *Searaven*. William ("Bull") Wright in *Sturgeon* got there first. He closed to within 13 miles of the coast, heard two ships pinging, promptly went to 250 feet, and rigged for depth charge. He noted in his log, "This area is too closely patrolled, I believe, to risk staying closer inshore." A few days later, Wright spotted a tanker with a destroyer escort. He did not attack either ship. Next day, December 18, he picked up a large convoy: a Zinto-class cruiser and several destroyers escorting five big freighters. In accordance with the stated order of target priority, Wright made an approach on the cruiser. He got within 1,700 yards, but a destroyer came into view and Wright ducked to 200 feet without firing. The destroyer dropped a few depth charges which caused minor damage. On the night of December 21, Wright sighted a ship, remained on the surface and fired four bow torpedoes. All missed.

Searaven, commanded by Theodore Charles Aylward, reached the Formosa area shortly after Sturgeon. Aylward was not in the best of health. For some years, his blood pressure had been climbing. During the patrol, he suffered pains in his chest, dizziness, and headaches. One consequence was that his exec, Francis David Walker, Jr., a classmate of Dusty Dornin, assumed much of the command load. Aylward, also fighting very heavy weather, fired at two ships, expending three torpedoes. All missed.

The boat sent to Hong Kong was the old Pike, first of the modern generation of fleet boats, commanded by William Adolph New. Billy New found plenty of junks and sampans but few targets. On the night of December 17, cruising in bad weather, he sighted a freighter and fired one torpedo from 3,000 yards. It missed. He saw no other targets.

Swordfish, commanded by Chester Carl Smith, a deceptively mild, conservative officer, headed for the island of Hainan. On the way from Manila to station, Chet Smith encountered two separate freighters, sailing alone. He fired two torpedoes at the first with a depth setting of 40 feet. The ship, Smith believed, sank. His two-torpedo salvo at the second ship, set for 40 feet, missed.

Working the south coast of Hainan, Smith found the area teeming with enemy vessels. On December 14, he attacked two separate steamers, one at dawn, one in late afternoon. He fired two at the first, believing he sank her. He fired three at the second with a depth setting of 30 feet. The first torpedo exploded prematurely close aboard, but Smith believed the others hit, sinking the ship, raising his score to three. On December 16, Smith came across an eastbound convoy of six big transports. His position was unfavorable, but he fired three torpedoes from a range of 2,800 yards at the last ship in line. One torpedo exploded prematurely; the other two, Smith believed, hit and sank the ship, bringing his score to four. Later that night, Smith got off a contact report on the convoy to John Wilkes in Manila.

The three boats assigned to patrol near Camranh Bay, Indochina—a big Japanese navy base—were *Pickerel,* *Spearfish,* and *Sargo.* *Pickerel,* commanded by Barton Elijah Bacon, Jr., got there first. The weather was rough and miserable. On December 14, Bacon saw a Japanese submarine coming out of Camranh Bay, its rising sun ensign flapping from a halyard. Bacon started his approach but then saw a destroyer. Believing this to be a superior target, he shifted to the destroyer. In the switch, however, the fire-control party became confused and both targets pulled off unharmed. On December 19, Bacon foolishly let fly five torpedoes at a small gunboat not worth one. All missed. Toward the end of his brief patrol, he noted in his log, "Seventeen days is about proper length for a patrol because twenty-one days is too long. Personnel become weary under constant strain and tempers become touchy."

Spearfish, commanded by Roland Fremont Pryce, arrived next in "mountainous" seas. On December 20, Pryce sighted three Japanese submarines standing out in column. While making the approach, a green helmsman remained on the wrong course for eight minutes before the error was discovered. The approach was botched, but Pryce fired anyway: four torpedoes from 9,000 yards—4½ miles—one of the longest torpedo shots of the war. A little later, Pryce spotted another submarine but could not reach a favorable firing position. After a few days, Pryce was ordered to Hainan Island.

The third boat into the Camranh Bay area was *Sargo,* commanded by Tyrrell Dwight Jacobs, who had spent two years at the Naval Academy doing postgraduate work in ordnance engineering. By the time Jacobs got on station, the codebreakers were tracking some Japanese fleet movements. On December 14, *Sargo* was vectored to intercept three cruisers. They appeared as predicted, but Jacobs was unable to maneuver into position to attack.

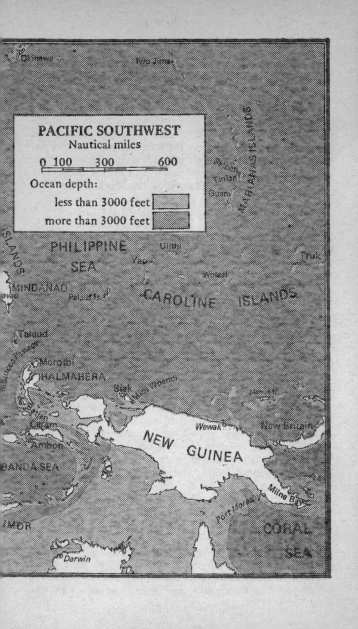

PACIFIC SOUTHWEST
Nautical miles

0 100   300   600

Ocean depth:

less than 3000 feet

more than 3000 feet

Assuming the cruisers were escorting troop transports or freighters, Jacobs moved in to intercept. That night he picked up a freighter, and fired one torpedo. Eighteen seconds after shooting, a violent explosion shook *Sargo*. The torpedo had prematured.

The explosion destroyed Jacobs's faith in the Mark VI magnetic exploder. Either there was something drastically wrong, he believed, or the Japanese had devised something to set it off before the torpedo reached its target. After a thorough discussion with his exec and his torpedo officer, Cassius Douglas Rhymes, Jr., Jacobs decided to deactivate the influence feature of the Mark VI and rely solely on contact.

On December 24, Jacobs sighted two fat cargo vessels through his periscope. At a range of about 1,000 yards, he fired two torpedoes at the lead ship and one at the trailing ship, with depth settings of 13 and 16 feet respectively. No explosions. During the attack, the diving officer lost control and *Sargo* broached to 45 feet, exposing her conning tower. The merchantmen saw her and turned away. Jacobs got off two quick shots from his stern tubes at the lead ship, range 1,800 yards, depth setting 10 feet. No hits. On the following day, he spotted two more merchantmen but couldn't get into position to attack.

Later, Jacobs found two more merchantmen sailing together. From a range of 900 yards, he fired two stern torpedoes at the rear ship, depth setting 10 feet. Both missed. An hour later, two more merchantmen came into sight. This time Jacobs, who had now fired eight torpedoes at four separate targets with zero results, was determined to do all in his power to ensure a hit. He dragged out the approach for fifty-seven minutes, inviting his exec to alternate on the periscope. The theoretical bearing on the TDC seemed to match the periscope observations perfectly. When he was absolutely certain, Jacobs fired two torpedoes at the lead ship and two at the rear ship, average range about 1,000 yards, depth setting 10 feet. All four torpedoes missed.

Jacobs was angry, baffled—and technically curious. After analyzing all the data on his attacks with Doug Rhymes, he concluded that the Mark XIV torpedo was running *deeper* than prescribed in the manuals. This was so, he reasoned, because the warheads were heavier than the exercise heads they had practiced with in peacetime. Accordingly, Jacobs ordered Rhymes to adjust the rudder throws to make the torpedoes run at a shallower depth.

The next day, an opportunity loomed for Jacobs to test his theory. About dusk, he sighted two more merchantmen. Before he could get off an attack, he lost them in the darkness. He surfaced and regained contact about 10 P.M. However, instead of attacking in darkness, he decided to run ahead, dive, and attack in daylight when he could be absolutely sure of his firing data. He carried this plan forward, but rough seas arose, and when the two ships reappeared Jacobs could not get into firing position. Several days later, he sighted a big slow-moving tanker. Again, the approach was dragged out, with Jacobs and his exec alternating on the periscope. In the thirty-five-minute period, the two men made seventeen unhurried periscope observations. Finally, at a range of 1,200 yards, depth setting 10 feet, Jacobs fired one torpedo. No explosion.

Jacobs was exasperated. He broke radio silence to send Wilkes a message raising serious questions about the reliability of the Mark XIV torpedo. He informed Wilkes that he had deactivated the Mark VI exploder and adjusted the rudder throws to make the torpedo run shallower. Even so, he reported, in six separate attacks during which he fired thirteen torpedoes, none had exploded. But Wilkes ignored this—and other—evidence of torpedo malfunction. No tests were conducted.

The remaining five boats deployed to westward were stationed along the western coast of Luzon. Wilkes sent *Saury* and *Sailfish* northward to the vicinity of Vigan, *S-36* was positioned in Lingayen Gulf, considered for decades the most likely invasion area, while *Perch* and *Permit* were stationed in the south, off Subic Bay.

Sailfish (formerly *Squalus* which had sunk and been raised in prewar years) was a difficult command. Some superstitious sailors considered her jinxed. If she sank once, she could sink again. Twenty-six men had drowned inside her hull; the memory was not easily erased. A sailor with a morbid sense of humor had informally christened her "Squailfish." To help improve her image, the navy had hand-picked one of the ablest of the peacetime skippers to command her, Morton Claire Mumma, Jr. Mumma, a strict disciplinarian, had imposed his strong personality on the boat; anyone referring to her as "Squailfish" would be court-martialed. But for all his zeal, competence, and emphasis on spit and polish, the boat remained "different."

On the morning of December 10, the Japanese landed a small force at Vigan. The landings were supported by small naval units, including a cruiser and several destroyers. Mort Mumma in *Sailfish* saw the cruiser and destroyers but was unable to get into firing position. *Saury*, commanded by John Lockwood Burnside, Jr., was cruising farther north and made no contacts with the enemy. The Japanese landed unopposed by U.S. naval forces.

Three nights later, Mort Mumma sighted two destroyers off Vigan and submerged to make a sonar approach. The destroyers evidently picked up *Sailfish*. Two or three depth charges fell, slightly jarring the boat. Mumma fired two torpedoes from a depth of 100 feet, range 500 yards. Fifteen seconds after firing, *Sailfish* was rocked by an explosion. It was either a premature or another depth charge, no one could tell in the confusion and noise. Mumma preferred to believe one of his torpedoes had hit a destroyer and sunk it. "Following the explosion," he wrote in his report, "no screws were heard." In all probability, the destroyer had stopped to listen, or the force of the explosion and rush of water blanked out noise, or the destroyer had passed overhead to a new position.

Immediately after the attack, the destroyers began depth-charging *Sailfish*. About eighteen or twenty charges fell at considerable distance. During the counterattack, Mort Mumma went to pieces. He summoned his exec, Hiram Cassedy, ordered him to take command of the boat, and to lock him (Mumma) in his stateroom. Cassedy did as ordered, getting off a radio dispatch to John Wilkes which was picked up and decoded by some other submarines. Reuben Thorton Whitaker, Bull Wright's exec on *Sturgeon*, remembers that the message said approximately: ATTACKED ONE SHIP . . . VIOLENT COUNTERATTACK . . . COMMANDING OFFICER BREAKING DOWN . . . URGENTLY REQUEST AUTHORITY TO RETURN TO TENDER.

Wilkes ordered *Sailfish* back to Manila, sending *Seal*, commanded by Kenneth Charles Hurd, to replace her. He then relieved Mumma, giving command of the boat to Richard George Voge, who had lost *Sealion* in the Cavite bombing attack. Despite the thin evidence, Wilkes credited Mumma with sinking the destroyer and awarded him a Navy Cross. The citation (perhaps designed to save everybody embarrassment) extolled Mumma's "extraordinary heroism" and concluded, "By his forceful and inspiring leadership [he] enabled the *Sailfish* to complete successfully an extremely perilous mission."

For Mumma—or for anybody else—being relieved of command in peace or war was a shattering professional blow. Command of a combatant ship was the ultimate goal of all naval officers, usually the high point of their professional career. To fail in command usually spelled the end for an officer, denying him an opportunity for good jobs and advancement to flag rank. Mumma's humiliation before his classmates and fellow submariners was further heightened by the fact that he had no way to leave Manila for other duty. He had to remain and face them every morning.

Many officers, especially the younger ones, were appalled by Mumma's conduct in war. No one could understand it. At the Naval Academy, they had been exhorted to "go in harm's way" and give their lives for their country. But they were soon to discover that Mumma was no isolated case. All too many of his contemporaries in the submarine force showed a disinclination to attack the enemy boldly and persistently, an unforeseen circumstance that would plague the submarine force throughout the war.

All the while, *S-36*, commanded by John Roland McKnight, Jr., maintained a lonely patrol in the shallow waters of Lingayen Gulf. She carried a total of twelve torpedoes, enough for three or four shots at the enemy if, as believed, Lingayen Gulf turned out to be the most likely point to land the main Japanese invasion forces. Why Wilkes did not position the other five S-boats inside Lingayen Gulf has never been made clear.

On the night of December 11, Wilkes sent a radio

dispatch to McKnight. Because of a faulty calibration in
S-36's receiver—undetected at the time—McKnight did not
receive the message. Wilkes repeated the message again
and again that night and on subsequent nights. Fearing
that the boat might be in serious difficulty, or perhaps
lost, on the night of the sixteenth, Wilkes ordered Mc-
Knight to exit Lingayen Gulf and return to Manila. Mc-
Knight received that message and pulled out. To replace
S-36, Wilkes sent Stingray, commanded by Raymond Starr
Lamb. Stingray would take up station off the mouth of
Lingayen Gulf, in deeper waters.

The two boats stationed off Subic Bay were Perch and
Permit. Permit was commanded by Adrian Melvin Hurst.
Hurst left for patrol with only two of his four engines in
commission. After a few days on station, he and some
others developed "Guam blisters" (an extremely uncomfortable form of impetigo), prickly heat, and other minor
diseases. On the fifth day out, an electrician caught his
hand in some machinery, crushing bones and severing
tendons. Hurst returned to Manila on December 20 after
a nine-day patrol.

Perch, commanded by David Albert Hurt, guarded Subic Bay alone until December 18, when she was ordered
to proceed to Formosa to replace Bull Wright's Sturgeon,
then Manila bound. Near Formosa on Christmas Day,
Hurt sighted a steamer and fired four torpedoes; one
broached and circled back toward Perch, in what was
called a circular run, exploding off her beam. Two days
later, Hurt picked up a convoy consisting of a light
cruiser, two destroyers, and a tanker. The approach was
botched, and a destroyer attacked. Hurt took Perch to the
bottom in 170 feet of water and lay quiet until the destroyer moved off. It was not the recommended form of
evasion. It would have been better if Hurt had maintained
his mobility and evaded the destroyer by creeping away.

On station off Lingayen Gulf, Ray Lamb in Stingray, who had been plagued with leaky pipes for some
time, noted a new infirmity in his boat: a small air leak
that sent a steady stream of little bubbles to the surface.
Believing this would be a dead giveaway to the enemy
in a glassy sea, Lamb ordered his crew to fix it. They

couldn't. After all efforts failed, Lamb radioed Wilkes, requesting permission to return to Manila for repairs. Wilkes granted the request.

At 5:13 on the afternoon of December 21, Lamb, coming to periscope depth preparatory to surfacing for the trip to Manila, spotted smoke on the horizon. He immediately turned *Stingray* toward the smoke. Moments later, he made out *columns* of smoke. He had sighted a submariner's dream (or nightmare): the main Japanese invasion force, headed in for Lingayen Gulf.

What happened in the following hours brought little credit to Lamb or the submarine force. In Lamb's words:

Turned to approach course but saw it would be impossible to intercept the column. Came to forty-eight feet and sent contact report to Commander in Chief, Asiatic Fleet . . . message sent twice but no receipt heard. . . . At this time heard distinct echo ranging, could no longer make out smoke due to darkness, turned and ran north for several miles to clear echo ranging, as I considered it of primary importance to ensure contact report reached the Commander in Chief. Surfaced, repeated contact report and sent amplifying report. . . . Turned to pursue enemy but could not make him out.

On receiving the message, Wilkes canceled Lamb's orders to return to Manila and told him to attack. For several hours, while the most luscious submarine target of the war approached the gulf, Lamb thrashed about in a manner that led many of his crew to believe him less than aggressive. At about three the following morning, he sighted a light on a Japanese ship. He turned to bring *Stingray*'s stern tubes to bear, but the light went out and he lost the ship in the darkness. Half an hour later, Lamb spotted a destroyer close by. Instead of shooting at it, Lamb, who believed himself to be in the middle of a screen, dived and went to 200 feet to evade. While submerged, Lamb heard echo ranging all around him, but no depth charges fell. When it seemed prudent, he eased away from the destroyers. At dawn, he came to periscope depth and searched the seas. They were empty. The invasion force had slipped past him and landed.

Instead of fighting into the gulf, Lamb turned in the opposite direction, standing out to sea at low speed at a depth of 100 feet. Later he would explain that his crew was "exhausted" and needed a rest. During this crucial period in the history of the Philippines, Lamb remained submerged, far from the Japanese, for 14 hours and 36 minutes, surfacing at about six on the evening of the twenty-second.

That evening, Lamb made a halfhearted attempt to slip by a Japanese destroyer screen which had now taken station at the mouth of the gulf. However, when a searchlight—presumably mounted on a destroyer—some 2 miles distant swung toward *Stingray*, Lamb dived and went deep. He heard four distant explosions—depth charges or torpedoes from another submarine, he was not sure. He lay quiet again, then slipped away to seaward. At 10:42 P.M. he surfaced and went farther out to sea to charge his batteries. While so engaged, Lamb found several more leaks that caused him concern.

Later he wrote in third person, "At [that] time the commanding officer believed it would be impossible to remain at deep submergence for a period of time necessary to pass under enemy screen and penetrate Gulf without continuously pumping bilges and leaving oil slicks on surface, therefore request was made to return to Manila for repairs."

Lamb arrived back in Manila without having fired a single torpedo at the enemy. Wilkes relieved him of command.

Upon receiving Ray Lamb's contact report, John Wilkes rushed six boats to the scene: two of the S-boats patrolling Verde Island Passage, *S-38* and *S-40; Salmon;* Adrian Hurst's *Permit,* now ready for a second patrol; *Porpoise,* which had been replacing her battery at Olongapo when the Japanese attacked; and Burnside's *Saury,* ordered south from Vigan. Wilkes's orders were explicit: enter Lingayen Gulf and attack the enemy landing forces.

Moon Chapple, another varsity football player (and heavyweight boxer) at the Naval Academy, was patrolling Verde Island Passage in *S-38* when the order came. He charged north like a fullback going up the middle.

On the morning of December 22, just before dawn, he dived and took his boat inside. The water in the gulf was shallow, full of uncharted reefs and humps. Later Chapple conceded he was "scared," but he gave no hint of his true feelings to his fired-up—and exhausted—crew.

Inside the gulf, just after daybreak, Chapple raised his periscope to find four fat transports standing in. Chapple put his crosshairs on the transports and ordered all four bow tubes made ready. When the ships reached a range of 1,000 yards Chapple fired, confident of his aim, but no explosion followed. The torpedoes had missed! A Japanese destroyer spotted Chapple's torpedo wakes. It charged over S-38, pinging with sonar gear, but dropped no depth charges.

When it moved off, Chapple got under way and moved deeper into the gulf toward the main landing area. While his crew reloaded the four forward tubes, he raised his periscope and saw dozens of ships. This time he picked a big transport that was anchored, a sitting duck. Believing his first four torpedoes had been set too deep, he now set them for 9 feet. He fired two torpedoes from a range of 500 yards. Thirty seconds later, there was a thundering explosion and the target settled to the shallow bottom. It was a 5,445-ton transport, Hayo Maru.

Moments later, two destroyers counterattacked. Chapple took S-38 to 80 feet and lay quietly in the water while depth charges exploded hither and yon—none close. After two hours, he got under way, evading. But S-38 went aground, stuck fast in the muddy bottom. Chapple let her stay where she was most of the day, while Japanese ships, small craft, and landing craft buzzed overhead. Later he dislodged the boat from the mud and crept away. That night, well clear of the landing force, he surfaced to air the boat and charge batteries. At dawn, he submerged and lay on the bottom all day to give his crew a rest and reload the empty tubes.

The following morning, Chapple again came to periscope depth to do battle. Almost immediately, he saw a column of six transports standing into the gulf and set up to fire. On the final approach, almost at the moment of firing, the boat was wracked by an awesome explosion. Evidently a Japanese plane had spotted S-38 and dropped a string of bombs. Chapple broke off the attack, went deep—180 feet—and lay on the bottom the rest of the day.

After sunset, he surfaced again. Chapple had been on the bridge only a few moments when he heard a jarring internal explosion. Hydrogen gas in the after battery, which had not been properly ventilated, exploded. Three men were seriously injured, and the after battery was a shambles. Chapple withdrew from the gulf, eluding the screen of destroyers patrolling at the mouth.

All five other boats attempted to penetrate the destroyer screen.

On the night of December 22, Johnny Burnside in *Saury* charged down from Vigan. Off San Fernando—on the north end of the gulf—Burnside ran into what seemed a squadron of Japanese destroyers "all over the place." (Later he wrote, "It is too bad Lingayen Gulf was not mined. We can't foresee everything.") Finding one stopped in the water, Burnside closed to 1,500 yards and fired a torpedo. It missed.

The next night, Burnside tried again to penetrate the screen, but a destroyer picked him up and drove him under. He was worried about his position, fearing he had wandered into the areas reserved for *Permit* and *Porpoise*. But Wilkes ordered Burnside to clear the area and make way for *Salmon*.

Salmon was commanded by Eugene Bradley McKinney, a soft-spoken officer who had taken his postgraduate work in law, earning a degree. McKinney said later, "At first, my crew didn't accept me. They asked why the navy would send a damned lawyer to command a submarine. When we came into Manila from Pearl Harbor, I made the crew put on whites and go on deck. One of the men said scornfully, 'New battleship arriving on Asiatic Station! U.S.S. *Salmon*.' When the war came, I guess I wanted to prove to them a lawyer could fight a submarine as well as anybody else."

On the night of December 23, McKinney moved in toward the destroyer screen. He was detected immediately. Coolly remaining on the surface, turning and dodging, McKinney got boxed in. He said later, "I confess I felt a lot like diving. But I was curious. We stayed on the surface and the destroyers came on. I guess the Jap skippers were just as inexperienced and puzzled as I was." When one of the destroyers crossed *Salmon*'s stern, McKinney fired two torpedoes from 2,500 yards. The destroyer turned aside; the torpedoes missed. McKinney's exec urged McKinney to dive and evade. But McKinney remained on the surface.

One of the destroyers turned toward *Salmon*, coming directly up the stern. McKinney ordered two stern tubes made ready. He would allow the destroyer to come very close, then fire a down-the-throat shot. McKinney let the destroyer come within 1,200 yards and then fired. He saw an explosion and believed, like Mumma, that he had sent one enemy destroyer to the bottom.

After firing, McKinney dived. The destroyers charged over, unleashing a barrage of depth charges. The boat shook, the lights went out, the crew hung on in terror. Later, McKinney recalled, "It was awful . . . it went on for hours."

Next to charge the line was Nicholas Lucker, Jr., in *S-40*. Lucker's exec was Thomas Kinkaid Kimmel, younger of two sons of the admiral who had commanded at Pearl Harbor, both of whom were in submarines. In the dark of night, Lucker boldly crept by the patrolling destroyer screen into the gulf. Later, Kimmel said, "We adjusted speed so we would be able to cross the entrance (which is quite long) at dawn. As soon as it commenced to get light we visually sighted several ships in the gulf and immediately submerged and commenced an approach to gain torpedo attack. It was extremely rough, and as diving officer I had considerable difficulty in maintaining depth control."

Even so, Lucker got into range and set up on a group of ships at 1,000 yards. He fired four torpedoes at one ship. "Just before firing," Kimmel recalled, "there was some discussion as to whether the torpedoes should be spread. Our doctrine called for no spread at a range of one thousand yards. I remember volunteering, 'You'd better spread them,' but the doctrine prevailed." All missed. Later Lucker said, "I couldn't believe it."

After firing, Kimmel lost control of the boat, and she broached in broad daylight, within sight of several escorts. A destroyer charged in; Lucker went "deep" (80 feet) to evade. However, the engine room reported a serious leak in the exhaust valves, a calamity that forced Lucker to make use of his noisy trim pump. The destroyer heard the pump, located S-40 by sonar, and came over, delivering a shattering depth-charge attack. The boat bounced around like a cork, but Kimmel kept her from broaching again. Lucker evaded and made his way to a small cove outside the gulf. After dark, he surfaced and found much of the superstructure from the engine-room hatch aft blown away. He reported the damage to Wilkes.

Back in Manila, Wilkes had no clear picture of what was going on at Lingayen Gulf. He was unable to establish radio contact with Gene McKinney in *Salmon*. Burnside in *Saury* reported McKinney had taken "about 180" depth charges and was surely lost. There had been no word from Moon Chapple. On the night of December 24, nevertheless, Wilkes issued orders to withdraw to *Saury* and *Salmon*, as well as S-38 and S-40, and ordered *Permit* and *Porpoise* to take their place and penetrate the gulf.

Porpoise, commanded by Joseph Anthony Callaghan, was next to assault the line. He delayed a few hours, finishing a battery charge, then headed in. He was immediately picked up by a destroyer which dropped eighteen depth charges, Callaghan reported, "seeming to explode directly overhead." He went north to "escape" and, upon reflection, decided that a further attempt to penetrate Lingayen Gulf was "impractical at this time." Callaghan's reasons, as listed in his patrol report, were: strong enemy defense at entrance; can't go in submerged; can't go in on surface at night; enemy carrier and cruiser no longer in gulf; reduced number of enemy vessels in gulf; necessity of passing through *Salmon* and *Saury* areas. He concluded, "Believe from general information in dispatches that a true picture at Lingayen not known by higher authority." Wilkes ordered *Porpoise* to go to Hainan Island.

The last boat to make the try was *Permit*, commanded by Adrian Hurst. Approaching the gulf submerged in daytime, Hurst sighted two destroyers. From a range of

1,500 yards, he fired two stern tubes. Both torpedoes missed ahead. Hurst went deep—to 200 feet. Fourteen depth charges fell, none close. The next day, Hurst tried to enter the gulf, evading a destroyer and going deep. He received a report that the main induction—the main air line to the engines—had flooded topside. *"Permit,"* he wrote, "became heavy at 220 feet, requiring a 12-degree up-angle to keep her from sinking to the bottom." Like Nick Lucker, he had to use a noisy trim pump. He gave up the attempt, writing, "Slightly inside Gulf . . . in view of inability of this vessel to maintain deep depth control and at the same time run silently, the decision was made to leave Gulf, stand out to sea and report." Later he added, "Everybody has been on board since 8th of December under trying conditions and an opportunity to rest and relax in the sunshine is rapidly becoming imperative for maintenance of good health, morale and efficiency." *Permit* returned to Manila after six days, the shortest patrol of the war.

There were at least nine other fleet boats within easy reach of Lingayen Gulf: Hurd's *Seal* off Vigan; Wright's *Sturgeon* and Alyward's *Searaven,* returning from Formosa; Voge's *Sailfish* and Hurt's *Perch,* en route to Formosa to relieve *Sturgeon* and *Searaven;* New's *Pike,* returning from the Hong Kong area; *Snapper,* commanded by Hamilton Laurie Stone, en route to Hong Kong to relieve *Pike;* Bacon's *Pickerel,* returning from Camranh Bay; and Freddy Warder's *Seawolf,* coming around from Aparri to Manila. None was pressed into the battle for Lingayen Gulf.

Thus the boats deployed to the west had no better luck than the boats deployed to the east. Bull Wright and Dave Hurt both missed opportunities to sink cruisers in Formosa waters; Tyrrell Jacobs missed three cruisers near Camranh Bay; Bart Bacon missed a submarine and a destroyer; Roland Pryce missed three submarines; Ray Lamb missed the entire Lingayen Gulf invasion force. Although Mumma and McKinney were each credited with sinking a destroyer off West Luzon, Japanese records failed to confirm these sinkings and they were later withdrawn. Hurst, Callaghan, and Burnside also missed opportunities to sink Japanese destroyers.

And thus the Japanese landed on Luzon virtually un-

PT boat

opposed—at least by the Asiatic submarine force. Only
two Japanese ships had been sunk, one of them already
unloaded in Lingayen Gulf. In a matter of a few days,
the Philippine ground forces under General Douglas Mac-
Arthur were driven into the Bataan Peninsula, Manila
was declared an "open city" and the Asiatic submarine
force compelled to withdraw to the south. During the
next few weeks, it was called on to help defend Java.
Several more Japanese ships were sunk, but generally it
was another dismal failure. Finally, all the Asiatic Fleet
submarines were withdrawn to Fremantle on the west
coast of Australia. Three more boats had been lost in
combat: *Shark* with all hands, *S-36* and *Perch*. The crew
of *S-36* was rescued but the crew of *Perch*, deliberate-

ly scuttled, was captured by the Japanese, and spent the remainder of the war in P.O.W. camps. In four months of war, the Asiatic submarine force sank only ten Japanese ships. The Japanese had overrun the entire Far East, the Solomon Islands, and now threatened Australia itself.

The surviving twenty-five boats of the Asiatic Fleet, many in miserable mechanical shape, now fell under the command of General Douglas MacArthur, who had escaped from the Philippines in a PT boat, and had been named Commander of Allied forces in the Southwest Pacific. The submarine arm of "MacArthur's Navy," based at Fremantle, was a sad, dispirited lot, badly in need of fresh, imaginative leadership. They were angry, too. Clearly there was something drastically wrong with the submarine torpedoes. But the smug Bureau of Ordnance in Washington refused to concede error or make further tests. They blamed torpedo failures on the skippers and crews.

3

PRICELESS INTELLIGENCE

In Pearl Harbor, Admiral Chester W. Nimitz, Jr., a one-time submariner, took command of what remained of the U.S. Pacific Fleet. In due time, he reorganized the Pearl Harbor submarine force under a new commander, Rear Admiral Robert H. English. By that time, nine new boats had arrived, giving English a total force of thirty submarines, mostly newer models. The new skippers patrolled with mounting aggressiveness, reflecting the new air of optimism Nimitz had brought to Pearl Harbor.

Charles Cochran Kirkpatrick, class of 1931, became the youngest officer yet to command at Pearl Harbor. His boat was *Triton*. "They told me to go out there and raise hell," Kirkpatrick said later. "Believe me, considering I was sort of a 'youth experiment,' had made no war patrols, I was really determined to show them I could cut the mustard."

Triton was sent to the East China Sea. Kirkpatrick found action a few days later. Passing north of Marcus Island, he was astonished to see a Japanese ship lying to, all alone and brightly lighted. He went to battle stations and fired one torpedo at point-blank range. It missed. Coming about, Kirkpatrick fired a second: another miss. On close inspection, the ship turned out to be a small trawler, not worth a torpedo. Angry at this misjudgment, Kirkpatrick ordered his crew to man the 3-inch deck gun. Within the space of eighteen minutes, *Triton* fired nineteen rounds plus a hurricane of small-arms fire. The trawler, estimated to be 2,000 tons—the first Japanese vessel to be sunk by deck gun—went down.

Pressing on to his patrol station in "Tung Hai," as

37

sailors call the East China Sea, Kirkpatrick found glassy, shallow waters, poor sonar conditions. On May 1, a six-ship convoy with a single small escort came into view. Manning the periscope, Kirkpatrick closed and unhesitatingly attacked, firing two torpedoes at two freighters. The first two hit, the second two missed, leading Kirkpatrick to believe—generally—that the torpedoes were running deep. *Taei Maru*, 2,200 tons, sank. Shifting targets, Kirkpatrick fired a single torpedo at another freighter. It ran under without exploding, but a second single, *set at a shallow depth* and aimed at another freighter, exploded, breaking the back of the vessel, the *Calcutta Maru*, 5,300 tons.

A few nights later, Kirkpatrick, cruising on the surface amid swarms of junks and sampans, came upon another convoy. He fired two torpedoes at a trailing ship, both set for shallow depth. One sank upon leaving the tube; the other went ahead of the target. Kirkpatrick launched a second attack against this same ship, firing two shallow-set torpedoes from 1,200 yards. One hit, blowing up *Taigen Maru*, 5,660 tons. Later, Kirkpatrick fired two torpedoes at two more ships in this convoy. One of the torpedoes hit the first ship, the second ship evaded, and a destroyer charged in, forcing Kirkpatrick to break off the attack.

To the north of *Triton,* Willis ("Pilly") Lent in *Grenadier* came across a beautiful target: a convoy of six freighters, plus one magnificent passenger vessel Lent recognized as *Taiyo Maru,* 14,500 tons. He went to battle stations, firing four torpedoes at *Taiyo,* one to explode on impact, two to run under and explode by magnetic influence, the last to explode on impact. The two torpedoes set to run under failed to explode. The other two hit and *Taiyo* went down, carrying about 1,000 Japanese oil technicians, scientists, and engineers who were en route to Java and Sumatra to restore the Dutch oil fields to full production.

Lent did not see *Taiyo* sink. Two minutes after firing, a string of bombs exploded over *Grenadier*. Then came destroyers, which dropped a total of thirty-six depth charges over the next four hours. Lent stayed deep—below 250 feet—and the charges did no damage. (Fortunately for U.S. submarines, the Japanese set their depth charges too shallow.) But the destroyers kept him from taking another shot at this valuable convoy. The surviving ships presumably picked up most of the oil technicians and continued on their way.

Back at Pearl Harbor, Lent complained bitterly about torpedo performance. Two of his torpedoes set to run deep under *Taiyo Maru* and actuate the magnetic exploder had failed to go off. Something was obviously wrong. His division commander agreed, pointing out that three other skippers of his division had reported magnetic exploder failures. He recommended that the Mark XIV torpedo be set to run at a much shallower depth, barely beneath the keel (as Kirkpatrick in *Triton* had done).

Bob English did not agree at all. Stubbornly following the policy of his predecessor, English unstintingly supported the torpedo and exploder. Like John Wilkes, he refused to take time out for a live test, blaming most torpedo failures on skippers and crews. He gave eight possible reasons for failures—including errors in estimated range, speed, and course of enemy target; inexperience with TDC; "guess and snap decisions"; and "physical condition" of the skippers—and concluded, "Commanding Officers will continue to set torpedoes at a depth not less than five feet greater than the maximum draft of the target." In other words, continue to rely on the magnetic exploder.

Two new boats, *Drum* and *Silversides,* patrolled off the east coast of Honshu and racked up impressive scores. *Drum,* commanded by Robert Henry Rice, arrived off Nagoya, south of Tokyo Bay, about May 1. One of his officers was Manning Marius Kimmel, son of the admiral and brother of Thomas Kimmel on *S-40.* Like his brother, Manning was eager for blood—to help clear the family name.

Rice was a bold and aggressive skipper. Guided by an Ultra, shortly after midnight, Rice spotted a ship "with considerable top hamper" and immediately fired two torpedoes. One hit; one missed. A destroyer charged out of the darkness. Rice crash-dived, firing a torpedo at the destroyer on the way down. It missed. Hearing no depth charges, Rice cautiously came to periscope depth. The destroyer was lying to, 1,500 yards distant, probably listening on passive sonar. Rice fired three more torpedoes at it. All missed.

Later, Rice's division commander gave him credit for damaging the ship he first shot at, calling it "medium-sized." However, one of the codebreakers had been eavesdropping on the Japanese radio report of this attack. He knew—and passed word—that the ship Rice had hit with one torpedo had sunk. It was not a "medium-sized" freighter but a major Japanese naval vessel, the seaplane carrier *Mizuho*, 9,000 tons, the largest Japanese combatant vessel sunk by submarines up to that time.

A week later, Rice made a day periscope attack on a ship he believed to be a naval auxiliary of perhaps 6,000 tons. It was loaded and "exceptionally neat and new looking." Rice fired four torpedoes. There was a violent explosion. The identity of this ship was never determined, but Rice was credited with an "unkown maru" of 4,000 tons. Four days later he sank 5,000-ton *Shonan Maru* with a single torpedo and, two weeks later, 2,300-ton *Kitakata Maru,* also with one torpedo. On May 28, he sighted a large auxiliary or merchant ship, fired five torpedoes, and missed. Rice's score for the patrol, confirmed by postwar records: four ships for 20,000 tons. This was the most productive patrol so far by any submarine.

Silversides was commanded by a classmate of Rice's, Creed Cardwell Burlingame. Burlingame was one of the more colorful skippers, swashbuckling and devil-may-care. His exec, Roy Milton Davenport, was an oddity in the submarine force, a teetotaler and devout Christian Scientist who played a trombone (badly). Burlingame kidded Davenport about his religious zeal and took along a buddha which he "worshiped" ostentatiously.

Burlingame boldly cruised most of the way to Japan on the surface. Six hundred miles from the coast, *Silversides* found herself embroiled in the tail end of a typhoon. About that time, a Japanese trawler came into view. Burlingame attacked in pitching seas with his deck gun. The trawler returned fire and killed an enlisted man, Michael Harbin, the first man to die in a submarine gun action. A few days later, Burlingame spotted a Japanese submarine. He fired one torpedo—with Harbin's name chalked on the side—heard an explosion, and claimed a hit, but postwar records failed to verify the loss of a Japanese sub at this time and place.

In action off the coast of Japan during the next few weeks, Burlingame seemed fearless. On May 17, while threading his way through an armada of sampans laying out fishing nets, Burlingame found a small convoy. Making an approach, *Silversides* got enmeshed in one of the nets, buoyed by a glass ball with a Japanese flag attached. Trailing the Japanese flag, Burlingame went on, firing at a freighter. It came apart in a massive explosion of fire and flames and sank. He fired at a second but missed. Later he damaged another freighter and a tanker. After the last attack, *Silversides* was pinned down by a destroyer, which dropped thirteen depth charges.

"During the depth-charging," Burlingame recalled, "I rubbed the belly of the buddha. Roy Davenport put his faith in the Lord, claiming He had placed an invincible shield between the boat and the Japanese. Afterward, I needled him. 'Roy, who do you think got us out of that one, Buddha or Mary Baker Eddy?' "

While these boats, and others, were on patrol, the codebreakers provided Nimitz and MacArthur with two of the most valuable intelligence intercepts of the entire war in the Pacific.

The first was a warning that the Japanese would attempt an amphibious landing at Port Moresby, an Australian outpost in southeastern New Guinea. This was dire news. If the Japanese successfully seized Port Moresby, it would provide a bomber base within easy reach of Australia. Acting on this intelligence, Nimitz sent the carriers *Yorktown* and *Lexington* to intercept the Japanese forces. They met—in what was called the Battle of the Coral Sea—in early May. The Nimitz forces turned back the Japanese, but in the battle *Lexington* was so badly damaged she had to be sunk. Nimitz's forces sunk a light carrier *Shoko* and damaged a heavy carrier, *Shokaku*. No U.S. submarines participated in the battle.

The second intercept, no less valuable, revealed plans for the boldest Japanese thrust of the war: an amphibious invasion of Midway Island about one thousand miles west of Pearl Harbor, together with a diversionary thrust into the Aleutians. Again, Nimitz mobilized his limited forces—the carriers *Enterprise, Hornet,* and *Yorktown,* and support vessels. This time, the Pearl Harbor submarine force was called upon to assist in the battle. Twenty-five boats were able to answer the call. It was yet another dismal chapter in the submarine war.

Tracked by the codebreaker, the Japanese invasion force bore down on Midway Island. At 9 A.M. on June 3, a Midway patrol plane spotted the Japanese invasion force 700 miles west of the island, not far from *Cuttlefish,* commanded by Martin Perry ("Spike") Hottel. Air Force B-17s, basing out of Midway, made a bombing attack on the force that afternoon, but their aim was off; they got no hits. In the early hours of June 4, torpedo planes based on Midway also attacked the invasion force, damaging one ship slightly.

Shortly after that attack, Hottel in *Cuttlefish* sighted what he believed to be a tanker and sent off a report to English—the first contact between U.S. submarines and the Japanese in the Battle of Midway. Believing the tanker to be a unit of the invasion force, English ordered Hottel to stalk it and send in position reports, a key assignment.

Hottel was uneasy. His lookouts believed they saw aircraft. Dawn was coming up fast. There was no way he could trail in broad daylight. The aircraft—friend or foe—would attack, he was certain. He had already performed his primary task, reporting the oncoming enemy. There was no way he could pull ahead and make an attack without being detected.

Hottel dived, losing contact with the enemy.

While this skirmish was in progress, on June 4, the Japanese striking force, composed of Carrier Divisions One (*Akagi, Kaga*) and Two (*Soryu, Hiryu*), all veterans of the Pearl Harbor attack, reached its assigned position undetected, about 150 miles northwest of Midway, and launched planes against the island. Meanwhile, planes on Midway took off to find the Japanese. At 6:35 A.M., Japanese planes attacked Midway. At 7:05, Midway planes attacked the striking force. Neither side inflicted decisive damage.

The Japanese had backup planes on the carrier decks armed with torpedoes in case U.S. naval vessels were sighted. None of the Japanese planes, as yet, had spotted any U.S. ships. Believing them to be elsewhere, the Japanese now ordered the backup planes rearmed with bombs for a second strike against Midway. While this work was in progress, Midway-based dive bombers and B-17s attacked the Japanese again, doing little damage but causing much distraction. In the midst of this attack, a Japanese plane reported sighting a U.S. carrier to the northeast. The Japanese again changed plans, ordering the backup planes reloaded with torpedoes instead of bombs.

Meanwhile, all three U.S. carriers had launched air strikes against the Japanese carriers. *Hornet*'s dive bombers and fighters made a wrong turn, headed south, and never found the enemy. But her torpedo planes, together with torpedo planes from *Enterprise* and *Yorktown*, found the Japanese force and attacked at 9:28. Altogether there were forty-one torpedo planes. Of these, thirty-five were shot down by the Japanese. Not a single torpedo found the mark. (The aerial torpedoes had all the defects of the submarine torpedoes, plus others.)

The Japanese were jubilant. The striking force seemed invincible. They had beaten off everything the Americans had thrown at them—land-based and carrier-based torpedo planes, high-level bombers. Now they prepared to launch a strike against the American carriers and bring to a conclusion what was certainly to be the greatest Japanese naval victory in all history.

At that moment, 10:24, dive bombers from *Enterprise* and *Yorktown* pushed over and attacked the striking force, finding *Akagi, Kaga,* and *Soryu* in their sights. (The fourth carrier, *Hiryu,* was to the northward, somewhat detached from the main group.) "Within three minutes," as naval historian Wilfred Jay ("Jasper") Holmes wrote later, "what had been a Japanese victory became a Japanese disaster." *Akagi, Kaga,* and *Soryu,* shuddering under the impact of dive bombers, burst into uncontrollable flames.

Hiryu, off to herself, was not bombed in this assault. She launched her dive bombers against the American carriers. They found *Yorktown* and disabled her with two bombs. In a second attack, later in the day, *Hiryu*'s torpedo planes, fighting through a withering wall of antiaircraft fire that destroyed half their number, managed

to fire four torpedoes against the damaged *Yorktown,*
two of which hit. With *Yorktown* listing and fires raging, her captain gave the order to abandon ship. At
about the same time, dive bombers from *Enterprise* and
Yorktown found *Hiryu* and hit her with four bombs.
She was left a flaming wreck.

Sixteen Japanese submarines were assigned to the Battle of Midway, disposed in two groups. Ten were stationed to the northeast of Midway and four between
Midway and Pearl Harbor, considerably south of the
three submarines English had placed between the two islands. For various reasons, all the Japanese submarines
arrived on station late and therefore missed making contact with the U.S. carrier task forces.

The codebreakers tracked the Japanese submarines by
means of codebreaking and RDF (Radio direction finding
stations were established to home in on U-boat radio
transmissions. When two or more of these stations picked
up a U-boat broadcast, it was possible to obtain an exact
fix on the U-boat location.), relaying reports to English,
who in turn relayed information to his submarines. On
June 4, the day of the major engagement, English informed his submarines that a Japanese submarine tender
was servicing Japanese submarines 700 miles west of Midway. Four times in the next three days, English sent further information on the position of Japanese subs.

Knowing the position of the Japanese submarines enabled Nimitz to make what otherwise might have been a
risky, even reckless move. After *Yorktown* had been
abandoned, her men were recovered by escorting cruisers
and destroyers. These ships were encumbered by the survivors. On the afternoon of June 4, Nimitz ordered
the submarine tender *Fulton* to get under way and bring
back the survivors, thus freeing the other ships for further
combat. *Fulton,* alerted to known positions of Japanese
submarines, raced to the rescue. She returned to Pearl
Harbor on June 8 with 2,025 survivors of *Yorktown*
and other U.S. vessels.

In spite of all the codebreaking and RDF-ing, one
Japanese submarine, *I-168,* scored a victory. She had left
Japan behind the others, delayed by overhaul. Main-

taining radio silence as she cruised more or less independently of the main Japanese submarine force, on June 5 she bombarded Midway, until driven down by U.S. destroyers. Later that night she picked up a report on the damaged *Yorktown* and headed for her position.

On the morning of June 6, *I-168* found *Yorktown*. By then the carrier's fires had been brought under control and a tug, *Vireo*, was attempting to tow her back to Pearl Harbor. The U.S. destroyer *Hammann* was alongside, supplying electric power. *I-168* fired four torpedoes at this overlapping formation. One torpedo hit *Hammann*. The destroyer broke up and sank immediately. Two torpedoes hit *Yorktown*. Added to her other damage, this was enough to send the carrier to the bottom. *I-168* was heavily counterattacked by other U.S. destroyers, but she managed to evade and limp back to Japan, having made the biggest kill yet by any submarine in the Pacific.

The role played by U.S. submarines in the Battle of Midway was one of confusion and error.

On June 4, Midway-based aircraft had spotted and reported the position of the Japanese striking force at 5:45 A.M. Thereafter, a flood of contact reports giving the location, range, speed, and course of the striking force filled the airways. English sent his submarines a report at 7:15 A.M. indicating a contact with an enemy carrier, giving a range and bearing from Midway. Some of the submarines deployed at Midway intercepted these reports and began moving toward the enemy on their own initiative. But *four hours* went by before English actually ordered nine of his twelve submarines (less *Cuttlefish, Flying Fish* and *Cachalot*) to close the enemy. This was shortly after the carrier-based torpedo planes attacked the striking force and long after the initial attack from the Midway-based aircraft.

The submarines nearest to the reported position of the striking force were Hap Lyon's *Gudgeon*, William Herman Brockman, Jr.,'s *Nautilus*, and Claren Emmett Duke's new boat, *Grouper*, all to the north or northwest of Midway.

Duke intercepted English's 7:15 A.M. contact report. He turned toward the reported position on the surface, going to battle stations at 7:26. Five minutes later, he sighted planes on the horizon that appeared to be taking off from a carrier. Duke dived and went in, but, he reported later, he was frustrated by the enemy. At 7:51, a plane machine-gunned and bombed his periscope. This attack, Duke reported, was followed up by a destroyer attack with depth charges over the next few hours. Duke fired two torpedoes from a deep depth, inflicting no damage on the destroyer.

While Duke stayed deep, important time passed by. At 11:40 he inched back to periscope depth. Sighting smoke pouring from what he believed to be two burning carriers, Duke again went deep, inching toward the targets. At 1:14 P.M., he heard several heavy explosions. Thinking that one of the carriers might be exploding overhead and might sink on *Grouper*, he went deep again and evaded.

In the hours following, Duke and *Grouper* were very nearly lost, not to enemy forces but by bad luck. During a quick dive to escape an aircraft, Duke lost depth control and *Grouper* plunged downward at a terrifying angle. As the officers and men struggled to bring her out of her fatal-seeming dive—blowing tanks, backing "emergency" (full power astern)—the depth gauge needle swung past 200 . . . 300 . . . 400 . . . 500 feet, far below *Grouper*'s test depth. At 600 feet, deeper than any fleet boat had ever gone, Duke pulled her out and climbed back to a normal depth. A large quantity of water had leaked in through the stern tubes, Duke reported, "and everyone had a few more gray hairs."

Later, Duke's division commander, Willard Merrill Downes, wrote:

From the report, it is evident that many golden opportunities to inflict severe damage on the enemy were missed. The Commanding Officer chose in many instances to use evasive tactics rather than aggressive tactics. It is unfortunate that an unseasoned ship, so far as combat is concerned, should gets its baptism of fire in an engagement of the magnitude of the Battle of Midway. It is felt that this initial introduction to combat together with the inadvertent deep dive of Grouper *colored the decisions of the Commanding Officer throughout the patrol.*

English added, "It is regretted that the attack on two burning carriers [at Midway] was not pressed home. It hardly seems conceivable that 100 depth charges [the number reported by Duke] were dropped on *Grouper* on the morning of June 4 and another 60 to 70 that afternoon."

When Hap Lyon in *Gudgeon* got the 7:15 contact report, he was not far from the Japanese. He turned south to run on the surface. "He was no chicken," said Dusty Dornin, who had moved up to be *Gudgeon*'s exec. "The problem was, Hap was blind as a bat." At 8:42, *Gudgeon* picked up the "pagoda masts" of two battleships on the horizon. Whether Lyon or Dornin sighted these masts is not clear. Dornin said he saw them and that Lyon "couldn't see a damned thing." In his patrol report, Lyon said, "The Commanding Officer alone sighted these vessels," and then he discounted them as doubtful sightings, adding, "The Commanding Officer has had a long history of defective vision which has grown progressively worse with each patrol until now he has difficulty recognizing his friends beyond 30 paces. He therefore views with suspicion anything he sees himself which is not verified."

Hap Lyon turned *Gudgeon* toward the targets and remained on the surface, going in. Dornin, who had already proved himself to be one of the most courageous men in the submarine force, said later, "Frankly, I urged Hap to dive. God! There were planes all around. There's a line between bravery and recklessness. You have to draw that line."

Lyon dived, closing at top speed. He remained on a normal approach course for forty-five minutes. When he raised the periscope, the battleships were nowhere in sight. There were Japanese planes overhead, so he decided to remain where he was, believing he must be on—or near—the rendezvous point for the Japanese carriers. He waited two hours but saw no carriers. He wrote in his patrol report, "Felt I should proceed to a better station but had no idea where to go." He waited on station until 4 P.M., hoping to see the Japanese carriers, but he had no further contact with enemy ships. At dusk, he poked up his radio antenna to see if English had any new instruc-

tions, but a plane (Japanese or U.S.) bombed *Gudgeon*
and Lyon went back down.

William Brockman in old *Nautilus* picked up a contact report from U.S. aircraft at 5:44 A.M. He plotted
the position and concluded that if the report were accurate the Japanese striking force was close by, on the
northern boundary of his sector. Remaining submerged,
he guided slow, clumsy *Nautilus* toward the position.

At 7:55, Brockman saw masts on the horizon. While
making this observation, his periscope was strafed by an
aircraft. At 8 A.M. he sighted a formation of four ships:
a battleship and a cruiser in column with two "cruisers"
on the bow, escorting. (The "cruisers" were probably
destroyers; many submarine skippers confused destroyers
for cruisers in the early days of the war.) Before
Brockman could get off a shot, one of the destroyers
turned and attacked, dropping twenty depth charges and
forcing *Nautilus* deep.

Twenty-four minutes later, Brockman was back at
periscope depth, taking another look. As he wrote later:

*The picture presented on raising the periscope was one
never experienced in peacetime practices. Ships were on
all sides moving across the field at high speed and circling away to avoid the submarine's position. Ranges
were above 3,000 yards. The cruiser had passed over
and was now astern. The battleship was on our port
bow and firing her whole starboard broadside battery at
the periscope. Flag hoists were being made; searchlights
were trained at the periscope.*

Brockman coolly fired two torpedoes at the battleship,
which was now evading at high speed. One torpedo failed
to fire; the other missed.

The destroyer charged in again, pinging. Brockman
dropped to 150 feet, with depth charges exploding all
around. When the Japanese broke off the attack, he came
back to periscope depth, astonished to find a Japanese
carrier barreling along on a converging course. As he was
looking, the destroyer charged in again. Brockman set
up and fired one torpedo at the destroyer, forcing it to
change course, but it returned in a moment, dropping

eight more charges. Brockman took *Nautilus* deep, creeping along the converging course for the carrier. When the depth-charging stopped, he promptly returned to periscope depth. The seas were empty.

Half an hour later, at 10:29, Brockman spotted four "large clouds" of smoke on the horizon. This was five minutes after navy dive bombers had hit *Akagi*, *Kaga*, and *Soryu*. At the same time, he picked up a message that a carrier had been damaged. Brockman turned toward the smoke, which he estimated to be about 10 or 11 miles distant. At 11:45, he saw clearly the smoke was coming from a burning carrier, range 8 miles. He continued on submerged at 3 to 4 knots. The burning carrier seemed to be motionless.

As they came up on the target, Brockman's exec, Roy Stanley ("Ensign") Benson, and others had a good look through the periscope. They compared the carrier silhouette to recognition pictures of Japanese ships pasted on the bulkhead in the conning tower and decided the carrier was *Soryu*. Its fires seemed to be under control; two cruisers (or destroyers) stood by. Men in whaleboats were apparently trying to pass a tow line.

Brockman ordered four torpedo tubes made ready. In the six minutes between 1:59 and 2:05, he fired four carefully aimed torpedoes. Three functioned; one failed to leave the tube. At the periscope, Brockman watched the torpedoes streak 2,700 yards toward the carrier. "Red flames," he reported, "appeared along the ship from bow to amidships . . . many men were seen going over the side." All five officers in the conning tower took turns looking through the periscope at the target. Then the destroyers charged *Nautilus*, and Brockman, satisfied he had sunk a damaged carrier, went to 300 feet. "The Commanding Officer believes that she was destroyed at this time by fire and internal explosions," Brockman later wrote. "He did not, however, actually see her sink."

Brockman's performance on June 4, in terms of courage and persistence, was outstanding, and he received a Navy Cross. Credited with sinking *Soryu*, Brockman was later to be denied. In a careful postwar analysis, the U.S. Navy determined, after comparing position reports of *Nautilus* and the Japanese forces, that the carrier Brockman shot at was not *Soryu* but *Kaga*. Japanese survivors provided proof. Three rescued from *Kaga* reported seeing three torpedoes fired from a submarine at 2:10, about the time Brockman fired. Two of the torpedoes missed. The third struck amidships but failed to explode. It shattered, throwing loose the air flask, which floated free and served for a while as a life preserver for several of *Kaga*'s crew. Survivors of *Soryu* reported no submarine torpedoes fired at that vessel.

The eight other submarines patrolling close by Midway that day were too far removed to close the enemy. Pilly Lent in *Grenadier*, patrolling in the sector south of *Nautilus*, intercepted a contact report at 6:15 A.M. After a quick plot, Lent realized the force "was already beyond us." At 8:37 he surfaced and proceeded toward Midway, "hoping to intercept retiring enemy units." A plane drove him down at 8:55. After a few minutes, he again surfaced and continued on.

To the south of *Grenadier*, even farther from the striking force, Eliot Olsen in *Grayling* had little chance at making an attack. He milled around, hoping to intercept something worthwhile. While so doing, he unwittingly became a target for U.S. aircraft.

On the afternoon of June 7, a formation of twelve B-17s based on Midway caught *Grayling* cruising on the surface. The bomber pilots—all green—believed they had found a retreating Japanese cruiser. Although Olsen flashed a proper recognition signal with his searchlight, the three leading B-17s dropped a string of twenty 1,000-pound bombs. Olsen immediately crash-dived. When the B-17 pilots returned to Midway, they triumphantly reported sinking "one Japanese cruiser which went down in fifteen seconds."

To the south of *Grayling*, the remaining four boats—*Gato, Trout, Dolphin,* and *Tambor*—were frustrated and ineffectual. While trying to run on the surface toward the enemy force, they were machine-gunned or lightly bombed by enemy (or friendly) aircraft. They dived to avoid being hit. None was able to make enough distance to meet the enemy.

After the June 4 battle, there remained a huge Japanese naval force somewhere on the seas to the west of

Midway: the main body of battleships, some light carriers, many cruisers and destroyers, plus the invasion force. (This force included an extraordinary vessel, *Yamato*, the largest warship ever built. She and two sister ships, *Musashi* and *Shinano*, were designed by Japanese naval architects in 1935, after Japan renounced the arms limitation agreement. Each ship was to be about 59,000 tons, mounting nine 18-inch guns—more firepower than any ship in history. Built in secret, *Yamato* was completed in December 1941, after Pearl Harbor. *Musashi* came later. Before *Shinano* was completed, the Japanese decided to convert her to an aircraft carrier—the world's largest. All three ships had heavy armor plating and were considered, by the Japanese, unsinkable. The codebreakers did not know about them for a long time.) Nimitz did not believe the Japanese would now attempt the Midway landing, but the possibility could not be disregarded.

At 2:15 A.M. on June 5, John Williams Murphy, Jr., in *Tambor*, 90 miles to the west of Midway, made contact with a group of ships. It was dark. Neither Murphy nor his officers was certain what they had found. Murphy got off a vague contact report to Bob English, mentioning "many unidentified ships," but did not give a course.

This message actually led to a major mistake in the Battle of Midway. Admiral Raymond A. Spruance, commanding U.S. forces, assumed the "many unidentified ships" must be the Japanese invasion force and that the invasion was still on. The carrier forces redeployed to the north of Midway to gain a favorable position to attack the invasion force as it closed. Bob English ordered his Midway submarines to fall back to a 5-mile radius from the island and repel landing forces. He also ordered the three boats standing by between Midway and Hawaii— *Trigger*, *Plunger*, and *Narwhal*—to join the Midway force.

In fact, however, Yamamoto, the chief of the Japanese navy, had given up the attempt and had ordered his forces to fall back, regroup, and leave the area. The "many unidentified ships" that Murphy had sighted were merely four cruisers and two destroyers which had been previously ordered to bombard Midway. About forty minutes after Murphy sent off his report, Yamamoto ordered them to rejoin the retreating forces. When they turned to do so, a

Japanese lookout sighted *Tambor* and gave the alarm. In maneuvering to avoid, two of the cruisers, *Mogami* and *Mikuma,* collided. *Mogami* severely damaged her bow; *Mikuma* trailed oil from a ruptured fuel tank. The other two cruisers retired to the northwest, leaving *Mogami* and *Mikuma* and the destroyer escort proceeding on a westerly course, speed reduced to 17 knots.

Although Murphy had been in visual contact with the cruisers and destroyers for two hours, he had not got off a torpedo. He was afraid, he said later, that they might be friendly forces, reported to be in the area. However, at 4:12 A.M., with visibility increasing, he recognized the ships as Japanese and saw that *Mogami* was badly damaged. With dawn coming on, Murphy submerged. He was unable to gain attack position, but at about six he got off another contact report, this time correctly identifying the vessels as two *Mogami*-class cruisers on a westerly course.

Four valuable hours had gone by between *Tambor's* first and second reports. During that time Admiral Spruance, anticipating an invasion, had moved about 100 miles to the northeast of Midway, and the submarines had pulled back eastward to stations about 5 or 10 miles from Midway. During the same four hours, Yamamoto's major forces had moved about 100 miles farther west and were increasing the gap by about 25 miles every hour. Two or three more confused hours went by before land-based Midway planes reported positively that there was no sign of an invasion. On the contrary, every contact they found indicated the Japanese forces in full retreat.

Thus Murphy's report sent all U.S. forces capable of pursuing and attacking the badly disorganized Japanese forces *in the wrong direction.* Aircraft sank the limping *Mikuma,* badly damaged *Mogami,* and unsuccessfully attacked a destroyer, *Tanikaze.* But the rest of the Japanese force got clean away, withdrawing toward Wake, where Japanese land-based aircraft could provide protection. Now low on fuel and aware of Japanese planes concentrating on Wake, the U.S. carriers broke off the chase, and the opportunity to inflict a coup de grace on the Japanese navy was irretrievably lost.

Some naval historians make the case that this was a lucky break for Admiral Spruance. The codebreakers had no knowledge of the superbattleship *Yamato.* Had Spru-

ance pursued instead of retiring, it is possible that he
would unwittingly have brought his two remaining carriers, *Enterprise* and *Hornet*, within range of *Yamato*'s
18-inch guns in darkness, when he was unable to launch
planes. *Yamato* might well have sunk both carriers, turning the Midway victory for the United States into a draw.

On the brand-new *Trigger*, commanded by Jack Hay-
den Lewis, there was a tremendous surge of excitement
as she raced to engage the landing force supposedly bearing down on Midway. In the early hours of June 6, with
the lights of Midway visible on the horizon, Edward Latimer ("Ned") Beach had the watch. "We got orders to
change course," said another officer, reservist Richard S.
Garvey. "Ned reported land ahead and sent for the skipper. After a few minutes, Lewis came from the bridge to
study a chart wearing red goggles, the new invention to
preserve night vision. There were some reefs on the chart
marked in red. We weren't experienced with night-adapta-
tion goggles then. We didn't realize that red goggles
blanked out the red on the chart."

Having studied the chart, Lewis went back to the
bridge to conn the ship into its proper position. "The next
thing you know," Garvey said, "somebody yelled down
that we were either running into land or the wake of a
huge ship."

In fact, *Trigger* was going aground. Beach later described the moment: "suddenly, catastrophically, with a
horrible, shattering smash, *Trigger* ran head on into a
submerged coral wall! Her bow shot skyward. Her sturdy
hull screamed with pain as she crashed and pounded to a
stop . . . here poor *Trigger* lay, bruised, battered, and
hors de combat."

Below decks, all was turmoil. "I was sleeping in the
wardroom with Willie Long, another officer," Garvey recalled. "There was a terrific crash. Long and I were
thrown out of our bunks. All the lights went out. The
collision alarm went off. The watertight doors slammed
shut. We were sealed in the compartment. I thought we
had been torpedoed. Long said, 'Hell, we can't do anything about it. We may as well go back to bed.' "

Lewis, dismayed, surveyed his ship. *Trigger* was stuck
fast, with the Japanese invasion fleet expected any mo-

ment. Feverishly, the crew lightened ship, emptying the trim tanks and dumping fuel. After a call for help, a tug came from Midway. Backing emergency, and with the tug straining, *Trigger* broke free and refloated. There was a "gaping hole" in a ballast tank, the sonar heads had been wiped away, but *Trigger* was still seaworthy. She took up her patrol station.

For the next several days, English shifted his boats here and there, trying to intercept various Japanese vessels, damaged and otherwise. Most of the submarines returning from distant patrol were pressed into this elusive hunt. They had various minor adventures. *Cuttlefish* was bombed by planes; *Grouper* fired a torpedo at a "submarine periscope" but missed; *Greenling* tried to find two cruisers returning to Wake Island; *Drum* was sent to find a "burning battleship" and "damaged cruiser" retreating to the west. None did any damage to the Japanese.

So ended what was later to be called the "incredible victory." Yamamoto had failed abjectly. He had drawn Nimitz into a decisive battle which the United States, not the Japanese, won. Credit for the outcome was largely due the codebreakers.

Years later, Chester Nimitz, in collaboration with Professor E. B. Potter of the U.S. Naval Academy, wrote in *The Great Sea War:*

Midway was essentially a victory of intelligence. . . . Since the United States was intercepting and reading Japanese coded messages, American intelligence of the enemy's plans was remarkably complete. Nimitz's information indicated the Japanese objectives, the approximate composition of the enemy forces, the direction of approach, and the approximate date of attack. It was this knowledge that made the American victory possible.

The submariners had done little in the battle. Only two or three got off a torpedo, and none hit anything. One sent an incomplete contact report that misled Admiral Spruance and prevented the possible sinking of more major Japanese ships. The skippers blamed Bob English's plan; Bob English blamed the skippers.

4

VITAL TORPEDO TESTS

John Wilkes and the Asiatic submarine force in Fremantle were still in despair. In April, although Wilkes managed to get seven boats on patrol, two of the seven, *Pike* and *Porpoise*, returned to Pearl Harbor for overhaul; three, *Swordfish, Sailfish,* and *Searaven,* had been assigned to special missions to Corregidor and Timor; and only one boat, *Skipjack*, commanded by James Wiggins Coe, achieved any success. Off Camranh Bay, Coe sank three confirmed ships for 12,800 tons. In terms of confirmed ships sunk, this was the best score achieved on a single patrol by any Asiatic skipper. All the others turned in zero results.

While the April boats were out, Wilkes, who was long overdue for rotation to the States, received a radio dispatch stating his replacement was on the way. The man was Charles Andrews Lockwood, Jr., recently detached from the job of naval attaché in London and promoted to rear admiral. He had spent his life in submarines.

Lockwood, an eternal optimist and man of good cheer, was almost overcome by the depression and fatigue he found all through the command. He buzzed here and there, giving pep talks. He leased two small hotels for submarine rest camps, the Ocean Beach at the seashore and the King Edward in downtown Perth. Then he launched an informal inquiry to find out why Asiatic submarines had not done a better job of stopping the Japanese in the Philippines and Java, summarizing his findings in a personal letter to an old friend in Washington, Admiral Richard S. Edwards, right-hand man to the Navy's Chief, Admiral Ernest J. King.

The boys here [Lockwood wrote] *have had a tough
row to hoe in the last four months. Why they didn't get
more enemy ships is a highly controversial point but my
reading of all war diaries thus far submitted has convinced
me that among the causes are: (a) bad choice of stations
in that most likely invasion points were not covered soon
enough nor heavily enough, (b) bad torpedo performance,
in that they evidently ran much too deep and had numerous prematures . . . , (c) buck fever—firing with ship
swinging when he thought it was on a steady course; set
up for one target and firing at a totally different one, (d)
lack of or misunderstanding of aggressiveness; many
evaded destroyers in the belief that they should save torpedoes for convoy following; one said he thought a sub
should never "pick a fight with a destroyer."*

Shortly after Lockwood arrived in Fremantle, Coe in
Skipjack returned from his fifty-day patrol off Camranh
Bay. Coe, a methodical as well as a courageous officer,
submitted a careful analysis of Mark XIV torpedo performance for his patrol. There was every indication, he said,
that torpedoes were running much deeper than set. He
added a bitter postscript. "To make a round trip of 8,500
miles into enemy waters, to gain attack position undetected within 800 yards of enemy ships only to find that
the torpedoes run deep and over half the time will fail to
explode, seems to me to be an undesirable manner of gaining information which might be determined any morning
within a few miles of a torpedo station in the presence of
comparatively few hazards."

After reviewing Coe's report, Lockwood decided to take
action beyond his letter to Edwards. His first official
action was within proper channels; he inquired of the
Bureau of Ordnance if there was any information or re-
cent tests to indicate deep-running in the Mark XIV
or defects in the exploder. He received in reply a prompt
—and lofty—pronouncement which, in effect, accused the
skippers of using torpedo defects as an alibi for poor
marksmanship. Receiving this, Lockwood was enraged. "I
decided to take matters into my own hands," he wrote
later.

Lockwood chose to conduct his own tests, as Tyrrell
Jacobs in Surabaya, had proposed. Wilkes had been in

Australia for almost three months, and still this had not been done. "All the skippers wanted to make the tests," a submariner said. "But you have to remember that the Bureau of Ordnance was a mighty bureaucracy. A naval officer, conditioned to believe the bureau's word was infallible in matters of ordnance, did not lightly challenge it. They could snow you with technical data, incomprehensible to the average line officer. It took Charlie Lockwood —plus flag rank—to take that bull by the horns."

Lockwood got in touch with James Fife, Jr., chief of staff of the Asiatic Submarine Force, based in Albany with the submarine tender *Fulton,* refitting submarines after patrol. The two men discussed the possibility of a test. Fife suggested that he obtain a fishnet from one of the many Portuguese fishermen working from Frenchman's Bay, Albany, and fire some of Coe's remaining torpedoes into it. Lockwood agreed.

This test—considered historic by many submarine skippers—was conducted on June 20, 1942, more than six months after the Japanese attack on Pearl Harbor. By that time, the three submarine commands had fired over eight hundred torpedoes in combat. Not one had been fired in a controlled test.

Under Fife's direction, the net was submerged in the calm, quiet waters of Frenchman's Bay. Ted Aylward (ex-*Searaven*), who had served a tour at Newport in 1928 and was now torpedo officer of *Holland,* was an official witness. Coe brought *Skipjack* to within 850 yards of the net and submerged to periscope depth. His torpedomen had loaded into a tube one of the Mark XIV torpedoes Coe had carried for the last seventy days. It was fitted with an "exercise head," weighted with calcium chloride solution to approximate the weight of a live warhead. They set the torpedo to run at 10 feet.

On signal from Fife, Coe fired. The torpedo swished from the tube, bearing down on the net. When it had been recovered, its built-in depth recorder showed that it had run at a depth of 25 feet. When the net was hauled up, there was a ragged hole punched in it at a depth of 25 feet. Both sets of data showed the torpedo (which follows a porpoising path) had run 15 feet deeper than set.

This test proved what most skippers had suspected. But the professorial Fife was not satisfied. One test was not a "scientific sample." On the following day, with Fife officiating, Coe fired two more torpedoes at the net. The first, set again for 10 feet, was fired from a shorter range, 700 yards. It cut the net at 18 feet. The second torpedo was set for zero feet and also cut the net at 18 feet. After taking ranges, the porpoising track of a torpedo, and other factors into account, the three tests indicated to Fife that the Mark XIV ran an average 11 feet deeper than set. On the day following the second test, June 22, Lockwood sent off a message to the Bureau of Ordnance, describing the tests and the results.

In Pearl Harbor, Bob English, who monitored Lockwood's transmissions, must have been startled to read the message to BuOrd, going over the air as it did only four days following English's own message on torpedo policy (listing eight reasons for torpedo failure, most of them the fault of skippers or crews). After he read Lockwood's message, English did a complete about-face. He informed BuOrd that some of his skippers reported deep-running torpedoes and inquired, HAVE NET TESTS INDICATED THAT TORPEDOES RUN GREATER THAN FOUR FEET BELOW SET DEPTH?

The Bureau of Ordnance responded to Lockwood on June 30. "Instead of thanking us," Lockwood wrote, "they scorned our inaccurate approach to obtain these findings." Specifically, BuOrd stated "no reliable conclusions" could be drawn from Lockwood's tests "because of improper torpedo trim conditions introduced." Lockwood, privately furious, reported that he would repeat the tests with proper trimming. He also asked that the bureau request Newport to make its own test and inform him of results by urgent dispatch.

Lockwood then set up another, "more scientific" field test. In Albany, Jimmy Fife made arrangements to restring the fishing net. On July 18, *Saury,* in Albany for refit, fired four Mark XIV torpedoes at the net from a range of 850 to 900 yards. The first shot was wasted; the fishing net had been carried away during the night. After the net was reset, the other three torpedoes were fired, set to run at 10 feet. All three punched holes in the net at 21 feet. Fife concluded, as in the first test, that the torpedoes ran an average of 11 feet deeper than designed.

Lockwood considered this second series of tests conclusive. Two days later, he sent off a dispatch to the Bureau of Ordnance, reporting the results. In addition, he wrote another personal letter, this one to William Henry ("Spike") Blandy, then chief of the Bureau of Ordnance. Blandy was a year junior to Lockwood and an old friend. Lockwood told him, "We haven't gotten very far in our exchange of punts and I am very desirous not to start a radio controversy with your Bureau. Please lend us a hand to clear the air and give us the dope we need." He asked Blandy to devote some of his "valuable time" to the project and request that the Newport Torpedo Station make backup tests.

Admiral King and Admiral Edwards, meanwhile, were making a special effort to help the submarine force solve its torpedo problems. Roland Pryce (ex-*Spearfish*) returned to Washington and, working with Edwards, prepared an analysis of all torpedo attacks to date. "Our conclusion," he said later, "was that no matter what blame the Commanding Officer assumed, or what questionable claims were made, we should have had about 100 percent more hits."

On the day after Lockwood radioed the results of the test, Admiral King, who received a copy of the dispatch, lit a blowtorch under the Bureau of Ordnance. In a letter to Blandy, King requested that the Bureau proceed immediately to recheck the tactical data for all torpedoes. King stressed that "it was of utmost importance not only to supply submarine personnel with correct data but in addition to take steps to restore their confidence in the reliability and accuracy of the performance data furnished them."

In Pearl Harbor, Bob English, who had also received a copy of Lockwood's latest dispatch, officially informed his skippers that the Mark XIV torpedoes ran 11 feet deeper than set. He ordered his boats to continue to rely on the Mark VI magnetic exploder but to subtract 11 feet to obtain the correct depth setting.

With this convergence of pressure, Spike Blandy was moved to action. Newport ran a new series of tests, this time firing from a submerged submarine, *Herring,* rather than from a "torpedo barge." On August 1, almost eight months after the Pearl Harbor attack, Newport conceded that the Mark XIV ran 10 feet deeper than set. In a follow-up memo six weeks later, Newport admitted that its depth-control mechanism had been "improperly designed and tested" and passed along instructions for making modifications so that the Mark XIV torpedo could be "trusted" to run within 3 feet of the actual depth settings.

In one sense, all this was immensely gratifying to Lockwood and his skippers. They had browbeaten the Bureau of Ordnance into conceding, officially, what was already known, and all skippers could now fire torpedoes at a uniform depth without fudging their official reports. Yet those who had already been setting torpedoes to run much shallower than authorized were far from satisfied. They believed the magnetic exploder to be defective as well, and they urged further tests to determine what caused prematures, duds, and other erratic torpedo behavior.

Here Lockwood, like Bob English, demurred. He believed that the deep-running fault had been the major cause of the apparent failure of the magnetic exploder. The torpedoes had been running too deep to enter the magnetic field of the target, and so they failed to explode. Now the torpedoes would be set to run shallower, the magnetic exploder—potentially a marvelous device—would work. Lockwood held to this view even though he knew, like others, that the British and Germans had discarded their magnetic exploding devices after a long period of unsatisfactory performance.

One overriding reason for holding to the magnetic exploder was that the warheads on the Mark XIV torpedo were relatively puny; 500 pounds. If the force relied solely on contact exploders, it could never hope to penetrate the armor of the glamorous targets: battleships and aircraft carriers. Moreover, one 500-pound warhead was not likely to finish off even a sizable merchantman. A positive sinking would require at least two or three torpedoes—perhaps four—an unacceptable expenditure, considering the acute shortage and the slow production rate in the United States. Finally, the contact exploder was not the best to use against shallow-draft vessels—destroyers, for example. The torpedo would have to be set to run so shallow it might broach and run erratically, perhaps even circling back to the submarine that fired it.

During the four-month period May–August 1942, Lockwood's Fremantle submarine force consisted of twenty boats. Four arrived from Pearl Harbor: *Gar, Grampus, Grayback,* and *Tautog.* Three returned to Pearl Harbor for overhaul: *Pickerel, Stingray,* and *Permit.* The five old S-boats were sent to Brisbane, on Australia's east coast. In all, Lockwood mounted twenty-eight patrols from Fremantle, spreading his small force thin at Indochina, Manila, Davao, Java, Borneo, and other areas conquered by the Japanese. The results were—predictably—very poor. One reason: the assertion that the skippers lacked aggressiveness appeared to be correct in all too many cases.

Snapper, commanded by Hamilton Stone, was a troubled boat. The exec, Carl Tiedeman, and the junior officers were unhappy. On May 27, Lockwood made an entry in his personal diary: "Investigated *Snapper* most of the morning and was very sorry to tell her skipper that I am going to relieve him of command. No other solution possible."

To replace Stone, Lockwood picked Harold Edward Baker, then only thirty-three and the second youngest officer to be chosen to command a fleet boat (after his classmate of 1932, Richard Victor Gregory in *Sargo*). Baker had stood 8 of 421 in his class and had been literary editor of *The Log.* He had been exec of *Permit* under Adrian Hurst and Moon Chapple.

Young Baker took *Snapper* on her third patrol to the Celebes Sea. The cruise was a bust. During the forty-nine days at sea, *Snapper* sighted only small Japanese patrol vessels and returned to port without having fired a torpedo. The next time out, Baker went to the South China Sea and was on patrol for seventy-nine days. He fired two torpedoes at a freighter and missed. On the way back to Fremantle, *Snapper* was bombed by a friendly navy patrol plane.

Lockwood had adopted the Pearl Harbor custom of appending endorsements to the patrol reports. Baker's endorsements for this patrol were scathing. Jimmy Fife wrote, "The past two cruises of *Snapper* have been devoid of aggressive hunting for the enemy. This submarine had not been fought to expected effectiveness." Lockwood wrote in his personal diary that he "met *Snapper* . . . and was depressed by her showing. We'll have to pull out skipper." Next day, after lunch with Baker, Lockwood noted, "Told him . . . I'd have to relieve him because he hasn't done a proper job."

Baker returned to the States for further assignment. *Snapper* sailed on into an unhappy future.

Baker's classmate, young Rich Gregory on *Sargo*, was not doing much better. On his second patrol in command of *Sargo*, he patrolled the South China Sea. In his only attack, he fired three torpedoes at a freighter and missed. Fife wrote in the endorsement, "It is evident that three torpedoes were wasted. This is particularly censurable considering current shortage."

Lockwood's operations officer, Heber Hampton ("Tex") McLean, requested permission to make a patrol with Gregory on *Sargo*. This was a radical idea; no senior officer in Pearl Harbor or Fremantle had ever made a regular war patrol on a submarine. Lockwood gave the proposal a "fair breeze." It would not only give McLean an opportunity to observe Gregory, it would also provide McLean with combat experience that might be helpful in planning future operations.

Gregory made his third patrol in the South China Sea. McLean was not impressed. Later he said, "Gregory was a hell of a fine guy, personally. But he was more the engineering type." Under the watchful eye of McLean, Gregory fired two torpedoes at a freighter. When it did not sink, he fired three more torpedoes, which missed. One circled back at *Sargo* and exploded close by the stern. Gregory then surfaced and pumped thirty-five rounds of 3-inch ammunition at the ship. Finally, *Teibo Maru*, 4,472 tons, went down.

When *Sargo* returned from patrol, McLean recommended that Gregory be relieved of command. To Lockwood he said privately, "You ought to give the *Sargo* cook a medal. He's the best morale builder on the boat." Lockwood agreed. He wrote, "*Sargo*'s patrol was not conducted with sufficient aggressiveness. Torpedoes were wasted, opportunities were lost to inflict damage on the enemy indicating a lack of basic training."

Gregory was relieved of command and assigned to the Submarine Repair Unit, Fremantle.

One of the exchange boats, *Grampus*, commanded by Edward Shillingford Hutchinson, made its third patrol off Manila Bay. When Hutchinson arrived on station, he found a full moon shining brilliantly, making *Grampus* a good target for antisubmarine vessels. Without asking Fremantle, Hutchinson shifted to Lingayen Gulf, where he found the weather bad. He then withdrew westward 60 miles—into open ocean. During the course of the patrol, many of his crew became ill with catarrhal fever and suffered from food and water poisoning. Hutchinson sighted several juicy targets—including a seaplane ferry and a tanker—which he fired at but missed.

Hutchinson's patrol report endorsements were also harsh. His division commander, Charles Dixon ("Shorty") Edmunds, said, "The Commanding Officer's reasoning in conducting the patrol off Lingayen Gulf instead of Manila Bay is not understood." His squadron commander, Allan Rockwell McCann, wrote, "Of six contacts reported only two attacks were made; approaches on the others were broken off because the range could not be closed sufficiently while submerged for an attack. In no case was an attempt made to gain a firing position by using high speed on the surface." Lockwood added the final chilly note. "This patrol of *Grampus* was not conducted in a sufficiently aggressive manner."

Also relieved of command, Hutchinson returned to the States for new construction. But he would be heard from again.

Willard Arthur Saunders, commanding another exchange boat, *Grayback*, patrolling off Camranh Bay, also conducted a less than distinguished patrol. Saunders found five targets. He was unable to close two, but on August 7 he fired two torpedoes at a small trawler from a range of 2,050 yards. On August 12, he fired three more at another target. None of the torpedoes hit. Saunders cut his patrol short and came home.

Grayback's patrol report endorsements were not glowing. "The Commanding Officer and the Executive Officer showed marked symptoms of physical fatigue on return to port." Another: "The Commanding Officer states that physical endurance of officers and crew was heavily taxed by this patrol, and discontinued the patrol a few days early on this account." Lockwood admonished Saunders for not patrolling closer to the coast and said, "The decision to fire torpedoes at a small armed trawler was not sound."

Saunders was relieved. He returned to the States for new construction.

Chet Smith, taking *Swordfish* on her fourth patrol, cruised in the South China Sea and Gulf of Siam. Smith, as usual, conducted an extremely aggressive patrol, sinking two confirmed ships for 6,500 tons. However, he came down with a bad cold, and when he returned to Fremantle he asked Lockwood to let him remain in port during *Swordfish*'s next patrol.

To replace Smith for this one patrol, Lockwood picked Albert Collins ("Acey") Burrows, a lawyer like Gene McKinney. Burrows, who had made one war patrol on Hurd's *Seal* as a Prospective Commanding Officer (PCO), took *Swordfish* to the Celebes Sea. He fired eleven torpedoes, achieving no damage. All officers and about 90 percent of the crew came down with an acute stomach disorder which was thought to be caused by food poisoning but was later traced to bad drinking water.

On return to Fremantle, Burrows was severely criticized. Jimmy Fife fumed over the profligate expenditure of torpedoes, resulting in zero damage, complaining that Burrows "allowed four valuable targets to escape." Lockwood grumped that Burrows spent time submerged "in the wrong area" and that Burrows's conduct of the patrol showed "lack of experience and seasoned judgment."

Burrows returned command of *Swordfish* to Chet Smith and reported for duty on Lockwood's staff. Burrows, too, would be heard from again—in spectacular fashion.

John Burnside in *Saury* had a difficult time on his third patrol. Setting off in late April, he was forced to return to Fremantle to repair a broken tank. He got under way again in early May to patrol off Manila. His exec was

Harry Meakin Lindsay, Jr., Hockett William Hazzard, who had left *S-37* to join *Saury,* believed Lindsay to be a detriment to Burnside. "Off Manila," Hazzard said later, "Lindsay fudged the navigation to make it look as though we were closer to shore than we were. Lindsay thought Burnside was rash to get in too close. In the hands of a better exec, Burnside might have done much better."

Returning from Manila, Burnside received an Ultra on an aircraft ferry carrying planes and aviation stores to Kendari. Burnside planned to intercept off Davao Gulf. On station, he ordered periscope looks every fifteen minutes. On one of these looks, Bill Hazzard spotted the ship. After a brief approach, Burnside fired but then lost depth control, exposing the periscope shears. "We were too far off the track and too late," Hazzard said. "An aggressive exec would have insisted on more frequent looks."

On return to Fremantle, Burnside was relieved. He went to surface forces and then was stricken by Hodgkin's disease, spent most of the war in hospitals, and died in 1946.

Lockwood appointed Leonard Sparks ("Tex") Mewhinney, an enthusiastic Texan, to replace Burnside, and *Saury* got another lawyer. Mewhinney, another lawyer, had served on S-boats in peacetime and had gone along on Burnside's last patrol as a PCO. He took *Saury* back to the Manila area, keeping Lindsay for his exec—temporarily. (Lindsay was later sent to general service.) Off Manila, Mewhinney bungled an attack on a huge fast-moving tanker. He fired two torpedoes, hitting the tanker's propellers. The tanker stopped dead, but Mewhinney, fearing an air attack, went deep, and when he returned to periscope depth the tanker was gone.

Mewhinney made up for the bungle on the way home. One night, while *Saury* was cruising on the surface in Makassar Strait, the bridge watch picked up a target. Bill Hazzard, who had good night vision and saw the target, urged a night surface attack. As Hazzard recalled, Mewhinney demurred. His night vision was poor; he preferred a periscope. However, time ran out. Mewhinney "grudgingly" shot quickly, on the surface, in darkness, firing three torpedoes. Moments later, there was an awesome explosion. Flames shot 1,000 feet straight up into the air as the aircraft ferry *Kanto Maru,* 8,600 tons, filled with aviation gasoline, blew up and sank.

Even old hands who had demonstrated no lack of aggressiveness came in for criticism.

Gene McKinney took *Salmon* on her third patrol off Indochina, where he nailed two handsome targets—his first confirmed ships. The first vessel he believed to be the light cruiser *Yubari;* it turned out to be even better, the repair ship *Asahi*, 11,400 tons, one of the largest ships sunk by any submarine up to that time. The second was a transport, *Ganges Maru*, 4,400 tons.

On his next patrol, McKinney was not so lucky. Cruising northeast of Borneo in Palawan Passage, he intercepted a huge converted whale factory, set up, fired—and missed. When he returned to Fremantle, Jimmy Fife's endorsement was frosty, blaming the miss on "personnel failure in the operation of the TDC, which caused torpedoes to go out on the wrong gyro angle and pass astern of the target."

Freddy Warder, taking *Seawolf* on her fifth patrol, cruised off Manila Bay, near Corregidor. Ever aggressive, Warder made seven separate attacks against seven ships, including an armed merchantman and a destroyer. Even so, Lockwood was critical of the patrol, suggesting that Warder might have gained better firing position on these ships if he had not patrolled *so close in*. He refused to credit Warder with a sinking, but postwar Japanese records gave Warder one small freighter of 1,200 tons. This was the first confirmed ship sunk by Warder.

On the next patrol, Warder took station near Borneo. He made six attacks and was credited with sinking two ships, confirmed in postwar records, and damaging one. Both Fife and Lockwood were again critical. "*Seawolf* obtained two hits out of seventeen torpedoes fired," Fife complained. "This is far below the expected standard of performance." Lockwood bore down harder. "The failure of *Seawolf* to inflict greater damage on the enemy can be attributed principally to improper solution of fire-control problems. Decisions to fire were made when excessive ranges existed [and] when lack of reliable data indicated that only a bare possibility of hitting would result." To all this, Warder later responded, "The goddamned torpedoes were no damned good. That was the problem."

Moon Chapple in *Permit*, patrolling in the Java Sea off Surabaya and northward in Makassar Strait, had a luckless time. He was directed by two separate Ultras to intercept tankers coming into Tarakan and Balikpapan but missed both and ran *Permit* aground on DeBril Bank. He returned to port without having fired a torpedo.

On the next patrol, Chapple took *Permit* to Pearl Harbor for overhaul by way of Davao Gulf. Again, no attacks. Bob English, who wrote the endorsement in Pearl Harbor, criticized Chapple for remaining submerged too much and for failing to make more frequent periscope observations.

Kenneth Hurd took *Seal* on her third and fourth patrols in the waters off Indochina. On the third patrol, he sank one small freighter for 2,000 tons; on the fourth, he made eleven contacts but managed to damage only one, a freighter estimated at 4,000 tons. Both Fife and Lockwood were critical. "More damage," Lockwood wrote, "should have been inflicted on the enemy." Hurd had declined to attack a destroyer. Lockwood called this a mistake and urged all skippers to take on destroyers.

William ("Pete") Ferrall returned *Seadragon* to the Indochina coast for her third patrol. It was a good one. In six attacks, Ferrall sank three ships for 16,000 tons, all confirmed in Japanese records. Both Fife and Lockwood wrote approving endorsements. Ferrall had topped Jim Coe's record, set in *Skipjack* in May, of three ships for 12,800 tons.

On the fourth patrol, Ferrall returned to the same area. He made contact with eighteen enemy ships, including two heavy cruisers, attacked five ships, and claimed two sunk. However, this was reduced in postwar records to one for 2,500 tons. Lockwood was not pleased with *Seadragon*'s performance, noting, "With targets as scarce as they are, submarines must take what comes rather than wait for something better, and must relentlessly pursue all contacts." He was particularly critical of Ferrall's attack on the two heavy cruisers, which resulted in no damage. Ferrall blamed it on faulty magnetic exploders, but Fife disagreed, stating that Ferrall had made a mistake in the speed estimate.

One episode on this patrol became submarine legend. While off Indochina, one of Ferrall's crewmen, Seaman First Class Darrell Dean Rector, fell to the deck unconscious. The ship "doctor," Pharmacist's Mate First Class

Wheeler B. Lipes, diagnosed Rector's malady as appendicitis—a bad case.

What to do? The prescribed procedure was to put the man in bed, pack him with ice, and keep him on a strict liquid diet until the submarine returned from patrol. Saunders on *Grayback* had had a case of appendicitis on his last patrol and had done just that. But Lipes did not think Rector could last. In his opinion, there was only one way to save him—operate.

Ferrall was torn. Lipes was no doctor. He had never operated on anyone for appendicitis. Yet Rector was in agony. Lipes said to Rector, "I can do it, but it's a chance. If you don't want me to go ahead . . ."

"Let's go," Rector said.

That settled it. Ferrall gave his approval and ordered preparations. He took *Seadragon* to 120 feet to ensure a smooth platform. The wardroom was converted to an operating room. Ferrall's exec, Norvell Gardiner ("Bub") Ward, served as Lipes's chief assistant. Other *Seadragon* officers stood by. Lipes devised surgical instruments from the wardroom silverware—bent spoons for muscle retractors, for example—sterilized in torpedo alcohol.

There followed a tense two and a half hours in *Seadragon*'s wardroom. Devising a mask from a tea strainer, Lipes knocked Rector out with ether. Then he operated, following instructions and diagrams in his medical books. He removed the appendix, stitching up the incision with catgut. Rector not only lived; he recovered fully.

When Ferrall reported the operation in Fremantle, the squadron medical officer was appalled. Jimmy Fife's endorsement was typically unenthusiastic. "While this had a happy ending, it is hoped that his success on this occasion will not encourage others to take unnecessary risks." But the story made good publicity.

In sum, the twenty-eight war patrols mounted from Fremantle during the period May through August 1942 produced a total of seventeen sinkings—little better than half a Japanese ship per war patrol, a miserable return. There was no great upsurge in kills after the deep-running defect of the Mark XIV torpedo was positively confirmed. The nine boats going on patrol in May—before the tests—accounted for seven enemy ships in thirty attacks. The ten boats going on patrol in July—after the tests—accounted for four enemy ships in fifteen attacks. Success still depended on many factors: position, sea conditions, depth control, coolness and skill at the periscope and TDC, torpedo maintenance—and the performance of the magnetic exploder.

In his management and deployment of Fremantle submarines, Lockwood displayed no more imagination or resourcefulness than his predecessor, Wilkes. He followed the procedure, already established, of positioning boats off the most likely (and heavily defended) traffic points, supplying them with Ultras when available. He made no special effort to blockade the oil exports from Borneo and Sumatra or any other specific strategic raw materials. It was "catch as catch can," with much hope and wishful thinking involved. As Lockwood's patrol report endorsements of the period reveal, most of his effort was expended in finding ways to improve the courage and shooting skill of the officers and crews so they would sink more shipping when—or if—the opportunity presented itself. The submarine force was still finding its way.

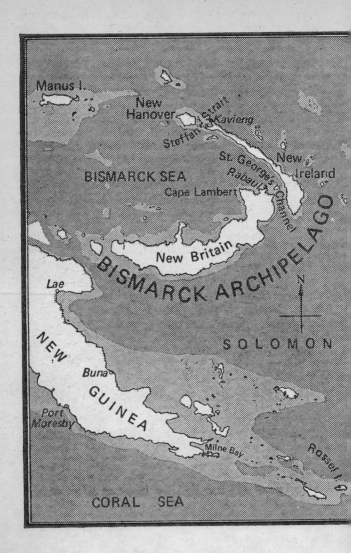

BISMARCK AND SOLOMON ARCHIPELAGOS

Nautical miles

0 30 60 90 120   180   240

Ocean depth:

less than 3000 feet

more than 3000 feet

Buka

Bougainville

Kolombangara

SOLOMON ISLANDS

hartland

Vella Lavella

Gonongga I.

New Georgia

THE SLOT

Savo

Tulagi

Cape Esperance

SEA

Guadalcanal

5

SUBMARINE WAR
IN THE SOLOMONS—I

Defeated in the battles of Coral Sea and Midway, the Japanese now renewed pressure in the Southwest Pacific. This took the form of new invasions in New Guinea (with the object of seizing Port Moresby by an overland route) and the Solomon Islands, notably Guadalcanal and Tulagi. These new thrusts were designed to provide bomber bases to interrupt the flow of war materials from the U.S. to Australia, now a major staging base for a counteroffensive against the Japanese. In both instances, the codebreakers provided advance information on Japanese plans, enabling Nimitz and MacArthur to conceive countermeasures. MacArthur reinforced New Guinea and staved off the assault on Port Moresby; Nimitz (through a subcommander, Vice Admiral Robert L. Ghormley) invaded Guadalcanal and wrestled the airfield from the Japanese. But the action did not stop there. The Japanese in turn reinforced both New Guinea and the Solomons and for the next six months bloody fighting ensued on land, in the air, on the sea, and beneath the sea. Most U.S. submarines in the Pacific would ultimately be drawn into the fearful naval contest in the Solomons.

When the Japanese drove into the Solomons, the island chain was being patrolled by the five old S-boats (formerly of the Asiatic Fleet) based in Brisbane. They were joined by six other S-boats hastily sent out from the States. This force of eleven World War I submarines was commanded by Captain Ralph W. Christie, a handsome and capable officer who had played an important role in the development of the submarine torpedo and its magnetic exploder.

The S-boat patrols from Brisbane were nightmares that no one would ever forget. The equatorial heat was intense; the temperature inside the submerged boats ranged from 105 to 120 degrees. Only one of the eleven boats—*S-44*—had air conditioning, a makeshift unit bought in Philadelphia with private funds and installed by the crew.

William James Ruhe, an artist and musician then a junior officer on *S-37*, later described the life:

The bunks beyond the wardroom are filled with torpid, skivvy-clad bodies, the sweat running off the white, rash-blistered skin in small rivulets. Metal fans are whirring everywhere—overhead, at the ends of the bunks, close to my ear. . . . I am playing cribbage with the skipper, mainly because I don't like to wallow in a sweat-soaked bunk most of the day. I have my elbows on the table near the edge and I hold my cards with my arms at a slight angle so the sweat will stream down my bare arms . . . without further soaking the pile of cards in the center. . . . Over-head is a fine net of gauze to catch the wayward cockroaches which prowl across the top of the wardroom and occasionally fall straight downward . . . they live in the cork insulation which lines the insides of the submarine's hull . . . we've killed over sixteen million cockroaches in one compartment alone. . . . The deck in the control room is littered with towels, used to sponge up the water drip-ping off the men and the submarine itself. . . . The food is routine—something canned. The dehydrated potatoes, powdered onions, and reconstituted carrots have the same general taste—like sawdust.

The boats had countless mechanical failures. (*S-45* was plagued with engine trouble; *S-46* experienced a main motor failure at sea.) All had electrical problems, inten-sified by the tropical humidity; most leaked oil from the riveted tanks. The diving planes were noisy, the sonar gear inadequate. *S-37*, which had been "saved" on the retreat from Manila by the engineering talent of James Richard Reynolds, was almost a complete wreck, the worst of the eleven boats. On arrival in Brisbane, she spent six weeks in overhaul. At sea, someone accidentally punched another hole in her fragile hull.

Three skippers overcame these hardships and delivered attacks on the Japanese: John Raymond ("Dinty") Moore on *S-44*, his successor Reuben Whitaker, and Henry Glass ("Hank") Munson on *S-38*. Moore, who had sunk a ship on his first patrol in April, was something of a character. "He was born in Tennessee," said a submariner, "and affected a hayseed front. But underneath he was very intelligent—he stood thirty-three in a class of two hundred and forty—and a very no-nonsense type of guy." Moore was helped considerably by his exec, Thomas Slack Baskett, with whom Moore worked in close harmony. Baskett, who stood 8 out of 422 in the class of 1935, was an urbane, low-key, thoroughly competent officer, no less aggressive than Moore.

Moore sank his second ship on his second patrol, north of Guadalcanal. It was a nerve-shattering adventure. He fired from close range and then stayed at the periscope to watch the results. The ship, converted gunboat *Keijo Maru*, 2,262 tons, sank with her stern high in the air. Moore could see people running along the slanting deck, jumping into the water. He took a final look and ordered *S-44* deep.

As the boat was going down, there was a sudden cataclysmic explosion overhead. Apparently *Keijo Maru* blew up just as Moore was sliding beneath her. Inside *S-44* there was terror and chaos. Glass gauges shattered. The spare torpedoes were torn from their racks, the small conning tower flooded. All through the hull the men could hear the nightmarish sounds of the ship they had torpedoed breaking apart and sinking—presumably on top of them. But Moore maneuvered *S-44* away, turning and diving deep, escaping without further damage.

On his third patrol, off Kavieng, Moore got his third ship—a big one. On the morning of August 10, four of the Japanese cruisers that had decimated the U.S. Navy in the Battle of Savo Island came into view, returning home. Moore set up on the last cruiser in line, opened the range to get a better shot, and fired four torpedoes at 700 yards. Thirty-five seconds later the first torpedo hit with a shattering explosion.

"Evidently all her boilers blew up," Moore said later. "You could hear hideous noises that sounded like steam

hissing through water. These noises were more terrifying
to the crew than the actual depth charges that followed.
It sounded as if great chains were being dragged across
the hull, as if our own water and air lines were bursting."

The Japanese heavy cruiser *Kako*, 8,800 tons, plunged
to the bottom. Although Warder, Brockman, Wright,
Voge, McKinney, and others had already been given credit
for sinking major Japanese men-of-war, *Kako* was, in fact,
the first major combatant ship lost to U.S. submarines
in the war. When Moore returned to Brisbane, he was
awarded a Navy Cross. By sinking one ship on each of
his three patrols, Moore had created an S-boat record
that would never be equaled, let alone beaten.

After that patrol, command of *S-44* went to Reuben
Whitaker, who had been Bull Wright's exec on *Sturgeon*.
Whitaker proved to be a fitting choice to command the
hottest S-boat in Brisbane. On his first—and only—patrol
as an S-boat skipper, Whitaker fearlessly attacked a column of three Japanese destroyers off New Georgia. He
fired three torpedoes at one and believed he sank it.
Afterward, *S-44* received a brutal depth-charging. Whitaker was credited with a kill, but it could not be found in
Japanese records.

Hank Munson on *S-38* got his ship in St. George's
Channel near Bougainville after the initial American landing on Guadalcanal. About midnight on August 8, while
on the surface, Munson picked up a Japanese convoy—
six transports, plus escorts—steaming down to Guadalcanal. Munson chose a target, a large freighter escorted
by a destroyer. He submerged, underran the destroyer, and
fired two torpedoes from deep submergence.

It was, Munson said later, a lucky shot. Both torpedoes
hit the 5,600-ton *Meiyo Maru*, a key vessel of the Japanese
expeditionary force. With the loss of this ship, the Japanese temporarily recalled the other five transports, giving the marines on Guadalcanal a little more time to
consolidate their defenses.

Ralph Christie also believed that some of his skippers
were not putting forth their best effort. Three were relieved for "not producing," as Christie wrote Lockwood—Nick Lucker on *S-40* (who missed a good target

off Savo Island), George Michael Holley, Jr. on *S-41*, and Edward Robert ("Irish") Hannon on *S-43*—and James Reynods on *S-37*, who sank a 2,800-ton ship off New Ireland, said later that he requested his own relief.

Later, Lucker wrote, "I felt that I would never accomplish much on *S-40*, as most of our time was spent in trying to keep the ship running, and . . . I believe I was completely worn out." Wrote George Holley, "I rather suspect that I may have been criticized for lack of aggressiveness. . . . No excuse can be offered." Wrote Hannon, "The mental strain and worry over not being able to rely on the engines [on *S-43*] to charge the batteries each night apparently took their toll, for when the *S-43* returned from its second patrol I was simply exhausted."

Not everybody thought Christie should relieve these men. Excessive caution on a fleet boat was reprehensible, but caution on these old buckets of bolts was not only condoned but forgiven. Said Thomas Kimmel, who was on *S-40*, "Nick Lucker was an intelligent competent submariner. . . . I believe [he] was a good submarine commanding officer who was one of those victimized by the frustration of the early part of the war."

One S-boat was lost during this period: *S-39*, commanded by Francis Elwood Brown. Leaving Brisbane, Brown twice suffered major breakdowns and was forced to return for repairs. When *S-39* finally got to sea and seemed well on her way, her exec came down with pneumonia. Brown radioed Christie for instructions. Christie told him to put the exec ashore in Townsville. After this was done, Brown proceeded toward his patrol area north of Guadalcanal.

Three nights later, while *S-39* was traveling on the surface minus one executive officer, she ran aground on a reef off Rossel Island. Jolted up and down by heavy seas breaking over the afterdeck, the boat immediately took a 35-degree list to port. Brown blew his ballast tanks dry, dumped fuel, and backed emergency, but *S-39* was stuck fast.

During the next twenty-four hours, Brown and his crew did everything possible to save the ship, including dumping more fuel and deactivating and firing the four bow torpedoes. Meanwhile, the boat was twisted sideways to the sea and pounded fiercely. Brown sent a call for help. The Australian naval vessel *Katoomba* responded.

On the morning of August 15, when *S-39* was thrown violently on her side, Brown passed the word that anyone who wanted to abandon ship and swim through the crashing surf to a nearby reef might do so. No one did. Then a young lieutenant volunteered to swim to the reef with lines. Joined by one of the enlisted men, he made it and tied the lines to one of the jettisoned torpedoes which had lodged on the reef. Using these lines, thirty-two of the crew transferred to the reef. The remaining twelve stayed on board, awaiting rescue by *Katoomba*.

Katoomba appeared, and by ten the following day all hands had been rescued from the reef or the stricken sub. The codebooks and other classified material were removed or destroyed. Satisfied that *S-39* would soon be torn to pieces on the rocks, Brown did not request that *Katoomba* destroy her by gunfire. He and his crew were dropped in Townsville, from where they made their way back to Brisbane. Meanwhile, Christie sent aircraft out to ensure *S-39*'s destruction by bombing.

Christie was impressed by Brown's coolness and his efforts to save his ship. Although some on his staff (and higher up) suggested a court-martial, Christie headed them off and gave Brown command of Irish Hannon's *S-43*.

The battles for Guadalcanal—and the Solomons— quickly became the focal point of the naval war in the Pacific. By mid-August, the marines were operating aircraft from the captured air base—which they named Henderson Field—and Admiral Ghormley was gamely hanging on. The Japanese, on the other hand, were determined to drive the U.S. forces from Guadalcanal. They threw the whole weight of the Japanese navy, including the surviving heavy carriers *Shokaku* and *Zuikaku*, the light carrier *Ryujo*, and eight battleships, into the South Pacific.

The war continued to go badly for the U.S. Navy. After the disaster of Savo Island came the Battle of the Eastern Solomons. The three Japanese carriers (*Shokaku, Zuikaku,* and *Ryujo*), supported by eight battleships plus nine cruisers, thirteen destroyers, and thirty-six submarines, steamed

to meet Ghormley's force of three carriers (*Enterprise,
Wasp,* and *Saratoga*), one battleship (*North Carolina*),
four cruisers, and ten destroyers. Just before the forces
met, Ghormley was misinformed by the codebreakers on
the location of the Japanese force and sent *Wasp* off to
refuel, thinking it had plenty of time to get back into
battle.

The two forces met on August 25. The Japanese lost the
light carrier *Ryujo,* a transport, and a destroyer. Two ships
were badly damaged, one of them the cruiser *Jintsu,*
which Freddy Warder believed he had sunk at Christmas
Island. The United States lost no ships, but *Enterprise*
was severely damaged by dive bombers, and a few days
later, in an epilogue to the battle, *Saratoga* was torpedoed
for the second time by a Japanese submarine and put out
of action for three crucial months. Because his forces had
sunk the light carrier *Ryujo,* Ghormley claimed a victory.
But her loss was less serious than the operational losses
of *Enterprise* and *Saratoga* due to damage.

The worst was yet to come. Two weeks after *Saratoga*
was hit, Japanese submarines struck again. On September
15, *I-15* and *I-19* found *Wasp* and the recently arrived
Hornet and their support groups in the Coral Sea, south
of Guadalcanal, bringing reinforcements to the island. *I-19*
fired four torpedoes at *Wasp.* Three hit. *Wasp* burst into
flames and was abandoned; a U.S. destroyer polished her
off. *I-15* fired at *Hornet* but missed. However, one of her
torpedoes hit the battleship *North Carolina,* tearing a 32-
foot gash in her hull. Another blew off the bow of the destroyer *O'Brien. North Carolina* survived; *O'Brien* limped
into Espiritu Santo for temporary repairs but foundered
on the way to California.

After September 15, the United States had only one
operational fleet carrier left in the Pacific—*Hornet*—and
one undamaged battleship—*Washington.* Taken together,
the naval actions in the Solomons over the three-week
period August 25—September 15 amounted to another
severe defeat for the U.S. Navy.

The only good news came from Port Moresby. General MacArthur's ground forces beat off the Japanese
troops that crossed the Owen-Stanley Range to attack
from the rear. This victory was the first positive Allied suc-

cess against Japanese troops. It was due, in large measure, to the codebreakers.

With all this Japanese naval power concentrated in the Solomons, the area seemed ripe for U.S. submarines. The S-boats were obviously ineffectual. "These vessels are twenty years old," Christie wrote. "The character of service in this theater is beyond the capability of S-boats." He suggested that they all be returned to the States for overhaul and reassigned to "areas where heavy antisubmarine measures may not be met." His superior agreed. They ordered that the S-boats, plus the tender *Griffin,* be prepared for return to the States. Most of Lockwood's boats at Fremantle were transferred to Brisbane to replace them.

When the first three boats reported to Brisbane from Albany in late August, Christie, with Lockwood's blessing, made some changes in command. Dick Voge on *Sailfish* had long-standing orders to report to Bob English to become Pearl Harbor's operations officer, so Christie gave the boat to Dinty Moore as a reward for his outstanding performance on *S-44.* Bull Wright on *Sturgeon* returned to the States to command a new division of Manitowoc-built boats. Christie gave *Sturgeon* to an officer with an M.A. in ordnance engineering and a nearly unpronounceable surname: Herman Arnold Pieczentkowski. "Pi," as he was called, had made one war patrol as Dick Voge's exec. Chester Nimitz, Jr., moved up to be Pi's exec. These two, plus Lucius Chappell's *Sculpin,* joined five S-boats for war patrols in the Solomons.

Up to then Ralph Christie, torpedo expert, father of the magnetic exploder, had had no wartime experience with the Mark XIV torpedo. His S-boats used the old Mark X with the contact exploder, which worked fine. Some of the skippers and crews on the fleet boats arriving from Fremantle raised questions about the Mark XIV torpedo and the exploder, but Christie would hear none of it. He believed (like English) that—apart from the now-corrected deep running—any defects in Mark XIV torpedoes could be laid to poor maintenance, improper settings, or

errors by the skipper or the TDC team. All fleet submarines under his command would continue to use the
magnetic exploder.

Before the boats left for patrol, Christie inspected them.
"I found the torpedoes in appalling condition," Christie
said later. "Afterbody syphons uncapped. Exploder mechanisms frozen. Scoops plugged with grease. Reversed
torpedo locks. Many of the torpedo officers and men had
not been properly trained. From that time on, there
was conscientious maintenance of torpedoes—according to
the book."

The three pioneer fleet boats at Brisbane turned in
mixed results. Lucius Chappell, patrolling in *Sculpin* off
New Britain and New Ireland in confined waters swarming with enemy destroyers, made five aggressive attacks.
He believed he had sunk three ships for 24,000 tons, but
postwar records credited him with two ships for 6,600
tons. Toward the end of the patrol, he attacked the light
cruiser *Yura* but failed to inflict serious damage.

Pi, in *Sturgeon*, made three attacks and sank one ship;
it was *Katsuragi Maru*, 8,000 tons, an aircraft ferry. Following that attack, *Sturgeon* received a vicious depth-
charging.

Dinty Moore, in *Sailfish*, evidently had a tough time shifting from his S-boat to a fleet boat. Getting under way,
he bent a propeller, delaying his start. Patrolling the Solomons, he sighted at least twenty Japanese destroyers,
perhaps more, plus a seaplane tender. He made one attack against a minelayer, firing three torpedoes. All missed.
The minelayer responded with a depth-charge attack,
dropping eleven well-placed missiles. Moore wrote in his
report, "The large number of contacts with no results is
disappointing. Lack of results may be attributed to strong
antisubmarine measures, many glassy calm days, bad management and bad luck. Just how much to one and just how
much to the other, I can't say."

On their August and September patrols, none of the S-
boats scored sinkings. One by one, as the fleet boats reported for duty, the Ss were pulled from combat and
returned to the States for other duty. Many of their skippers and execs went on to commission new fleet boats.

In his deployment of the fleet boats, Christie displayed little imagination and ingenuity. By September, when the first three left Brisbane, it was clear from codebreaking information and other intelligence that the Japanese were using Palau and Truk as bases for operations in the Solomons. There was heavy traffic—both men-of-war and merchant shipping—between those islands and Rabaul and Kavieng. Rather than attack this traffic on the high seas, with open water and plenty of leg room, Christie chose to position the boats off the terminal points, where air and sea antisubmarine measures were heaviest. As a result, the skippers were forced to remain submerged a great deal of the time in shallow and dangerous waters, wasting two prime assets of the fleet boat: speed and mobility.

In making his decisions on deployment, Christie was influenced by the existing target priority established by Admiral King in Washington. Japanese carriers, battleships, cruisers, and other major combatant units were still top, with merchant ships, tankers, destroyers, and auxiliaries taking second place. The waters were teeming with Japanese aircraft carriers, battleships, and cruisers, most of them being tracked by the codebreakers. In his eagerness to help the beleaguered and thin U.S. surface forces, Christie constantly shifted his boats to intercept these prime Japanese targets. However, it was all wasted effort. Except for Chappell's inconclusive shot at the light cruiser *Yura*, none of the boats found or attacked major Japanese units.

While Christie's boats patrolled the Solomons from Brisbane, Nimitz instructed English to send Pearl Harbor boats to the Japanese base at Truk, a major staging base for Japanese operations in the Solomons. The idea was to throw a submarine "blockade" around Truk and shut off the flow of supplies and ships to the Solomons. In response to this order, English sent eleven boats to Truk during the period July through September, 1942.

In general, the operation was another failure for Pearl Harbor submarines. The eleven boats at Truk operating independently of one another and close to the island, where antisubmarine activity was intense, sank only eight confirmed ships. Many boats were badly bombed or depth-charged. On at least three occasions, the submarines attacked major Japanese carriers or battleships, but for one reason or the other the attacks resulted in no sinkings. On other occasions, a battleship and carriers were sighted but no attacks could be made.

The first wave of six boats left for Truk in July. Bob Rice in *Drum*, who had scored heavily on his first patrol in Empire waters, was one of the earliest. He had a miserable patrol. He missed one freighter—perhaps due to erratic torpedo performance—and damaged another. While he was preparing a second attack on the damaged ship, Japanese aircraft delivered a bombing attack on *Drum*, forcing him to break off. English, who had praised Rice's aggressiveness on his first patrol, criticized him this time for failing to follow up.

Eliot Olsen in *Grayling*, who had been roasted for missing the carrier *Hosho* at Truk in February and had made a lively second patrol in Empire waters, had an experience at Truk similar to Rice's. He fired at a ship, perhaps a submarine tender, achieving two hits. When he tried to follow up the attack, he was bombed by aircraft. Bedeviled by a squealing port shaft, air leaks, and other matériel failures, Olsen terminated the patrol early, returning to Pearl Harbor after forty-three days. English criticized Olsen for not following up the attack on the supposed submarine tender and sent *Grayling* to a long navy yard overhaul. Olsen went to duty in the Atlantic.

Greenling, commanded by lawyer Henry Chester Bruton, whom English had rebuked for his performance on his first patrol off Truk, seemed destined at first to rack up more failures. On his first attack against a group of enemy vessels, Bruton fired three torpedoes; all missed. An escort counterattacked; Bruton fired; another miss. He found a tanker and fired four torpedoes; all misses. The score was nine torpedoes, no hits.

This pattern changed dramatically for Bruton on the night of August 4. While running on the surface, he saw what he believed to be an aircraft carrier. He set up fast and fired four stern torpedoes, all apparent misses. He continued tracking, hiding in rainsqualls. Four hours later, he made a second night surface attack, firing three

bow tubes and achieving two solid hits. The target fired a
deck gun at *Greenling*, then sank swiftly.

Cruising through the wreckage, Bruton picked up a survivor. He told Bruton the ship was not an aircraft carrier
but the huge 12,000-ton *Brazil Maru*, which had been
carrying 600 passengers, 400 of them soldiers bound for
the Solomons. *Brazil Maru*, the largest ship sunk to date
by any U.S. submarine, had been scheduled for conversion to a light aircraft carrier on her return to Japan.
The survivor also reported to Bruton that earlier that night
the ship had been struck by torpedoes that had failed to
go off.

With this and subsequent successes, Bruton's aim improved considerably. The next night he spotted another
ship, *Palau Maru*, 5,000 tons. He closed to point-blank
range—800 yards—and fired three torpedoes for three
hits. The ship sank. Later, he sighted and closed other ships
but was driven off by escorts and aircraft. On return to
Pearl Harbor, English credited Bruton with two ships for
24,000 tons (later reduced to 17,000) and gave him a
Navy Cross, but his endorsement was, on the whole, luke-
warm. He criticized Bruton for overcautious use of the
periscope, for remaining deep on one attack when he
might have followed up, and other matters.

Three exchange boats routed to Fremantle by way of
Truk all had new skippers. *Gudgeon* was commanded by
William Shirley Stovall, Jr. Dusty Dornin, who remained
as Stovall's exec, could have commanded *Gudgeon*, but
English was not yet ready to give that responsibility to a
Naval Academy graduate of the class of 1935.

Stovall and Dornin had a furiously active patrol. The
first target was a small patrol craft at which Stovall fired
three torpedoes. All missed. A few nights later, he made
a night surface approach on a convoy of two destroyers
and three tankers. Before he could get off a shot, one of
the destroyers sighted *Gudgeon* and charged, firing a torpedo. Stovall went deep. *Gudgeon* took twelve depth
charges, none close. A week later, Stovall made a night
surface attack on a cargo vessel escorted by a single destroyer, firing three torpedoes, two of which seemed to hit.
Stovall escaped on the surface. On August 3, Stovall made

a day periscope attack on an unescorted merchantman, firing three torpedoes, scoring two hits.

The climax of *Gudgeon*'s busy patrol came on August 17, when Stovall found two large transports and two destroyers, escorted by a screen of three aircraft from Truk. Making a day periscope attack, he fired three torpedoes at each transport. Three hit the first, two hit the second. Then the destroyers counterattacked, dropping no less than sixty depth charges, many close. "Minor leaks occurred throughout the boat," Dornin reported later with understatement, and "the crew was shaken up considerably."

When *Gudgeon* reached Fremantle, Lockwood credited Stovall with four ships sunk for 35,000 tons, one of the best performances of any submarine to date. There were many congratulations all around. However, JANAC, Joint Army-Navy Assessment Committee, trimmed the actual sinkings to one, the 4,858-ton cargo vessel *Naniwa Maru*. Said Dornin later, "It was the same old defective torpedo story all over again."

Stovall, shaken by the depth charges and the heavy responsibilities of command, requested that Lockwood relieve him. Lockwood noted in his diary, "Very poor story. Skipper cracked up and asks to be relieved." However, after a rest in Perth, Stovall changed his mind and got ready for another patrol.

Of the other two new skippers on the exchange boats, Stephen Henry Ambruster on *Tambor* and Bruce Lewis Carr on *Grenadier*, Ambruster conducted the more aggressive patrol. Lockwood credited him with sinking two big freighters for 12,000 tons (although Japanese postwar records cut the total tonnage in half). Carr was credited with sinking a tanker (denied postwar), but Lockwood criticized him for missing a number of other opportunities.

The second wave of five boats left in August and September and prowled Truk during the heaviest movement of major Japanese ships to and from the Solomons. Though all five found major Japanese vessels, aircraft carriers and battleships, the results were disappointing. Nevertheless, two of them could claim "firsts."

Trout was now commanded by Lawson Paterson ("Red") Ramage, another member of the class of 1931.

Ramage had made one war patrol with Pilly Lent on *Grenadier*. A genial backslapper and popular with his crew, Ramage had very nearly failed his submarine physical because of poor sight in his right eye. "But it turned out this was a great advantage," he said later. "I didn't have to fool around with the focus knob on the periscope. Before I raised it, I turned the knob all the way to the stop [extreme focus]. When the scope came up, I put my bad eye to the periscope and could see perfectly."

Alerted by an Ultra, on August 28 Ramage intercepted a Japanese task group consisting of the light carrier *Taiyo* (*Otaka*), plus cruisers and destroyers. Relentlessly aggressive, Ramage closed to short range and fired five torpedoes at the carrier. He believed some of the five hit, reporting, "A large volume of smoke was pouring out of the starboard side near the waterline and pouring up and over the flight deck." Postwar Japanese records confirmed that *Taiyo* (*Otaka*) suffered medium damage from a submarine attack on the day and at the place Ramage claimed. It was the first hit any U.S. submarine had actually scored on a Japanese aircraft carrier; had the warheads been more powerful, *Taiyo* (*Otaka*) might have sunk.

A few days later, while making a periscope navigational fix, *Trout* was caught by Japanese aircraft. A tremendous explosion shook her from stem to stern. One man was thrown from his bunk. Others froze in shock. Ramage went deep, where he found the bomb had wrecked both periscopes. He cut his patrol short and set a course for Brisbane to have the periscopes replaced.

On the same day Ramage attacked *Taiyo* (*Otaka*), Glynn Robert ("Donc") Donaho in *Flying Fish* spotted a battleship of the *Kongo* class, escorted by two destroyers and aircraft from Truk. Donaho moved in to attack, planning to fire four bow tubes at the battleship and two bow tubes at a destroyer. The four bow torpedoes streaked toward the battleship. Donaho, manning the periscope, saw two hits, the first for the submarine force on a Japanese battleship. He believed he saw fire along the waterline and later reported to English: SET ON FIRE, ONE BATTLESHIP. Before he could fire at the destroyer, one of the aircraft escorts attacked *Flying Fish* with a bomb which fell close and forced Donaho deep. Four destroyers or patrol craft attacked with depth charges.

Two hours later, Donaho shook the destroyers and returned to periscope depth for a look. While he was searching the horizon, a "nervous torpedoman" in the after torpedo room accidentally fired a torpedo in Number 7 tube with the outer door closed. As the report of that accident reached Donaho, another Japanese bomb fell close aboard, forcing *Flying Fish* deep again. Number 7 torpedo was jammed in the tube. Donaho could not open the outer door to get rid of it. Two engines flooded due to leaky exhaust valves.

When the sun set, Donaho returned to periscope depth. He found two destroyers close by and prepared torpedo tubes forward. Working quickly—perhaps too quickly—Donaho set up and fired three torpedoes at one of the destroyers. All missed. He did not follow up. After dark, Donaho surfaced. One of the destroyers charged at *Flying Fish*, forcing Donaho deep again, and dropped eleven close depth charges. Later, Donaho surfaced again, saw the two destroyers 1½ miles astern, and dived. He did not attack.

After midnight, he surfaced and left the area. For the next two days he remained at sea, trying to get rid of Number 7 torpedo. His men were finally able to pull it back inside the after torpedo room, but in the process they partially flooded the compartment.

On September 2, with all machinery back in commission, Donaho returned to the Truk area for more combat. Finding a patrol vessel, he fired two torpedoes from 700 yards. Both missed. The patrol boat charged at *Flying Fish*, dropping eight charges very close and causing serious damage. The next night, Donaho played tag with the patrol boat, firing two torpedoes at it, achieving one hit. "We watched it sink," Donaho reported. On the morning of September 4, at dawn, Donaho closed another patrol boat on the surface. It opened fire on *Flying Fish* with a 3-inch gun. Donaho cleared all personnel from the bridge, then closed to 600 yards and fired a torpedo. It missed. As the patrol boat charged in, Donaho dived. *Flying Fish* went down with a terrific angle. The patrol boat dropped eight charges, all close.

Two destroyers joined in the hunt. They pinned *Flying*

Fish down for four and a half hours, dropping fifty-four depth charges, many of them very close. Donaho went deep—to 350 feet. In order to maintain depth, he held the damaged *Flying Fish* at an 18-degree up-angle, making standing almost impossible. Finally, he shook the destroyers and slipped off into the darkness, having survived one of the worst depth-chargings of the war. Donaho requested permission to leave station early. It was granted.

On return to Pearl Harbor, English gave Donaho a hearty "well done" and a Navy Cross. He credited Donaho with two hits on a battleship but picked nits in the endorsement, criticizing Donaho for firing not six but four torpedoes at the battleship and for failing to fire at the two destroyers when he surfaced later that night.

Wahoo was a new boat with a new skipper, Marvin Granville ("Pinky") Kennedy. He patrolled Truk after *Flying Fish*. Kennedy had a fine wardroom. His exec was Richard Hetherington O'Kane, and the third officer was George William Grider.

Like Donc Donaho, Pinky Kennedy ran a taut ship. He was a "perfectionist and a slave driver," Grider wrote later. After commissioning and shakedown, Kennedy had trained his crew relentlessly. "We were on the fine edge of exhaustion all around," Grider wrote, "training all day and working all night." To complicate matters, Kennedy did not have complete faith in O'Kane. O'Kane struck Grider, and possibly Kennedy, as a young man who was "overly garrulous and potentially unstable."

Off Truk, Kennedy's first target was a lone freighter. He fired three torpedoes, missed, and, in Grider's words, "kept going," fearful of a counterattack from the air. "After the exhausting months of drills," Grider wrote, ". . . it was demoralizing to creep away submerged from that first target." A week later, while on the surface at night, Kennedy found his second target—another lone freighter. He chose to make a cautious submerged periscope attack and fired four torpedoes, one at a time. The first three missed; the last hit. Kennedy claimed a freighter of 6,400 tons. English later credited it, but postwar analysis showed no sinking at this time and place.

A short time later, Kennedy missed two of the best targets of the war. The first was the aircraft tender *Chi-*

yoda, which came along without an escort. "The Japs were just begging someone to knock off this tender," Kennedy later wrote, "but it was not our lucky day"; Kennedy did not have time to get into position to shoot. The next was an aircraft carrier which Kennedy believed to be *Ryujo,* sunk six weeks earlier in the Solomons. Whatever it was, it came into sight, escorted by two destroyers. Kennedy later wrote in his report:

Made approach which, upon final analysis, lacked aggressiveness and skill . . . watched the best target we could ever hope to find go over the hill untouched. . . . Had I but required a more rigorous and alert watch we might have picked it up sooner. Had I correctly estimated the situation and made a more aggressive approach we could have gotten in a shot.

When *Wahoo* returned to Pearl Harbor, English was furious. "Opportunities to attack an enemy carrier," he wrote in Kennedy's patrol report endorsement, "are few and must be exploited to the limit with due acceptance of the hazards involved."

Richard Cross Lake patrolled Truk in *Albacore,* another new boat, and he too missed opportunities to attack Japanese men-of-war. The first was a small Japanese submarine, which turned directly toward *Albacore* at the last minute. The second—and the heart-stopping one—was a *Zuikaku*-class carrier picked up on October 9, escorted by one heavy cruiser and a destroyer. Lake closed to 8,000 yards, but he was detected. The cruiser and destroyer pinned *Albacore* down, dropping eleven close depth charges which badly shook the boat. Lake prepared a sonar attack from deep submergence, but exploding depth charges and screws from the cruiser and destroyer "spoiled" the sonar bearings and he withheld fire.

Amberjack, commanded by another new skipper, John Albert Bole, Jr., patrolled the sea lanes south of Truk, dropping down as far as Rabaul and Kavieng. Guided by a flow of Ultras, Bole and his exec, Bernard Ambrose ("Chick") Clarey (ex-*Dolphin*), picked up a battleship escorted by a cruiser. In a night periscope attack, Bole fired four torpedoes at the cruiser and then got set to swing the boat and fire four stern tubes at the battleship. But Bole had "badly underestimated" the speed of the cruiser, and all torpedoes missed. Alerted, the battleship turned a searchlight on *Amberjack*'s periscope. Believing the battleship would zig away before he could fire his stern tubes, Bole fired his last remaining other two bow tubes at the battleship. Both missed.

Continuing this extremely aggressive patrol, Bole later sank a 2,000-ton transport. Then, off Kavieng Harbor, Bole fired four torpedoes at long range into the anchorage. One damaged a freighter; others sank the huge 19,000-ton whale factory, *Tonan Maru II*, the largest ship sunk by a U.S. submarine to date. (However, she sank in shallow water and was salvaged, towed to Japan, and returned to service.) Low on fuel and torpedoes, Bole followed *Trout* into Brisbane for refit and replenishment. Christie, who endorsed the patrol report, gave Bole high marks.

6

SUBMARINE WAR
IN THE SOLOMONS—II

None of the submarine activity at Truk had made an appreciable dent in the Japanese reinforcements bound for the Solomons. Except for the light carrier *Taiyo* (*Otaka*) damaged by Red Ramage, carriers, battleships, cruisers, and most of the troop transports and freighters got by unscathed.

On October 11–12, the Japanese and U.S. naval surface forces met again in the Solomons in what would be known as the Battle of Esperance. Naval historian Morison wrote that "it might have been called the Battle of Mutual Errors." In the darkness, both sides became confused, misidentified ships, gave orders to fire, and then gave orders to withhold fire. The Japanese lost the heavy cruiser *Furutaka* and the destroyer *Fubuki*, and the heavy cruiser *Aoba* was severely damaged. The United States lost a destroyer, *Duncan,* and a light cruiser, *Boise,* was badly damaged.

After this battle, Admiral Nimitz gave a dark estimate of the situation. "It now appears that we are unable to control the sea in the Guadalcanal area. Thus our supply of the positions will only be done at great expense to us. The situation is not hopeless, but it is certainly critical." Feeling the need for "a more aggressive commander," Nimitz relieved Admiral Ghormley, replacing him with Admiral William ("Bull") Halsey. Halsey took over from Ghormley at Noumea, he said later, with feelings of "astonishment, apprehension, and regret."

Halsey had no sooner assumed command than he was faced with a major sea battle, later known as the Battle of Santa Cruz. Admiral Yamamoto, with headquarters at Truk, was determined, once and for all, to blast the U.S. Navy out of the Solomons. For this purpose he had assembled the largest Japanese naval force since the Battle of Midway. It consisted of four carriers (*Shokaku, Zuikaku, Zuiho,* and *Junyo*), five battleships, fourteen cruisers, and forty-four destroyers. To oppose the force, Halsey had *Enterprise* (back in action, but still not completely repaired) and *Hornet,* plus one battleship, six cruisers, and fourteen destroyers.

The battle, fought on October 26–27, was yet another devastating defeat for the U.S. Navy. The only remaining undamaged carrier, *Hornet,* was lost to air attack and the destroyer *Porter* to submarine attack. *Enterprise* was severely damaged, as was the battleship *South Dakota* and the cruiser *San Juan.* The loss of *Hornet* left the United States only two carriers in the Pacific—*Saratoga* and *Enterprise,* both damaged. The Japanese lost no ships. However, the carriers *Shokaku* and *Zuiho* were damaged, as were a cruiser and two destroyers.

Japanese submarines, prowling the Solomons in October, scored only minor successes compared with their September performance. On October 20, *I-176* believed she had torpedoed a battleship; her target turned out to be the cruiser *Chester. Chester* survived the attack, but she was put out of action for many months. After the battle of Santa Cruz, *I-21* found the brand-new battleship *Washington* and attacked. One of her torpedoes was right on target but exploded prematurely 400 yards short. But for that, *Washington* might have gone to the bottom.

After Halsey relieved Ghormley, he requested that, in addition to the submarine blockade of Truk, Nimitz send more fleet boats to operate from Brisbane, augmenting those moved around from Albany. Nimitz concurred. He ordered English to send the bulk of his modern submarines to Brisbane along with the tenders *Fulton* and *Sperry.*

English complied with these orders as rapidly as possible. In October, four boats, *Tarpon, Plunger, Pollack,* and *Stingray,* maintained the Truk blockade, and English sent three boats—*Silversides, Growler,* and *Flying Fish*—to Brisbane by way of Truk. *Plunger,* damaged off Truk, made an unscheduled stop at Brisbane. *Grayling*, an exchange boat bound for Fremantle, patrolled off Truk on the way. The next month, November, English sent five boats to Brisbane by way of Truk: *Gato, Wahoo, Tuna, Grouper,* and *Albacore. Fulton* and *Sperry*, loaded with torpedoes and spare parts, sailed from Pearl Harbor in early November, reaching Brisbane in mid-month. In December, English sent another three boats, plus *Argonaut* and *Nautilus* for special missions.

Counting the boats bound for Brisbane and Fremantle, plus those returning to Pearl Harbor, English mounted a total of eighteen patrols off Truk, or to the south toward the Solomons, during the period October through December. They had little luck.

David Charles White in *Plunger*, returning to combat after a second long period in overhaul, patrolled south of Truk toward the Solomons. He received an Ultra directing him to intercept a Japanese task force. A few hours later, while cruising on the surface at night, White picked up what he thought was an island on his new SJ radar. It turned out to be a *Natori*-class cruiser.

Exec David Hayward McClintock was standing watch on the bridge. In a snap decision, McClintock fired four torpedoes at the cruiser, believing he had scored for damage. Then White dived and went deep. At 130 feet, he hit bottom with a bone-jarring crash. The grounding badly damaged the hull and wiped off the sonar heads. When White radioed his plight, he was ordered into Brisbane for repairs, having been on station only five days.

In his endorsement, Christie went out of his way to congratulate McClintock for the snap firing but criticized White for precipitous diving after the attack, urging skippers to remain on the surface after a night attack and make repeated SJ radar attacks. In his endorsement, Admiral Halsey also congratulated McClintock.

Tarpon, returning to service after long overhaul with a new skipper, Thomas Lincoln Wogan, patrolled the sea lanes south of Truk. One of the junior officers on *Tarpon* this trip was William Robert Anderson, class of 1943 (graduated, June 1942 on the accelerated wartime program) and fresh from sub school, which had now been

SUBMARINE WAR IN THE SOLOMONS—II

telescoped to three months. Many years later, Anderson would achieve fame as the skipper who guided the first nuclear-powered submarine, *Nautilus,* beneath the Arctic ice cap.

"Wogan was extremely ambitious and very capable," Anderson said later. "But he had trouble putting it all together. We were almost run down by a tremendous convoy—ten ships, three destroyer escorts—going to the Solomons. It came right out of the blue, a complete surprise. Wogan shot some torpedoes but didn't hit a thing. The escorts held us down until the convoy was out of range. Wogan was plenty disappointed."

So were Bob English and the Pearl Harbor high command. The endorsements stated, "The fifth war patrol of *Tarpon* was most disappointing. The attack on November 7 was not pressed home. . . . [Wogan] failed to take advantage of a golden opportunity."

Dinty Moore patrolled Truk in another old Asiatic boat returned from overhaul, *Stingray.* Moore, too, had trouble getting it all together. He made contact with twenty-one enemy vessels, including a light aircraft carrier which he attacked twice on November 13, firing two torpedoes on each attack. All missed. He was credited with damage to one freighter. The attack was conducted by Moore's exec, Paul Edward Summers, a youngster from the class of 1936.

Moore, relieved of command, said later, "It was at my own request." He spent most of the rest of the war at the General Motors engine factory in Cleveland.

Donc Donaho set off in *Flying Fish* for Truk and Brisbane. After his fearless attack on the battleship at Truk, Donaho was held in new regard by his fellow skippers.

It was another frustrating patrol. On November 14, Donaho received an Ultra directing him to intercept an enemy task force. He found it—an awesome formation of four heavy cruisers and one light cruiser escorted by five destroyers—dived boldly beneath the destroyer screen, and fired six torpedoes at the second heavy cruiser in line from a range of 1,600 yards. All missed. On November 30, another Ultra moved him to intercept Japanese vessels off New Georgia. He found them, too, but was unable to gain a firing position. Admiral Halsey wrote in his endorsement, "This [patrol] shows how radio intelligence may be capitalized on. The fact that the contacts did not culminate in successful attacks does not detract from the utility of such procedure."

Pinky Kennedy's *Wahoo* had a new face in the wardroom. He was Dudley Walker ("Mush") Morton, on board as a Prospective Commanding Officer.

Below Truk, Kennedy found a southbound convoy of three ships, escorted by a destroyer. He first tried to attack the destroyer, on the theory that once it was out of the way he could pick off the three heavily laden freighters one at a time. However, he was unable to attain firing position on the destroyer, so he shot at the largest freighter, *Kamoi Maru*, 5,300 tons. It sank.

Immediately, the destroyer charged over *Wahoo* and dropped about forty depth charges, none close. Kennedy went deep and evaded, remaining submerged until sunset. When he came up for a periscope observation, he saw one freighter going off in the distance and the other stopped to pick up survivors from *Kamoi Maru*. The destroyer was zipping back and forth on patrol.

Mush Morton and Kennedy's exec, Dick O'Kane, urged him to mount a second attack. After dark, on the surface, using the new SJ radar, they argued, it would be easy to knock off the freighter. With luck, they might also get the destroyer. However, Kennedy had had enough. As George Grider wrote later, with a note of disappointment, "We left without a try at the other freighters."

When *Wahoo* arrived in Brisbane, the crew, Grider noted, was "more discouraged" than it had been at the end of the first patrol. "The *Wahoo* . . . was not making much of a record, and we knew it. We . . . had waited in the wrong places at the wrong time like unlucky fishermen; . . . we still felt thoroughly discouraged."

Pinky Kennedy lost his command—to Mush Morton. Later, Kennedy wrote that he was relieved because his superior believed that "a more aggressive conduct of the first two war patrols would have resulted in more enemy sinkings. In retrospect, I can see he was right, but I was not so philosophical about it at the time." Kennedy went

on to command the destroyer *Guest*, on which he served
with distinction, winning a second Silver Star.

Dick Lake in *Albacore*, making his second patrol, attacked several transports and destroyers, none successfully
until December 18. On that day, while cruising off the
north coast of New Guinea, Lake picked up what he
thought to be one transport escorted by one destroyer.
Closing to 2,000 yards, he fired three torpedoes at both.
The "destroyer" blew up and exploded in a mass of flames.
The freighter appeared to sink too. In Brisbane, Lake was
credited with a destroyer and a freighter. Later it was
realized that the "destroyer" was actually the light cruiser
Tenryu, 3,300 tons. *Tenryu* was the second Japanese cruiser
sunk by U.S. submarines in the war, after the heavy
cruiser *Kako*, 8,800 tons, sunk by Dinty Moore in *S-44*.

The last wave going to Brisbane did better. These boats
were skippered by old hands. Chester Bruton, having just
completed a dazzling patrol in *Greenling* off the coast of
Japan (four ships sunk, one light carrier damaged), sank
four ships on the way to Brisbane, including an old 800-
ton destroyer serving as an escort. C. C. Kirkpatrick, returning *Triton* from overhaul, was sent first to Wake
Island to serve as a "beacon" for a U.S. carrier attack on
that place; then, on the way to Brisbane, he sank two
ships for 6,500 tons. (One was an Ultra which showed up
right on the dot, with *Triton* in perfect position.) Bill
Brockman in *Nautilus*, en route to a special assignment
to evacuate twenty-nine Catholic missionaries from Bougainville, sank a small freighter, damaged a tanker and a
freighter, and fired two torpedoes down the throat at an
attacking destroyer.

Admiral Yamamoto was determined to retake Guadalcanal, no matter what the price in human life and suffering. After the Battle of Santa Cruz, where *Shokaku*
and *Zuiho* were damaged, he withdrew his carriers and
prepared his battleships and cruisers for the most furious and decisive battle of all. The plan was to annihilate
Admiral Halsey's forces with battleships and heavy cruisers,
supported by land-based aircraft, and then embark about

12,000 troops in a dozen first-rate transports for a new assault on Guadalcanal.

The engagement—known as the Battle of Guadalcanal —raged over three days, November 12–15. Before and during the battle, the codebreakers provided detailed radio intelligence to Admiral Halsey which enabled him to anticipate Japanese movements and attack accordingly, and as a result the U.S. Navy achieved a substantial victory in thwarting the Japanese plan. Losses were heavy on both sides. One Japanese battleship, *Hiei*, was sunk; another, *Kirishima*, was so badly damaged she had to be scuttled. In addition, the Japanese lost the heavy cruiser *Kinugasa*, two destroyers, and six—perhaps more—of the twelve big transports lifting the troops to Guadalcanal. The United States lost two light cruisers, *Atlanta* and *Juneau* (sunk by a Japanese submarine, *I-26*), and seven destroyers. In a subsequent last-gasp battle known as Tassafaronga, the Japanese lost another destroyer; the United States lost the heavy cruiser *Northampton*, and there was major damage to the heavy cruisers *New Orleans, Minneapolis,* and *Pensacola*.

After these battles, Yamamoto gave up all further efforts to recapture Guadalcanal. Most of the surviving Japanese naval units were withdrawn to Rabaul and then to Truk and the homeland for battle-damage repairs and upkeep, becoming the nucleus of a second-generation Japanese navy coming off the launching ways. Guadalcanal marked the end of the Japanese offensive action in the South Pacific and also of their threat to the New Hebrides, New Caledonia, and Australia. From November 1942 onward, the Japanese went on the defensive, trying to hold what had been gained during the drive that began on December 7, 1941.

During this period, the many fleet boats of Squadrons Two, Eight, and Ten, plus the tenders *Holland, Fulton,* and *Sperry*, arrived at New Farm Wharf in Brisbane. What had once been a small base, built around Christie's tender *Griffin* and his force of ten surviving S-boats, suddenly became an enormous enterprise, the largest concentration of U.S. submarine power in the Pacific.

There was a struggle on the higher levels for control of the boats. General MacArthur wanted them to support his campaign in New Guinea; Halsey wanted them to support his campaign in the Solomons. In this tug-of-war, Ralph Christie proved to be a diplomat of considerable skill, serving both commanders but retaining operational control of the boats himself. "The setup of a task force operating under two different commands was unique," the official submarine historian observed, "but proved extremely satisfactory in that [Christie] was able to shift his units to support both the Solomons and the New Guinea campaigns and comply with the wishes of both his superiors."

The problem was, however, that the large concentration of submarines at Brisbane was still being employed *tactically* and *reactively* against Japanese fleet movements. In most cases, they were shunted here and there on Ultra contacts, often into the teeth of massive destroyer screens or against well-defended harbors at places where the Japanese had clear superiority in the air. It was Java all over again, and no one appeared to have learned the lesson.

Every Japanese ship in the southwest Pacific was dependent on oil to keep its engines running. The oil came from Borneo, Sumatra, and Java to the Palaus or Truk and then to Rabaul and other bases. A well-conceived strategic submarine offensive against Japanese tankers coming from these oil ports would almost certainly have done far more to immobilize Japanese naval units in the Solomons than all the futile chasing about. None of the tanker convoys was as heavily escorted as the Japanese fleet units in the Solomons. By utilizing radar they could have been attacked on the high seas north of New Guinea at night with relative ease and with far more rewarding results.

From October through December 1942, while the final battles for Guadalcanal were being played out, Christie mounted twenty-four war patrols from Brisbane. Nineteen of these were conducted by fleet boats new to the command, the other five by the last of the S-boats. Nine of the twenty-four patrols were carried out by Squadron Two boats returning to Pearl Harbor for overhaul. Of the twenty-four patrols, most in areas infested with Japanese destroyers and aircraft, only three achieved anything. Although there were many Ultras, especially on Japanese submarines operating to and from Truk and Rabaul, and many ships and convoys were sighted, only six Japanese ships—two of them submarines—were sunk. These six were sunk by three fleet boats.

Tex Mewhinney, who had done much to lift spirits on *Saury,* patrolled off Rabaul with a new exec, Doug Rhymes. There he received many Ultras on Japanese forces preparing for the Battle of Guadalcanal. One bright moon-lit night he intercepted a task force of several big ships, including a light carrier which, as the third officer, Bill Hazzard, recalled, was *Hosho.* Mewhinney maneuvered to attack the force while submerged, choosing *Hosho* as his target. He fired four torpedoes, but according to Hazzard a premature explosion gave away the game and *Saury* was driven off by destroyers.

After that, *Saury* headed for Pearl Harbor for over-haul. En route Mewhinney decided (without orders) to reconnoiter Nauru and the Ocean Islands, which lie between the Solomons and the Gilberts. There he found a sitting duck, but another premature spoiled the attack.

When he arrived in Pearl Harbor, Mewhinney was crit-icized by Bob English in his endorsement for poor torpedo shooting (thirteen fired, one possible hit). Later, Mew-hinney said, "In my post-patrol interview with Admiral English, I told him that some of our torpedoes were ex-ploding prematurely or not exploding at all. He replied that SubPac [Submarines Pacific] had never had a pre-mature explosion."

Snapper, with two skippers in four patrols, sailed on her fifth with yet another, Augustus Robert St. Angelo, in-evitably nicknamed "The Saint."

The Saint did no better than his predecessors, Ham Stone and Harold Baker. He was shunted to likely areas to intercept Japanese forces aimed at recapturing Guadal-canal, but *Snapper* saw nothing of consequence and mounted no attacks. The Brisbane high command was not happy. One endorsement stated, "The scarcity of contacts is noted. However, it is known that a major 12-ship trans-port convoy [the main Guadalcanal invasion force] with heavy escort passed through *Snapper*'s area three times be-tween 12 and 14 November without being detected by the submarine."

Grampus, commanded by a new skipper, John Rich Craig, landed four coast-watchers on an island before conducting her regular patrol. In contrast to *Snapper*, *Grampus* must have seen almost every Japanese ship in the area—twice. Craig's official log listed twenty contacts with major Japanese forces, comprising forty-four cruisers and seventy-nine destroyers. Craig launched six torpedo attacks. He was credited with sinking one destroyer and damaging another, but postwar records failed to substantiate the sinking. In his endorsement, Admiral Halsey wrote that he was sorry that Craig had not sunk more ships, but the patrol was distinguished by the fact that the "Commanding Officer was thinking all the time, clearly and correctly."

On his second patrol, in December, Craig again sighted an astounding number of Japanese ships: forty-one. In seven attacks, Craig fired at six of these vessels, including two freighters, two transports, a small destroyer, and a submarine. He was credited with sinking three ships for 24,000 tons and damage to one for 1,500, but postwar records failed to credit the sinkings.

Grayback, commanded by a new skipper, Edward Clark Stephan, patrolled in the same area. Stephan made eight attacks, firing all twenty-four torpedoes. Five of the eight attacks failed. Christie credited him with sinking two ships.

When Stephan returned to port, Christie was ready to relieve him, but his boss, Arthur Schuyler ("Chips") Carpender, stood in the way. Christie wrote Lockwood:

Grayback had many opportunities and fired twenty-four torpedoes. The results were, to say the least, disappointing. My frank opinion is that Stephan is not well suited for the responsible job of Commanding Officer. You may well ask, then, why not take steps to relieve him. The answer to that is a pusillanimous one. My diplomacy is unequal to the task. I frankly told Admiral Carpender . . . before the patrol that Stephan was not in my opinion suited for the job but that I had previously so stated officially and had been overruled. . . . Now . . . there is no change.

Lockwood, ever eager to go to the mat with Carpender, replied:

I . . . agree that twenty-four torpedoes is a terrific number
to accomplish the sinking of one ship . . . a second patrol
after some intensive training [may] result better. If it
doesn't then certainly he should be relieved. . . . I will
certainly back your judgment in this or other cases if you
desire to draw me into the argument.

Postwar records failed to credit Stephan with the two
ships Christie credited, but he retained command.

On his second patrol, in December, Stephan did not improve his aim by much. In six attacks, he fired twenty
torpedoes, sinking one ship, the Japanese submarine *I-18*,
2,000 tons. During the patrol, terminated after forty-seven
days by a matériel failure, Stephan's pharmacist's mate,
Harry B. Roby, removed an inflamed appendix from a
crewman, W. R. Jones, in a replay of the appendectomy
on Pete Ferrall's *Seadragon*.

Chet Smith reassumed command of *Swordfish* from
Acey Burrows after the latter's one unfortunate patrol.
Smith had recovered from his cold, but he found the
crew of *Swordfish* still suffering from what he believed
to be bad drinking water. On this patrol, *Swordfish*'s sixth,
all hands were troubled by queasy stomachs, Smith reported. About one third of the crew vomited for days.
Smith made two attacks, claiming one ship damaged, one
sunk. However, postwar records failed to bear out the
sinking.

When Smith returned from this, his fifth war patrol, he
was the high scorer for Asiatic submarines with what was
then believed to be eleven ships sunk for 68,000 tons, four
damaged for 27,000 tons. He was promoted to command
a division in Al McCann's Squadron Six in Fremantle.

Gudgeon, commanded by Shirley Stovall, had another
fiercely active patrol, making contact with four separate
convoys. One escaped in a rainsquall, but Stovall, assisted
by his exec, Dusty Dornin, attacked three, hitting perhaps
five or six ships. Christie credited Stovall with sinking
three ships for 22,000 tons and damage to another, but
postwar records denied any sinkings. In two patrols, Stovall's credited score was seven ships for 57,000 tons,
only one of which was later confirmed. Again, Dornin

blamed poor torpedo performance. In his glowing endorsement to the patrol, Admiral Halsey singled out Dusty Dornin for special praise.

Red Ramage in *Trout*, bound for Fremantle when his periscopes were damaged at Truk, made a brief unscheduled patrol out of Brisbane to the Solomons and got into the thick of the Battle of Guadalcanal, November 12–15. On November 12, Christie sent him an Ultra to intercept an important Japanese combatant force. The following morning at 7:39, the battleship *Kirishima*, escorted by a ring of destroyers, came along right on schedule. Ramage submerged and closed from 6 miles to 3, but when he was ready to fire, *Kirishima* zigged away. Later in the afternoon, Ramage found the battleship again, fending off a U.S. air attack. Ramage closed to 1,800 yards and fired five torpedoes—only the fourth time in the war (after *Nautilus, Flying Fish,* and *Amberjack*) that a U.S. submarine had attacked a Japanese battleship. None of the five torpedoes hit, and a destroyer drove *Trout* deep. After twenty-eight days, Ramage returned to Brisbane. *Trout* was ordered to Fremantle for refit and more patrols.

Pieczentkowski in *Sturgeon* and his exec, young Chester Nimitz, patrolled from Brisbane to Pearl Harbor by way of Truk. Pi made nine contacts, comprising thirteen enemy vessels. He attacked three, firing nine torpedoes and obtaining one hit for damage. When he arrived in Pearl Harbor, Bob English was furious. "This and many other patrol reports," English fumed, "show that too many targets are getting by at close range without well-aimed shots being fired at them before the situation is hopeless."

While the boat was in Pearl Harbor preparatory to returning to the States for overhaul, Admiral Nimitz took pride in pinning a Silver Star on his son's chest. Back at Mare Island, Pi retained command of *Sturgeon*, but young Nimitz went to the Electric Boat Company to become exec of a new boat.

Pete Ferrall in *Seadragon* patrolled near Rabaul on the way to Pearl Harbor. He was loaded with old Mark X torpedoes left over from the S-boats because Christie

wanted to keep all the available Mark XIVs for the
Brisbane boats. Along the way, Ferrall fired nineteen
torpedoes at a multiplicity of targets including two destroyers, a submarine, and a freighter. The Mark Xs
were a nightmare. Ferrall had prematures, erratic running, and other problems. During a failed attack against a
Japanese sub off Rabaul, the enemy fired a torpedo at
Seadragon.

In Pearl Harbor, Ferrall was credited with sinking a
freighter and one submarine, but postwar records credited
only the submarine, *I-4,* 2,000 tons. The powers that be
carped at Ferrall's shooting—four hits out of nineteen
torpedoes—and for missing several other opportunities to
attack. On return to the navy yard for overhaul, Ferrall
was sent to the Bureau of Ships.

Lockwood—and others—were not happy at Ferrall's
new assignment. All too many good skippers were being
yanked out of the submarine force and sent to other duty.
Lockwood believed that these older men, who had made
many patrols, should be retained as instructors for the
younger ones. Later, Ferrall did return to the force (as
force matériel officer and division commander), but all
too many, encouraged by the Bureau of Personnel to di-
versify their careers and experiences, did not.

Lucius Chappell in *Sculpin* patrolled home by way of
Truk. Alerted by an Ultra, he made contact with a light
aircraft carrier on the night of December 17 and closed
from 12 miles to 9. At that point, two destroyer escorts turned toward *Sculpin.* One pinned her with a
searchlight; both opened fire. Chappell dived to evade,
sweating out a depth-charge attack. The following night,
he attacked a tanker, achieving damage.

Dave White in *Plunger,* who had put into Brisbane
to repair damage after grounding on the bottom, patrolled back to Pearl Harbor. Along the way, he sighted
two submarines and four groups of destroyers. He attacked the destroyers, receiving credit for sinking one and
damaging one; however, the sinking was not credited in
postwar Japanese records. At Pearl Harbor, both White
and his exec, Dave McClintock, were detached and returned to the States to fit out and commission a new boat.

The last five S-boats patrolling from Brisbane achieved little. Two made one attack each, resulting in damage to two ships. After these patrols, the boats returned to the States for extensive overhaul and reassignment to Alaska or to training duties. The S-boat tender *Griffin* left Brisbane November 11, returning to San Diego for conversion to a fleet boat tender.

Silversides, commanded by Creed Burlingame, was the last boat to leave Brisbane in 1942. She was assigned to patrol Truk and then return to Pearl Harbor. When she pulled away from New Farm Wharf, many of the officers and men were wearing strictly nonregulation "Digger" hats, obtained from Australian soldiers. The exec, Roy Davenport, broke out his trombone and played a miserable version of "Waltzing Matilda." Later, the teetotaler Davenport said, "The men on the tender looked at us kind of funny. I guess they were saying, 'Oh, well, they'll sober up in a few days.' "

This fourth patrol put Burlingame and his raffish, combat-hardened crew to the test in more ways than one. Off Rabaul, one of the crewmen, George Platter, complained of a serious stomachache. "We had left port nearly a week ago," Burlingame later wrote, "so upset stomachs resulting from hangovers were a thing of the past." Platter had acute appendicitis. For the third time a submarine pharmacist's mate, here Thomas Moore, twenty-two, performed an appendectomy. Roy Davenport quoted scripture. Platter survived.

A few hours after the operation, Burlingame brought *Silversides* to the surface. The bridge watch spotted what was believed to be a Japanese submarine. Burlingame went to battle stations, fired two stern torpedoes, and dived. One of the torpedoes, perhaps disturbed by *Silversides'* wake, exploded prematurely. "This blew our stern out of the water," Burlingame said later, "and us out of our wits." The target—in reality a Japanese destroyer—kept *Silversides* down until dawn, when Burlingame surfaced and poked up his periscope.

At that moment, *Silversides* was rocked by a thunderous explosion. An aircraft from Rabaul, perhaps called in by the destroyer—still unharmed and patrolling warily—dropped three bombs directly on top of the boat. "In a year of being depth-charged," Burlingame wrote later, exaggerating his time in combat, "we had never had one so close. . . . I thought the conning tower was being wrenched loose from the pressure hull." The men—including Platter, still anesthetized—were thrown violently from their bunks. Light bulbs shattered. *Silversides,* bow planes frozen on hard dive, plunged toward the bottom with a frightening down-angle. "Just short of collapse depth," Burlingame wrote, "we managed to get things under control and leveled off as deep as we could." For the remainder of the day—Christmas Eve—the destroyer passed overhead, dropping depth charges. When he finally went away, Burlingame broke out the medicinal whiskey. "We added it to powdered eggs and canned milk," Burlingame wrote later, "and with a lot of imagination, it tasted almost like eggnog."

After this, Burlingame moved north to Truk to patrol his assigned area. He found numerous targets. The first was an I-class Japanese submarine, which he believed he sank but which was not confirmed in postward records. The second was a huge tanker which blew up in spectacular fashion. It was confirmed at 10,000 tons by JANAC.

In late January, while submerged, Burlingame picked up a convoy at twilight: four fat freighters, guarded by two escorts. He fired five torpedoes at three of the overlapping freighters (the sixth wouldn't fire), heard five hits, then went deep to avoid the escorts. During the evasion, the crew heard breaking-up noises from the direction of the targets but were unable to observe any ships sinking.

When Burlingame shook the escorts, his crew discovered an astonishing—and nerve-chilling—fact: the sixth torpedo had stuck half out of its tube. Had it armed? No one could be sure. It might blow up at any moment, taking Burlingame, Davenport, and the crew down forever. There was only one way to get it out: refire it. Burlingame gave the fateful order, with additional orders that the buddha's belly be rubbed. He backed *Silversides* emergency, to get as far from the torpedo as possible. It sizzled out of the tube and bore away.

Postwar analysis would show that Burlingame's attack on the convoy was one of the most perfectly executed of the war. His five torpedoes hit the three freighters, sinking them all. Counting the big tanker, Burlingame had actually sunk four ships for 27,798 tons—the best patrol of the war by tonnage to date—according to Japanese records. However, lacking positive verification of the convoy sinkings, Pearl Harbor credited only the tanker, plus damage.

Following this patrol, *Silversides* required a navy yard overhaul, and Roy Davenport was detached, with orders to command his own boat. Burlingame and Davenport parted company without shedding tears. Burlingame was happy to have no more of Davenport's religion, while for his part Davenport was delighted to leave the harddrinking wardroom of *Silversides* for his own command.

In late November, Ralph Christie, reveling in his job of commanding the largest congregation of submarines in the Pacific, received despairing news. Back in the States, torpedo production—and development—had turned into a fiasco. There was a hopeless logjam at Newport. The bureaucracy there seemed unable to gear itself for war. As a consequence, the United States was running out of torpedoes for submarines, destroyers, and aircraft. A proposed electric torpedo, which held so much promise, was not moving forward. BuOrd's chief, Spike Blandy, had requested that Ralph Christie return to the States at once as Inspector of Ordnance in Charge, Newport, to clear up the mess. Lockwood's Chief of Staff, James Fife was named to succeed Christie.

On the whole, the great concentration of submarines in the Solomons—and at Truk—had achieved very little.

7

DISAPPOINTING SCORES

The diversion of forces to the Solomons seriously impeded the submarine war against Japanese maritime shipping. During the four-month period July through October, English could mount only twenty war patrols from Pearl Harbor to Empire, East China Sea, and Alaskan waters. Six of them were conducted *like* antiques feeling the strain of war.

Narwhal, commanded by Charles Warren (Weary") Wilkins making his third patrol, was seriously in need of modernization. Nevertheless she went to heretofore unexplored territory: the island of Etorofu, northeast of Hokkaido, the northernmost of the main Japanese home islands. The route was called "the Polar circuit."

Wilkins conducted a most aggressive patrol. Penetrating the Sea of Okhotsk, he boldly sank two small interisland freighters and shifted southward to patrol off northeast Honshu, where the waters were dense with shipping. Wilkins fired at one juicy target, but a torpedo prematured twelve seconds after leaving the tube, badly jarring *Narwhal* and alerting the target, which immediately evaded. An hour later, Wilkins sank the 3,000-ton *Meiwa Maru* and fired at another ship. Aircraft and surface vessels counterattacked. Wilkins counted—and logged—124 depth charges, a record; one of his crewmen, unnerved by the charges, went berserk. A week later, Wilkins sank the 2,500-ton passenger freighter *Bifuku Maru*. He was attacked by a group of Japanese destroyers but managed to evade. Back at Pearl Harbor, English sent *Narwhal* off for a long period of modernization.

Willis Manning Thomas took command of *Pompano*. Even though Thomas had made no war patrols, both Slade Deville Cutter, another Naval Academy football star, and *Pompano*'s third officer, David Rikart Connole, who had made two war patrols, were "absolutely delighted" to have him for skipper.

This third patrol for *Pompano* was conducted off Honshu, where the old boat very nearly came to grief. On August 9, she was caught on the surface by a destroyer, which promptly opened fire. Thomas crash-dived, and the destroyer closed for a savage depth-charge attack. An engine exhaust valve sprung loose. Seawater poured in. *Pompano* sank below 250 feet, with water rising over the engine-room floor plates. Thomas put on more speed and started the pumps. The noise brought on another savage depth-charging. Minutes later, *Pompano* ran aground submerged, wiping off her sonar heads.

Thomas believed that his ship was doomed. She seemed trapped in shallow water with no hope of getting away. Thomas called Cutter and Connole separately to his cabin and told them quietly to prepare the boat for scuttling.

Cutter and Connole did not want to give up the ship without a last fight, and so they prevailed on Thomas to cancel the scuttling and make one more try. It was successful. Surfacing the boat a mere 1,000 yards from the Japanese coast, Thomas was able to clear the area and elude the destroyer.

The third antique to put to sea was Spike Hottel's *Cuttlefish,* now commanded by Elliott Eugene ("Steam") Marshall, another of the class of 1931. He wound up with two execs, Carter Lowe Bennett and John Day Gerwick. Bennett and Gerwick shared a bottle of bourbon one night and divided the duties: the senior man, Bennett, to be exec and navigator, Gerwick to be engineering officer.

Off Japan, Steam Marshall's first contact with the Japanese came in a near collision with a destroyer. The two ships met, nose to nose, about midnight. Marshall crash-dived. On the way down, the conning tower hatch failed to close properly. Carter Bennett and the quartermaster, Richard F. Breckenridge, fought their way through a stream of water; by the time they got the hatch shut there was three feet of water in the conning tower.

Later, Marshall, bedeviled by heavy seas, attacked two ships, the first a 10,000-ton steamer and the second a 19,600-ton *Tonan Maru*-type whale factory, converted to a tanker. Marshall fired three torpedoes at the steamer and was certain it sank, but to make sure, he shot an extra torpedo. He believed he sank the whale-factory tanker. On return to Pearl Harbor, English credited Marshall with both ships, totaling 29,600 tons, but postwar records confirmed neither of the big sinkings.

English was generous with awards. Marshall received a Navy Cross, Bennett and Gerwick Silver Stars. In addition, Quartermaster Breckenbridge received a Navy Cross for "extraordinary heroism" in remaining in the conning tower and helping Bennett close the hatch. This was one of three Navy Crosses awarded to enlisted men in submarines during World War II.

Cuttlefish returned from this third patrol in atrocious mechanical shape. As was her sister ship *Cachalot*, the fourth antique, which had made a luckless patrol in the Aleutians, she was withdrawn from combat service and sent to New London to serve as a school boat.

The fifth antique, *Dolphin*, commanded by Royal Lawrence Rutter, followed *Cachalot* into Alaskan waters. On the way, she encountered a terrifying North Pacific storm and for days was buffeted by huge seas. Going into Dutch Harbor for voyage repairs, Rutter was galvanized by a cry over the PA system, "Torpedoes dead ahead!" Rutter said later, "I hit the bridge just in time to see two parallel torpedo tracks. . . . We thread-needled them and got out fast."

Rutter made a long patrol in the Sea of Okhotsk, where Wilkins had taken *Narwhal* some weeks earlier, but found nothing worth a torpedo. On return to Pearl Harbor, *Dolphin* was assigned to training duty at Pearl Harbor and later followed *Cachalot* and *Cuttlefish* to New London as a school boat.

The sixth antique, *Nautilus*, patrolled off the east coast of Japan. Her skipper, Bill Brockman, ever aggressive, launched his cruise by blasting two fishing trawlers off the face of the sea with his huge deck guns. On the night of September 27, he attacked a six-ship convoy, firing both torpedoes and deck gun into the Japanese force. When one freighter turned to ram, Brockman, still on the surface, countered with gunfire and torpedo fire, sinking the ship, *Ramon Maru,* 5,000 tons. In the ensuing days he sank two more big freighters, totaling 7,500 tons. All three ships were confirmed in postwar records.

On return to Pearl Harbor, English decided that *Nautilus* and her sister ships *Narwhal* and *Argonaut* were too big and clumsy for war patrol in Empire waters. From then on the three old boats were reserved for special missions such as landing guerrillas, spies, ammunition, and supplies in the Philippines.

The other fourteen patrols from Pearl Harbor to Empire and East China Sea waters during July through October were conducted by the newer boats. One of these, *Haddock,* commanded by Arthur Howard Taylor, was equipped with a new type of radar known as the SJ. The first radar set carried by U.S. submarines—the SD—was nondirectional, purely an aircraft warning device. The SJ, a major improvement technically, was a "surface search" radar, designed specifically for picking up enemy shipping. It provided exact range and bearing, enabling the submarine to "see" at night or in rain, fog, or snow.

For a historic trial of submarine radar, English sent Taylor to the lower East China Sea. The radar helped him sink two Japanese ships. Off Formosa on August 12, Taylor made a conventional daylight periscope attack against a large freighter, inflicting damage. That night, he tracked the damaged ship by radar, made an end around and carried out a successful night surface attack. The ship was never identified, but Taylor was credited with 4,000 tons. Two weeks later, in the Formosa Strait, Taylor's radar picked up another ship. He made another end around and waited. When the ship caught up, Taylor fired four torpedoes. All missed. He fired two more, sinking *Teishun Maru,* 2,250 tons. On return to Pearl Harbor, English credited Taylor with sinking three ships for 24,000 tons, but postwar analysis reduced this total to two ships for 6,251 tons.

This was not an overwhelming score. However, during much of the patrol the SJ was out of commission or calibration. Nor had they had much time to practice with the set. Even though it had not performed consistently, Taylor was enthusiastic. The SJ had obvious potential, both for attack and for navigating in tricky enemy waters. As fast as SJ radar became available to the submarine force it was installed in the boats, and extra technicians, skilled in radar repair, were added to the ship's table of organization. It would prove to be a decisive weapon.

Of the skippers departing Pearl Harbor in August on first patrol, one was destined to win instant fame and glory. This was mild-mannered, soft-spoken Thomas Burton Klakring, commanding a new boat, *Guardfish*. Klakring's exec was Herman Joseph Kossler, a big, affable officer, Klakring's opposite in temperament. The two men got along famously.

On the way out to Pearl Harbor, *Guardfish* nearly came to grief, Klakring remembered. "In Panama, at Cristobal on the Atlantic side, there was a minefield with a narrow gate, maybe 150 feet wide, operated by the army. When you gave a certain signal, the army opened the gate for a brief period. Very brief. Then you barreled through. I gave the proper signal and rang up flank speed. Something malfunctioned. The gate didn't open. At the last minute, I backed full on both engines to avoid hitting the gate. The bow swerved. The next thing I knew, we were backing into the minefield. Before we could get out of there, we sliced a mine in half with the port propeller. For some inexplicable reason, it didn't explode. The force of the blow even bent the propeller. It was a terrible, terrifying experience."

English assigned Klakring to the northeast coast of Honshu; it was dense with shipping of all kinds. Nosing into the area, Klakring picked up a large naval auxiliary with an escort and fired three torpedoes. All missed. An escort held *Guardfish* down with a desultory, ineffectual depth-charging until the auxiliary was beyond range. Klakring then engaged two fishing trawlers with his deck gun and sank them both.

In the days following, Klakring seemed to spot a ship nearly every day—or hour. One reason was that he maneuvered *Guardfish* extremely close to shore in order to get between the beach and the close-in shipping lanes.

"This was a difficult technique to master," Klakring

said later. "In the early morning, after we got our battery charge in, we made a high-speed run at the beach, sort of groping toward the mountainous coast in the pitch dark. There were tricky currents—some northbound, some southbound. We got so we could time it just right. Get right in there on the beach just about daybreak when we had to submerge. Then we were in ideal position."

Within a space of eleven days, Klakring believed he sank six fat vessels. Four of these, he thought, went down in one day, September 4. One was a freighter anchored inside a harbor. Klakring fired from a range in excess of 7,500 yards. It was the longest shot of the war that resulted in a sinking.

When *Guardfish* returned to Midway for refit, Bob English was ecstatic. Klakring, considered by most an engineering specialist of modest promise, had turned out to be a submarine force commander's dream. English gladly and uncritically credited him with what he claimed, six big ships for 50,000 tons—four of these (34,000 tons) sunk in a single day. From a tonnage standpoint, this bag was nearly twice that achieved by any submarine in any of the three forces: Pearl Harbor, Brisbane, or Fremantle. No one had sunk six ships on a single patrol; no one had sunk four in a single day. Klakring received a Navy Cross, Kossler a Silver Star.

In addition, English authorized a rare event for the submarine force, a press conference. War correspondents regularly went to sea and interviewed surface-ship officers and men, but up to then they had been more or less barred from the submarine force, which they had dubbed "The Silent Service." There were two reasons. First was security: the submarine force, fighting in Japanese waters, did not want inadvertently to reveal operational or technical secrets; in particular, submariners wanted to safeguard the secrets of Ultra, the magnetic exploder, and the fact that Japanese depth charges were set to explode too shallow. The second reason was political: nobody wanted the press digging deep into submarine force problems—nonaggressive skippers, malfunctioning and scarce torpedoes, and the failure to stop the Japanese forces at Manila, Java, Midway, and the Solomons.

The press conference—heavily censored—gave rise to another submarine legend that died hard. Herman Kossler remembered its origin. "One Sunday, we came in very close to the Japanese coast. On the chart, we saw a notation: 'race track.' Through the periscope, we saw a train crossing a trestle. We could see people on the train, all dressed up as if they were off on a picnic. Somebody in the conning tower made a feeble joke: 'Maybe they're going to the races.'"

During the press conference, Klakring, having a little fun, recalled the race track and told reporters that the officers on *Guardfish* "placed some bets on the ponies." Said Kossler, "I could have killed him for saying that . . . but, what the hell! We'd had a great patrol. He was entitled to spin a sea story if he wanted to. It was a good story—good for the morale back home." English was pleased. It was almost as good a stunt as shelling the Emperor's summer palace.

Guardfish thereafter became famous as the submarine that "watched the horse races." As the story was told and retold, it grew in drama and dimension. In the final version, it was said that *Guardfish* entered Tokyo Bay and watched horse races from there. The New York State Racing Commission appointed Klakring an honorary member. There was a "Klakring Day" at Pimlico racetrack. Stuck with the story, the *Guardfish* crew tired of denying it—or perhaps even came to believe it.

The tonnage *Guardfish* sank was also exaggerated with the telling. *Life* magazine added 20,000 tons to what Klakring had claimed and published a long article on his first patrol under the subtitle, "U.S. sub patrols the Jap coast, watches Jap horse races and sinks 70,000 tons of shipping." In the postwar analysis, Klakring's tonnage score was reduced by about two thirds, to five ships for 16,600 tons.

Another Pearl Harbor boat operated close to the Japanese shores during the fall of 1942. Because of the torpedo shortage, John Behling Azer, commanding the new boat *Whale*, was ordered to lay mines off Kii Suido. It was the first such mission for any Pearl Harbor skipper, and it turned out to be a spine-chilling assignment.

The orders were to lay the mines 20 miles offshore, in fairly deep water. But Azer's exec, Frederick Joseph ("Fritz") Harlfinger, observed that enemy ships were running close to shore and suggested that Azer plant the mines as far in as possible. Azer was hesitant, as would be any prudent man making his first submarine war patrol within spitting distance of the Japanese beach. Harlfinger pressed; Azer gave his consent. "We were a bunch of wild Indians in that wardroom," Harlfinger said later.

Whale planted her minefield very close to the beach—by moonlight. The next day they saw a convoy. Azer attacked, hoping to sink ships with his torpedoes or drive them into the minefield. As he was attacking, an escort charged in. Bedlam followed, with torpedoes, mines, and depth charges all going off at once. In the ensuing days, Azer and Harlfinger believed they had accounted for four freighters, and so radioed English. But postwar analysis discredited the entire claim.

On the way home, *Whale* was viciously attacked by a patrol craft and almost lost. The first salvo opened valves, flooding part of the boat and standing her on her tail with a tremendous up-angle. Said Harlfinger, "We barely held our own with the leaks. All available spare men were sent to the forward part of the boat in a desperate effort to regain an even keel. Charge after charge was dropped. We were pursued by the patrol boat for seventeen hours."

Finally, *Whale* got away.

On the whole, the newer boats going to Empire waters or the East China Sea on regular patrols sank twice as many ships as the boats going to Truk. There were more targets and—with experience—the skippers had learned where to look for them. Skippers felt more confident with Dick Voge handling operations. Antisubmarine measures near Japan were less intense. The deep-running defect in the Mark XIV had been cured. Now, when a torpedo was fired, it usually ran as directed. If the magnetic exploder worked (or if a skipper violated orders and set for contact hit), there was a good chance for a sinking.

The transfer of boats to Brisbane, plus a decision to retire *Cachalot, Cuttlefish, Dolphin, Nautilus,* and *Narwhal* from regular patrol, drastically reduced Bob English's submarine force and virtually brought the war against Japanese shipping in Empire waters to a halt. In November and December, English mounted only ten Empire and East

China Sea patrols. Because so many torpedoes had been sent to Brisbane, most boats departed with less than a full load. Three were assigned to lay minefields. Three were antiques: *Pike, Porpoise,* and *Pollack.* All ten ran into foul winter weather.

The three boats assigned to lay mines were *Drum, Trigger,* and a new boat, *Sunfish. Drum* had a new skipper, Bernard Francis McMahon. On the way to his area, McMahon stumbled blindly on a major target: the light aircraft carrier *Ryuho,* with destroyer escorts, bound for Truk on her maiden voyage. (A hard-luck ship, she had been hit while being worked on in Tokyo Bay during the Doolittle raid and capsized.)

McMahon set up quickly and fired four bow tubes at the carrier. The other two forward tubes were filled with mines. One hit. Before he could bring his stern tubes to bear, the destroyers drove him deep. One of the main motors went out, and in the ensuing moments McMahon lost depth control, plunging toward the deep ocean floor. By the time McMahon regained control of the vessel and brought her to the surface, Japanese planes overhead drove him back down. He was unable to get another shot at the carrier, but his one hit forced her to return to a navy yard in Japan for lengthy repairs.

McMahon went on to lay his minefield and make two more attacks. He sank no ships, but his aggressive attack on *Ryuho* earned him a Silver Star and a reputation for boldness.

Sunfish, commanded by Richard Ward Peterson, who had never made a war patrol, and *Trigger,* now commanded by Roy Benson, who had been Brockman's exec on *Nautilus* at the Battle of Midway, were the second and third minelayers. No known sinkings resulted from *Sunfish*'s mines. However, Benson laid his off Inubo Zaki, a few miles north of Tokyo Bay, and then watched as a freighter with an escort steamed right into the field and blew herself up. Benson believed the escort had sunk too, but there was no Japanese record of it. The ship sunk was *Teifuku Maru,* 5,198 tons. This was probably the only ship sunk by any of the Pearl Harbor minelaying missions in 1942.

A few nights later, Christmas Eve, *Trigger* nosed quietly into Sagami Nada, just outside Tokyo Bay. One of the enlisted men proposed that the ship's record player be hooked to the PA system so the crew could hear Christmas carols. When this was done, the familiar music chorused throughout the boat—and also from the two speakers on the bridge. As the sound drifted across the dark waters toward Tokyo Bay, Ned Beach, standing watch on the bridge, felt a lump in his throat "the size of a watermelon." He wrote, "For the few minutes that those magic, so-well-remembered strains filled the air we were transported away from the battle, and the danger, and the lurking terror." There is no record that the Japanese heard the carols, but for many on *Trigger* the episode was an act of defiance, reflecting the bold spirit she now displayed under Roy Benson.

During this aggressive patrol, Benson attacked a freighter outside Tokyo Bay, a second freighter loaded with aircraft a little farther offshore, and the destroyer *Okikase*. In all, he was credited with sinking four ships for 24,000 tons, but JANAC reduced his score to the one freighter sunk in the minefield plus the destroyer *Okikase*.

The three antiques, *Pollack*, *Porpoise*, and *Pike*, all made difficult and dangerous voyages.

Pollack, commanded by Robie Ellis Palmer, was hit by bad weather and left station early—with 44,000 gallons of fuel, enough for ten more days. The Pearl Harbor command was not happy about this. *Porpoise*, commanded by John McKnight, was caught in the same typhoon. McKnight did mount several attacks and managed to sink one ship for 5,000 tons, but he also left station early without telling anybody.

Billy New, returning *Pike* from long overhaul, had the worst of it. Following an unsuccessful approach on a Japanese vessel, he was trapped by a destroyer which delivered what Pearl Harbor judged to be the worst depth-charging of the war up to then—a total of seventy-one charges. *Pike* was forced to 365 feet and suffered near-fatal damage. Everything leaked.

Luckily, few Japanese depth-charge attacks were persistently conducted. The Japanese apparently assumed their depth charges were finding their mark and that in most cases an attack resulted in a sinking. Few waited

around for confirmation, such as debris bubbling to the
surface, and many were apparently fooled by oil slicks
which came from leaks, not fatal ruptures. *Pike*'s attacker
left before the job was finished, and *Pike* returned to the
navy yard for extensive repairs. Billy New, an unlucky
skipper who had made six patrols (counting his eleven-
day sortie at the Battle of Midway) without ever having
sunk or damaged a ship, left submarines for good.

Three of the newer boats, all fighting the foul weather,
sank six ships. Philip Harold Ross in *Halibut,* who had
made two zero patrols in Alaskan waters, sank three for
12,500 tons. Vernon Long ("Rebel") Lowrance, making
his second patrol in *Kingfish,* sank two for 10,000 tons. Art
Taylor in *Haddock,* making his third and last patrol, sank
one for 4,000 tons. Jesse Lyle Hull in *Finback* got caught
in storms and flooded his conning tower. On this, also his
third and last patrol, he fired no torpedoes.

During the second half of 1942, following the Battle of
Midway and the foray to Alaska, Bob English had
mounted a total of sixty-one war patrols from Pearl Harbor. Twenty-nine of these had been at Truk or to the waters south of Truk, twenty-seven had been to Empire
or East China Sea waters, three were in Alaskan waters,
and two were the special missions of *Argonaut* and *Nautilus* to Makin Island.

In all, only thirty-four of the sixty-one patrols resulted
in sinkings—57 percent. There had been twenty-five bar-
ren patrols. No ships were sunk by the three fleet boat
patrols in Alaskan waters. The twenty-seven patrols in
Empire waters had accounted for forty-seven ships.
The twenty-nine patrols to Truk and vicinity had accounted for twenty-four ships, including three men-of-
war: Dick Lake's light cruiser, *Tenryu;* Burt Klakring's
fleet destroyer, *Hakaze;* and an "old destroyer" sunk by
Chester Bruton. In addition, Red Ramage had inflicted
positive damage on the light carrier *Taiyo* (*Otaka*), Barney McMahon had damaged the light carrier *Ryuho,*
and Donc Donaho had probably damaged a battleship. The
rate of sinkings in Empire waters remained twice that of
boats patrolling to Truk.

In Fremantle, Rear Admiral Lockwood was an unhappy warrior. The decision to transfer Squadron Two from Albany to Brisbane and return the boats to Pearl Harbor for overhaul temporarily reduced his force from twenty submarines to eight. He faced a critical shortage of torpedoes; the boats on patrol shot about seventy-five a month and Lockwood received about eighteen. When Lockwood complained to Washington, Admiral Edwards replied, "We will give you new tools to work with some day, but at present, the tool shed is empty. . . . If there is anything that you want done from this end please let me know and I will probably send you my deepest sympathy in return."

One item arriving in Fremantle made him happy: a shipment of three 5-inch submarine deck guns. For well over fifteen years, Lockwood had urged larger deck guns on submarines for defensive purposes, but he had always been turned down. Now, with a war on, they had been shipped to him as an experiment. He ordered the first two guns placed on *Gar* and *Thresher* and—somewhat imprudently—encouraged the skippers to use them *offensively* against suitable Japanese shipping.

During the four-month period September through December, while the great sea battles in the Solomons were taking place, Lockwood mounted seventeen war patrols from Fremantle. Five of the seventeen were conducted by Squadron Two boats that returned directly to Pearl Harbor without stopping for duty in Brisbane. Because of the torpedo shortage, five were the hated—and usually unproductive—minelaying missions.

Gar, commanded by Donald McGregor, set off with her new 5-inch deck gun and a load of thirty-two mines and torpedoes. After laying the mines in shallow waters near the edge of the Gulf of Siam, McGregor conducted a lackluster patrol off Indochina. He did not use his new 5-inch gun. He found few contacts. When *Gar* returned to Freemantle, both the exec, Allison John Fitzgerald, and the third officer, Maurice William ("Mike") Shea, asked for transfers.

The endorsements on McGregor's patrol report were blistering: "It is difficult to understand how a submarine

Deck gun

could spend thirty-nine days [off Indochina] and make only two contacts"; it was speculated that McGregor had either patrolled too far off the coast or spent too much time submerged. Lockwood wrote, "The track of the ship during the last patrol indicates that the assigned areas in known traffic lanes were not sufficiently exploited," and relieved McGregor, Fitzgerald, and Shea in one fell swoop.

In contrast to *Gar*, William John ("Moke") Millican in *Thresher* (also with new 5-inch deck gun and mines) turned in a sizzling patrol. After planting his mines near the edge of the Gulf of Siam, he found many targets. He made four torpedo attacks, firing off eight torpedoes, all he had on board. None hit. Then, off the south end of Makassar Strait, he boldly attacked a 3,000-ton freighter with his 5-inch gun and drove her into shallow water, where she probably sank (Japanese records provided no specific information on her loss). This was the largest—and one of the few—Japanese vessels sunk solely by deck gun. Lockwood was immensely pleased.

On his next patrol, Millican was ordered to reconnoiter Christmas Island (the tiny dot in the Indian Ocean where Freddy Warder had attacked three cruisers in late March) and Sunda Strait. The codebreakers had picked up word that the Japanese intended to try to mount salvage operations on the cruiser *Houston*, sunk in shallow water during the Battle of Java Sea, and were concerned that the Japanese might recover U.S. Navy codebooks and machines or discover from documents on *Houston* that the U.S. Navy was reading Japanese codes. One of *Thresher*'s missions was to torpedo any Japanese salvage vessels found at the scene of *Houston*'s grave.

On this patrol, Millican had a new exec, William Schuyler Post, who was impressed by Moke Millican's aggressive spirit. "I learned everything I knew from him," Post said later. "He had a TDC in his head. He was a scrapper—he'd been a bantamweight fighter at the Academy. He was not too articulate, but he knew what he was doing."

Off Christmas Island, Millican had a near catastrophe. While "routining" the torpedoes, Number One tube was accidentally fired with the outer door closed. The torpedo made a "hot run" (the motor ran, the propellers turned furiously), and then it pushed halfway out the outer door.

After dark, Millican surfaced and removed the torpedo. However, the outer door was jammed full open and wouldn't close. Millican returned to Fremantle to have it fixed.

Thresher returned to Christmas Island and then swung north through Sunda Strait. There was no sign of salvage vessels at *Houston,* so Millican went around to the Java Sea. On Christmas Day off Surabaya, he found a five-ship convoy and attacked, believing he sank one 7,000-ton freighter despite some torpedo failures. On the following day in the same area, alerted by an Ultra, Millican sighted a heavy cruiser and a "first-class" carrier, probably *Shokaku* or *Zuikaku,* returned from the Solomons. He closed to 6,000 yards, but before he could set up and fire, a destroyer drove him off.

A few nights later, near Lombok Strait, *Thresher* picked up a large freighter sailing alone. Millican, who had a master's degree in ordnance engineering, was by now convinced that the magnetic exploder was defective. He tried an experiment with the freighter, closing to 800 yards and firing one torpedo. No explosion. Millican again ordered his crew to man the 5-inch deck gun. Using binoculars strapped to the gun for a sight, the crew fired off eighty-five rounds. When the freighter failed to sink, Millican fired four more torpedoes at her. Down went *Hachian Maru,* 2,733 tons.

Lockwood gave Millican glowing endorsements: "He is really a remarkable type, and I wish I had a couple dozen more like him."

Grenadier, Tambor, and *Tautog* planted minefields along the coast of Indochina—two off Haiphong—and then made undistinguished regular patrols.

After laying his mines, Bruce Carr, with eight torpedoes on *Grenadier* for his second patrol, made seventeen contacts. He fired three torpedoes at the same ship; all missed. An Ultra from Lockwood directed him to intercept two Japanese cruiser divisions coming up from Singapore to Manila; Carr couldn't find them. On return to Fremantle, Lockwood was critical of Carr and relieved him of command. Later Carr wrote, "Having been awarded the Silver Star for *Grenadier*'s second patrol [under Pilly Lent], the Commendation Medal for her third, and having, on her fourth, successfully completed her primary mission, the laying of an effective minefield off Haiphong, I feel that my contribution to the war effort was fully positive."

Stephen Ambruster on *Tambor* laid his minefield and then patrolled aggressively, making four torpedo attacks, during which he sank one confirmed ship. However, on his next patrol in Sunda Strait (to drive any salvage vessels from the site of the *Houston* sinking), Ambruster apparently let down, for when he returned Lockwood wrote, "The results of this patrol are disappointing not only because of lack of results but also because the area was not thoroughly exploited."

Joseph Harris Willingham in *Tautog* planted his minefield and then made one gun and six torpdeo attacks, the last of which brought on a severe depth-charging. Most of the torpedo attacks failed. On one, Willingham even heard the torpedo hit the side of the ship's hull, but it did not explode. McCann, one of Lockwood's staffers, wrote, "There have been numerous reports of torpedoes failing to explode when passing under the target but this is the first report of a failure to function on actual impact. Every effort is being exerted to insure the proper function of exploders."

Willingham was relieved for new construction, and Lockwood gave command of *Tautog* to William Bernard ("Barney") Sieglaff. Sieglaff, who had never made a war patrol, turned in a splendid first effort. Taking advantage of Ultra reports—which he said later he did not fully trust —he intercepted two light cruisers in separate engagements. Finding the first off Ambon Island, he stopped it with one quick shot and then fired two more for hits. The damaged cruiser opened up on *Tautog*'s periscope with 5-inch guns before limping into Ambon. The second cruiser was in Salajar Strait on the south coast of Celebes. Sieglaff fired four bow tubes in heavy weather from an unfavorable position, but all missed, and a destroyer escort pinned *Tautog* down until the cruiser got away. In addition to these attacks, Sieglaff intercepted several convoys and sank two confirmed ships, earning a reputation for extreme aggressiveness.

Jim Coe in *Skipjack* returned to Pearl Harbor by way of Ambon, Halmahera, and the Marshall Islands. He

carried twelve Mark XIV torpedoes and four antique
Mark IXs, predecessors to the old Mark X, which had not
been test-fired for twenty-three years. Along the way, 75
percent of the crew came down with nausea and loss of
appetite, probably caused by bad drinking water. Even so,
Coe managed several attacks, including one on a tanker,
firing twelve torpedoes, three of them Mark IXs. Only two
hit. Bob English commended Coe's aggressiveness but
criticized his shooting.

Freddy Warder in *Seawolf* returned to Pearl Harbor
by way of Davao Gulf and the Palaus, an island group no
submarine had yet investigated and where the codebreakers reported carrier activity. Warder, making his
seventh and last patrol of the war, might have chosen to
take it easy. But Warder was Warder, and his final patrol
was one of the most aggressive and productive of all.

Warder headed for Davao by way of Makassar Strait.
Off Makassar City, he attacked a freighter but missed. Off
Balikpapan, he found a tanker but was unable to get into
firing position in time. He boldly poked *Seawolf*'s bow into
Davao Gulf and within a few hours had sunk *Gigu Maru*,
3,000 tons. In nearby Talomo Bay, he sank a large trans-
port, *Sagami Maru*, 7,000 tons. After evading subchasers
and aircraft, he sank *Keiko Maru*, 3,000 tons, off Davao
Gulf. When one of his torpedoes made a circular run,
Warder coolly evaded it by going deep.

Seawolf moved east to the Palaus, arriving November
11. No sooner had she got there than two destroyers came
charging out. Warder began an approach. While swinging
the periscope around, he spotted a big aircraft carrier—
Shokaku or *Zuikaku?*—coming out of the rain and twilight. Unfortunately, Warder could not attain a favorable
attack position, but after dark he surfaced and pursued the
carrier at full speed, trying to raise Pearl Harbor to report.
The carrier got away. Eventually Pearl Harbor received
the report.

At Pearl Harbor, Bob English gave Warder a "well
done" and sent *Seawolf* to Mare Island for overhaul and
modernization.

Kenneth Hurd in *Seal*, returning to Pearl Harbor, followed Warder to the Palaus. As he was nearby when War-

der got off his contact report on the carrier, Dick Voge ordered Hurd to close and try to find it.

Hurd promptly ran into a large convoy and attacked from close range, shooting at a large freighter. A few seconds after firing, *Seal* was shaken to her keel by a terrifying explosion or other noise—no one was sure what had happened—and she broached, then plunged deep. A destroyer came over, dropping depth charges, holding *Seal* down until the convoy had proceeded beyond range. When Hurd surfaced that night, he found one periscope bent over at right angles and the other frozen in its mount. There was red bottom paint on the bent periscope. The destroyer had collided with *Seal*, smashing the periscope.

Because *Seal* was now blind, Hurd received permission to cut his patrol short. When he arrived at Pearl Harbor he met a cool reception. He claimed to have sunk one ship, but Voge decided the evidence was too slim. However, postwar records revealed that Hurd was right. In the wild melee that almost destroyed *Seal*, his torpedoes had found *Boston Maru*, 5,500 tons, and he was later credited with sinking her. Hurd relinquished command of *Seal* and reported to the Pearl Harbor staff.

Red Ramage in *Trout* set off for patrol in Indochina waters near Camranh Bay. Along the way, he received an Ultra ordering him to intercept a huge tanker, *Kyokuyo Maru*, 17,000 tons, loading oil at Miri, on the west coast of Borneo. Ramage found the ship at anchor. After dark, he fearlessly slipped into the channel on the surface, closed to about 3,000 yards, and fired four torpedoes. Two hit amidship, causing a tremendous explosion and brilliant flames. One torpedo prematured; one, Ramage claimed, was a dud.

Believing the ship had sunk, Ramage proceeded on to Camranh Bay, sinking two schooners with gunfire and a 3,000-ton freighter with two torpedoes. Then he attacked a destroyer from the point-blank range of 900 yards, firing three torpedoes. He watched them run hot, straight and normal toward the target, but they were, as Ramage reported, "DUDS!"

After that, Ramage received another Ultra, directing him to the Singapore–Manila sea lanes to eastward.

While there, he saw three large tankers but was unable to make an attack. He commented in his report, "Sad day. With two cents' worth of luck we could have had a picnic. But here is the race track and the field is fast."

Ramage received yet another Ultra, directing him to return to Miri, where another huge tanker, *Nisshin Maru,* 17,000 tons, was expected. He found her at anchor. Believing the Japanese would now have defenses against night attacks, this time Ramage went in submerged in daylight. He fired two torpedoes, set on low speed, from a range of 5,000 yards. Then, on second thought, Ramage surfaced to man his deck gun, but *Nisshin Maru* opened fire with her own guns, driving Ramage under again. Exiting to sea, Ramage heard two explosions and saw smoke rising from the ship's stern.

Ramage swung north and rounded Borneo, then went south through Makassar Strait. There he received two Ultras, one informing him to take position north of Lombok Strait for expected enemy traffic, the second canceling the first, ordering him back near Balikpapan to intercept traffic. Right on schedule, Ramage found a 2,000-ton freighter off Balikpapan and fired two torpedoes from 700 yards. The first hit, blowing off the bow of the ship; the second was another "DUD!" as Ramage noted in his report.

Ramage battled-surfaced and closed the wildly maneuvering ship. It fired back with accurate machine guns, spraying the deck. Seven of Ramage's gun crew were struck during the fusillade. He hauled off, got the wounded below, submerged, and went in for a second torpedo attack, firing one torpedo from 700 yards. It hit and the ship sank.

When Ramage reached Fremantle, he was furious. Of the fourteen torpedoes he had fired, one had prematured and five were duds. This, he estimated, was about a 43-percent failure rate. Al McCann was concerned but not sure that all the failures could be blamed on the exploder; "control errors or firing at too close range might have accounted for them." However, the disparaging torpedo reports from Millican and Red Ramage led both McCann and Lockwood to believe that there might be something amiss in the exploder. But nothing was done.

Information from the codebreakers corroborated Ramage's claim that he had hit both *Nisshin Maru* and *Kyo-kuyo Maru*. However, they reported, *Kyokuyo* had been salvaged. Ramage received credit for damage to both ships for 35,000 tons, plus credit for sinking two other ships for 10,000 tons and the two schooners. Postwar records confirmed the two sinkings but trimmed the tonnage to 4,900 tons.

One Fremantle boat, Shirley Stovall's *Gudgeon*, refitted at Brisbane after her fifth patrol from that port and then proceeded to Lockwood's area for her sixth. Stovall was ordered to the Philippines, where he was to land a guerrilla party of six, commanded by a Filipino war hero, a Major Villamor.

The patrol seemed jinxed from the beginning. Leaving Brisbane, *Gudgeon* had a crankcase explosion in one of her Fairbanks-Morse engines, forcing a return to port. After repairs she set off again, landing her guerrillas on Negros Island. Then she traveled farther north into the Philippines to have a look at Manila Bay and Lingayen Gulf. Although the area was teeming with Japanese shipping, Stovall found nothing to shoot at. Dornin, relentlessly aggressive, believed that *Gudgeon* should penetrate Lingayen Gulf, but Stovall refused.

Moving southward, *Gudgeon* received an Ultra that a big Japanese tanker would put into Davao Gulf on January 19, so Stovall set a course to intercept, taking station off the entrance to the gulf. Either the tanker failed to show up or Stovall didn't see it; he remained in the area a few days, patrolling carefully, but found nothing.

After this fruitless running about, *Gudgeon* was ordered off Ambon Island. There she was spotted by a small subchaser with an exceptionally capable and aggressive skipper. In a near-perfect sonar approach, the subchaser attacked *Gudgeon*, dropping eight depth charges, all terrifyingly close. *Gudgeon* was severely damaged. One charge dished in the hull in the after torpedo room, putting the torpedo tubes out of commission. Most of the gauges and lights were smashed. The concussion knocked men off their feet. Many were cut by flying glass. There were countless leaks.

Fortunately for *Gudgeon*, a heavy rainstorm fell during the attack, and the drumming of rain on the surface of the sea interfered with the subchaser's sonar. During the storm, Stovall evaded and ran for safety. In Dornin's opinion, the storm "may have saved the boat." After withdrawing to open ocean, Stovall's crew spent three days repairing the damage.

Stovall next received orders to carry out a second special mission: sneak to a designated point on the coast of Timor and evacuate a party of guerrillas who had been fighting on the islands for seven and a half months. The guerrillas—twenty-one Australians, one Portuguese, one Britisher, and five natives, many with malaria and other jungle diseases—were picked up successfully by rubber boats, and Stovall delivered them to Australia.

When *Gudgeon* returned to Fremantle, Stovall and Dornin were at swords' points. Said Dornin later, "Stovall had won a couple of Navy Crosses and wanted to go home. I put him on report for not being aggressive enough. Al McCann felt he should have penetrated Davao Gulf like Freddy Warder had done. So did I. We had not shot a single torpedo on this patrol and we'd gotten hell knocked out of us. The upshot was, they relieved us both."

Little had been achieved. In their seventeen war patrols, Lockwood's forces sank only sixteen ships, including one (Millican's) by deck gun and none—so far as Japanese records revealed—by minelaying. All too many skippers had been found wanting.

Although Lockwood's operations were hampered by the extreme shortage of torpedoes and the small number of submarines available, he had been in the best position to mount a strategic offensive against the flow of oil to the Japanese fleet units in the Solomons. Red Ramage in *Trout* had made a good contribution in this direction at Miri. But why hadn't Lockwood concentrated *all* available submarines off known oil ports? These ports could have been mined, perhaps causing havoc—or at least considerable confusion. Why bother with Indochina and Manila? "The answer," a submarine skipper said, years later, "was simple. There was too much concentration on the numbers racket. Lockwood wanted 'Bags.' Tonnage sunk. The more the better. He didn't care what kind or where it was found. He assumed, I suppose, that his boats would find better bags off Indochina and Manila."

Too much time was expended on special missions—for example, *Gudgeon*'s patrol. These missions, primarily supporting guerrilla activity in the Philippines, were pet projects of General MacArthur and his intelligence officers, who were, perhaps, bedazzled by the glamour and secrecy surrounding them. In theory, the missions helped sustain "unrest" in the occupied territories. This may have been true, to a point. But at this stage of the war, a few tanker sinkings off Borneo would have been far more valuable to the overall war effort than support of a handful of brave but jungle-bound operatives on Luzon. However, MacArthur was Lockwood's boss and he was not in the best position to deny MacArthur the submarine support he requested for these missions. There is strong evidence, too, that Lockwood was also mesmerized by the glamour of spying and guerrilla activities and enthusiastically joined in the game.

8

SUMMARY: 1942

So ended the first year of the submarine war against Japan.

During 1942, Pacific-based submarines had made a total of about 350 war patrols. They had been employed for coastal defense (Lingayen Gulf, Java, Midway), for blockading (Truk-Solomons), for intercepting Japanese capital ships via Ultra, for interdicting merchant shipping, for commando raids, for delivering and retrieving guerrillas and spies in Japanese-held territory (mostly the Philippines), for minelaying, for reconnaissance (primarily in the Marshalls), for delivering supplies and evacuating personnel (Corregidor), for shifting staff around in the Asiatic theater, and for "beacons" and weather forecasting in support of a few carrier strikes (Doolittle raid, bombing of Wake Island).

In pursuit of these missions, seven submarines had been lost in the Pacific: three S-boats by grounding (*S-27, S-36,* and *S-39*), one fleet boat (*Sealion*) in the Cavite Navy Yard, and three most likely by enemy countermeasures (*Perch,* scuttled after being trapped in shallow water; *Shark* and *Grunion* to unknown causes, probably depth-charge attack).

Only one of these kinds of missions did real harm to the Japanese, and the harm was, on the whole, slight. This was interdiction of Japanese maritime shipping. During the 350 patrols, the three submarine commands (Pearl Harbor, Fremantle, Brisbane) claimed they had sunk 274 Japanese ships for 1.6 million tons. According to postwar Japanese records (incomplete in some cases), the figures were 180 ships sunk for 725,000 tons. This figure was about equal to what thirty-eight operating German U-boats in the Atlantic sank during the two months of February and March 1942.

This effort had not seriously interfered with Japanese imports and exports. Imports of bulk commodities—coal, iron ore, bauxite, rice, lead, tin, zinc, and so on—for 1942 remained about the same as for 1941, about 20 million tons. While U.S. submarines were sinking ships, more were being built. Japan began the war with 5.4 million tons of merchant marine shipping, excluding tankers. By the end of December 1942, the figure stood at 5.2 million tons, excluding tankers, a net loss of only 200,000 tons. As for tankers, Japan began the war with 575,000 tons, built more during the year, and by the end of December 1942 the figure stood at 686,000 tons—an *increase* of about 111,000 tons. Combining the figures for merchant ships and tankers, the Japanese suffered a net loss in shipping of about 89,000 tons, a figure so slight as to be meaningless.

The considerable effort—there is no way of figuring the precise number of patrol days involved—expended in chasing Japanese capital ships from glamorous Ultra reports was likewise largely unproductive. Including the Battle of Midway and the Truk blockade, these reports (plus lucky finds) resulted in about twenty-three individual sight contacts on major Japanese units—five on battleships and eighteen on aircraft carriers. Four of the five battleship contacts were developed into attacks, resulting in slight damage to one—Donaho's at Truk. Ten of the eighteen carrier contacts were developed into attacks, resulting in slight damage to three, those by Red Ramage at Truk and Chester Bruton and Barney McMahon in Empire waters. Only two major Japanese naval vessels were sunk in all of 1942: Dinty Moore's (*S-44*) heavy cruiser *Kako* and Dick Lake's (*Albacore*) light cruiser *Tenryu*.

By contrast, Japanese submarine effort against U.S. surface forces was rewarding—for the Japanese. Japanese submarines sank the damaged carrier *Yorktown* at Midway and the carrier *Wasp* and the light cruiser *Juneau* in the Solomons. The carrier *Saratoga* was twice torpedoed and put out of action for most of the year. In addition, Japanese submarines inflicted heavy damage on the brand-new battleship *North Carolina* and the older heavy cruiser *Chester*. Thanks in part to Ultra, Japanese submarine losses in 1942 were heavy: twenty-three. Six of these were sunk by U.S. submarines: *Gudgeon, Tautog* (two), *Triton, Grayback,* and *Seadragon*.

By far the most successful U.S. submarine effort of 1942 was the fifty-four fleet boat war patrols mounted from Pearl Harbor to Empire, East China Sea, and Formosan waters. These fifty-four, amounting to about 15 percent of all war patrols, accounted for eighty-one confirmed ships, about 45 percent of all sinkings. Had all the fleet boats been concentrated at Pearl Harbor at the beginning of the war and sent to these same waters—and Luzon Strait—to prey on merchant shipping (as Doenitz was doing in the Atlantic), they could probably have carried out an additional two-hundred-odd patrols accounting for an additional three hundred ships, a truly meaningful inroad in Japanese shipping services. The concentration of submarines in the Philippines, Java, Fremantle, Midway, Alaska, Truk, Brisbane, and Solomons achieved little compared to Empire patrols.

Much of the submarine failure in 1942 could be laid to poor skipper performance and poor torpedo performance. During 1942, the three commands relieved about 40 skippers out of 135—almost 30 percent—because of poor health, battle fatigue, or nonproductivity, mostly the last. Many younger officers from the class of 1931 and three from 1932 became skippers, but the three commanders chose these younger men all too slowly and cautiously, still obsessed by the peacetime emphasis on seniority. During 1942, Lockwood made a substantial contribution by confirming the deep-running fault of the Mark XIV torpedo—and getting BuOrd to admit it officially—but all three commands were derelict in follow-up investigations of the magnetic and contact exploders. At the end of December 1942, a full year into the war, no live controlled tests of the exploders had been conducted, in spite of the almost universal belief in the submarine force that something was wrong with both magnetic and contact types.

The major reason for the submarine failure of 1942 was not mechanical, physical, or psychological. It was, to put it simply, a failure of imagination on the highest levels. No one had set up a broad, unified strategy for Pacific submarines aimed at a single specific goal: interdicting

Japanese shipping services in the most efficient and telling manner. The lessons of the German U-boat campaigns against Britain in World Wars I and II—the latter in progress almost on Washington's doorstep—had apparently not yet sunk home. The military and maritime theories of Clausewicz and Mahan were ignored. The U.S. submarine force was divided and shunted about willy-nilly on missions for which it was not suited, while the bulk of Japanese shipping sailed unmolested in Empire waters and through the bottleneck in Luzon Strait.

9

ASSETS AND DEBITS

In January of 1943, Bob English was killed in an airplane crash. Charles Lockwood was named to command the Pearl Harbor submarine force under Nimitz. Ralph Christie was ordered to replace Lockwood in Fremantle. James Fife retained command of the submarine force in Brisbane.

The war in Europe had slowly turned in favor of the Allies. The Nazis had been stopped in Africa at the Battle of El Alamein, in Russia at the Battle of Stalingrad. Losses to the U-boat were still high, but radio intelligence, radar, and hundreds of new antisubmarine surface vessels and aircraft, plus the convoy system, promised an end to the carnage.

In January, Roosevelt and Churchill had met in Casablanca for a strategy conference. During these talks, the defeat of the Axis in Europe had remained the number-one goal, but there were discussions on Pacific strategy, anticipating the time when there would be sufficient military power to go on full offensive there.

Everybody seemed to have a different idea about how to defeat Japan. Admiral King believed there should be a two-pronged effort of equal weight: MacArthur to push up through the Solomons and New Guinea to the Philippines; Admiral Nimitz to advance through the mid-Pacific in an island-hopping campaign from Hawaii to the Gilberts (Tarawa-Makin), to the Marshalls (Kwajalein), and then to the Marianas (Guam-Saipan). General Mac-Arthur—who had sworn publicly to return to the Philippines—did not like this plan. He believed the greater weight should be given his campaign, with the mid-Pacific drive only a diversionary action. Many naval planners thought the Philippines, Gilberts, Marshalls, and Marianas should be bypassed, with the main drive at Truk and Iwo Jima. The British wanted to push through Burma, recapture Singapore and Hong Kong, and then bomb Japan into submission from bases in China. Roosevelt favored the last scheme as a supplement to King's two-pronged strategy.

The submarine force had not played a very large role in these discussions. Submarines, the strategy papers stated, would merely continue to maintain pressure on Japanese lines of communication. No serious consideration was given the idea of a massive submarine blockade of Japan such as Germany had mounted against Britain in World Wars I and II. Most of the emphasis—and priority —was placed on air power (land and carriers), amphibious forces, and ground troops.

The decisions on Pacific strategy that had come from the Casablanca Conference were, in fact, rather vague. MacArthur would continue pressure on the Japanese in the Solomons and New Guinea, driving to Rabaul. What came next was left up in the air. Nimitz would continue pressure on the Japanese in the Alaskan area, with the aim of dislodging them from Attu and Kiska, meanwhile planning for a move westward toward the Gilberts, the Marshalls, Truk, and the Marianas.

The plans Nimitz conceived for a mid-Pacific drive were influenced by one overriding factor: the shortage of aircraft carriers. During 1942, Nimitz had lost four first-line carriers: *Lexington, Yorktown, Wasp,* and *Hornet.* By January 1943 only two remained in service, *Enterprise* and *Saratoga,* both committed to the struggle in the Solomons.

The Arsenal of Democracy was turning out more aircraft carriers. Seven new first-line carriers, authorized by the 1940 Two-Ocean Navy bill, had been launched and were fitting out. In addition, nine light cruisers were being converted to light aircraft carriers. Finally, the navy was in the process of converting about three dozen merchant ships to jeep carriers, designed specifically to support amphibious landings. However, few of these ships would be ready for combat before summer or fall of

1943. No mid-Pacific drive could be launched until this naval power arrived.

When Charles Lockwood arrived at Pearl Harbor in January, he found it "vastly different." Everywhere there were new buildings, Quonset huts, supplies, aircraft, and new ships. The gloom that had hung over the base when he passed through on his way to Australia in April 1942 had disappeared. He felt a "spirit of confidence," positive thinking, a determination to get on with the war—and win it. After his bags were unpacked, Lockwood "went into a huddle" with the staff "which lasted practically twenty-four hours" as they hashed over all the credits and debits of the Pearl Harbor submarine ledger.

The major asset was intelligence. The Joint Intelligence Center was now a booming operation, with its own two-story quarters "on the hill" at Pearl Harbor. Hundreds of people worked there behind tight security guard. Hundreds more were on the way. The center's most valuable core, the codebreakers, was well organized and operating with exceptional efficiency.

On the debit side of the ledger there were several items, none small. The first and most critical was the extreme shortage of submarines. This had been caused by three principal factors: the diversion of fleet boats to Brisbane, the failure of the H.O.R. engines in the new Squadron Twelve, and the diversion of four fleet boats to Scotland for Atlantic service. With so few submarines available, Dick Voge, the very able operations officer, could not take full advantage of the information from the codebreakers. The second and no less critical debit concerned torpedoes. It was a three-headed problem.

First, the shortage. In spite of all efforts on the part of the Bureau of Ordnance, submarine torpedo production had not yet caught up with expenditures. During all of 1942, the three submarine commands had fired 1,442 torpedoes. During that same period, the Bureau of Ordnance had manufactured about 2,000 submarine torpedoes, many of which had not yet even reached the submarine bases. If the shortage continued, it was clear that submariners would be forced to resort again to unpopular—and ineffective—minelaying missions.

Second, exploders. The magnetic exploder was now more controversial than ever. Many submarine skippers in Pearl Harbor favored deactivating the magnetic feature and trying for direct contact hits. However, Lockwood was still loath to do this.

Third, the Mark XVIII electric torpedo. It had been promised to the submarine force by summer of 1942 but had not yet arrived. What was going on? After a dazzling beginning by Westinghouse, it appeared to be now going the way of all torpedo development.

Because of the shortage of submarines and the need to overhaul many that had been diverted to Brisbane, Lockwood mounted only twenty-eight patrols from Pearl Harbor during the first three months of 1943. The majority of these patrols—sixteen—were conducted at Truk, Palau, and the Marianas, from which the Japanese were reinforcing their possessions in the Solomons. Only twelve boats went to Empire and East China Sea waters to interdict Japanese commerce and oil shipments. All suffered from a shortage of Ultras brought on by a Japanese switchover in codes.

Off Kyushu, Eugene Thomas Sands, commanding the new boat *Sawfish,* sank two ships he wished he hadn't. Russia and Japan were still at peace. By mutual agreement, Soviet shipping from Vladivostok usually left the Sea of Japan through La Pérouse Strait, the body of water lying between Hokkaido and Sakhalin. But now, February, La Pérouse was frozen over. Unknown to either Sands or Dick Voge, Soviet shipping from Vladivostok had been routed to the south, leaving the Sea of Japan through Tsushima Strait and then moving to the open sea via the south end of Kyushu.

Early on the morning of February 17, the watch on *Sawfish* saw a light. Closing the range, Sands found two ships in company, both lighted. Somewhat mystified, and suspecting a trap, Sands pulled ahead, dived, and waited. About sunrise, he saw the outlines of a freighter and fired. About noon, another ship came along. She had Russian markings. Sands let her go by, very reluctantly, not convinced it was not a Japanese trick. That same night, Sands found another freighter with lights and sank her. During the remainder of the patrol, he approached four more ships with Soviet markings and let them all pass safely. Later he believed he sank a third Japanese freighter, but it was not confirmed in postwar records.

On return to Pearl Harbor, Sands received a glowing endorsement to his patrol report. Lockwood congratulated him for a "highly successful" patrol, during which the officers and crew "carried out their mission like seasoned veterans," and gave him credit for sinking three Japanese freighters. However, the two lighted ships turned out to be Russian, *Ilmen* and *Kola*. The Soviets lodged a strong protest. Sands was hauled on the carpet, but owing to the unusual circumstances of the sinkings, he escaped a reprimand and retained command of his boat. After this episode, the Soviets improved recognition markings and furnished more and better information on general traffic routing and individual ship movements.

Thomas Wogan, commanding the hard-luck *Tarpon* which had never yet sunk a ship, left Pearl Harbor under a cloud for the abysmal performance on his first patrol, south of Truk. This time he was determined to do better. En route to patrol station in Empire waters, Wogan kept his communications officer, William Anderson, working like a slave. Said Anderson, "Wogan insisted that *Tarpon* break *all* the traffic from Voge, every message for every boat. I stood eight hours on watch, then four hours in the yeoman's shack, locked up, decoding Ultras."

For a while it looked as though *Tarpon* would turn in another zero patrol; off Tokyo, she was caught up in a severe gale, with huge seas, and Wogan kept *Tarpon* at 120 feet to maintain depth control. However, after the storm subsided, Wogan picked up a contact on SJ radar. He closed and submerged, keeping the radar antennas above water. In two separate attacks, he fired six torpedoes, sending the 10,935-ton *Fushimi Maru* to the bottom. A week later, in a similar attack, Wogan sank the huge 16,975-ton passenger liner *Tatsuta Maru,* en route to Truk loaded with soldiers. In these two attacks, Wogan catapulted his own score—and *Tarpon*'s—from zero to 27,910 confirmed tons. In terms of tonnage, it was 110 more than Burlingame's fourth patrol off Truk and therefore the best of any submarine in the war so far.

Rebel Lowrance taking *Kingfish* on her third patrol off Formosa, very nearly failed to return. Lowrance made five attacks—many ruined, he believed, by poor torpedo performance. An Ultra put him on the trail of a big troop transport, the 8,000-ton *Takachiho Maru,* taking reinforcements to the Philippines. She was escorted by what Lockwood would later describe as the "Dean Emeritus of the Tokyo Sound School."

Lowrance sank the troopship (which managed to get only one lifeboat away), but the Dean got on *Kingfish's* track and delivered one of the severest depth-chargings of the war. When Lowrance went deep to evade, a squealing propeller shaft gave his position away, and the escort unleashed a heavy barrage of depth charges that forced *Kingfish* to the bottom at 300 feet. While Lowrance lay still, one salvo smashed and flooded the main induction lines. Another bashed in the pressure hull. During the attacks, which kept the boat pinned down sixteen hours, Lowrance vowed that if he got out of this scrape alive he would personally lead the entire crew to church to thank God for deliverance.

Lowrance got away, finally, and limped to Pearl Harbor. "That *Kingfish* came back at all is miraculous," Lockwood wrote later. Lowrance and the crew went to church and then took *Kingfish* to Mare Island for overhaul.

Augustus Howard Alston, Jr., took *Pickerel* to northeast Honshu, where Klakring on *Guardfish* had earned fame. In an aggressive series of attacks, Alston fired all his torpedoes. However, most missed and Alston received credit for only one sinking. Lockwood described the patrol as "disappointing" but was willing to give Alston a second chance.

On his second patrol, Alston asked for the same area. He topped off *Pickerel's* fuel tanks at Midway on March 22—and was never heard from again.

Postwar analysis of Japanese records helped piece together part of *Pickerel's* last days. On April 3, Alston sank a small subchaser off the extreme northeast tip of Honshu. Four days later, he sank a 1,000-ton freighter. Several Japanese antisubmarine attacks were conducted in the area during that period. Although no specific proof of her loss was ever found, Dick Voge believed that *Pickerel* was lost to depth charges during one of these attacks. Not counting *Grunion,* lost in Alaskan waters, *Pickerel* was the first fleet boat Pearl Harbor had lost in sixteen months of combat.

Whale, commanded by John Azer, with Fritz Harlfinger as exec, patrolled the Marshalls. Off Kwajalein, Azer found a huge transport, evidently bringing in troop reinforcements; through the periscope he could see hundreds of soldiers crowding the decks. In a series of attacks, Azer fired nine torpedoes at the ship for an estimated seven or eight direct hits. Yet the target sank slowly. When it finally went under, *Whale* cruised submerged among eight lifeboats.

"One boat was passed close aboard," Azer reported, "and survivors made ready to hit the periscope with their oars." The ship was *Heiyou Maru,* 10,000 tons. Azer and Harlfinger subsequently got two more confirmed ships, totaling 9,000 tons.

All during this patrol, Azer had been feeling miserable; his ankle and wrist joints were swollen and painful. When he returned to Pearl Harbor, he checked in at the hospital. "The diagnosis," he said later, "was arthritis."

It thus became necessary to relieve Azer from command. Casting about for a qualified skipper, the staff lit on Acey Burrows, the lawyer who had fouled up his first patrol on *Swordfish* while Chet Smith was out with a cold.

Before Burrows set off for his second chance, Lockwood took him aside for a private chat, saying he must perform this time—or else. As Lockwood wrote Fife, "If no wishbones, curtains for Acey." Fife returned, "Hope [he] kicks through this time . . . will cheer loud if he does with *Whale* what he failed to do with *Swordfish.*"

Burrows and Harlfinger patrolled the Marianas, making nine attacks, firing off all but one torpedo. This time, Burrows received glowing endorsements and was credited with sinking four ships for 33,500 tons, making him one of the high scorers in the Pearl Harbor command. However, postwar records confirmed only one ship for 6,500 tons on this patrol.

Two antiques—*Porpoise,* commanded by John Mc-Knight, and *Pike,* with a new skipper, Louis Darby ("Sandy") McGregor—patrolled Truk.

McKnight turned in a luckless patrol. Old *Porpoise* was feeling her age. He had got as far as Wake Island, which he intended to reconnoiter, when oil leaks and other matériel failures forced him back to Pearl Harbor for repairs. Twenty days later, he restarted the patrol, this time going to Truk by way of the Marshalls. McKnight found plenty of good targets, twenty-three in all, including a seaplane tender and a tanker. However, he failed to capitalize on his opportunities. When he returned, Lockwood criticized him for missing the seaplane tender and "regretted" that McKnight had not attacked more targets. McKnight left submarines for good, going to communications duty.

Sandy McGregor in *Pike* also found many targets and tried to sink them all. However, he had a run of bad luck. On his first attack against a small convoy off Truk, all torpedoes missed. McGregor wrote, "All hands feel terrible. First chance we get, we drop the ball." McGregor also bungled another attack against a small convoy, again missing with all torpedoes. *Pike* received a terrific depth-charging, her second in a row. But although he had failed to sink anything, Lockwood praised McGregor for a "well-conducted patrol."

When Roy Davenport took command of his own boat, he told the crew about his devout Christian Scientist faith and said he believed God would place a protective shield between *Haddock* and her enemies that would save them from fatal counterattacks. On Sundays, Davenport conducted religious services in the forward torpedo room. "The first Sunday," he said later, "eighteen men showed up. Thereafter, the attendance rose to an average of about twenty-five, about half of the men not on watch."

Davenport took *Haddock* to Palau, by way of Truk. Off Truk, he found many targets, including two heavy cruisers. However, he was unable to get into position to fire. Davenport bucked up his crew, telling them God meant it to be that way and that perhaps He was saving *Haddock* for something bigger and better.

Moving to the Palaus, Davenport sank a large passenger-cargo vessel, *Arima Maru*, and a smaller freighter, *Toyo Maru*. Following the attack on *Arima Maru*, an escort counterattacked, forcing *Haddock* far below her test depth. At about 415 feet, Davenport saw a hair-raising sight: the chart desk in the conning tower moved inward! Believing that the conning tower was on the verge of imploding, Davenport immediately ordered it evacuated. He tried to close the lower hatch into the control room, but it was warped out of shape; Davenport bashed it shut with a sledgehammer. The conning tower held and *Haddock* escaped. Davenport set a course for Pearl Harbor.

Davenport told his crew that he now understood why God had not enabled them to attack the two heavy cruisers at Truk. If they had, *Haddock* would most certainly have received a punishing depth-charging from the escorting destroyers which would surely have collapsed the conning tower and sunk the boat.

While Davenport was on the way back to Pearl Harbor, the codebreakers re-established contact with Japanese carrier movements. They learned that the new Japanese Carrier Division Two, composed of two new first-line carriers, *Hiyo* and *Junyo* (converted from big merchant ships), were en route to Truk by way of the Marianas, bringing aircraft for the Solomons. Voge directed Davenport—despite the infirm conning tower—to close Saipan and look. At 9 A.M. on April 7, while submerged in a flat calm sea, Davenport picked up the targets: one large carrier, one auxiliary carrier, range 12,000 yards, moving fast. They zigged toward him, then away. By 9:43 the range was 20,000 yards. Said Davenport later, "With the calm sea, a long-range slow-speed shot would never have been successful."

After returning to Pearl Harbor, *Haddock* went into a long period of overhaul. There it was determined that the shipbuilders had made an error in the design and construction of the conning tower, undetected until this patrol. Davenport was credited with sinking *Arima Maru*, but *Toyo Maru* was denied until postwar records confirmed her sinking. Even though Davenport had failed to attack two heavy cruisers at Truk and two aircraft carriers at Saipan, the patrol was judged successful.

Suspected torpedo failure continued to plague the patrols and still sparked plenty of controversy within the service. Rebel Lowrance had reported two prematures, one observed dud, and a probable dud in seventeen torpedoes fired on *Kingfish*. Willis Thomas, on old *Pompano*, had fired six torpedoes at a carrier, and three of them had prematured.

John Addison Scott, on the new boat *Tunny*, had been convinced on his first patrol that poor performance of the magnetic exploder had robbed him of some sinkings, and his distrust of it led him to change the settings when he went out again. Off Wake Island he managed to damage a 10,000-ton transport (this transport was later destroyed by John Augustine Tyree, another youngster from the class of 1933, commanding *Finback*) and later sank two large cargo ships. But bigger game lay ahead.

On the night of April 8, Dick Voge sent Scott an Ultra, reporting the two carriers, *Hiyo* and *Junyo*, that Davenport had seen at Saipan. Ably assisted by his exec, Roger Myers Keithly, Scott moved to intercept. The force appeared at night on schedule. As Scott saw it, there was one large aircraft carrier, one escort carrier, and another "large ship" which was probably the auxiliary carrier *Taiyo* (*Otaka*), guarded by two destroyers. Scott and Keithly boldly remained on the surface, working the radar and TDC, and maneuvered *Tunny* into the midst of the formation in position for a triple-header: they planned to fire the bow tubes at the escort carrier and "large ship" and the stern tubes at the largest carrier. Still distrusting the magnetic exploder, Scott set his torpedoes to run at a depth of 10 feet. If the magnetic exploder failed, the torpedoes would explode on contact.

Coolly watching his three magnificent targets approach, Scott got ready to shoot. But at the last moment, three smaller escorts, possibly torpedo boats, appeared dead ahead. This forced Scott to change the attack plan and settle for two out of three. Within the next few minutes, he fired ten torpedoes at two of the carriers from an average range of 800 yards. Going deep to evade, Scott believed he heard at least seven hits. The crew cheered wildly, believing *Tunny*'s unparalleled attack had sunk at least one and possibly two Japanese capital ships.

When Scott returned to Pearl Harbor, the endorsements on his patrol report were ecstatic, and the attack on the carriers became the classic of the war. "The efficiency and aggressiveness with which this attack was carried out reflects the outstanding ability of the entire *Tunny* organization," Lockwood wrote. "The audacity combined with superb judgment of the Commanding Officer on remaining on the surface is an illustrious example of professional competence and military aggressiveness."

But disappointing news came from the codebreakers. The auxiliary carrier *Taiyo* (*Otaka*) had been damaged slightly but, according to the Japanese account, all four torpedoes aimed at the other carrier exploded prematurely some 50 meters away. *Hiyo* and *Junyo* had escaped unharmed. Evidently this time the torpedoes had worked as designed. "The shallow setting," Scott said later, "thus caused the torpedo to reach the activating flux density of the exploder some fifty meters from the target. The settings I had used worked well on lighter, less dense targets but backfired on these heavier men-of-war."

The twenty-eight patrols leaving Pearl Harbor during the first three months of 1943 produced a disappointing bag. Twenty-seven patrols accounted for only twenty-five ships. The eleven other Empire patrols accounted for ten ships (for a grand total of nineteen ships in Empire waters), the twelve patrols to Truk-Palaus produced fifteen sinkings. Clearly, there was now sufficient evidence to conclude that something was definitely wrong with torpedo exploders. The matter could have been resolved with a simple series of live tests at Pearl Harbor. And yet, nothing was done. Lockwood was still hoping that Spike Blandy would produce a miracle that would fix the magnetic exploder's apparent defects.

10

SHOWING THE WAY

Soon after James Fife took command of submarines in Brisbane, the naval war in the Solomons began winding down. Admiral King ordered that most of the boats and tenders return to Pearl Harbor. This order, in effect, left Fife with only twelve boats.

Fife believed the generally poor showing of U.S. submarines basing in Brisbane up to then was due to over-caution. When he had his feet firmly planted beneath his desk, he abandoned caution. Each of his skippers would give a good account of himself or else he would be summarily relieved.

Up to then, most of the skippers had been assigned an area to patrol and left pretty much on their own. Before the Japanese changed the codes in February, there was a steady flow of information from the codebreakers about Japanese maritime forces reinforcing the Solomons from Palau and Truk. Fife believed the submarine force could better capitalize on this information if the boats were more tightly controlled from Brisbane and shifted about frequently as targets became known. He believed he should take a direct—and firm—hand in the shifting or, as he told his staff, "playing checkers" with submarines. In many respects, his new policy resembled that of Doenitz in the Atlantic. It led to many disasters and near disasters.

When Fife took command, the ancient and clumsy *Argonaut,* commanded by John Reeves Pierce, was en route from Pearl Harbor to Brisbane to help carry out the many special missions General MacArthur demanded of submarines. She had landed troops on Makin, but she had

144

never made a real war patrol, firing torpedoes at Japanese ships.

Fife, believing *Argonaut* capable of combat, ordered her to patrol against Japanese shipping in the hazardous area between New Britain and Bougainville, south of St. George's Channel. On January 10, Fife directed Pierce to attack a convoy of five freighters with destroyer escorts. By happenstance, a U.S. Army aircraft, out of bombs, was flying overhead and witnessed the battle, *Argonaut's* first and last. Pierce apparently attacked the destroyers first, hitting at least one for damage. The destroyers counterattacked, churning the water with depth charges. The crew of the aircraft saw *Argonaut's* huge bow suddenly break water at a steep angle, hanging. One of the depth charges had obviously inflicted severe damage. The Japanese destroyers circled like sharks, pumping shells into *Argonaut's* hull. She slipped below the waves, never to be heard from again. One hundred and five officers and men went down with her.

Argonaut's loss, a sad event in its own right, caused further problems for the Australian submarine command. She had been sent there to carry out special missions—for MacArthur and his intelligence operations. Her loss meant that regular fleet boats would continue to be diverted from normal patrol for many of these time-consuming (and hazardous) chores, meaning fewer torpedo tubes on the firing line.

In the same month Howard Gilmore in *Growler*, "born under an unlucky star," as one buddy put it, left Brisbane for his fourth patrol. Fife, manning his radio nightly, chivied *Growler* around, trying to put Gilmore in the path of known convoys or other targets. On January 16, Gilmore got a big one: the 6,000-ton passenger-cargo ship, *Chifuku Maru,* his sixth confirmed sinking. On the last day of the month, he attacked a 2,500-ton converted gunboat with a single torpedo that ran under the target without exploding. A few nights later, Fife put Gilmore on the trail of a small convoy, but escorts, and mechanical failures on *Growler,* prevented an attack.

On the night of February 7, while charging batteries, Gilmore saw what he believed to be the converted gunboat he had unsuccessfully attacked the week before.

Actually, it was *Hayasaki*, a 900-ton provision ship. Manning the bridge, Gilmore went to battle stations and began closing, but *Hayasaki* spotted *Growler* from a mile away and charged in to ram. *Growler*'s crew was slow to detect the target's change in course.

Gilmore's unlucky star now shone brightly. The small ship suddenly loomed out of the darkness. On the bridge, Gilmore sounded the collision alarm and then shouted, "Left full rudder!" His intent was probably to avoid both ramming and being rammed. However, the swing left put *Growler* on a collision course and *Growler*, making 17 knots, hit *Hayasaki* amidships.

The impact was massive. *Growler* heeled 50 degrees, throwing everyone belowdecks off his feet. The crew of the damaged *Hayasaki* manned machine guns, directing a withering fire at *Growler*'s bridge. The assistant officer of the deck, young Ensign William Wadsworth Williams, and a lookout, Fireman W. F. Kelley, were killed instantly. Howard Gilmore, wounded, clung to a bridge frame. Above the roar of machine gun fire, he shouted, "Clear the bridge!"

The officer of the deck, the quartermaster, and two wounded lookouts hurried down the hatch into the conning tower. Arnold Frederic Schade, the exec, stood at the foot of the ladder, waiting for Gilmore. Then came another shout from Gilmore—one that would become submarine legend:

"Take her down."

Schade hesitated for thirty seconds. Save the ship or save the captain? Schade decided to follow his captain's last order and save the ship. He gave orders to dive. *Growler* went down, leaving Howard Gilmore, along with the bodies of Williams and Kelley, topside. No one knows how long Gilmore lived in the water. The Japanese on *Hayasaki* apparently made no effort to capture him. He probably drifted away in the darkness, borne along by the winds and current. For sacrificing his life to save his ship, Gilmore was posthumously awarded the Medal of Honor, the first man of the submarine force to be so decorated.

Beneath the waves, Schade, dazed and bruised from a fall from the conning tower to the control room, had his hands full. The impact of the collision had bent 18 feet of

Growler's bow at right angles to the submarine, rendering her forward torpedo tubes useless. Salt water poured through bullet holes in the conning tower. Schade gave orders to battle-surface and sink *Hayasaki*, but when *Growler* came up the seas were empty. Schade believed the ramming had sunk her, but she was only damaged and lived to fight on.

So did *Growler*. Schade got the leaks repaired and limped slowly back to Brisbane. On the endorsement to this patrol report, Fife wrote, "The performance of the officers and crew in effecting repairs and bringing the ship safely back to base is one of the outstanding submarine feats of the war to date. . . . *Growler* will be repaired and will fight again."

The next disasters befell three of the five boats leaving Brisbane for patrol in February. These were John Bole's *Amberjack*, out for blood, according to Fife; John Craig's *Grampus;* and *Triton*, now commanded by George Kenneth MacKenzie, Jr. The three boats were manned by battle-wise crews.

Fife controlled these boats strictly, repeatedly moving them around on his checkerboard. *Amberjack*, for example, was first moved from west of New Guinea to west of Shortlands, then to west of Buka. She was next ordered west of Vella Lavella. En route, she was ordered west of Ganongga Island. A few days later she was ordered north to cover traffic to the Shortlands. Then she was ordered farther north, and subsequently to the area between New Ireland and Bougainville. She was then shifted north of New Ireland, then ordered to a position west of New Hanover. Her last station was west of Cape Lambert.

In the course of all this jumping about, the three boats achieved little. Bole reported sinking a 5,000-ton freighter, but postwar records failed to substantiate it. MacKenzie attacked a convoy and sank one freighter, confirmed in postwar records at 3,000 tons, and damaged another of 7,000 tons. Craig in *Grampus* may have damaged one large vessel but sank none.

None of the three boats returned from patrol. All were declared "overdue, presumed lost," taking down Bole, Craig, MacKenzie, and 214 other officers and men. After the war, U.S. naval authorities made an intensive hunt in Japanese records to determine the causes for each loss. There were clues, giving rise to various speculations, but nothing positive was ever learned about any of them.

A sixth boat, *Gato*, commanded by Robert Joseph Foley, was very nearly lost. Fife had assigned Bub Ward to be Foley's exec. On their first patrol together, Foley and Ward had made eight attacks, claiming four ships sunk for 27,600 tons, a performance that led Halsey in his endorsement to compare Foley with the best of the submarine commanders. Postwar Japanese records credited Foley with three and a half ships for 11,500 tons, the half credit shared with naval aircraft.

On the second Foley-Ward patrol from Brisbane, *Gato* was first diverted to a special mission: twenty-seven children, nine mothers, three nuns, and a dozen commandos were delivered from Bougainville to a ship waiting off Tulagi. After that, Foley went on regular patrol, a piece on Fife's checkerboard.

On April 4, Fife directed Foley to intercept a freighter escorted by a destroyer. While making the approach, the destroyer detected *Gato* and turned to attack. Foley ordered deep depth, but before *Gato* responded the destroyer came over, dropping depth charges that fell close—and *beneath*—the boat. The blast was violent. *Gato* rocked and plunged out of control toward the bottom. Ward, helping the diving officer, caught the boat at 380 feet. The charges knocked out all propulsion and caused hot runs in the torpedo tubes and bad leaks. Said Ward later, "We almost came to the end of the road."

Foley terminated the patrol and limped into Brisbane. After a drydock inspection, it was determined that all of *Gato*'s stern torpedo tubes would have to be replaced. *Gato* was ordered to return to Pearl Harbor for the work.

Fife's reaction to the loss of four fleet boats with all hands was cold-blooded. "Tough luck," he wrote Lockwood, "but they can't get Japs without taking chances . . . don't think the time has arrived to inject caution into the system because it is too difficult to overcome again."

The transfer to Squadron Ten and the remnants of Squadron Two to Pearl Harbor set in motion a backward

Torpedo room

trek for the submarines that had come down to Brisbane. During the spring, seven (including two Squadron Two boats) returned: *Flying Fish*, *Wahoo*, *Gato*, *Grayback*, *Snapper*, *Swordfish*, and *Nautilus*. *Nautilus* went direct, without conducting a war patrol. The other six patrolled home, along the equator, in the Marianas, and elsewhere. With the exception of *Wahoo*, the patrols produced nothing spectacular.

Donc Donaho on *Flying Fish* had a new exec, his third in four war patrols, Reuben Whitaker. Whitaker said later, "*Flying Fish* was the most miserable boat I ever saw. . . . Donaho had cut off all the water to the enlisted men's showers. If a man made a simple mistake, he would fly into a rage and say he never wanted to see him again. After I had been on board a few days and met the officers in the wardroom, I said to Donaho, 'What the hell are you talking about? You've got a really fine bunch of officers.' Donaho just didn't know how to handle people."

Donaho's *Flying Fish* and St. Angelo's *Snapper* patrolled back to Pearl Harbor by way of the Marianas. Donaho, relentlessly aggressive, poked *Flying Fish*'s nose right into the harbors at Guam and Tinian and fired off ten torpedoes. The Saint torpedoed and sank one ship that Donaho had damaged in the Guam harbor, *Tokai Maru*, 8,350 tons, so both skippers shared credit for her. In addition, Donaho sank the 1,000-ton Freighter, *Hyuga Maru*. *Snapper* seemed unable to shake the dark spell that had dogged her since the beginning of the war. On return to Pearl Harbor, St. Angelo was criticized for remaining submerged too much on the patrol, and when *Snapper* went in for overhaul, St. Angelo was relieved of command and sent to the staff of John Grigg's Squadron Twelve. Reuben Whitaker left *Flying Fish* for new construction.

Chet Smith's *Swordfish* was turned over to Jack Lewis, who had made the first luckless patrols of *Trigger* at Midway and in Alaska. Like Hottel, Lewis was being given a second chance because of the skipper shortage. Off Bougainville, he conducted a well-executed attack on a convoy, sinking a 4,000-ton freighter, but a few days later *Swordfish* was strafed by a U.S. B-17 which inflicted enough damage to require Lewis to terminate the patrol early. At Mare Island, Lewis went to new construction.

Before *Wahoo* left Brisbane on her first patrol under Mush Morton, the new skipper called the crew to quarters on deck and gave them a flaming pep talk. *"Wahoo* is expendable,"* Morton said, according to her yeoman, Forest J. Sterling. "We will take every reasonable precaution, but our mission is to sink enemy shipping. . . . Now, if anyone doesn't want to go along under these conditions, just see the yeoman. I am giving him verbal authority now to transfer anyone who is not a volunteer. . . . Nothing will ever be said about your remaining in Brisbane."

Nobody asked for a transfer. After the speech, Sterling reported, he became aware of

a different Wahoo. . . . *I could feel the stirring of a strong spirit growing in her. The officers acted differently. The*

*men felt differently. There was more of a feeling of free-
dom and of being trusted to get our jobs done. A high
degree of confidence in the capabilities and luck of our
ship grew on us and we became a little bit cocky. It was
a feeling that Wahoo was not only the best damn submarine in the Submarine Force but that she was capable
of performing miracles.*

Wrote George Grider, a junior officer:

*Mush . . . was built like a bear, and as playful as a cub. . . .
The crew loved him. . . . Whether he was in the control
room, swapping tall tales . . . or wandering restlessly about
in his skivvies, talking to the men in the torpedo and
engine rooms, he was as relaxed as a baby . . . constantly
joking, laughing, or planning outrageous exploits against
the enemy.*

All this must have required considerable effort, for Mush
Morton was not a well man; he suffered from prostate
trouble. Young John Griggs recalled, "During our periods
in port he would be hospitalized and on patrol he had to
have semiweekly prostate massages. Yet he did not let
this deter him from his goal, sinking Japs."

The wardroom—Grider, Roger Warde Paine, Jr., young
John Griggs—considered Mush "magnificent" but still
had reservations about the exec, Dick O'Kane. Grider
wrote:

*He talked a great deal—reckless, aggressive talk—and it
was natural to wonder how much of it was no more
than talk. During the second patrol Dick had grown harder to live with, friendly one minute and pulling his rank
on his junior officers the next. One day he would be a
martinet, and the next he would display an overlenient,
what-the-hell attitude that was far from reassuring. With
Mush and Dick in the saddle, how would the Wahoo fare?*

Fife gave Morton orders to reconnoiter Wewak, a
Japanese supply base on the north coast of New Guinea.
Morton kept *Wahoo* on the surface. "It was a strange and
unfamiliar experience," Grider wrote, "to see enemy land
lying black and sinister on the port hand, to feel the

enemy planes always near us, and yet it was invigorating."

There was one large problem about reconnoitering Wewak: *Wahoo* had no charts of the harbor. However, it turned out that one of the motor machinists, D. C. ("Bird-Dog") Keeter, had bought a cheap school atlas while he was in Australia. It had a map of New Guinea with a small indentation labeled "Wewak." With that as a reference, Morton located the unmarked area on a larger navy chart, and George Grider, an amateur photographer, made a blowup of the navy chart with an ingenious device composed of camera and signal lights. "It might have made a cartographer shudder," Grider wrote, "but it was a long way ahead of no chart at all."

Morton found Wewak. Then, to everyone's amazement, he announced that his interpretation of "reconnoiter" meant penetrate the harbor and sink whatever ships could be found. "Now it was clear," Grider wrote, "that our captain had advanced from mere rashness to outright foolhardiness."

Among the many innovations Morton had put in effect on *Wahoo* was one suggested by Fife: the exec, not the captain, manned the periscope. According to Grider:

This, he explained, left the skipper in a better position to interpret all factors involved, do a better conning job, and make decisions more dispassionately. There is no doubt it is an excellent theory, and it worked beautifully for him, but few captains other than Mush ever had such serene faith in a subordinate that they could resist grabbing the scope in moments of crisis.

The trip into the harbor was long and perilous. Throughout, Morton remained almost irrationally casual. "The atmosphere . . . would have been more appropriate to a fraternity raiding party than so deadly a reconnaissance," Grider wrote. "Mush was in his element. He was in danger, and he was hot on the trail of the enemy, so he was happy. . . . Mush even kept up his joking when we almost ran aground."

Wahoo moved ahead, silently, boldly, dodging patrol craft. Nine miles inside the harbor, O'Kane saw a destroyer he believed to be at anchor, with several small Japa-

nese submarines nested alongside. While O'Kane made
periscope observations, Morton sent the crew to battle
stations and prepared to attack this sitting duck. Grider
wrote:

*I found . . . myself marveling at the change that had
come over Dick O'Kane. . . . It was as if, during all the
talkative, boastful months before, he had been lost, seek-
ing his true element, and now it was found. He was calm,
terse, and utterly cool. My opinion of him underwent a
permanent change. It was not the first time I had observed
that the conduct of men under fire cannot be predicted
accurately from their everyday actions, but it was the most
dramatic example I was ever to see of a man trans-
formed under pressure from what seemed almost adoles-
cent petulance to a prime fighting machine.*

As Morton prepared to shoot, O'Kane reported the duck no longer sitting. The destroyer was getting under way. Morton shifted his plan, firing three torpedoes at the moving target. All missed. The destroyer headed directly for *Wahoo,* its superstructure crowded with a hundred or more men on lookout duty. Morton, keeping the periscope up to lure the destroyer, prepared for a down-the-throat shot. When the destroyer closed to 1,200 yards, he fired another torpedo. It too missed. *Wahoo*'s crew was frozen in terror, expecting final disaster. Wrote Forest Sterling, "I had an almost uncontrollable urge to urinate." Morton fired a sixth torpedo at a range of 800 yards. It hit, with a massive explosion. Morton was certain the destroyer sank. He withdrew from the harbor, navigating by sonar.

That night after passing out a ration of brandy to the crew, Morton put *Wahoo* on a northwest course, following the convoy route from Wewak to Palau. The next day, slightly north of the equator, he found a four-ship convoy: two freighters, a huge transport, and a tanker. Morton fired two torpedoes at each of the freighters and three at the transport, achieving hits on all three ships. One freighter, with an unusually aggressive skipper, turned toward *Wahoo* to ram. At the last minute, Morton let her have two more torpedoes down the throat. Then he went deep to avoid being run down.

When *Wahoo* surfaced again, one freighter had sunk, the second was limping away slowly, and the transport was stopped dead in the water. Morton closed to 1,000 yards and fired another torpedo at the transport. It failed to explode. Morton fired another. The transport blew "higher than a kite," Morton wrote, and the thousands of soldiers aboard her "commenced jumping over the side like ants off a hot plate."

Meanwhile, the other freighter had pulled away beyond range, joining up with the tanker. Morton pursued, submerged, but could not overtake. "Mush cursed philosophically," Grider wrote, "swung the *Wahoo* around, and brought her to the surface to resume the chase afloat at a higher speed while we charged our batteries."

When *Wahoo* surfaced, Morton ordered all deck guns manned. He found himself in a "sea of Japanese." The survivors of the transport were hanging on the flotsam and jetsam or huddling in about twenty boats, ranging from scows to little rowboats. Grider wrote:

The water was so thick with enemy soldiers that it was literally impossible to cruise through them without pushing them aside like driftwood. These were troops we knew had been bound for New Guinea, to fight and kill our own men, and Mush, whose overwhelming biological hatred of the enemy we were only now beginning to sense, looked about him with exultation at the carnage.

Yeoman Sterling, who was topside, remembered the scene this way:

The water was filled with heads sticking up from floating kapok life jackets. They were scattered roughly within a circle a hundred yards wide. Scattered among them were several lifeboats, a motor launch with an awning, a number of rafts loaded with sitting and standing Japanese fighting men, and groups of men floating in the water where they had drifted together. Others were hanging onto planks or other items of floating wreckage. A few isolated individuals were paddling back and forth toward the center in search of some human solidarity.

Sterling remembered, roughly, an exchange between Roger Paine and Mush Morton:

"There must be close to ten thousand of them in the water," said Roger Paine's voice.
"I figure about nine thousand five hundred of the sons-a-bitches," Morton calculated.

Whatever the number, Morton was determined to kill every single one. He ordered the deck guns to open fire. Some of the Japanese, Morton said later, returned the fire with pistol shots. To Morton, this signaled "fair game." What followed, Grider wrote, were "nightmarish minutes." Later, Morton reported tersely, "After about an hour of this, we destroyed all the boats and most of the troops."

Leaving the carnage, Morton now took up the pursuit of

the remaining two ships. He caught up at dusk, submerged, and fired three torpedoes at the tanker, obtaining, he thought, at least one hit. After dark, Morton surfaced and started after the obstinate freighter. He then observed that the tanker was still going. He shifted targets and fired two of his four remaining torpedoes at the tanker. The torpedoes hit and Morton believed the tanker sank. After another hour of pursuit, Morton hastily fired his last two torpedoes at the freighter, which was firing shells at *Wahoo*.

In the conning tower, Grider said to Roger Paine, "If either one of those torpedoes hits, I will kiss your royal ass." Both hit. The freighter sank instantly. Wrote Grider, "Exulting on the bridge at his final victory . . . Mush missed the most unusual ceremony ever performed in the conning tower of the mighty *Wahoo*."

That night, Morton drafted a triumphant report for Pearl Harbor: IN TEN HOUR RUNNING GUN AND TORPEDO BATTLE DESTROYED ENTIRE CONVOY OF TWO FREIGHTERS ONE TRANSPORT ONE TANKER. . . . ALL TORPEDOES EXPENDED. "Let's head for the barn, boys," he said.

On the way to Pearl Harbor, Morton found yet another convoy and tried to attack one small lagging freighter with his deck gun, but a destroyer counterattacked *Wahoo*, forcing her down. That night, Morton got off another report to Pearl Harbor: ANOTHER RUNNING GUN BATTLE TODAY. DESTROYER GUNNING, WAHOO RUNNING.

Wahoo nosed into the Pearl Harbor sub base on February 7, twenty-three days after leaving Brisbane. Topside, she had embellishments to celebrate her victory. There was a straw broom lashed to her periscope shears to indicate a clean sweep. From the signal halyard fluttered eight tiny Japanese flags, one for each Japanese ship believed to have been sunk in all three of *Wahoo*'s patrols. "She had left Brisbane a comparative nonentity," Sterling wrote, "and returned to Pearl Harbor a celebrity."

Sudden fame came to Mush Morton too. The story of his exploits was released almost at once to the press. By the time the crew reached the Royal Hawaiian Hotel, Sterling recalled, the Honolulu newspapers had headlines proclaiming *Wahoo*'s deeds. Lockwood nicknamed Morton "The One-Boat Wolf Pack" and gave him a Navy Cross. From Port Moresby, General MacArthur sent an

Army Distinguished Service Cross. This patrol, one of the most celebrated of the war, gave the whole submarine force a shot in the arm—or a kick in the pants. "More than any other man," Ned Beach later wrote, "Morton—and his *Wahoo*—showed the way to the brethren of the Silent Service."

After analyzing the attacks, Pearl Harbor credited Morton with all he claimed: the destroyer at Wewak, the transport, the two freighters, and the tanker, a grand total of five ships for 32,000 tons. In the postwar analysis, however, this total was sharply reduced. The destroyer did not sink—it was beached and repaired—nor did the tanker. In the final tally, Morton received credit for the transport, *Buyo Maru*, 5,300 tons; a freighter, *Fukuei Maru*, 2,000 tons; and an "unknown maru," 4,000 tons. Total: three ships, 11,300 tons.

In his patrol report, Morton described the killing of the hundreds (or thousands) of survivors of the transport. To some submariners, this was cold-blooded murder and repugnant. However, no question was raised abut it in the glowing patrol report endorsements, where policy was usually set forth. Many submariners interpreted this—and the honors and publicity showered on Morton and *Wahoo* —as tacit approval from the submarine high command. In fact, neither Lockwood nor Christie nor Fife ever issued a policy statement on the subject. Whether other skippers should follow Morton's example was left up to the individual. Few did.

Mush Morton's second patrol as skipper of *Wahoo* was another bellringer. This time *Wahoo* sailed without George Grider, who had gone to *Pollack* as exec. O'Kane still served on *Wahoo*.

For this patrol, Dick Voge assigned Morton an area never before penetrated by U.S. submarines: the extreme northern reaches of the Yellow Sea, in the vicinity of the Yalu river and Dairen. One reason no submarines had been sent there before was that the water is extremely shallow, averaging 120 feet. But the "wading pond" barely fazed Morton. He welcomed the virgin territory.

En route from Pearl Harbor to the Yellow Sea, Morton kept *Wahoo* on the surface, except for routine morning dives. He wandered through the boat restlessly, talking to the enlisted men, telling them that this time *Wahoo* would make a killing.

Off Kyushu, the watch picked up a ship that was going around in circles and giving off dense smoke. Morton went to battle stations warily. He thought the ship must be a decoy, a Q-ship. Almost reluctantly, he fired a single torpedo. It missed. O'Kane, manning the periscope, urged Morton to fire again. Morton said no, he suspected a trap. When O'Kane pressed, Morton grew suddenly angry and, as the yeoman, Sterling, remembers, said approximately, "Goddamit, when you get to be a captain in your own sub you can shoot all the torpedoes you want, at whatever you want. . . . Break off the attack." Sterling added, "It was the first time I had seen Morton angry."

Entering the Yellow Sea, Morton found the area dense with sampans and junks—and unsuspecting targets. On March 19, he attacked two ships, believing that he sank one and the other got away. In the next four days he sank four more. On the twenty-fifth, when two torpedoes fired at a freighter prematured, Morton surfaced and sank it with the deck gun. While he was at it, he sank another freighter with the deck gun and then attacked a trawler, sampans, and junks. Leaving the area, he fired his last two torpedoes at a freighter, which sank.

When Morton reported his results to Pearl Harbor, Lockwood replied: CONGRATULATIONS ON A JOB WELL DONE. JAPANESE THINK A SUBMARINE WOLF PACK OPERATING IN YELLOW SEA. ALL SHIPPING TIED UP.

Returning to Midway for refit, Morton claimed eight ships for 36,700 tons, plus damage to the ship he believed got away. In fact, however, as postwar analysis would reveal, the damaged ship did not get away. It sank too, giving Morton a confirmed total of nine ships sunk on this single patrol, for about 20,000 confirmed tons. In terms of numbers of ships sunk, no skipper had ever come close to this record.

During January through July of 1943, the few boats under Christie's command in Fremantle mounted twenty-two war patrols in Southeast Asia, an average of three per month. The patrols produced twenty-three confirmed sinkings, an average of slightly more than one vessel per patrol, one of the best averages for any command to date. However, nine of the patrols—41 percent—produced no confirmed sinkings. Two boats were lost.

Moke Millican in *Thresher* returned to Christmas Island and Sunda Strait. Because of the shortage, he carried only twenty torpedoes instead of twenty-four. Millican conducted five aggressive attacks, sinking a big freighter and a tanker near Balikpapan. He shot—and hit—a Japanese submarine, but the torpedo, Millican asserted, was a dud.

On return to Fremantle, Millican for the second time criticized torpedo performance, stating that on the submarine attack he had "clinked 'em with a clunk." This time Al McCann sided with Millican. In his endorsement, he denigrated torpedo design and made some suggestions of his own. Upon reading McCann's endorsement, Christie went down to Pelias. There was to be no "wrangling in print" about torpedoes. The torpedoes, Christie said, were fine. Millican was ordered back to the States for rest and new construction.

Red Ramage on *Trout*, who had also complained bitterly about torpedo performance, visited Christie just before leaving on his fourth patrol. *Trout* had been selected to lay mines off Borneo, a long-overdue effort to stop the flow of oil to the Solomons.

"What's your armament?" Christie asked Ramage.

"Sixteen torpedoes and twenty-three mines," Ramage replied.

"I want you to sink sixteen ships with those torpedoes," Christie replied lightheartedly.

This remark enraged Ramage. He said icily, "If I get 25 percent reliable performance on your torpedoes, I'll be lucky, and you will bless me."

Now it was Christie's turn for anger. He railed against those who were creating distrust and suspicion about the torpedoes.

"It got a little bit rough," Ramage recalled. "Tex McLean grabbed me by the neck and pulled me out of there, saying, 'It's time to leave.' When we got outside Christie's office, McLean said, 'You're goddamned lucky to be going to sea.' I said, 'It's the other way around, Tex. With these torpedoes you're giving us, I'll be goddamned lucky to get back. If you think I'm so lucky, how about packing your bag and coming along with me?' That cooled him."

Ramage laid his mines off Miri, Borneo. Afterward, his patrol was unlucky. He made four attacks for zero results, firing fifteen of his sixteen torpedoes. One torpedo hit a freighter, but Ramage reported it to be a dud. Later he fired three torpedoes each at three different ships—all misses.

Back in Fremantle, Ramage again complained about poor torpedo performance, but Christie blamed his failure on shooting errors and wildly maneuvering targets, noting in his diary, "Red had a miss last patrol—many chances and many failures. He is due for a relief and will be sent back to the U.S. for a new boat and rest at the same time."

Barney Sieglaff in *Tautog* conducted two patrols, each no less aggressive than his first. In February he carried a mixed load of mines and torpedoes. He laid his minefield off Balikpapan, in Makassar Strait. No ships struck the minefield immediately, but according to Jasper Holmes the Japanese destroyer *Amagiri* was sunk by one of these mines in April 1944. (*Amagiri* was the destroyer that rammed and sank *PT-109*, commanded by John F. Kennedy.)

Tautog had been fitted with the third 5-inch gun from the old V-class boats, and during this patrol Sieglaff made four battle surfaces to test it out. The first, a night attack on a ship, failed when the flash of the gun blinded both crew and skipper. On the second and third, Sieglaff sank small trawlers. On the fourth, he tried to sink a ship at anchor inside a harbor, but the gun jammed and he had to break off the attack.

In addition, Sieglaff conducted three torpedo attacks. In the first, he fired a single torpedo at a beached ship, to make certain she wasn't salvaged. Next, he fired three torpedoes at a freighter. All missed. For his third attack, he plowed into a small convoy, firing nine torpedoes and sinking two confirmed ships, a 5,000-ton freighter and a 2,000-ton destroyer, *Isonami*.

Sieglaff's second patrol took him back to Pearl Harbor, dropping off two agents en route. Though it included three gun attacks and six torpedo attacks, he sank only two freighters for 5,500 tons.

William Post, commanding *Gudgeon,* did the most to account for the respectable score made by the Fremantle boats during the first half of 1943. He and his exec, Mike Shea, were both post-Midway "rejects": Post had been surfaced from *Argonaut,* and Shea had been relieved on *Gar.* Although *Gudgeon* carried only sixteen torpedoes, Shea and Post were determined to make each one count.

They found plenty of targets. Off Surabaya, they attacked a seven-ship convoy with two escorts. Post fired two torpedoes each and believed he sank two and probably all three.

A few days later, while on the surface, Post saw a small vessel and ordered battle surface, gun action. As *Gudgeon* closed in, Post realized the vessel was a small destroyer; it turned to attack. Post kept charging, with deck gun manned and four bow tubes ready. At 1,800 yards he fired the bow tubes. The destroyer maneuvered to avoid. All the while, the deck gun crew pumped shells at the weaving target, scoring at least four good hits. However, Post elected to break off the attack and clear the area.

Later, Post attacked another convoy, firing five torpedoes at one tanker and two at another. He obtained good hits, leading him to believe he had sunk both. With only two torpedoes remaining, Post set course for Fremantle, arriving home after a twenty-four-day patrol. He had nothing but praise for the Mark XIV torpedo and its magnetic exploder. Christie was ecstatic. He credited Post with four ships for 29,600 tons (reduced postwar to two ships for 15,000 tons), by far the best score of any Fremantle skipper that year.

Post got a Navy Cross and went out again in April to earn another. This time *Gudgeon* returned to Pearl Harbor. Along the way, Post also was to conduct a special mission, putting ashore a party of four guerrillas and their three tons of equipment on Panay Island. Going north through Makassar Strait on the night of April 25, Post picked up a contact. In two separate attacks, he fired six torpedoes at the target, obtaining, he believed, several hits. But further attempts to close and attack were thwarted by an escort.

Shortly before reaching Panay, while running on the surface at night, Post spotted an enormous ship all alone. In the darkness, it looked like a battleship but turned out to be an ocean liner, zigzagging at 17½ knots on a southerly course. From the size and silhouette, Post correctly identified the ship as *Kamakura Maru,* 17,500 tons, which had often visited Hawaii prior to the war.

Post bent on flank speed, trying to gain a position ahead for firing, but the liner was too fast. She was pulling away. The best Post could do was come directly in from astern and fire the opposite of a down-the-throat shot—what he later named an "up-the-kilt" shot. He let go four torpedoes and dived. Going under, he heard three hits.

Coming to periscope depth, Post closed the range, maneuvering to bring his stern tubes to bear. But in his first periscope observation he saw that the target was stopped. On the next, he was astonished to see her bow rising high. *Kamakura Maru* went down stern first, like a rock.

Gudgeon surfaced. The waters were strewn with flotsam, lifeboats, and shouting survivors, military government personnel en route to Surabaya. The Japanese disclosed the loss of the liner in their newspapers, including photographs, as Jasper Holmes put it, of "government typists [rescued by Japanese vessels] looking very sexy in their wet dresses." *Kamakura Maru* was the largest ship sunk by U.S. submarines up to that time.

Post's patrol was not yet over. He landed his guerrillas and looked for more enemy ships. On May 4, he battle-surfaced on a small trawler and sank it. During the action, one of his officers was knocked overboard by a cartridge case ejected from the deck gun—a freak accident and a fatal one, since the officer was lost despite Post's two-hour search.

The following day, Post battle-surfaced on a freighter, scoring some hits. Later he saw what he believed to be a tanker and swung in, deck gun manned. The "tanker" turned out to be an armed ship that attacked *Gudgeon.*

Post dived and went deep. The ship pummeled *Gudgeon* with close depth charges, which caused extensive minor damage.

Three days later, while on the surface, Post tangled with another trawler. With no time to man the deck gun, he fired off one quick torpedo; when it missed, he swung ship and fired a second from the stern tube; when this, too, missed, he dived and went deep. The trawler unleashed eleven depth charges, none close.

On May 10, reduced to only one or two torpedoes, Post spotted a fat freighter. He closed and fired. Down went *Sumatra Maru*, 5,800 tons. After that triumph, Post set a course for Pearl Harbor.

Lockwood credited Post with sinking three ships for 19,600 tons, with damage to another 9,000 tons of shipping. In fact, Post had sent two ships down for 23,000 tons. With a second Navy Cross in his possession, he took *Gudgeon* to Mare Island for overhaul. In two patrols on *Gudgeon*, Post had sunk 39,000 tons of confirmed shipping, twice as much as his predecessors, Grenfell and Stovall, on five patrols.

Grenadier, like *Snapper*, was a boat seemingly unable to shake the dark cloud that had dogged her since the beginning of the war. In four patrols, she had had three skippers: Allen Joyce, Pilly Lent, and Bruce Carr. Setting off on her fifth patrol from Fremantle, she had a fourth, John Fitzgerald, who had been transferred from Don McGregor's *Gar*. Fitzgerald proved to be aggressive and fearless. Patrolling the Java Sea, he made six attacks, receiving credit for sinking one ship and damaging another.

On his second patrol in *Grenadier*, Fitzgerald was sent to an area no U.S. submarine had ever patrolled—Malacca Strait, the body of water lying between Malay and Sumatra—to interdict the flow of Japanese shipping between Rangoon and Singapore. Ordinarily this piece of geography fell under British control, but the British had asked for a U.S. fleet boat to explore the area. Tex McLean was opposed; the waters were confined and shallow. But he was overruled.

The area proved a disappointment. Although Fitzgerald patrolled aggressively off Rangoon, remaining on the surface a great deal of the time, he found no targets and moved southward. On the morning of April 21, he closed the port of Penang on the west coast of Malay. While only a few miles from shore, lookouts sighted a two-ship convoy. Remaining on the surface within sight of the Malay coast, Fitzgerald gave chase. At eight o'clock in broad daylight, a lookout suddenly shouted, "Aircraft on port quarter!"

Fitzgerald cleared the bridge and dived. At 130 feet, Fitzgerald's exec, George Harris Whiting (ex-*Triton*), relaxed and said, "We ought to be safe enough now." His statement was followed by a violent explosion that rocked *Grenadier* and pushed her to the bottom at 270 feet. A bomb had exploded over the maneuvering room. It twisted *Grenadier*'s stern out of shape and set off a fire in the electrical section. The main induction and some after hatches and sea valves were unseated and warped, causing leaks.

"Steady, men," Fitzgerald said over the PA system. "Everything is under control." He sent men wearing fire-fighting gear into the maneuvering room to extinguish the flames. He set up a bucket brigade and pumps to carry off the flooding water. Inspecting the boat, Fitzgerald found conditions worse than he had imagined. The hull was bashed in four inches, the shafts and after torpedo tubes bent out of line. Throughout the day, work parties, suffering heat prostration and exhaustion, worked to make repairs.

That night, Fitzgerald brought *Grenadier* to the surface. He tried to get off a radio dispatch to Christie, reporting the damage, but couldn't get through. Meanwhile, the engineering officer tried to make the bent and misaligned shafts turn. He couldn't. When Fitzgerald received this news, he put his men to work making a canvas sail, intending to sail *Grenadier* close to the shore and then blow her up. With luck, the crew might slip into the Malay jungle and obtain help from guerrillas or sympathetic natives.

At dawn, Fitzgerald was dismayed to find there was not a breath of air, no hope that *Grenadier* could come close to the shore. They would have to swim. He gave orders to prepare to abandon ship. While lookouts kept a sharp watch for planes and men manned the deck guns, others below destroyed the radio, radar, sound and TDC gear, and decoding machines, tossing the codebooks over the side.

While this work was in progress, a Japanese aircraft appeared on the horizon, making a beeline for *Grenadier*. Fitzgerald withheld fire until the last minute. When the gunners let go, the plane veered up and away, damaged. Coming in for a second run, the pilot dropped his bomb. It fell harmlessly into the water, 200 yards away. (Later Fitzgerald learned that this futile attack cost the Japanese pilot his life. Wounded, he crashed on returning to base and died.)

Preparing to abandon ship, Fitzgerald lined his men on deck in life jackets. Meanwhile, a Japanese merchant ship and small escort came into sight, headed for *Grenadier*. Fitzgerald gave orders to scuttle. The vents were opened and *Grenadier* sank by the stern. The men jumped or floated off into the water, while the Japanese ships circled, taking pictures. When the last man from below reached the deck, he and Fitzgerald went into the water together.

The men on the Japanese merchant ship rescued *Grenadier*'s men and took them to Penang. For many weeks thereafter, Fitzgerald and his men were treated brutally by Japanese interrogators, who tried to elicit technical information. Fitzgerald was tied to a bench with his head hanging over the end. The Japanese elevated his feet and then poured water into his nostrils, holding his mouth shut so he was forced to swallow the water. When they judged him sufficiently full of water, they clubbed him repeatedly and denied him food for a week.

In spite of all this, Fitzgerald maintained his sanity and composure. He left encouraging messages for his crew on the walls of the toilet room: "Don't tell them anything. . . . Keep your chins up." One of his men said later, "I think as much of Commander Fitzgerald, our skipper, as I do my father. He went through hell for us. They beat him, jumped on his stomach, and tortured him by burning splints under his nails. He never talked."

The *Grenadier* crew was removed to the prison camp in Ofuna, Japan, where they underwent further relentless interrogation. After the war, for "extraordinary heroism" and "unflinchingly withstanding the cruelties of his cap-

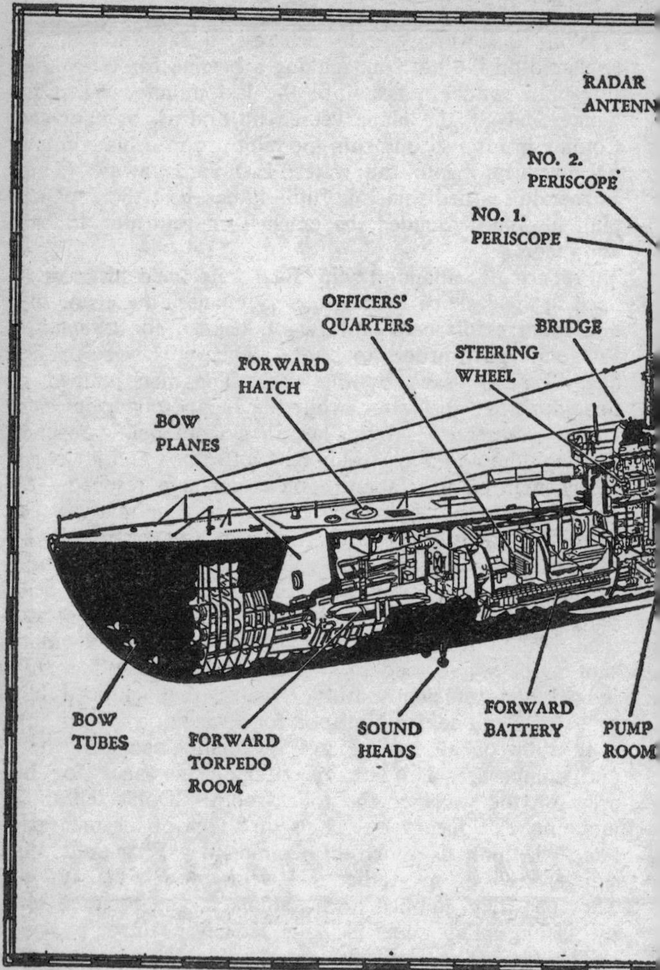

RADAR
ANTENN

NO. 2.
PERISCOPE

NO. 1.
PERISCOPE

OFFICERS'
QUARTERS

BRIDGE

FORWARD
HATCH

STEERING
WHEEL

BOW
PLANES

BOW
TUBES

FORWARD
TORPEDO
ROOM

SOUND
HEADS

FORWARD
BATTERY

PUMP
ROOM

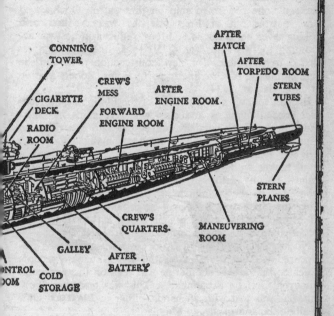

CONNING TOWER

CIGARETTE DECK

RADIO ROOM

CREW'S MESS

FORWARD ENGINE ROOM

AFTER ENGINE ROOM.

AFTER HATCH

AFTER TORPEDO ROOM

STERN TUBES

STERN PLANES

CREW'S QUARTERS.

MANEUVERING ROOM

GALLEY

AFTER BATTERY

CONTROL ROOM

COLD STORAGE

TYPICAL U. S. SUBMARINE

CUT-AWAY SHOWING COMPARTMENTATION

tors," Fitzgerald was awarded the Navy Cross. Four enlisted crewmen died in the POW camp, but Fitzgerald, Whiting, and seventy others were released.

Grayling was also lost during this period. After Eliot Olsen, John Elwood Lee had taken command, patrolling to Fremantle by way of the Gilberts and the Marshalls. Lee sank one confirmed ship on that patrol. On his next three patrols out of Fremantle, he was credited with sinking seven ships for 34,600 tons, reduced in postwar accounting to two ships for 4,750 tons. Lee had then returned to the States for new construction, and Christie gave command of *Grayling* to a youngster, Robert Marion Brinker, class of 1934.

Brinker took *Grayling* by way of the Philippines, to conduct special missions and sink whatever ships he could find. On July 31, he delivered supplies to guerrillas on Panay. On August 19, he reported damaging a 6,000-ton freighter near Balikpapan. The following day he sank a small tanker with the deck gun and took a prisoner. On August 23, he delivered further supplies at Panay and proceeded to the Manila area. Four days later, Brinker sank the 5,500-ton passenger-cargo ship *Meizan Maru* off Mindoro. It is possible that a few days later he attacked another passenger-cargo vessel, *Hokuan Maru*.

Nothing was ever heard from *Grayling* again. She disappeared without trace. After the war, Japanese records indicated that a U.S. submarine was seen on the surface in Lingayen Gulf on September 9. This was probably *Grayling*. She was lost with all hands, either in Lingayen Gulf or along the approaches to Manila.

11

TORPEDO DEFECTS ISOLATED

The Combined Chiefs of Staff held another series of meetings on Pacific strategy, culminating in yet another conference, Trident. These conferences attempted to resolve the conflicts between the MacArthur view and the King-Nimitz view about how to defeat Japan and to determine what the first offensive steps would be. Again, the conclusions were limited and controversial. However, positive agreement was reached for the Pearl Harbor forces: Nimitz should retake Attu and Kiska and proceed with plans to invade the Gilberts (Tarawa-Makin) on or about November 1943.

The Pacific Fleet aircraft carrier inventory—crucial to the proposed invasion—was steadily swelling. In May, the battle-worn *Enterprise* was released from the Solomons for stateside overhaul and then reassignment to Nimitz (the *Saratoga* remained in the Solomons). That same month the first of the big new carriers, *Essex*, arrived in Pearl Harbor. She was followed by four new sister ships. In addition, two light carriers reported at Pearl Harbor, followed soon by three new sister ships.

These additions boosted the Pacific carrier force to twelve, seven heavy and five light. Most (including *Enterprise* and *Saratoga*) were earmarked for the Gilberts invasion.

In April 1943 fleet boats produced on an assembly-line basis at Electric Boat, Portsmouth, Mare Island, and Manitowoc began arriving at Pearl Harbor in significant numbers. The remainder of Squadron Fourteen boats reported in, followed almost immediately by the long-delayed H.O.R.-powered boats of Squadron Twelve. In addition, week by week the older boats of Squadron Two returned from overhaul, modernized with SJ radar, new sonar gear, new engines, and trimmed-down silhouettes.

Counting all the new arrivals, and the older boats of Squadron Four, Lockwood soon had about fifty fleet boats under his command. A few of these were sent temporarily or permanently to Australia to maintain that submarine force at twenty boats, but the majority based from Pearl Harbor. During the four-month period April to August 1943, Lockwood mounted ninety-one war patrols with these boats—an average of almost twenty-two per month, twice the average for a similar period in 1942.

The target priority for Pearl Harbor submarines remained fixed: Japanese carriers and battleships, followed by lesser ships. With Admiral Koga basing at Truk with his major fleet units, and with carriers and other vessels bringing in aircraft and supplies for the campaign in the Solomons, Truk remained an important patrol area for Pacific submarines. In addition, Lockwood continued to send submarines to the Marshalls, the Marianas, and the Palaus, also engaged in resupplying the Solomons. However, for the first time in the war, more submarines went to Empire and East China Sea waters than to the islands, fifty-three versus thirty-eight (including six boats patrolling to Australia).

The "bags" (as Lockwood called them) produced by these patrols maintained the usual trend: more for Empire boats, less for boats going to Truk and Palau. The fifty-three Empire–East China Sea patrols produced sixty-four confirmed sinkings, the thirty-eight patrols to the islands only twenty-one. Based on past statistical averages, the Empire boats should have produced even more sinkings. However, this group of boats was hobbled by a variety of problems, including the continuing shortage of torpedoes, torpedo failures, inexperienced fire-control parties, breakdowns of H.O.R. engines, inept or nonproductive skippers, and a flood of Ultras on major Japanese fleet units that brought on time-consuming—and usually futile—interceptions and chases.

Even so, the U.S. submarine force was beginning to inflict serious damage on the Japanese shipping services. In the spring of 1943, the seventy-odd fleet boats patrolling from Pearl Harbor, Fremantle, and Brisbane reached a confirmed sinking level of 100,000 tons per month. For the first time, the Japanese began to worry about this steady attrition. Merchant ship captains who had heretofore preferred to sail alone rather than in convoys showed interest in convoying, despite its disadvantages. The Imperial Naval Staff requested 360 frigates for convoy escort (the high command authorized only 40) and laid plans for a central convoy escort command.

In April and May, the United States mounted its offensive against Attu and Kiska. Forewarned by the codebreakers that the Japanese intended to counter the Attu invasion by a major sortie of the fleet, Lockwood sent his top skipper to the Kuriles to intercept it: Mush Morton in *Wahoo*.

The *Wahoo* crew found this far-north area stark and bitterly cold. Yeoman Sterling wrote:

Each day, like a Chinaman, I added another piece of clothing to go up on lookout. . . . I came off . . . shivering, teeth chattering, and my nose and ears so cold I was afraid to touch them for fear they would shatter into crystallized fragments. It had begun to sleet and snow, and I stood helplessly trying to peer into a darkness that was not penetrable with the human eye.

Later, when the weather cleared, he wrote:

There was no ocean to be seen but instead a vast thin ice plain. Jagged rock islands pierced this ice at irregular intervals. . . . Wahoo's nose was clearing a pathway through the six or eight inches of ice so smoothly that the surface seemed to part at her approach. It gave the illusion that Wahoo was standing still and the ice was moving.

While U.S. troops stormed ashore on Attu, Morton took station near Etorofu Island in the Kuriles, waiting for the Japanese fleet. When the sortie was canceled, Morton was released for general patrol, helped along by the codebreakers, who were tracking Japanese ships bringing reinforcements to the Kuriles and Paramushiro. On May 4, they positioned him to intercept a seaplane tender,

Kamikawa Maru. While Dick O'Kane manned the periscope, Morton closed to 1,300 yards and fired three torpedoes. One passed ahead, the second hit amidships, but the third failed and the tender got away. Morton wrote, "It must have been erratic or a dud. It is inconceivable that any normal dispersion could allow this last torpedo to miss a 510-foot target at this range."

Another Ultra directed Morton to Banten Zaki. On May 7, Morton intercepted two big northbound ships, one freighter and one large escort, right on schedule. He closed to 900 yards and fired six torpedoes, two at the freighter, four at the escort. The freighter, *Toman Maru,* 5,260 tons, went down, but the escort avoided the four torpedoes and escaped harm.

The following day, Morton shifted south to Kobe Zaki for another interception. On the afternoon of May 8 he picked up a three-ship convoy, two escorts and a large naval auxiliary. Morton closed to 2,500 yards and fired three torpedoes at the auxiliary. The first torpedo prematured after fifty-one seconds, halfway to the target. This evidently deflected the second torpedo, or else it failed to explode. The third hit at the point of aim but failed to explode. This ship, too, got away and Morton was forced deep by escorts. Later he wrote, "Both sound operators reported the thud of the dud at the same time that a column of water about ten feet high was observed at the target's side abreast of her foremast as the air flasks exploded."

That evening Morton surfaced, received new information from the codebreakers, and then reversed course northward to Kone Zaki. Early on the morning of May 9, he picked up two ships on radar. Closing to the point-blank range of 1,200 yards, Morton identified them as a tanker and freighter. He fired six torpedoes, three at each ship. The torpedoes hit, and down went *Takao Maru,* 3,200 tons, and *Jinmu Maru,* 1,200 tons.

Three days later Morton found two more freighters and attacked, firing four torpedoes from 1,200 yards. The two aimed at one ship missed. Of the two aimed at the other ship, one hit amidships and the other was not heard from. Morton wrote, "The second torpedo, fired at his stack amidships, is believed to have been erratic or a dud.

The target course and speed had been most accurately determined and it is inconceivable that any normal dispersion could cause it to miss."

Morton surfaced to pursue the ship he damaged. He closed to 1,800 yards and fired his last remaining bow tube. "Nothing was seen of the bow torpedo or its wake," he wrote, "and the enemy apparently did not know he had again been fired upon." Morton turned and fired his last stern tube. "It hit under the bridge with a dull thud much louder than the duds we have heard only on sound, but lacking the 'whacking' which accompanies a whole-hearted explosion. It is considered that this torpedo had a low-order detonation."

Having shot off all his torpedoes, Morton manned his deck gun, planning to polish off the damaged freighter by gunfire. However, the other freighter charged *Wahoo*, firing heavy guns and forcing Morton to break off the attack. He terminated the patrol and returned to Pearl Harbor after twenty-six days.

This patrol of *Wahoo*, Morton's third, was one of the most important of the war—not for what it achieved but for what it didn't achieve. Morton stormed into Lockwood's office on May 21 in a towering rage. He denounced the Mark XIV torpedo in salty language, detailing his prematures, duds, and erratics. Mush Morton was Lockwood's star; he had conducted a brilliantly aggressive patrol. *Wahoo* had one of the best fire-control parties in the submarine force. Had the torpedoes not failed, *Wahoo* would have sunk not three but six ships.

This patrol—following hard on the heels of the problems experienced by Rebel Lowrance in *Kingfish*, John Scott in *Tunny*, and Willis Thomas in *Pompano*—finally destroyed Lockwood's faith in the magnetic exploder. Now, after eighteen months of war, he decided it should be deactivated—but still he delayed a little longer, hoping his pressure on Spike Blandy might produce a quick fix that would save it.

On inspection, *Wahoo* was found to need a navy yard overhaul. Morton himself appeared tired and not in the best of health; in fact, he was still suffering from prostate problems. Lockwood ordered *Wahoo* to Mare Island. There, Dick O'Kane was detached to new construction.

Much farther to the south, the boats patrolling off Honshu in May, also alerted by Ultra dispatches, attempted to intercept and sink Admiral Koga and his fleet returning from Truk to Tokyo Bay for the sortie to Alaska. Eugene Sands in *Sawfish*, at the tail end of his second patrol south of Tokyo, was first to sight the force. He found it on radar at about 12,000 yards, speed 18 knots, on the night of May 20. It consisted, he believed, of three battleships, a large aircraft carrier, two destroyers, and two other ships. The weather was foul, and Sands was unable to get a clear picture of the formation or produce a fast firing solution. When he finally figured it all out, he reported later, "the chance of shooting had passed."

Lying in wait on the projected track off Tokyo, Roy Benson, making his fourth patrol in *Trigger*, picked up the task force on the morning of May 22. As Benson ticked off the targets—an aircraft carrier, three battleships, numerous cruisers and destroyers—his exec, Stephen Stafford Mann, Jr., and Ned Beach, serving as diving officer, could hardly believe their ears. It was, Beach later wrote, "an appreciable segment of the main Japanese battle fleet."

Benson was cool and soft-spoken at the periscope. He let a cruiser go by, waiting for the carriers and battleships. But at the last minute, these prizes zigzagged out of range. Benson, Beach reported, "watched helplessly." Short of a suicidal surface attack, there was nothing Benson or anyone else in *Trigger* could do. It was a bitter disappointment for all hands.

Two weeks later, the boats off Japan received another Ultra: several aircraft carriers were leaving Tokyo Bay, southbound. There were three boats nearby, *Trigger*, *Salmon*, and *Sculpin*, the last two being Squadron Two boats returned from long overhaul.

Roy Benson in *Trigger* was first to find the force, picking it up during the night of June 8 on radar, range 12 miles. He went to full power on all main engines, trying to reach firing position, but one engine was in bad shape and refused to put out maximum power. Benson was still 6 miles away. He could see the two carriers from the bridge but was not able to close the gap. Once more the *Trigger* crew missed a golden opportunity.

Nicholas John Nicholas, formerly exec of *Drum*, lay to the south of *Trigger* in *Salmon*. While waiting for the oncoming prizes, a convoy of three freighters and a destroyer passed by. Unable to resist this temptation, Nicholas chased the convoy, hitting two ships for damage. While *Salmon* was thus involved, the carrier force appeared on schedule, but Nicholas was too far away and couldn't catch up. Later, Lockwood wrote that it was "unfortunate" Nicholas went after the convoy instead of waiting for the carriers.

Farther south, Lucius Chappell on his seventh war patrol in *Sculpin* waited near Sofu Gan (Lot's Wife), a rock-like island in the ocean used by many navigators as a landfall for approaching and departing Japan. Chappell picked up the force on June 9 around midnight, range 6 miles. He identified the targets as two carriers escorted by a cruiser. Ringing up flank speed, Chappell tried to close, but the task force pulled away. In desperation, Chappell fired four torpedoes from a range of 7,000 yards. One prematured, advertising his presence. He tried to bring his stern tubes to bear but it was too late. It was the second time in two consecutive patrols that Chappell had fired at—and missed—an aircraft carrier. Chappell was promoted to John Herbert ("Babe") Brown's training staff at Pearl Harbor.

Roy Benson in *Trigger*, alerted by yet another Ultra, remained on station off the mouth of Tokyo Bay. On the afternoon of June 10, his last day on station, a junior officer standing periscope watch suddenly shouted and sounded the battle alarm. He had picked up Koga's flagship, the carrier *Hiyo*, standing down the bay at 21 knots, with a destroyer on port and starboard bows.

Benson ducked under the destroyer screen and fired six bow tubes at *Hiyo* from 1,200 yards. Immediately after shooting, he went deep to avoid the destroyer escorts. On the way down, Benson counted four solid explosions and, as Ned Beach wrote, "we jubilantly credited ourselves with a sure sinking." A destroyer immediately counterattacked.

On board *Hiyo*, there was surprise, confusion—and error. One of the Japanese staff officers wrote Beach after the war:

At that time, just two minutes before sunset, the duty officer on the bridge saw the big white bubbles of torpedoes in the middle of the calm cobaltic seas and on the right at about 1,500 yards from the ship. He cried: "Torpedoes! This direction." We looked at it, six white tracers were coming at us. The Commanding Officer ordered the destroyers by the flag signal "Attack the enemy submarine." The Captain ordered "Port side helm. Full rudder."—These events occurred instantaneously . . . the skipper should have ordered "starboard helm" in this case. But I did not suggest it because it would add to the confusion.

The third fish exploded itself after running about 1,000 feet and a big water column rose. The right side destroyer turned to the site of the bubbles and began a depth charge attack. Our ship turned to the left to avoid your torpedoes. But I thought it would be in vain; some of them would surely hit for you had a very favorable position to fire and the skipper failed to turn in the right direction. The first and second torpedoes passed before the bow. The fourth hit under the right hawse hole and splashed water higher than the bridge. The ship trembled terribly. The fifth one hit at the middle part between the bow and the bridge, but when it hit the torpedo's head dropped from the body and it flew along the side. . . . The last one hit just under the bridge for an instant. . . . All the crew on the bridge were staggered by the shock. The first hit did not do much damage; it only broke the chain locker. But the last hit damaged us vitally. It broke the first boiler room and the bulkhead of the second boiler room. . . . These rooms all took in water at once. The third boiler room leaked by and by. All fire was put out and all steam went out; the ship stopped.

In summary, of the six torpedoes Benson fired, two missed ahead and one prematured. Three hit *Hiyo*, but one was a dud and only two exploded, one forward in the chain locker doing slight damage, one in the boiler rooms doing major damage.

Benson's attack on *Hiyo*—well outside Tokyo Bay—gave rise to another submarine myth: that a U.S. submarine stole quietly into Tokyo Bay, lay on the bottom for a month watching workers in a shipyard putting the finishing touches on a brand-new aircraft carrier, and then, when the carrier was launched, came to periscope depth and sank it as it was coming off the ways.

Trigger reached Pearl Harbor on June 22. Benson reported four hits and a probable carrier sinking, but Lockwood knew from the codebreakers that *Hiyo* had not gone down. Furthermore, he knew from the same source that only one of *Trigger*'s torpedoes had caused any real damage.

This failure to sink an important target was the final straw. After talking with Benson, Lockwood decided to deactivate the Mark VI magnetic exploder. The order went out—under Nimitz's name—on June 24, two days after Benson reached Pearl Harbor.

The Bureau of Ordnance and Ralph Christie immediately queried Nimitz on his reasons for giving this order. Nimitz replied it had been done "because of probable enemy countermeasures, because of the ineffectiveness of the exploder under certain conditions, and because of the impracticability of selecting the proper conditions under which to fire."

In Fremantle, Christie held a conference with his staff and after much discussion decided *not* to deactivate the magnetic exploder. (He was able to take this divergent course because he reported to MacArthur not Nimitz.) Christie's reasoning: (a) the Mark VI magnetic exploder got *some* hits; (b) it was the only defense against very shallow draft antisubmarine vessels; and (c) if it were discarded, it was "gone forever" and any attempt to locate its possible defects would be terminated. Christie wrote in his diary, "Conference on Mark VI. . . . Decided to keep it activated. . . . This is at variance with Charles Lockwood . . . who is 'agin' the magnetic exploder. He is 'agin' the torpedo but brags about the tonnage sunk. What sunk them, spuds?"

The split caused a complication for submarine skippers: while they worked for Lockwood, they set the torpedoes one way; while working for Christie, another. A boat going from Pearl Harbor to Australia on the exchange program departed with the magnetic feature deactivated. On the way down, when the boat fell under the operational control of Fife or Christie, the skippers had to reactivate the magnetic feature. Boats returning from Australia followed the opposite procedure, starting out with the magnetic feature activated, then deactivating it after falling under Lockwood's operational control.

Lawrence Randall ("Dan") Daspit in *Tinosa* patrolled off Truk with orders to intercept the fleet tanker traffic plying between Palau and Truk. On July 20, the codebreakers put him on the track of a whale factory, *Nippon Maru*. Daspit found it and fired four torpedoes. All missed. Daspit later wrote, "Target had been carefully tracked and with spread used torpedoes could not have run properly and missed."

Daspit surfaced after dark and ran ahead. This time he found two targets on radar. One turned out to be a destroyer. Before Daspit could attack the target, the destroyer picked up *Tinosa* and opened fire with guns, driving her under. The tanker got away. Daspit spent the following day submerged, resting his crew and routining the torpedoes. "All torpedoes were checked during this and next day," he reported. "Exploder mechanisms were not touched."

The codebreakers gave Daspit another juicy target: *Tonan Maru III*, the 19,000-ton whale factory Edward Carmick had missed off Woleai in June. She was on an easterly course from Palau to Truk. Daspit found her on the morning of July 24. He made an end around and submerged ahead. When he got a good look at her through the periscope, he saw she was heavily loaded, making about 13 knots.

Daspit attacked, firing four torpedoes. He believed that two hit; he saw large splashes of water forward. However, the ship did not appear to be damaged. She turned away, leaving Daspit in a poor firing position. However, he fired two more torpedoes. Both hit, one aft, causing smoke. The target stopped with a port list, settling by the stern, but showed no signs of sinking.

Daspit studied his prey carefully. He could see her deck guns. Men were running around, dropping small depth charges over the side to intimidate him. There was still no sign of an escort, surface or air.

Daspit recorded what happened next in his patrol report:

1009.   *Having observed target carefully and found no evidence of a sinking, approached and fired one torpedo at starboard side. Hit, heard by sound to stop at same time I observed large splash. No apparent effect. Target had corrected list and was firing at periscope and at torpedo wakes with machine guns and one inch [gun].*

1011.   *Fired eighth torpedo. Hit. No apparent effect.*

1014.   *Fired ninth torpedo. Hit. No apparent effect. Target firing at periscope, when exposed, and at wake when torpedoes were running.*

1039.   *Fired tenth torpedo. Hit. No apparent effect.*

1048.   *Fired eleventh torpedo. Hit. No effect. This torpedo hit well aft on the port side, made splash at the side of the ship and was then observed to have taken a right turn and to jump clear of the water about one hundred feet from the stern of the tanker. I find it hard to convince myself that I saw this.*

1050.   *Fired twelfth torpedo. Hit. No effect.*

1100.   *Fired thirteenth torpedo. Hit. No effect. Circled again to fire at other side.*

1122.   *Picked up high-speed screws.*

1125.   *Sighted destroyer approaching from east. . . .*

1131.   *Fired fourteenth torpedo. Hit. No effect.*

1132½. *Fired fifteenth torpedo. Started deep. Destroyer range 1,000 yards. Torpedo heard to hit tanker and stop running by sound. Periscope had gone under by this time. No explosion. Had already decided to retain one torpedo for examination by base.*

In all, eleven of Daspit's torpedoes, fired under almost perfect conditions, had been duds. When he returned to Pearl Harbor, the normally cool and unflappable skipper was in a rage. "I expected a torrent of cusswords, damning me, the Bureau of Ordnance, the Newport Torpedo Station and the Base Torpedo Shop," Lockwood wrote, "and I couldn't have blamed him—19,000-ton targets don't grow on bushes. I think Dan was so furious as to be practically speechless. His tale was almost unbelievable, but the evidence was undeniable."

Daspit's attack on *Tonan Maru III* had been the nearest possible thing to a laboratory test. It was clear to him, to Lockwood, and to everyone else on the Pearl Harbor staff that the Mark XIV torpedo had yet another defect: something was wrong with the *contact* exploder. That defect had been obscured by dependence on the magnetic exploder, now deactivated. Lockwood ordered his force gunnery and torpedo officer, Art Taylor (ex-*Haddock*), to find out what was wrong. Everybody got in the act.

Charles Bowers ("Swede") Momsen, who, Lockwood wrote, "was always full of practical ideas," came up with a simple scheme. He proposed that they fire a load of torpedoes at the vertical cliffs on the little island of Kahoolawe. At the first dud, they could stop firing, recover the torpedo, dissect it in the torpedo shop, and find out what was wrong. This was, Lockwood wrote, "a thoroughly practical idea, but I suspected we would find ourselves shaking hands with St. Peter when we tried to examine a dud warhead loaded with 685 pounds of TNT."

Lockwood got approval from Nimitz and put Swede Momsen in charge of the tests. Momsen chose one of the new H.O.R. boats, *Muskallunge,* commanded by Willard Saunders (ex-*Grayback*), for the test bed. On August 31, three weeks after Daspit returned from patrol, Saunders set up and began firing torpedoes at the cliffs, including the one Daspit had brought back. The first and second torpedoes exploded. The third was a dud.

Saunders relayed word to Lockwood back at Pearl Harbor. The next day, Lockwood and Swede Momsen boarded the submarine rescue vessel *Widgeon* and steamed to Kahoolawe to help recover the dud. Everybody jumped in the water wearing goggles. A boatswain's mate, John Kelly, found it. Then he free-dived to 55 feet and shackled a line to the tail of the torpedo. Crewmen on *Widgeon* gingerly hauled the torpedo on board.

All hands conducted an examination on the spot. Lockwood reported, "The warhead was crushed in at the forward end and, when we got the exploder mechanism out of it, we found the firing pin had actually traveled up its badly bent guide lines and hit the fulminate caps, but not hard enough to set them off."

While experts in the torpedo shops on the sub base and *Holland* studied the exploder firing pin and guide lines, Lockwood ordered further tests on dry land. With the help of an ordnance expert, a reserve officer named E. A. Johnson, Lockwood and Momsen worked out another testing scheme. They dropped dummy warheads, fitted with exploders, from a cherry picker (a traveling crane) onto a steel plate from a height of 90 feet. These tests—conducted by Art Taylor—showed that when the warhead hit the plate at a 90-degree angle, a perfect shot, the exploder mechanism was crushed before it struck the caps. When the warhead struck the plate at 45 degrees, a bad shot, only about half were duds.

These tests—and follow-up ones—proved beyond doubt that the exploder was improperly designed and had been inadequately tested. The torpedo experts at Pearl Harbor immediately began devising new firing pin designs that would work. The reservist ordnance expert, Johnson, worked on an electrical device; the base and *Holland* torpedo shops concentrated on making a stronger, lighter, mechanical pin. Some of the latter were fashioned from a tough metal obtained from Japanese aircraft propellers found on the island. Bill Hazzard, exec of *Saury*, who lunched one day with a lieutenant who was working with the Japanese propellers, was struck by the irony. "We gave them scrap metal to build their ships," he said later. "Now they were providing us with scrap metal which would be used to sink those same ships."

In further dry-land tests, the new firing-pin mechanisms devised by Lockwood's torpedo experts worked fine. After these tests, Lockwood ordered all Mark XIV torpedoes equipped with the new exploder innards, meanwhile telling the boats already at sea to try for "glancing blows" to help the performance of the defective exploders they carried. When all this was done, he informed Spike Blandy at BuOrd. The Newport Torpedo Station conducted further tests against submerged steel plates and then ordered a redesign of the contact exploder.

After twenty-one months of war, the three major defects of the Mark XIV torpedo had at last been isolated. First came the deep running, then the magnetic influence feature, then the contact exploder itself. Each defect had been discovered and fixed in the field—always over the stubborn opposition of the Bureau of Ordnance.

Torpedo tubes

12

UPS AND DOWNS

The long-awaited boats of Squadron Twelve—with H.O.R. engines—had arrived at Pearl Harbor in May with their tender, *Griffin*. Every boat of the squadron had experienced engine problems, but they were sent into combat anyway. The result was one of the great fiascoes of the submarine war.

Hoe, commanded by Victor B. McCrea, was first to go on patrol—at Palau. During most of the patrol, McCrea suffered from engine problems, and before the patrol was out he lost Number 4 engine altogether. He made one attack on a 9,500-ton transport and received a Bronze Star medal for it. The citation praised his performance "despite the unreliability of the ship's main engines." Lockwood wrote, "The efficiency of this patrol was handicapped a great deal by the unreliability of the main engines."

In August, McCrea took *Hoe* to Truk. On September 1, assisted by an Ultra dispatch, he found an auxiliary carrier northeast of Truk, escorted by destroyers. He picked it up at 8½ miles but was not able to close. On return to Pearl Harbor, Lockwood wrote, "Faulty engine performance was a detriment to the performance and efficiency of this patrol."

John Sydney ("Junior") McCain, Jr. in *Gunnel*, whose father was head of the powerful Bureau of Aeronautics in Washington, patrolled in June. He had made only one Atlantic patrol—during the North African landings when all four H.O.R. engines broke down. The area of his second

183

patrol was the northern reaches of the East China Sea and the Yellow Sea, the "wading pond" where Mush Morton had pioneered. McCain conducted a fearlessly aggressive patrol, making three attacks which resulted in two large confirmed ships sunk: *Koyo Maru*, 6,400 tons, and *Tokiwa Maru*, 7,000 tons.

During the whole patrol McCain was plagued with engine breakdowns. After a mere eleven days on station, he radioed Lockwood that he must terminate his patrol early and return to base. Lockwood was furious. He wrote Washington:

Gunnel is returning from patrol with two of her H.O.R. engines out of commission due to idler gear failures. McCain also says that the idler gears on the other two engines are badly worn. His breakdown occurred in the Yellow Sea, which is a damned bad place for a lousy set of engines to demonstrate their unreliability. I note from the papers that Congress has appropriated seventy-one billion dollars for the war. I suggest you set aside some of that with which to buy new and different engines for the H.O.R. boats.

H.O.R. engine flaws existed in Charles Herbert Andrews's *Gurnard* too, but the skipper's particular doggedness and skill with machinery partly overcame them. Andrews was small—five foot four—and, as he said later, he had an inferiority complex. "When I was a little kid, I was considered a sissy. I was the only boy in a house with three older sisters. My mother dressed me in velvet pants and Buster Brown collars. Faced with going into combat, I felt a very strong drive to prove myself—to carry my own weight."

Gurnard was sent to the Palaus, where Andrews patrolled close to the harbor entrances. Although he conserved his engines and treated them with loving care, the Number 2 main engine broke all its gear teeth and had to be put out of commission for the duration of the patrol. Andrews, however, remained on station.

One day a convoy steamed out, just beyond reach. After that, Andrews patrolled even closer, almost bumping up against the reefs. When destroyers came out, he played cat and mouse, going deep, slipping beneath them, coming up, then going down. "I worked up a little contempt for them," Andrews said later.

One morning during a cat-and-mouse game, *Gurnard,* submerged at 90 feet, was hit by two bombs. "It was a hell of a blast," Andrews said later. "They went off *under* us, blowing us upward with a terrific up-angle." Andrews and his exec, Robert E. M. Ward, reached the control room about the same instant. Ward shouted, "Flood everything. Flood! Get her *down*." The bow planes had jammed. The electricity had been blown out. "For a while," Andrews said, "I was certain we were going right to the surface and that destroyer would ram us."

The engineering officer, Robert Carlisle Giffen, Jr., had been in the head when the bombs went off. The force of the explosion jammed the door. Giffen was big: six foot two, 225 pounds. He broke down the door and ran to the control room, arriving to see the diving plane wheels spinning wildly. He lunged for the spinning bow-plane wheel; it flung him across the control room, where he fell in a heap, knocked out.

To help bring the bow down, Andrews sent every available man rushing to the forward torpedo room. "About fifty men ran up there," Ward said later. "That's about eight thousand pounds. That did it. We started down like a rock."

Gurnard plunged uncontrollably downward at a steep angle. "We passed by three hundred feet," Andrews said later. "I knew we were going too fast. I backed emergency and yelled at Ward to get all the men aft to try to get the down angle off." The fifty men in the forward torpedo room tore through the boat to the after torpedo room. By the time they got there, the depth gauge in the control room registered 495 feet.

With all that weight in the stern, *Gurnard* now took a steep up-angle. With the control room showing 495 feet, Andrews calculated that the after torpedo room was probably 520 or 530 feet deep, far below test depth—ready to cave in. About this time one of the electricians, Chief W. F. Fritsch, had an inspiration; he laid a toothbrush between two electrical connections. This restored power to the diving plane wheels, enabling Andrews and Ward to get the boat under control.

During the postbattle damage inspection, Ward, who

was thin and wiry, volunteered to inspect the main induction piping. He got a flashlight, peeled down to his skivvies, and squirmed into the narrow pipe with a flashlight, inching his way from the engine room toward the control room. Returning, Ward got stuck near the engine room opening.

"I couldn't get out," he said later. "It was a very tight squeeze. This bothered me considerably. I hollered down and asked for a cigarette. They passed it up and I smoked and calmed down. Then I maneuvered my body into the same position I'd used to get in the pipe and wriggled out."

All in all, the damage to *Gurnard* was severe. "It was a miracle she wasn't lost," said Ward later. "I've never seen a better man than Herb Andrews under pressure. The whole time, he was cool and precise about what to do. Everybody did the right thing—Andrews, Giffen, Fritsch." Said Andrews, "Following this patrol, I recommended [Ward] for his own command."

Later, leery of going below 70 feet, Andrews got off several spectacular shots at the enemy. A convoy came out, heavily escorted. Andrews maneuvered in, firing at the freighters and a destroyer that got in the way. He hit the destroyer and two of the freighters, sinking all three, he thought. Afterward, *Gurnard* got another working over with depth charges.

A short time later, Andrews poked up the periscope again. There, to his astonishment, he saw an aircraft carrier standing out. "I was surprised," he said later, "because the Japs knew we were sitting right out there." Andrews set up and fired three bow tubes—all that were ready—from 1,800 yards. One torpedo prematured after twenty-four seconds. Andrews fired a stern tube. He thought he got two solid hits in the carrier. He returned to periscope depth and saw her motionless in the water, listed over and smoking. Escorts charged in and prevented another look—or another shot.

When Andrews returned to Pearl Harbor, all torpedoes expended, he received ecstatic patrol report endorsements. Calling it "one of the finest, most aggressive first patrols on record," his division commander wrote, "The customary expression that the area was well covered does not fit this case, as the *Gurnard* stuck her head in the bottleneck and stopped traffic at its source. This patrol offers an excellent example of what can be accomplished by taking the fight into the enemy's back yard."

Andrews received credit for sinking three ships, including a destroyer, for 15,583 tons and for damage to five, including the carrier (estimated at 17,000 tons), for 43,482 tons. When the awards were passed out, Andrews (who got a Navy Cross) saw that electrician Fritsch got a Silver Star for his toothbrush fix. Postwar analysis cut Andrews's sinkings to one freighter for 2,000 tons. However, after this patrol nobody would ever again think of calling Herb Andrews a sissy.

Jack, another boat with H.O.R. engines, was commanded by Thomas Michael Dykers, a tall aristocratic man from New Orleans. His exec was John Paul ("Beetle") Roach, who came from shore duty in Washington. Neither he nor Dykers had ever made a war patrol.

Dykers, assigned to patrol off Honshu, found the area dense with convoys. On June 19 one went by, but Dykers was caught flatfooted and he soon realized it had "given us the slip." The next day, a 1,500-ton trawler came out of the mist. More alert this time, Dykers fired three torpedoes from 1,000 yards. The first torpedo—Dykers's first shot of the war—prematured after thirty seconds. The other two missed.

A little angry at himself (and more so at the torpedoes), Dykers moved *Jack* to within 3 miles of the Japanese coastline. On June 26 a five-ship convoy, apparently unescorted, came into view about dawn. Dykers maneuvered into position and dived. He came in close, firing bow and stern tubes and getting good hits which led him to believe he had sunk three of the five ships and damaged one. The fifth ship ran around in circles, with "all hands dropping small depth charges."

To Dykers, all this had seemed a breeze. While his torpedomen were reloading, he watched through the periscope. He wrote later:

One boat load of survivors passed within twenty yards of the periscope. Some hid behind the gunwale when they saw it. There was a sprinkling of soldiers amongst those men. I then left the periscope up to let some of the officers and men look at the sinking ship and this prevented my getting Number 5 in column and almost cost us our lives.

It seems this last ship was an auxiliary and had been looking for us all the time. Just after we passed the lifeboat, I swung the periscope around and saw No. 5 belching smoke from his stack and swinging toward us—range 1,500 yards. We had two torpedoes ready forward so we swung towards him to shoot down his throat. The set-up had just been cranked into the TDC and I opened my mouth to say fire when all hell broke loose. . . .

Evidently there had been a plane escort that we hadn't heard from. The charge landed very close aboard on our port quarter (it must have landed practically on the lifeboat) and blew our stern out of water. Bow and stern planes went out. She nosed over about 25 degrees. By blowing . . . we caught her at 380 feet. I don't know what became of No. 5 ship. The depth charge or the lifeboat made him change course. Whatever it was definitely saved us from being rammed when we broached. . . . If I hadn't been so eager to gloat I could have gotten the No. 5 and saved this vessel the damage which may yet require early termination of this patrol.

Dykers returned to Pearl Harbor with one engine out of commission. He was credited with sinking three ships for 24,000 tons. Postwar records confirmed the sinking of three ships on this patrol but reduced the tonnage to 16,500 tons.

Another H.O.R. boat, *Harder,* was commanded by Samuel David Dealey. Dealey came from a famous Texas family; his Uncle George was a founder and publisher of the *Dallas Morning News.* Up to then Dealey had had a lackluster naval career: he was "bilged" from the Naval Academy for low grades, got reinstated, graduated with the class of 1930, and then went on to a series of routine peacetime duties, during which he demonstrated little interest in the navy as a career, often stating he might return to civilian life. In the spring of 1941, he finally got a command: *S-20,* an old noncombatant tub at New London detailed to various experimental tasks. When war brought on a pressing need for qualified skippers, Dealey was ordered to commission *Harder*.

Dealey, who was soft-spoken, clean-living, and family-oriented, had the good luck to wind up with an exceptional wardroom. His exec was John Howard Maurer, who had been exec to Lew Wallace on *Tarpon* during the first part of the war. The third officer, Frank Curtis Lynch, Jr., a football star from the class of 1938, was also extraordinarily able. Lynch was huge (and therefore called "Tiny"), bright, and had a gift for organization and technical innovation.

On the way from New London to Pearl Harbor, *Harder* suffered the fate of all too many submarines. In the Caribbean, headed for Panama, she was attacked by a friendly aircraft—a navy patrol bomber. Although the men on *Harder*'s bridge flashed a recognition signal, the plane roared in, machine guns winking. As the bullets whined into the water alongside *Harder*, Dealey dived. The plane then dropped two bombs, one close, one distant. That night Dealey wrote in his log, "The aviator's poor approach was exceeded only by his poor marksmanship . . . but whose side are these crazy aviators on?"

Lockwood sent *Harder* to an area off Honshu. On the night of June 21, Dealey made his first attack, firing four torpedoes at a two-ship convoy, with Maurer serving in the conning tower as assistant approach officer, Tiny Lynch in the control room as diving officer. The first torpedo prematured—"a bit disconcerting," Dealey noted in his diary. He believed the others hit. An escort counterattacked and Dealey went deep—too deep. The fathometer showed 300 feet of water, but Lynch let *Harder* overshoot. The boat crashed into the muddy bottom, throwing men, dishes, and other loose gear forward.

Much later, Dealey would joke, "That night *Harder* made her first landing on the shores of Japan." At the time, however, it was far from a joke. *Harder* was stuck fast, with a steep down-angle, her stern bobbing up and down as the escort worked her over, dropping thirteen depth charges. After the ship went away, it took Lynch forty-five tense minutes to work *Harder* out of the mud.

Two nights later, June 23, radar reported a huge pip. Dealey went to battle stations. As he closed on the surface, the big ship spotted *Harder* and opened fire with her guns. Dealey fired four torpedoes, but only one appeared to hit. However, it was a mortal blow. Down went the ex-seaplane tender *Sagara Maru*, 7,000 tons.

In the next four days, Dealey attacked three separate convoys, adroitly firing first bow and then stern tubes, twisting and turning *Harder* as though he had been doing it all his life. "He had the vision and mind of an artist," Tiny Lynch said later. "His imagination pictured situations so vividly and scenes photographed themselves so clearly on the retina of his mind that he really did not need a TDC solution."

In all, Dealey made seven attacks. When he returned to Pearl Harbor, with one H.O.R. engine completely broken down, Lockwood credited him with sinking three ships for 15,000 tons and damaging four others for 27,000 tons, more than sufficient for a Navy Cross. Postwar accounting confirmed only the sinking of *Sagara Maru*.

The engineers patched up the H.O.R.s, and by August *Harder* was ready for her second patrol—loaded with spare engine parts. Dealey returned to the area off Honshu and turned in a second splendid patrol. In fourteen days he made nine attacks, claiming four ships sunk for 25,000 tons. Postwar accounting readjusted this to five ships for 15,000 tons, making it, in terms of ships sunk, one of the best patrols of the war. Throughout the patrol *Harder* still had engine problems, and at Pearl Harbor the engineers again set to work. John Maurer was transferred back to the States to new construction, and Tiny Lynch fleeted up to exec.

As these H.O.R. boats returned from patrol, it soon became clear that they would have to have new engines before they could become adequate fighting machines. Admiral King ordered this done, and one by one the Squadron Twelve boats returned to Mare Island for Winton engines.

From Brisbane, Jimmy Fife wrote Lockwood, "The history of the H.O.R. engine in Squadron Twelve seems to be rather smelly. I suppose no one will be blamed for the long period of immobility which has resulted for those twelve boats and that no one will ever get a court-martial for the fiasco." No one did.

Years later, Tommy Dykers of *Jack* said, "The H.O.R. engines saved the Japanese thirty or forty ships."

Among the new skippers bringing new fleet boats to Pearl Harbor was Charles Otto ("Chuck") Triebel in *Snook* and his excellent wardroom: Sam Colby Loomis, Jr., son of a navy captain and onetime Naval Academy athlete, as exec, and reservist Vard Albert Stockton, a former All-American football player at the University of California at Berkeley, as third. To some, Triebel was an unlikely bet. Like his Medal-of-Honor-winning friend, Howard Gilmore, he still bore a scar from the time in Panama on *Shark*'s shakedown cruise when he got his throat cut by hoodlums. Triebel's capers ashore became legendary in the submarine force. At sea, however, he was a wholly different man: dedicated, shrewd, extraordinarily competent.

Between April and August, Triebel made three war patrols, mostly to the East China Sea. Each exemplified skill and aggressiveness, and each had good results.

On the first, Triebel began by laying a minefield off Shanghai. He had a difficult time getting rid of *Snook*'s twenty-four "eggs." The Yangtse River mouth was shallow and infested with sampans and junks. Approaching in daylight submerged, Triebel got stuck in the mud at 60 feet. He broke loose, bumping along the bottom until he found a hole 75 feet deep, where he lay until dark. Coming up that night, Triebel almost holed the bottom of a junk with his periscope. He laid his small minefield in two hours.

Following this, Triebel, who had only fourteen torpedoes, patrolled the Yellow Sea. In four aggressive attacks, he sank three freighters. In addition, he sank two sampans with his deck gun.

On the second patrol, Triebel carried a full load of Mark XIV torpedoes. On June 24, he attacked a convoy of six ships, escorted by two destroyers. He fired four torpedoes, damaging a tanker, but was driven under by the destroyers. On July 4, on a black, rainy night, he found a convoy of eight ships. In an epic three-hour night surface battle, Triebel got into the middle of the convoy and fired a total of nineteen torpedoes. Deciding that one of the ships was an aircraft carrier, he fired six

torpedoes at it and saw hits. He believed it sank. When
the codebreakers picked up reports of this attack, they
identified the target not as a carrier but a big whale-
factory tanker, *Nissen Maru,* 17,600 tons. It didn't sink, but
two others did, *Koki Maru,* 5,200 tons, and *Liverpool
Maru,* 5,800 tons.

On the third patrol, Vard Stockton replaced Sam Loomis
as exec. *Snook* was now fitted with a brand new gadget
for the radar known as the plan position indicator (PPI).
This device, commonly used today in weather telecasts,
translated information obtained from radar pulses to a
"picture" with *Snook* at the center. It helped the skipper
"see" the enemy formation relative to the position of the
submarine.

Triebel experienced poor torpedo performance on this
patrol. On September 12, alerted by the codebreakers, he
intercepted an eight-ship convoy and fired six torpedoes at
two ships. All missed. The following night, the codebreakers put him on another eight-ship convoy, and he again
fired six torpedoes at two ships. One spread missed, but the
other hit and sank *Yamato Maru.*

Later, on the night of September 22, he picked up a
couple of singles. He fired four torpedoes at the first, sinking *Katsurahama Maru.* In the second attack, he began
with four torpedoes, all of which missed. In another attack on this same ship, Triebel fired another four. The
first and fourth missed ahead and astern; the second ran
erratically to the left; the wake of the third was never
seen.

Having expended all his torpedoes, Triebel set course
for Pearl Harbor. On the way home, he battle-surfaced
on a trawler. During this battle, the trawler fired back,
wounding four of Triebel's men.

In three patrols, Triebel was credited with sinking six
ships for 42,000 tons and damaging four for 31,800 tons.
Postwar records showed that he actually sank seven. Triebel was on his way toward becoming one of the leading
skippers of the war. Lockwood forgave his excesses on the
beach.

Freddy Warder's famous old *Seawolf* returned from
overhaul commanded by Royce Lawrence Gross. Gross
had inherited Warder's exec, William Nolan Deragon, who

had been on *Seawolf* for her seven previous times out. In addition, he was assigned a prospective exec, Robert Dunlap Risser, who had been in graduate school for two years and had never made a war patrol.

Both Gross and Risser felt a strong duty to uphold *Seawolf*'s reputation. Between April 3 and September 15, Gross completed three war patrols in the East China Sea near Formosa, a turnaround record for the Pearl Harbor command.

Outbound on his first patrol, Gross received an Ultra reporting a freighter near Guam, so he submerged on the assigned position. The following day the ship, *Kaihei Maru*, escorted by a trawler, came along on schedule. Gross fired four torpedoes. The first—his first shot of the war—prematured at fourteen seconds, a performance that left him "amazed." This premature alerted the freighter, which dodged the other three. After dark, Gross surfaced and tracked the ship, firing three more torpedoes. He saw two explosions and believed he obtained two hits. He then turned on the escort, firing another two torpedoes. Both missed. He fired another two at the freighter, saw a big explosion, and went deep.

Some hours later, Gross returned to the surface. His radar still showed two pips. He was exasperated: he had now fired eleven torpedoes without sinking either of the ships. However, on closer inspection he saw that he had blown the bow off the freighter. He was tempted to battle-surface to polish it off, but Japanese aircraft appeared on the radar. Gross left the disabled freighter, which later sank.

Gross continued on to patrol area with only half a load of torpedoes. On April 19, he found a small tanker and fired two more. One hit and Gross saw the ship sink, bow down. He surfaced amid the debris and a lifeboat containing about thirty survivors, machine guns ready. He picked up three life rings, a briefcase, and charts and tried to find codebooks or other valuable intelligence without success. Somehow this ship must have remained afloat; there was no record of its loss in postwar Japanese accounts.

Three days later, Gross came upon another fine target, a big damaged ship escorted by a small old destroyer and a tugboat. Gross—running low on torpedoes—decided to sink the destroyer and then attack the damaged vessel with his deck gun. He fired three torpedoes at the destroyer. One hit amidships; the other two missed. He fired a fourth; it also missed. Again exasperated, Gross fired a fifth and a sixth. Both missed, but the destroyer (*Patrol Boat No. 39*, 750 tons) sank from the damage inflicted on the first salvo.

Gross now turned on the freighter and fired his last torpedo. When it failed to explode, he ordered his gun crew to prepare for action. However, about that time a fleet destroyer came on the scene and Gross decided discretion was the better part of valor. He turned east and headed for Pearl Harbor, arriving after a mere thirty days at sea. Lockwood, who blamed most of Gross's bad luck on defective torpedoes, heaped praise on this new skipper who seemed bent on outdoing Fearless Freddy Warder.

After only two weeks in port, Gross was on his way again. On this trip, Risser had replaced the exec, Deragon, who went to new construction. Gross returned to Formosa, circling around the north side into Formosa Strait. In a period of two weeks, *Seawolf* encountered five convoys composed of about thirty-seven ships. In five separate attacks, Gross fired sixteen torpedoes, but only two or three of these hit, sinking one confirmed ship, *Shojin Maru*, 4,739 tons.

Back in port, Bob Risser left the ship for new construction, replaced by Douglas Neil ("Red") Syverson, a youngster from the class of 1939. Returning to the East China Sea for a third patrol, on August 29 Gross found a fat convoy northeast of Formosa: five big freighters and escorts. In a dogged forty-eight-hour running battle—the most tenacious on record—Gross fired all his torpedoes for contact explosion, sinking two ships and damaging another which he finished off with his deck gun. He returned to port after thirty-two days. In his patrol report, Gross blamed himself for having missed with twelve of his torpedoes. His endorsers believed Gross had been a bit too severe on himself, taking pains to point out that many of his targets might have maneuvered out of the way.

In three patrols, Gross had fired about fifty-six torpedoes, sinking six ships. Like Triebel, Roy Gross was on his way to becoming one of the high scorers of the war.

Creed Burlingame took *Silversides* back to Brisbane on his fifth patrol. He was the same old jaunty, cocksure Burlingame and, like Triebel, legendary on shore leave. An entry in his patrol report for May 28 reads: "Proceeded on surface toward assigned position . . . a frigate bird made a high level bombing attack, scoring direct hit on the bare head and beard of the OOD. . . . No indication by radar prior to attack." Burlingame had a new exec, Robert Kemble Worthington, who stood 4 out of 438 in the class of 1938.

Silversides had two missions. The first was to lay a small minefield in Steffen Strait, between New Hanover and New Ireland. The second was to sink ships. Burlingame laid the field on the night of June 4 and hauled clear, reporting to Jimmy Fife in Brisbane. Fife ordered him northward to the intersection of the equator and longitude 150 degrees east, lying athwart the lane from Truk to Rabaul.

After Burlingame got into position, Fife sent an Ultra on a northbound convoy. While waiting for it to show up, Burlingame picked up what he believed to be a southbound convoy unreported by Fife. "In the belief that a southbound convoy was more valuable than the northbound one we were expecting," Burlingame wrote, "decided to surface and end around. . . . It then became evident that this group was northbound, whether the same convoy I do not know." He made his end around, taking advantage of generally poor weather, and waited on the surface. Shortly after midnight, the convoy reappeared. Burlingame fired four torpedoes at one of the largest ships in the formation. As he wrote later:

First hit looked to be a magnetic explosion. Ship seemed to jump out of the water and streak of flame twice ship's length on water line. Second hit under bridge, large column of water and smoke. Third hit and felt throughout ship but not observed . . . fourth missed . . . an explosion occurred on target, evidently gasoline as a bright flame shot up 200 feet in the air and completely enveloped ship. Also lit us up like a church.

An escort charged at *Silversides*. Burlingame let the ship close to 1,700 yards, fired a stern torpedo down the throat, and submerged. The torpedo forced the escort to turn away, which, Burlingame reported, "probably saved our necks." The escorts returned, pasting *Silversides* with several salvos of close depth charges that shook the boat violently but did no serious damage. Later, Burlingame surfaced and slipped away.

The ship Burlingame destroyed was *Hide Maru*, 5,200 tons, an important vessel probably being used as a destroyer or submarine tender. The codebreakers had followed her progress north and her final demise. Later, Burlingame learned there had been a Japanese admiral on board who was killed in the sinking, but Burlingame never discovered his name. In Brisbane, Burlingame relinquished command of *Silversides* and was promoted to command a division of new boats in Squadron Eighteen then under construction. In his five patrols he had sunk eight confirmed ships, ranking him high on the list of top scorers.

John Tyree took *Finback* on a round trip to Fremantle, a spectacular voyage in every respect. On the way down, he patrolled the Palaus, where he made eight relentlessly aggressive attacks which resulted in the sinking of three confirmed ships for 13,000 tons. When he reached Fremantle, Christie, who had served with Tyree on the aircraft carrier *Ranger*, was unstinting in his praise, noting in his diary, "Good boy!"

Tyree remained in Fremantle only briefly. After refit, Christie ordered him to return to Pearl Harbor via the Java Sea and have a look at Surabaya.

On July 30 Tyree found plenty of targets. The first contact was a pair of light cruisers, escorted by destroyers which Tyree picked up fourteen miles north of Surabaya in shallow water—140 feet. These ships passed *Finback* at 5,000 yards, too far to shoot. An hour later, Tyree spotted a "huge" freighter and fired three torpedoes: one prematured, one missed, one hit. Down went *Ryuzan Maru*, 4,700 tons.

In subsequent days, Tyree sank a large freighter and a small submarine chaser and inflicted damage on other ships. On most of these attacks, Tyree experienced erratic torpedo performance. Upon reaching Pearl Harbor, he claimed he had had five prematures. Lockwood was pleased by Tyree's aggressiveness but angered that Christie still insisted that the magnetic exploder remain activated.

In his round trip to Fremantle, John Tyree had sunk six confirmed ships for 24,000 tons.

The climax of Lockwood's submarine offensive in the summer of 1943 was a daring penetration of the Sea of Japan, the body of water lying between Japan and the Asian mainland.

Lockwood and Voge had been eying the Sea of Japan all spring, logically assuming that it was crowded with shipping. The problem was how to get at it. The Sea of Japan is virtually landlocked. It has three narrow entrances: Tsushima Strait in the south, Tsugaru Strait in the middle, and La Pérouse Strait in the far north. Each of those shallow, narrow passages was believed to be mined and heavily patrolled by surface ships and aircraft. In winter months, La Pérouse was frozen solid.

After studying the problem with his usual thoroughness, Dick Voge concluded that in summer months submarines might penetrate the Sea of Japan by the northernmost passage, La Pérouse. Lying between Japan and Russian-held Sakhalin, it was used by Russian ships from Vladivostok. If Russian ships could get through, Voge reasoned, U.S. submarines might do the same, either by clandestinely following a Russian ship or by choosing the most likely route a Russian ship would follow. It was risky, but not unreasonably so.

The real problem—on paper—was getting out. If U.S. submarines suddenly appeared in the Sea of Japan, the Japanese were certain to take vigorous measures to block the three passages and seal the submarines inside, where they could be systematically hunted down until they ran out of food and fuel. To minimize this possibility, Voge proposed that the first boats make a four-day hit-and-run assault. In addition, Frank De Vere Latta's *Narwhal* would be assigned to bombard Matsuwa To in the Kurile Islands, a diversion that might draw antisubmarine vessels away from La Pérouse.

For this unprecedented foray, Lockwood picked three submarines, old *Plunger* and *Permit* and the new H.O.R. boat *Lapon,* commanded by Oliver Grafton Kirk, supported by his exec, Eli Thomas Reich. *Lapon* had never made a war patrol.

Dave White on *Plunger* had been replaced by a remarkable young officer, Raymond Henry ("Benny") Bass, a fiercely competitive, cool-headed gymnast from the class of 1931. In 1932, he had won an Olympic Gold Medal for rope climbing, the last year that sport was counted as a single event.

Bass had taken *Plunger* on two patrols in the "quiet" Marshalls, each memorable. On the first, he sank a small freighter and damaged a large tanker. On the second, he picked up a convoy of five big freighters, escorted by two subchasers, and in an epic chase that dragged over two days and nights had chipped away at it until he believed he had sunk three of the five ships for 24,000 tons. Postwar analysis reduced his claim to two ships for 15,000 tons, but the persistence and bravery of the battle had earned Benny Bass high praise.

Permit was still commanded by the indefatigable Moon Chapple, who had led her on five patrols since taking command from Adrian Hurst in Surabaya in February 1942. After returning from Australia, *Permit* had had a long overhaul, but she was still cranky and somewhat infirm. On two patrols from Pearl Harbor, one to Empire and one to Truk, Chapple had had both bad luck and faulty torpedo performance. Most of his bad luck was his own fault. Chapple had undeniable courage—his penetration of Lingayen Gulf in old *S-38* proved that— but he was not an expert torpedo shooter.

One of Lockwood's older staffers, Babe Brown, who had been aching to make a war patrol, was given tactical command of the operation. He flew his flag in Latta's *Narwhal*, which Brown had put in commission in 1930. At age fifty-one, Brown, class of 1914, was the oldest and most senior officer to make a patrol during the war.

The four boats proceeded on the mission separately— *Narwhal* to the Kuriles to create the diversion; *Plunger*, *Permit*, and *Lapon* to La Pérouse Strait. On the night of July 4, *Plunger*, *Permit*, and *Lapon* went through the strait on the surface; it was crowded with lighted ships, presumably Russian. Benny Bass and Moon Chapple each made contact with what was believed to be an antisubmarine vessel and dived—Bass into what were believed to be mined waters, Chapple into uncharted shallow water. Chapple hit bottom and damaged his sonar head. Otherwise the boats were unharmed. Inside the Sea of Japan, Bass and Chapple remained concealed in their assigned areas, waiting for Kirk to reach his position, which was the southernmost.

While waiting, about half of Chapple's men came down with an "epidemic of food poisoning or water contamination," Chapple reported. "Symptoms are nausea and vomiting, which in most cases lasted from 5 to 10 minutes." The epidemic broke out again a week later. No explanation for it was ever discovered.

As the midnight firing time approached, Chapple and his exec, Frederick Leonard Taeusch, who had already let a dozen fat targets go by, grew impatient. They jumped the gun by an hour and a half and torpedoed a freighter. Shortly after midnight, they picked up a two-ship convoy. Chapple sank one and hit the other. Then he decided to surface.

Coming up, *Permit* was "pooped"—swept by a huge wave. Tons of seawater flooded the conning tower hatch and went down into the pump room, beneath the control room. For a while, many of the men on *Permit* believed she was lost. However, Chapple ordered emergency procedures to stop the flooding and managed to save the ship. But the conning tower was half full of water, and the SJ radar, located there, was put out of commission for the key ninety-six-hour period in the Sea of Japan. Chapple made four more night surface attacks, but with the radar out of commission he could only guess at the ranges. All torpedoes missed.

A few hours before he was due to leave his area and retreat through La Pérouse, Chapple sighted a small craft he believed to be a Japanese patrol vessel and ordered battle surface. After *Permit* fired a few well-placed shots, the men on the small vessel raised a large white flag. Coming alongside, Chapple discovered she was a Russian fishing trawler, manned by a crew that included women. One man had been killed and another mortally wounded and several of the women had been hit by shrapnel. The trawler was sinking. What to do?

Moon ordered the survivors, seven men and five women, to come on board *Permit* and then withdrew through

La Pérouse to the Sea of Okhotsk, where he radioed Lockwood news of the unfortunate incident and requested permission to land the survivors on Russian soil. Lockwood was stunned, both by the news and by Chapple's suggestion. The Russians, he felt, might intern *Permit* or retaliate, so he ordered Chapple to take his survivors to Dutch Harbor.

On the way, the survivors were treated royally. The crew made quarters for them in the forward torpedo room. The women took their meals in the wardroom; the men in the crew's mess. After a week Chapple had so charmed the women that they didn't want to get off *Permit* in Dutch Harbor. "They were crying when they left," Chapple said later. "We gave them all a U.S. Navy insignia, fifteen dollars apiece, shoes, and a little bag containing some clothes."

Moon got a chewing out for this attack. Everyone was sure it would lead to another international incident with the Russians, like the one Eugene Sands on *Sawfish* had caused. Conceivably, it might expose the secret of the penetration of the Sea of Japan. However, the Russian trawler captain rose to the occasion. Chapple said later, "In his official report, he stated that he had first been attacked by a Japanese submarine and that we came along and chased off the Jap sub and rescued them."

Like Chapple, Benny Bass on *Plunger* had seen many targets while awaiting "firing time." When it came, the seas were empty. About noon the following day, a small freighter came out of the fog. Bass attacked with torpedoes. When he saw men climbing down ropes into the lifeboats, he battle-surfaced to finish off the ship. However, the freighter fired back and radioed a distress call. Aircraft soon appeared, driving Bass under. Before the ninety-six hours expired, however, Bass found and sank a small freighter.

Oliver Kirk on *Lapon* cruised far to the south off Korea. The whole time *Lapon* was enveloped by an impenetrable fog and bedeviled by problems with the SJ radar. On the night of July 8, he fired four torpedoes by radar at an unknown target but missed. He withdrew through La Pérouse without having sunk anything.

Since Kirk had plenty of fuel and provisions remaining, Lockwood ordered him to patrol down the coast of Japan to the approaches to Tokyo on the way home. On July 23, while off Tokyo Bay, Kirk received an Ultra and picked up a magnificent sight in his periscope: a large aircraft carrier, and two destroyers, range 4 miles. Kirk went to battle stations, but, before he could fire, an attack by an aircraft and the two destroyers drove him deep. When he was able to come up again, the carrier was gone. After that, he set course for Midway, noting in his patrol report, "Disappointed on fruitlessness of patrol."

Narwhal, also plagued by fog, was not able to close Matsuwa To in time to provide the diversion for the three boats withdrawing through La Pérouse. However, when she finally got there, Babe Brown and Frank Latta decided to carry out the mission anyway. Latta battle-surfaced at 14,000 yards and got off a few shots with *Narwhal's* 6-inch guns, aiming at the Japanese airfield and hangars. However, the Japanese returned fire with salvos so accurate that Latta broke off and submerged. After some fruitless days of hunting ships in the Kuriles, *Narwhal* returned to Midway.

On return to port, both Moon Chapple and Oliver Kirk stepped down from command. Kirk's division commander wrote, "Results were disappointing." Lockwood said, "It is believed that more contacts would have been made had a patrol closer to the beach been conducted." Moon Chapple wrote in his patrol report, "In spite of the fact that the time submerged was negligible the health of the crew as a whole was poor. Several of the crew that have served aboard since the war began and have made nine successive war patrols show signs of needing a prolonged rest." Chapple himself had made eight war patrols, two on *S-38* and six on *Permit.* He returned to new construction. Oliver Kirk, who returned from patrol in ill health, was sent to the Bureau of Ordnance to work on torpedoes, specifically as officer in charge of testing the Mark XVIII electric at Newport. Kirk's exec, Eli Reich, went to new construction.

Although the results of this foray had been disappointing in the extreme—three small freighters sunk for 5,000 tons—Lockwood and Voge planned a second penetration.

The first man to volunteer was Benny Bass on *Plunger*. The second was Mush Morton. *Wahoo* had just returned from a long overhaul at Mare Island, and Mush himself was back from shore treatment for the chronic prostate problem that needed medical attention between every patrol.

There had been important personnel changes on *Wahoo*. The exec, Dick O'Kane, transferred to new construction, had been replaced by young Roger Paine, the third. However, when *Wahoo* reached Hawaii, Paine came down with appendicitis and had to be hospitalized. He was replaced by Verne Leslie Skjonsby, who stood seventh in the class of 1934. Skjonsby had come from a long tour of duty in the Bureau of Ordnance; he had never made a war patrol.

Morton did not tell Lockwood, but he had privately developed a new firing scheme for his trip into the Sea of Japan. He would shoot only one torpedo at each ship he attacked. If his marksmanship was as good as it had been in the past, Morton reasoned, he would probably sink fifteen or twenty ships, a record no one had ever achieved. He would do this in spite of the fact that he no longer had O'Kane on the periscope and Roger Paine on the TDC.

Bass and Morton were programmed to go through La Pérouse Strait together on the night of August 14. However, *Plunger* developed engine and motor trouble on the way. Morton went through La Pérouse as scheduled, at night, on the surface, full speed; Bass went through submerged during daylight, two days later.

Mush Morton found a convoy almost immediately and put into effect his single-torpedo concept. Each shot was fired for confact. A log of his attacks:

15 August. *Fired one torpedo at a freighter. Miss.*
            Fired one torpedo at a freighter. Dud.
            Fired two torpedoes at freighter. Both missed.
            Fired one torpedo at same freighter. Miss.
17 August. *Fired one torpedo at a freighter. Miss.*
            Fired one torpedo at a freighter. Miss.
18 August. *Fired one torpedo at a freighter. Miss.*
            Fired one torpedo at a freighter. Miss.
            Fired one torpedo at same freighter. Broach.

Blaming all his bad luck on torpedo performance, Morton noted in his patrol report, "Damn the torpedoes." He radioed Lockwood for permission to return to base for a torpedo reload, again damning the torpedoes. Lockwood gave his approval and on August 19, after four days in the Sea of Japan, Morton withdrew through La Pérouse Strait.

Benny Bass had only slightly better luck. His log:

17 August. *Fired four torpedoes at freighter. Miss.*
18 August. *Fired two torpedoes at freighter. Miss.*
20 August. *Fired two torpedoes at freighter. One hit.*
Crew abandoned, but ship didn't sink. Fired one more torpedo. No explosion. Fired another. Ditto. Fired another. Still no explosion. Fired one more. Hit. Ship sank.
22 August. *Fired two torpedoes at freighter. One hit, one dud. Second hit, blew off rudder. Fired a third. Hit. Ship sank.*

Bass withdrew from the Sea of Japan behind Mush Morton, returning to Pearl Harbor. Lockwood credited him with two ships for 9,000 tons and added a glowing endorsement to his patrol report which concluded, "More ships would have been sunk had the torpedo performance been better." Postwar analysis readjusted the credit upward to three ships. Bass took *Plunger* back to Mare Island for overhaul.

This time, the endorsements to Morton's patrol reports were not so glowing. For the first time, he had turned in a zero run. Although Morton blamed it on poor torpedo performance, Babe Brown blamed it on Morton's decision to only fire one torpedo at each ship. Brown wrote, "The decision of the commanding officer to fire single torpedoes, while understandable, is not concurred in. A minimum of two, preferably three, torpedoes, using a spread, should be fired at any target worthy of torpedo expenditure, taking into consideration the poor performance of the Mark XIV torpedo, the many unknowns in torpedo firing." Lockwood added, "Failure to use torpedo spreads during most of the attacks undoubtedly contributed materially to the lack of success. Torpedo spreads must be used to cover possible errors in data or possibility of duds."

The two forays into the Sea of Japan, from which so much was expected, produced very little. The six patrols involved (including *Narwhal*, on her diversionary raid) accounted for a total of five confirmed ships sunk for 13,500 tons, with Benny Bass doing most of the damage: three ships for 10,500 tons. It seemed hardly worth the risk.

13

TANKER OFFENSIVE

In June 1943, Allied forces in the southwest Pacific—following the strategic plan agreed upon at the Trident conference—went on the offensive against the Japanese. The drive was a two-pronged, mutually supporting effort. Admiral Halsey's forces moved northward on an island-hopping campaign in the Solomons; General MacArthur's forces launched the reconquest of New Guinea. Halsey's forces landed on New Georgia June 30 and then advanced to Bougainville; MacArthur, after capturing some outlying islands on his right flank, landed north of Buna, New Guinea, June 30, and at Lae in September. To support these campaigns, Allied aircraft made repeated attacks on the Japanese bases at Rabaul, Kavieng, and Wewak.

Each forward step brought on a Japanese reaction. Admiral Koga sent a steady stream of reinforcements and aircraft from Truk and Palau and attempted to break up the Allied landings with surface forces composed of heavy and light cruisers and destroyers. After Halsey landed on New Georgia, Japanese naval units counterattacked in two battles known as Kula Gulf and Kolombangara, July 6 and July 12. In these two engagements, the U.S. Navy came off second best, losing the cruiser *Helena* and two destroyers, *Gwin* and *Strong*. The cruisers *St. Louis* and *Honolulu* were damaged. The Japanese lost the cruiser *Jintsu* and two destroyers, *Nagatsuki* and *Niizuki*.

As Halsey moved north from his bases in New Georgia, there were four more noteworthy surface force engagements: Vella Gulf, Vella Lavella, Empress Augusta Bay, and Cape St. George. The U.S. Navy won them all except Vella Lavella. In the battles, the Japanese lost the light cruiser *Sendai* and eight destroyers; the U.S. lost one destroyer, *Chevalier*. In addition, several Japanese cruisers and destroyers were badly damaged during the air strikes on Rabaul.

Until the summer of 1943, the number of boats based in all of Australia was held to twenty—twelve in Brisbane under James Fife, eight in Fremantle under Ralph Christie. However, as the Allies pushed northward into the Solomons, the patrol areas available to the Brisbane submarines diminished accordingly. It was decided, therefore, to give Christie twelve boats, reducing Fife to eight. In addition, Washington ordered a new squadron to Fremantle, giving Christie another dozen boats, for a total of twenty-four. *(subs)*

Fife's boats found poor hunting, but Christie's boats, now belatedly concentrating on tankers in the South China Sea and elsewhere, turned in some spectacular patrols. *(Subs)*

Two of Christie's new boats were *Bowfin* and *Billfish*. *Bowfin* was commanded by one of the fine performers of 1942, Joe Willingham, who had won two Navy Crosses for his four patrols on *Tautog*. *Billfish* was commanded by Frederic Colby Lucas, Jr., a peacetime submariner who had been on the staff of Commander, Submarines Atlantic Fleet during the early months of the war and had never made a war patrol. His exec was Frank Gordon Selby, who had made the first two war patrols on Creed Burlingame's *Silversides*.

On their first patrol, *Bowfin* and *Billfish* conducted what might be described as an "extemporized" cooperative unit off Indochina, similar to Fife's experimental cooperative efforts with the Brisbane boats. There the two boats found a six-ship convoy.

Later, Willingham's exec, William Calhoun Thompson, Jr., wrote, "Willingham was a perfectionist. . . . We sank three ships, firing bow and stern tubes simultaneously—bow with the TDC but stern with his infallible eye and judgment. To the best of my knowledge this was an 'only feat' during the war." Postwar analysis trimmed these three ships to one, a transport, *Kirishima Maru*, 8,120 tons. Lucas in *Billfish* was credited with damage to two ships for 11,900 tons. His endorsement stated, "It is unfortunate that the attacks . . . were not productive of more visible results."

When Willingham returned *Bowfin* to Fremantle, Christie labeled his patrol "brilliant" and promoted him off the boat to command a division in Brisbane. Willingham recommended his exec, Thompson, for command, but Christie picked Walter Thomas Griffith, who had been exec on *Gar* and was a year senior to Thompson. Lucas retained command of *Billfish*.

Walt Griffith was, in Christie's words, a "studious-looking, red-haired, trim young man with blood pressure too high and a slight hand quiver." To his exec, Thompson, he was "absolutely fearless—maybe too much so" and a "reasonable and wonderful skipper and shipmate." Wrote Thompson, "I shared his cabin with him, at his suggestion, and one of us was 'always awake on feet' throughout the boat at all times. . . . Walt, at sea, was a fearless fighter; in port, a mild, kindly, even poetic type."

Going off on their second patrols, *Bowfin* and *Billfish* again operated as an extemporaneous unit off Indochina. On the way over, Griffith found a group of five two-masted schooners, steaming in company. He charged the formation at full speed, sending the crew to gun stations. Within one hour, three of the schooners were riddled and sinking. Each had been manned by about thirty people —men and women—and there were children aboard. All the schooners, Griffith reported later, were "heavily laden . . . each vessel sank like a stone after two good hits . . . no clue as to cargo." During the battle, a plane came over and dropped a small bomb, forcing Griffith to let the last two schooners go. However, later that night he found another, and after two hits it too "sank like a stone."

During this engagement, many women and children had been killed or drowned. Those who knew Griffith well said that in later years he regretted the attacks against these defenseless targets and brooded about it. Said Thompson, "I would not have sunk some of the sampans."

A few nights later, November 11, while going through Sibutu Passage, Griffith found two small unescorted tankers. Again he ordered battle surface. Within half an hour, he had holed both and set them afire. Wrote Griffith, "Nice fireworks for Armistice Day."

On November 20, Griffith joined up with Lucas in *Billfish* and began the wolf-pack operations, cruising toward the coast of Indochina near Camranh Bay. The weather turned foul. During the storm, *Bowfin* and *Billfish* separated and temporarily lost contact.

Early on the morning of November 26, Griffith, feeling his way through pitch blackness and solid sheets of rain, suddenly found pips on the radar ranging from 1,000 to 4,000 yards. At first he thought he had run right up on the beach. Then he realized he had steamed into the middle of a Japanese tanker convoy. He backed emergency to avoid colliding with one "enormous" ship.

A wild melee followed. Reversing to get range to shoot, Griffith made ready his torpedo tubes. He fired nine torpedoes (one tube door would not open) at two or three ships. (In the dark and confusion it was difficult to tell how many.) His magnetic exploders were activated. As Griffith maneuvered through the convoy, his torpedoes started exploding. Within the next few hours, three confirmed ships went down: a tanker of 5,000 tons and two freighters, one 5,400 tons and one smaller.

Two days later, Griffith made contact with Lucas in *Billfish*, who had been patrolling to seaward. Lucas picked up a convoy and helped put *Bowfin* on the track. A second furious close-in action ensued. Griffith sank two more big ships, including a tanker of 9,900 tons and a transport of 5,400 tons. One ship of the convoy fired back with a deck gun, piercing *Bowfin*'s main induction, and seawater flooded the engine room. Undaunted, Griffith set up and fired his last two torpedoes at another ship. One prematured after thirteen seconds, deflecting the second. Now out of torpedoes, Griffith withdrew from the convoy to repair the damages.

Lucas in *Billfish* was ready and waiting on the convoy track, but Griffith's attack had scattered it and alerted the escorts. Where Griffith had had the advantage of a dark land mass behind him, Lucas had open sea for backdrop. He trailed and got off one attack from long range, reporting damage to a 6,000-ton vessel.

On the way home, Griffith found another schooner, which he described as a "two-masted yacht, with jib, flying jib, foresail, mainsail and two topsails." He battle-surfaced and sank it, adding, "Did not observe crew closely but vessel was not a native craft. Looked like it might have been some planter's yacht taken over by the Japs."

Griffith arrived back in Fremantle after thirty-nine days at sea. When Christie heard the news of this patrol, he was awestruck, calling it in his diary the "classic of all submarine patrols."

It was. After carefully going over the accounts of the attacks, Christie credited Griffith with sinking a total of fourteen vessels—nine ships and five schooners—for 71,000 tons. This was 20,000 more tons than Klakring had been credited with on the first patrol of *Guardfish*, the largest single claimed score by any submarine up to then. Overnight the "poetic" Walt Griffith became a submarine superstar. Christie awarded him a Navy Cross and wined and dined the wardroom in spectacular fashion at his home, "Bend of the Road." He gave the exec, William Thompson, a Silver Star and pronounced him qualified for command of his own boat. And when his cocker spaniel had a puppy, Christie named it Bowfin.

In all his torpedo attacks, Griffith had kept the Mark VI magnetic exploder activated as instructed. Christie noted triumphantly in the patrol report endorsement, "The torpedo performance on this patrol was excellent. Nineteen hits were obtained from the twenty-four torpedoes fired." It seemed to Christie proof that the magnetic exploder—in the proper hands—was still a marvelous weapon.

In the postwar accounting, Walt Griffith's confirmed score for this patrol—like almost everybody else's—was trimmed. There was no doubt about the five schooners, but the bigger ships sunk were reduced from nine to five, for a total of 26,958 tons. In terms of confirmed tonnage sunk, this made his patrol the third best of the war to date, after Creed Burlingame's fourth in *Silversides* and Tom Wogan's second in *Tarpon*.

When Lucas in *Billfish* returned to Fremantle thirteen days later, he had a painfully candid talk with Christie. He explained that he had never been comfortable in submarines and he now believed that over the period of a war patrol this mild phobia adversely affected his performance. He therefore felt that he was not doing justice to this fine submarine and crew, and recommended that the command be given to one of several war-experienced officers then in Fremantle awaiting their chance at command.

Christie noted with regret in his diary, "I am obliged to detach Lucas from command of *Billfish* on his own request. He is convinced that he is temperamentally unsuited for submarine command. I have been quite well satisfied with him although he has had two unproductive patrols [and] I would not have removed him." Lucas went to Brisbane to serve on the staff of Squadron Eight.

Bluefish, commanded by George Egbert Porter, Jr., who had made three patrols on *Greenling* as exec to Chester Bruton, left on her first patrol from Darwin. Porter's exec was young Chester Nimitz, who began the war on *Sturgeon.* Porter and Nimitz conducted six attacks and were credited with sinking four ships for 16,200 tons and damage to one for 7,000 tons. It was one of the shortest war patrols on record: twenty-five days port to port.

On the second patrol, Porter patrolled near Indochina in company with another new boat, *Cod,* commanded by James Charles Dempsey, ex-*Spearfish.* On November 8, Porter picked up a big convoy near Dangerous Ground off Palawan in the South China Sea. Swinging in on the surface at night, Porter fired all ten tubes. The fifth torpedo to leave the tubes prematured right in the path of *Bluefish.* The others continued on, for what Porter believed were "eight or nine hits" in various ships.

After reloading, Porter swung around for another attack on a motionless ship that loomed large on radar. It turned out to be a big tanker, already disabled. Porter delivered three more attacks against the tanker, which finally blew up, sending a vast column of flame skyward. "This is the most beautiful sight I have ever seen," Porter exclaimed, watching his handiwork through the periscope. "This is beautiful." The ship was *Kyokuei Maru,* 10,570 tons. Porter retrieved a magnetic compass from a lifeboat and later presented it to Christie.

Dempsey in *Cod* was close enough to this battle to hear Porter's torpedo explosions, but he was unable to make an attack.

Ten days later, in the Celebes Sea, Porter and Nimitz found another tanker escorted by a destroyer. With only six torpedoes left, Porter cooked up an ingenious plan. He fired three torpedoes at the destroyer and one at the tanker, with the intent of sinking the former and damaging the latter, slowing it down. The destroyer blew up with an enormous explosion; the tanker, hit with one torpedo, slowed down as planned. Porter swung around and fired his last two torpedoes at the tanker, but he forgot to allow for the diminished speed, and both missed. He started to attack with his deck gun but broke off when the tanker fired back.

On the way home, Porter battle-surfaced on a small fishing sampan engaged in collecting turtles. Most of the crew dived overboard, but one old fisherman was badly burned in the flames that engulfed the craft. Porter brought him on board. One of *Bluefish*'s officers, James De Roche, reported later, "There was considerable division of opinion on the submarine as to whether we should bring this prisoner back or not. Some of the men who had been at Pearl Harbor and who had lost many shipmates from Japanese bombings and attacks felt that we should take no Japanese alive. One . . . felt that we should kill this man outright." The prisoner was not executed, however; he died of burns.

When Porter and Nimitz returned to Fremantle after thirty-two days, there was "much discussion" about what *Bluefish* had or had not sunk. Porter and Nimitz believed that they had sunk seven ships—a record performance—but Christie had Ultra information indicating otherwise. He credited Porter with sinking three ships for 22,800 tons and damage to five for 43,800 tons. Postwar records credited Porter with sinking only the tanker and the destroyer, which turned out to be an old 800-tonner.

After this patrol, Christie pulled Chester Nimitz from *Bluefish* for a rest. He went to the PCO pool, qualified for his own command.

Rasher was commanded by thirty-nine-year-old Ed Hutchinson, whom Lockwood had relieved of command of *Grampus* the year before for lacking aggressiveness. His exec was Stephen Henry Gimber, ex-*Trigger*. Patrolling in the Celebes Sea, Hutchinson, perhaps smarting from his previous relief, conducted an outstandingly aggressive patrol: eight attacks and four ships sunk, a claim sustained in postwar records. On the way home, *Rasher* was attacked by a friendly navy patrol bomber. Hutchinson dived. The bombs exploded when he was passing 47 feet, fortunately doing no serious damage. In Fremantle, Hutchinson stepped down as commanding officer and was promoted to command a division.

Command of *Rasher* went to Willard Ross Laughon, who came from the Atlantic and command of *R-1*, on which he made ten war patrols. Retaining Steve Gimber as exec, Laughon joined George Porter in *Bluefish* for a joint patrol in the South China Sea, along the approaches to the Gulf of Siam. Both boats would lay minefields and then conduct regular patrols. On the way to lay his field, Porter found a tanker in Karimata Strait and sank it.

On the night of January 3, after both Porter and Laughon had laid their minefields, Christie vectored them to intercept a convoy of three tankers. After making contact, Porter and Laughon talked by blinker tube. Porter, the senior skipper, generously offered Laughon the first attack. Laughon accepted.

Moving into position for a night surface attack, Laughon fired four torpedoes at one tanker. The first torpedo—Laughon's first shot of the war—prematured 400 yards out of the tube, alerting the convoy. The tankers began shooting at *Rasher*. But Laughon had got one hit and his target slowed down. Meanwhile Porter had attacked another tanker, which burst into flames. Laughon fired again—six torpedoes. Two prematured but one hit. Laughon reloaded and attacked again with four torpedoes. One prematured but others hit, and the tanker exploded in a mass of flames. Wrote Laughon, "Three attacks—five prematures. Were we unhappy!"

The combined attack had netted two of the three tankers: *Hakko Maru*, 6,046 tons, for Porter; *Kiyo Maru*, 7,251 tons, for Laughon. After sinking his tanker, Laughon patrolled off Camranh Bay, where he made two more attacks, one marred by a premature and the other by a TDC error. On the way home, he found a "beautiful" 10,000-ton transport which he chased for fifteen hours before firing his last torpedo at extreme range. It missed.

When Porter returned to Fremantle, Christie was waiting with sad personal news: one of his two daughters had drowned. Porter returned to the States for new construction, to be with his wife and other daughter for a while.

Crevalle was commanded by Hank Munson, who had commanded *S-38* for six patrols from Manila, Surabaya, and Brisbane. His exec was Frank Walker, who had made six patrols as exec of *Searaven*. Munson's third was Lucien Berry McDonald, and his torpedo officer was Bill Ruhe, who had served on *S-37* in the early days of the war and was, according to Munson, "one of the best TDC operators in the Southwest Pacific." Munson—at Fife's suggestion —had adopted the Mush Morton-Dick O'Kane technique for fire control: Frank Walker manned the periscope, leaving Munson free for overall direction.

Crevalle touched at Darwin and then went on patrol near Manila. On November 10, Munson attacked a three-ship convoy, firing ten torpedoes before an escort drove them down. Although a hit was observed, no claims were made. The next night, Munson battle-surfaced and sank a 750-ton freighter. On November 15, a huge passenger-cargo vessel came out of the mist. Munson set up and prepared to shoot. The target zigged, placing it only 900 yards away. Munson fired four torpedoes down the throat. The ship disintegrated.

Two nights later, while Munson was patrolling off the west coast of Luzon, radar picked up a high-speed formation, with one large pip. Munson closed to attack, trying to figure out what he had. He was never certain. It looked like an escort carrier, or a cross between an escort carrier and a large amphibious tender, escorted by a destroyer. Munson closed to point-blank range and fired six torpedoes, set to run at 6 feet. One torpedo prematured off the bow; several others hit.

Munson said later, "The outcome was never known, for about that time I got a damn sight more interested in saving my neck than collecting historical evidence. We came under violent and intense gunfire (five-inch stuff) from both the target and the escorting destroyer as we passed down beneath them, about five hundred yards abaft. We can only hope they scored some hits on each other. A hunk of shrapnel went through the bow buoyancy tank, but we didn't know it . . . we pulled the plug and reached test depth in considerably under contract specification time."

A week later, Munson picked up another ship, a 4,000-ton unescorted freighter, and attacked her with his last four torpedoes. He believed he got two hits and claimed she sank.

During the course of this patrol, Munson stopped a fishing boat to interrogate the Filipino crew about Japanese shipping traffic. The fishermen were terrified, Bill Ruhe recalled in a brief account of the incident, and thrust peace offerings—baskets of fruit, bunches of bananas, struggling livestock—at Munson. When the Filipinos insisted that Munson take something, he "apologetically accepted one little dirty-gray emaciated chicken." Looking over the pathetic little bird, Munson decided no one could get any meat from it, so he pronounced it *Crevalle*'s mascot.

The chicken wound up in care of the gang in the forward torpedo room. As Ruhe told it, the torpedo gang, dreaming of fresh eggs, began feeding the chicken bread crumbs and cornmeal. The chicken ate ravenously, Ruhe reported, "and then decided to be grateful for the good treatment and produce an egg." The gang drew straws to see who would get it. The chief torpedoman, Howard, won. When the chicken announced with a loud cackle that she meant business, Howard put his hand underneath to catch the egg. Out came not an egg but a revolting shell-less ooze—all in Howard's hand.

Another torpedoman, Crowley, who was to get the next egg, pondered this situation. Why had there been no shell? Not enough calcium, he concluded. He went forward to the crew's mess and got some shells from the ship's supply of frozen eggs, ground them up, and fed them to the chicken. Reported Ruhe, "A day later her cackle held a note of triumph as out came an egg covered with a nice hard white shell."

When Munson returned to Fremantle, Christie was much pleased with the patrol. He noted in his diary, "Munson in *Crevalle* in today and a fine story he has to tell. Result: 1 auxiliary carrier, 18,000; 1 large, 1 medium and 1 small freighter . . . brought back a chicken mascot." In all, Munson claimed four ships for 29,800 tons, for which Christie gave him a Navy Cross. However, postwar analysis wiped out the escort carrier and two other ships, leaving him only the freighter *Kyokko Maru*, 6,783 tons, sunk on November 15.

Munson's second patrol was a frustrating one. At dawn on January 7, while crossing the Java Sea, *Crevalle* came across a submarine. Munson thought it must be Dutch or English, so he flashed the current recognition signal. In return, Munson recalled, he received the correct reply. Yet there was something strange about the boat. When the sky became lighter, Munson realized belatedly that the sub was a Jap, a small RO-class. Munson set up and fired two stern tubes just as the submarine dived. Both torpedoes, set for 6 feet, prematured. After that Munson— on his own—deactivated the magnetic exploder on all his torpedoes.

Munson continued to patrol off Indochina. Near Camranh Bay he laid a small minefield. A week later, he picked up a cargo vessel with one escort. He fired four torpedoes and sank *Busho Maru*, 2,500 tons. On the way home, transiting Alice Channel between the Sulu and Celebes seas, Munson battle-surfaced on a small subchaser and sank it.

During this action, Munson received an important Ultra from Christie. A large convoy was leaving the island of Halmahera, east of Makassar Passage, northbound, and Munson was directed to take station south of Talaud Island to intercept. He waited round for two days with no sign of the convoy. On the morning of February 15, as he was telling Frank Walker to set a course for Fremantle, the periscope watch reported a contact. It turned out to be the expected convoy: seven ships.

Munson tracked it during the day, watching two more ships join up. After dark, he surfaced and attacked. In his first salvo, Munson fired nine torpedoes at several of the ships. He saw hits in at least three ships, but escorts firing big shells drove him under. He reloaded the bow tube with his last six torpedoes and fired them all at a single big target. The fire-control party misjudged the ship's speed, however, and only one of the five hit. Having expended all his torpedoes, Munson cleared the area and set course for Fremantle.

Upon completing this patrol, for which he received high praise and a second Navy Cross, Munson stepped down as skipper and went to the Squadron Sixteen staff. His exec, Frank Walker, moved up to take command.

Bonefish was a very special boat. She had been sponsored at launching by Mrs. Freeland Daubin at Electric Boat about the time Christie's wife christened another boat, *Corvina.* Christie chose *Bonefish* for his new "flagship." She was commanded by Thomas Wesley Hogan, who had made three war patrols on *Nautilus* under Bill Brockman. The exec was Guy Edward O'Neil, Jr., who had made five patrols on *Salmon* under Gene McKinney.

Jumping off from Darwin, Hogan patrolled off the Indochina coast. Helped by numerous Ultra reports, he found no end of targets. In eight dogged attacks, Hogan fired off all his torpedoes, returning to Fremantle after forty-five days. Christie had followed Hogan's progress by Ultra intercepts and, when he returned to port, credited him with sinking six ships for 40,000 tons. Postwar accounting cut this total to three ships for 24,000 tons, but it was still one of the best patrols of the war; two of the ships were large and important troop transports: *Kashima Maru,* 10,000 tons, and *Teibi Maru,* 10,000 tons.

Christie surprised Hogan, on his arrival in Fremantle, by visiting the boat at seven thirty in the morning to give him a Navy Cross, and he wrote ecstatically in his diary, "This morning, Hogan's *Bonefish* arrived—my flag—with 40,000 tons. . . . His patrol was exceptional in all respects . . . ship arrived clean and fit."

Christie, like Lockwood, was anxious to make a "brief" submarine war patrol. In October, a situation arose that seemed made to order. An air force B-24 crew went down on Celebes, where the men hid out, awaiting rescue. Mac-Arthur ordered a submarine sent there to pick up the crew, leaving from and returning to Darwin.

Christie proposed to his boss—by telephone—that he make this brief patrol. He believed he could fly to Darwin, join the submarine for the rescue mission, patrol Ambon, return to Darwin, and fly back to Fremantle, all in about twelve days. His boss denied this request as he had others. Christie sent instead one of the new Squadron Sixteen division commanders, Philip Gardner ("P.G.") Nichols.

The submarine selected for this special mission was a

new Squadron Sixteen boat, *Capelin*, commanded by Steam Marshall, who had made an Empire patrol on ancient *Cuttlefish*.

P.G. Nichols joined *Capelin* in Darwin. She got under way on October 30. En route, the special mission to pick up the downed aviators was canceled. Marshall patrolled in Molucca Sea, around Ceram. On November 11, Armistice Day, Christie sent Marshall an Ultra reporting an important convoy off Ceram, escorted by two destroyers. "It was fifteen minutes late," Nichols recalled.

While Nichols watched, feeling rather like a fifth wheel, Marshall attacked the convoy. His first two torpedoes prematured, one on one side of his target, the other on the other. "After that we disconnected the Mark VI magnetic exploder," Nichols recalled, "and shot again for contact. He was running for the beach at Ceram, but we blew him up." Marshall claimed a second ship, but postwar analysis confirmed only one for 3,000 tons.

In the wake of the attack, the two destroyers attacked *Capelin* with depth charges. "We had a noisy bow plane," Nichols recalled, "and a defective conning tower hatch and radar tube." Nichols believed it would be prudent for Marshall to return to Darwin for repairs before continuing the patrol. After seventeen days, *Capelin* put into Darwin.

While there, Nichols telephoned Christie to report on the results of this first leg of the patrol, asking permission to make the second leg. Christie refused permission, informing Nichols that during his absence Christie's chief of staff, Tex McLean, had been ordered back to the States to command a new squadron of boats and that Nichols had been selected as McLean's replacement.

Nichols was somewhat astonished by all this, and a little disappointed. He was not one of Christie's admirers. He got off *Capelin* and returned to Fremantle to his new job.

Steam Marshall took *Capelin* to Makassar Strait. On December 1 *Capelin* encountered Tom Hogan in *Bonefish*, who was slashing away at a convoy, and Walt Griffith in *Bowfin*, returning from his famous first patrol off Indochina. Hogan had sunk two ships. Griffith was out of torpedoes and, having sighted both *Capelin* and *Bonefish*, continued on to Fremantle.

Later Hogan wrote:

On December 2, we sighted Capelin . . . heading west about 10 miles off the coast. He was about 5 miles away and dove right away. By sonar I told him who I was, about the convoy, and named him by his nickname: "Steam." I told him that since he was in the area I was going to leave what was left of the convoy to him and would continue on to my patrol area. He receipted for the message by sonar. I left and did not see him again.

Nor did anyone else. *Capelin* disappeared without a trace with all hands.

Another new Squadron Sixteen boat met much the same fate. It was *Cisco,* under the much-loved and much-respected Jim Coe, who had commanded *S-39* and *Skipjack* during the first year of the war.

After touching at Brisbane, *Cisco* topped off her fuel tanks in Darwin. Coe and his exec, August Frederick Weinel (who stood first in the class of 1936) left Darwin on September 18. That same evening, *Cisco* returned with a faulty main hydraulic system. After repairs, Coe sailed again the following day. According to his orders, on September 28 Coe should have been in the middle of the Sulu Sea, but nothing was ever heard from him.

In postwar Japanese records it was learned that on that date and at that place the Japanese discovered a U.S. submarine and delivered a well-coordinated air and sea attack. One Japanese pilot reported, "Found a sub trailing oil. Bombing. Ships cooperated with us. The oil continued to gush out, even on the 10th of October."

All things considered—submarine losses, the great number of torpedo failures—Christie's offensive against the Japanese tankers produced good results. Of forty-three ships sunk in the fall, twelve were tankers. Others had been damaged. The loss or delay in arrival of this oil was beginning to be felt at Truk and also in Japan itself. The pity was that the offensive had not been launched sooner.

14

THE FIRST WOLF PACKS

On November 20, 1943, Nimitz's amphibian forces, supported by large fast carrier task forces, launched the long-awaited Central Pacific drive with the invasion of Tarawa and Makin Islands in the Gilberts. About a dozen of Lockwood's submarines were assigned to various roles in this offensive—"lifeguarding" (picking up downed naval aviators), photographing beaches, and standing by to intercept Japanese ships bringing reinforcements.

But the majority of Lockwood's boats pressed the war of attrition against Japanese maritime forces. Now that the Mark IV torpedo defects had been corrected and the long-overdue Mark XVIII electric torpedo (which left no wake) had begun to arrive, the Pearl Harbor submarine force began to inflict severe damage on the Japanese.

Mush Morton in *Wahoo*, smarting from his luckless fourth patrol in the Sea of Japan in August, asked to return there. Lockwood gave his permission, assigning Eugene Sands in *Sawfish* to go with him. Although the Mark XVIII electric torpedo had not yet been fully debugged, Lockwood suggested that Morton and Sands take along a mixed load of these and Mark XIVs.

Sawfish and *Wahoo* got under way about September 10, going by different routes to La Pérouse Strait. Morton went into the Japan Sea first, with Sands following by a few days. Nothing further was ever heard from Morton.

On October 5, the Japanese news agency Domei announced to the world that a "steamer" was sunk by an American submarine off the west coast of Honshu near

Tsushima Strait, with the loss of 544 lives. This was the 8,000-ton *Konron Maru*. In addition, JANAC showed that Morton sank three other ships for 5,300 tons, making the total for this last patrol four ships for about 13,000 tons.

Japanese records also reported that on October 11, the date *Wahoo* was due to exit through La Pérouse, an anti-submarine aircraft found a submarine and attacked, dropping three depth charges. After Lockwood examined these records, he concluded that this attack fatally holed *Wahoo* and that she plunged to the bottom in the strait, taking down "Mush the Magnificent" and all hands.

Meanwhile, Sands in *Sawfish* experienced enough torpedo problems to drive an ordinary man berserk. During his eighteen days in or near the Sea of Japan, he made contact with an estimated eighteen ships. He made seven attacks, three against one freighter. Three electrics fishtailed while leaving the tubes, struck the shutters, and "were not heard to run thereafter." One electric plunged straight to the bottom. Seven electrics ran astern of the intended targets. The first Mark XIV broached and ran erratically. In a spread of three Mark XIVs, two hit the targets but were duds.

In his seven attacks, Sands had inflicted no damage on the enemy. When he returned to port, his patrol was declared unsuccessful. In his endorsement to the patrol report, Charles Wilkes ("Gin") Styer wrote, "The fourth war patrol of the *Sawfish* is one of the first in which the Mark XVIII torpedoes were extensively employed. The results were disappointing, and indications are that considerable testing and proof firing will be necessary before the Mark XVIII is satisfactory for service use."

The loss of Morton and *Wahoo* caused profound shock in the submarine force. Lockwood and Voge ceased all further forays into the Sea of Japan. Morton was posthumously awarded a fourth Navy Cross. When he died, his claimed sinkings exceeded those of any other submarine skipper: seventeen ships for 100,000 tons. In the postwar accounting, this was readjusted to nineteen ships for about 55,000 tons, leaving Morton, in terms of individual ships sunk, one of the top three skippers of the war.

After Roy Benson left *Trigger*, Lockwood gave the boat to Dusty Dornin, who had made six war patrols on *Gudgeon*. He was the first officer from the class of 1935 to command a Pearl Harbor boat. Ned Beach, now a veteran of six war patrols, remained on *Trigger* as exec. In the fall of 1943 Dornin made two spectacular patrols, both in the East China Sea.

On the evening of September 17, Dornin found an unescorted two-ship convoy and attacked. Using the Morton-O'Kane technique of exec on periscope or on the bridge, Dornin fired four torpedoes—his first of the war as skipper —at one ship. He got two hits, but both were duds. The ship turned to ram, firing deck guns, and Dornin submerged, ordering tubes reloaded. Shortly after midnight, he swung in for a second attack by periscope, firing four torpedoes. Two hit. "The target sank in two minutes," Dornin reported. "All hands in the conning tower got a look. . . . Have heard of targets sinking fast, but this is the first time this ship or this Commanding Officer has ever experienced such a thing. It seems very unreal."

For the next few days, *Trigger* was buffeted and held down by heavy weather, the fringes of a typhoon passing to eastward. However, on September 21 *Trigger* picked up another convoy: six ships with air escort. It was composed of one very large tanker, two smaller tankers, and three old freighters. Dornin moved *Trigger* in for a night surface attack, firing the rest of his torpedoes in a period of three and a half hours. Three confirmed ships went down, two tankers and a freighter. Total for the patrol: four ships for 27,095 tons. In terms of confirmed tonnage sunk, it was the third best war patrol thus far—after Wogan on *Tarpon*'s sixth patrol (27,910 tons) and Burlingame on *Silverside*'s fourth (27,798).

Dornin returned *Trigger* to Midway on September 30. On that very day, his classmate and football buddy, Slade Cutter, assumed command of *Seahorse* from Donald McGregor. Both men had much to celebrate, and they did so with gusto.

Trigger and *Seahorse* set off for patrol two days apart, *Seahorse* on October 20, *Trigger* on October 22. Dornin retained Beach for his exec; Cutter's exec was John Patterson ("Speed") Currie. Cutter said later, "I trained my *Seahorse* crew the same way I did my battleship *Idaho* football team years before. On each training period we would start with the individual and the fundamentals, then on to department training, then molding all departments into a team for surface gunfire and another team for battle stations, torpedo. The important thing was to develop in each man self-confidence and confidence in his team."

On the way to station, while still several hundred miles off the coast of Japan, Cutter sighted an unarmed fishing trawler. He was hesitant about attacking this puny target, but his young officers were hungry for battle so he ordered battle surface. The trawler went down, leaving nine fishermen in the water. Later, the gun crew sank another from the same little fleet.

His officers, Cutter recalled later, "loved gun action." When another trawler came into sight, they made ready for battle again. However, Cutter had been sickened by the slaughter and decided not to attack. Later he said, "One of my officers came to me with our operation order, which said something like 'You shall sink all vessels encountered, by torpedoes or gunfire.' He argued that these boats were feeding the Japanese and might be serving as aircraft and submarine warning patrols. So I said, 'Oh, hell,' or something like that and ordered battle stations surface. Another trawler went down. No survivors." All this was too bloodthirsty for Cutter. He never authorized another gun attack.

While Dornin and Cutter were proceeding westward, Ignatius Joseph ("Pete") Galantin in *Halibut,* patrolling off Bungo Suido, got on the trail of a large well-escorted convoy. He made a daylight attack, but the convoy veered away, leaving *Halibut* out in left field. Galantin fired a long-range low-speed shot which may have hit a freighter. Escorts pinned him down, but after dark he surfaced, continued trailing, and got off a contact report to Lockwood.

On the night of November 1–2, both Dornin and Cutter (unaware of the other's presence) stumbled into this convoy and attacked. Dornin shot first, sinking a large transport and a freighter, damaging others. Cutter, somewhat mystified by Dornin's initial torpedo explosion, shot next, sinking a large freighter and transport, damaging others. Pete Galantin in *Halibut* finally caught up and also attacked, sinking one freighter. Total: five ships, 26,400 tons.

Because of a rare lapse in Dick Voge's efficient staff organization, there was an amusing aftermath to this engagement which gave rise to another submarine legend that died hard. After receiving word from both Dornin and Cutter on their attacks, a junior officer on Voge's staff wondered if they might not be claiming the same ships sunk, so without Voge's knowledge he naïvely—and stupidly—sent each skipper a dispatch raising the question. This was the first indication to both Cutter and Dornin that they had attacked the same convoy. Dornin reacted calmly, but Cutter, who could be a bull in a china shop on occasion, was indignant that Pearl Harbor had questioned his veracity. He responded with a furious message. The following night, Lockwood, having upbraided the junior officer who caused the flap, sent an apology to Dornin and Cutter. All submarines on patrol copied these messages, and many skippers had a good laugh. But the episode gave rise to a myth that Dornin and Cutter delighted in poaching on one another's areas.

Following this, Dornin and Cutter went on to adjacent areas in the East China Sea, while Galantin returned to Bungo Suido. Dornin sank two additional ships and Cutter three, including a big tanker. Dornin's total confirmed score: four ships for 15,114 tons; Cutter's: five ships, 27,579 tons, one of the best patrols of the war. In terms of confirmed tonnage, Cutter's patrol now ranked third—after Wogan's and Burlingame's.

During the invasion of the Gilberts, Lockwood placed two submarines, *Searaven* and *Sculpin*, directly east of Truk, near the islands of Oroluk and Ponape. Both boats were commanded by new skippers. Fred Connaway commanded *Sculpin*. Melvin Hulquist Dry commanded *Searaven*. Dry sank a 10,000-ton tanker off Ponape. Connaway was not so lucky.

Embarked on Connaway's *Sculpin* was a senior officer, John Philip Cromwell, then commanding Division 43. Lockwood had sent Cromwell on *Sculpin* in case he wanted to form a wolf pack of *Sculpin* and *Searaven* or possibly *Sculpin* and *Apogon*. Cromwell had been fully briefed on all the plans for the invasion and knew much more about Ultra than the ordinary submarine skipper.

On the night of November 18, Connaway picked up a convoy en route from Truk to the Marshalls. He bent on full power to make an end around and get into position for a submerged attack at dawn. As he was preparing to attack, the convoy saw *Sculpin*'s periscope and turned toward the submarine as if to ram. Connaway went deep. When the convoy had passed over, he surfaced to make another end around in broad daylight.

The convoy commander was a clever fighter. He had left a "sleeper" behind, the destroyer *Yamagumo*. It spotted *Sculpin* and attacked, forcing Connaway to make a quick dive. *Yamagumo* dropped a barrage of depth charges, causing some damage. Connaway went deep to avoid, remaining submerged for several hours.

About noon, Connaway decided to come up again and have a look around. As he was rising, the depth gauge stuck at 125 feet. Not realizing this, the temporary diving officer, Ensign W. M. Fielder, a reservist, kept pumping water overboard and planing up. So deceived, Fielder broached the boat, and *Yamagumo*, which was still lurking nearby, charged immediately.

As Connaway hurriedly took *Sculpin* back down, eighteen depth charges exploded all around the boat, inflicting severe damage. There were serious leaks, and the planes and steering gear went out of commission. Connaway decided his best course was to surface and try to brazen it out with his deck gun. He passed the order and brought *Sculpin* back to the surface.

It was a one-sided engagement, with *Sculpin* the loser. One of *Yamagumo*'s first salvos hit the bridge, killing Connaway, his exec, Nelson John Allen, and the gunnery officer, Joseph Rollie DeFrees, Jr. Command of *Sculpin* passed to the senior officer, Lieutenant G. E. Brown, Jr., another reservist. He decided to scuttle and passed the word: "Abandon ship." The crew struggled into life jackets, and the chief of the boat opened the vents.

Division Commander John Cromwell, only thirteen days at sea on his first war patrol, was in a predicament. If he abandoned ship and was taken prisoner, the Japanese might torture him and obtain not only the secrets of the invasion but also the secrets of Ultra. He told Brown that he "knew too much" and elected to go down with *Sculpin*. Ensign Fielder, perhaps feeling responsible for the disaster, made the same decision. These two and ten others—some dead, some probably fearing capture—rode the ship down for the last time.

In all, half of *Sculpin*'s total crew of eighty-four officers and men were rescued by the Japanese: Brown and two other officers and thirty-nine enlisted men. Of these, one crewman, badly wounded, was thrown over the side. Another, also wounded, managed to escape this fate by wrenching free and hiding among the other crewmen of *Sculpin*. The surviving forty-one were taken into Truk, where for ten days they were interrogated by Japanese intelligence officers. After this grilling, they were divided into two groups for transport to Japan on two of the carriers that had ferried aircraft to Truk: twenty-one on *Chuyo*, twenty on *Unyo*.

Later, when Lockwood learned what had happened on *Sculpin*, he recommended John Cromwell for the Medal of Honor. It was approved and awarded to his widow after the war.

Farther north, off Japan, lay *Sailfish*, making her tenth war patrol. Command of the boat had been given to Bob Ward, class of 1935, who had been exec to Herb Andrews on *Gurnard* during his famous rugged first patrol off the Palaus.

When *Chuyo* and *Unyo* left Truk for Japan, Voge flashed word on Ultra. Ward moved *Sailfish* into intercept position, fighting mountainous seas generated by a winter typhoon. Nearing Japan, the Japanese carrier force went on submarine alert, but when it entered the full fury of the typhoon the task force commander rescinded the alert and stopped zigzagging, believing the ships safe in such foul weather.

On the evening of December 3, after a long day submerged, Ward came to the surface. The typhoon raged. The seas were "tremendous"; winds blew at 50 knots. Near midnight, Ward picked up the carrier force on radar, range 9,000 yards. Owing to the weather, Ward abandoned any idea of a methodical approach. He submerged to radar depth and, at twelve minutes after midnight, fired four bow tubes at one of the largest radar pips, range 2,100 yards. He heard two distinct and solid hits.

A destroyer charged out of the howling darkness, forcing Ward deep. It dropped twenty-one depth charges, two close, nineteen distant. During this interlude, Ward reloaded his torpedo tubes, and at about 2 A.M. he returned to the surface to see what was going on. His radar showed pips all around, including one moving very slowly. Ward tracked, working in heavy seas to attain firing position, still not sure what he had hit or what the slow-moving target might be.

With morning light coming on, Ward hurried to shoot again. He fired three more bow torpedoes, range 3,200 yards. He heard and observed two torpedo hits, including a puff of fire. The target replied with a barrage of bullets, fired first willy-nilly, then directly at *Sailfish*. Ward submerged to reload and make another attack.

At 7:58 A.M., Ward finally got a glimpse of his wounded target. It was an aircraft carrier, unmoving, with a small list to port and slightly down by the stern. There were "enough people on deck aft to populate a fair size village." To Ward, it seemed they were preparing to abandon ship. To hurry them on, he fired three more torpedoes at the carrier, range 1,700 yards. The sonarman reported "tremendous" breaking-up noises, but high waves prevented Ward from obtaining visual confirmation of hits.

Passing down the side of the carrier, Ward suddenly saw another big ship: a heavy cruiser. The cruiser apparently saw *Sailfish*'s periscope. It charged dead on and Ward, fearing *Sailfish* might broach in the heavy seas, ordered 90 feet. He obtained sonar data on the cruiser, but by the time he could set up to fire she was astern and disappearing in the mountainous seas. Ward chastised himself, stating in his report that he "threw away the chance of a lifetime."

After reloading, Ward crept back to look for the wounded carrier but could find no sign of it: *Chuyo*, 20,000 tons, had gone down with all hands, taking with her the survivors of *Sculpin* she was carrying. She was the first Japanese aircraft carrier sunk by a U.S. submarine. When submariners learned later of the Americans aboard, they would remark on the irony. In 1939, *Sculpin* had found and stood by *Squalus* when she sank. Now *Squalus*, renamed *Sailfish*, had killed half the survivors of *Sculpin*. (But none of the original crew that found *Squalus* was among them. By that time—four and a half years later —all the old hands had rotated to other duty.)

Happily ignorant of this fact, Ward continued to his patrol station. On December 7, while cruising on the surface, he was caught by a Japanese plane and badly bombed and strafed. On December 13, he picked up a two-ship convoy with two escorts. He sank one, *Totai Maru*, 3,000 tons, and damaged the other. On December 21, he found another convoy: six big transports, escorted by three destroyers. He fired three stern tubes into the formation and sank the freighter *Uyo Maru*, 6,400 tons. During the attack, the diving officer lost control of the boat and broached. Ward sent all off-duty men to the forward torpedo room, and *Sailfish* went down like a rock to 327 feet before Ward could check her. The destroyers attacked, dropping thirty-one depth charges, some very close.

When Ward returned to Pearl Harbor, he was greeted by Lockwood, standing on the pier with a broad smile. Later, after presenting Ward his first Navy Cross, Lockwood wrote, "This patrol can be considered one of the most outstanding patrols of the war." Ward was credited with three ships for 35,729 tons and damage to one for 7,000 tons. Postwar analysis showed that his sinking claims were nearly accurate: three ships, 29,571 tons. In terms of confirmed tonnage, it was the best patrol of the war to date.

When George Herrick Wales returned *Pogy* from the Palaus, where his third patrol had resulted in damage to some ships and the sinking of a big transport, *Maebashi Maru*, 7,000 tons, he was transferred to staff and Lockwood gave *Pogy* to her former exec, Ralph Marion Metcalf, another from 1935.

Metcalf returned *Pogy* to the Palaus. On the way, he received an important Ultra on a big navy auxiliary and a submarine tender, *Soyo Maru*. Metcalf skillfully intercepted the ships east of the Marianas on the night of December 7, fired at both ships simultaneously, and obtained hits for damage. After dark, he surfaced and tracked *Soyo Maru*, attacking again after moonset while a destroyer circled nearby. She blew up and sank. Six days later, off the Palaus, Metcalf found a three-ship convoy standing out with escorts. Metcalf fired, sinking one 4,000-ton freighter. The escorts counterattacked, disabling *Pogy*'s fire-control system. Metcalf was forced to break off the patrol and return to Midway for repairs. Total time at sea: twenty-nine days. Total confirmed damage to the enemy: two ships sunk for 10,000 tons.

John Starr Coye, Jr., making his third patrol in *Silversides,* replaced Metcalf at Palau. On the night of December 29, Coye (who had sunk four ships on his previous patrol) picked up a convoy and methodically sank three freighters. On January 2, a Japanese submarine found *Silversides* and fired three torpedoes. The officer of the deck, who saw the periscope, turned *Silversides* to comb the track—run parallel with the torpedoes to reduce the target area and thus the chance of being hit. One torpedo passed down the starboard side, range 50 yards; another came down the port side, range 75 yards.

Between September and late January, Roy Gross in *Seawolf* completed two patrols to the Hong Kong area —his specialty. On the first he sank two ships. On the second, on January 10, he picked up a seven-ship convoy and engaged in one of the most dogged submarine attacks of the war.

For his first attack on the convoy, Gross got in close and fired seven torpedoes. With this salvo he sank two big freighters and damaged others. The convoy scattered, the ships firing deck guns willy-nilly. A destroyer found *Seawolf* and dropped nine close depth charges.

Gross was held down the rest of the afternoon by the destroyer escorts and aircraft circling overhead. After dark he surfaced in bright moonlight. Finding one crippled ship being towed by another, he set up on the towing ship and fired three torpedoes, obtaining a hit. Then he fired all four stern tubes at both the crippled ship and the now-damaged towing ship, again obtaining hits. Soon the towing ship disappeared. Dodging destroyers and lifeboats filled with survivors, Gross moved in to fire three torpedoes at the cripple. All three hit, and the ship went down. With destroyers pursuing and firing, Gross hauled clear and submerged, leaving the scene of attack.

Two days later, January 14, Gross received an Ultra from Dick Voge to intercept another convoy and left his regular patrol area in pursuit. On the way, he stumbled across another convoy, four freighters and two escorts. "Although assigned mission was important," Gross wrote, "decided to proceed on the bird-in-the-hand theory." Later he noted, "It is my recollection that very many Ultras were false alarms, whether from errors in decoding, uncooperative convoy commanders who changed their mind (and course) after the decoding, or maybe we on the boats made our own errors in copying the . . . schedules and/or in also decoding."

Gross made a night surface attack, firing his last four bow torpedoes. Two hits which started fires led Gross to believe the ship—a big freighter—was loaded with aviation gasoline. It sank. Wrote Gross, "This may keep some of the Rabaul fliers grounded for a while."

Having fired all his torpedoes, Gross sent off a contact report to Dick Voge. Voge alerted Acey Burrows, patrolling nearby in *Whale*, and Burrows hurried to close the convoy.

While trailing the convoy and waiting for Burrows, Gross decided to make a gun attack on one ship he believed to be a tanker full of aviation gasoline. He reasoned that one hit with his 3-inch gun might blow her up. He battle-surfaced and fired off six inaccurate rounds. When he heard shells "whistling close" Gross broke off the gun attack, dropped back out of range, and continued trailing.

In time, Burrows showed up. In his first attack, he sank *Denmark Maru*, a freighter of 5,870 tons. Standing off to one side, Gross watched and listened to the explosions with satisfaction. The convoy scattered. One ship, apparently intent on going on alone, came toward Gross.

Gross reasoned that a few rounds from his deck gun might turn the ship back toward *Whale*, so for the second time he sent his gun crews to battle station surface. His men fired off about thirty rounds. The ship returned the fire with big guns. However, Gross's gambit worked; the ship turned back toward *Whale*. Gross alerted Burrows, who attacked and sank the ship, *Tarushima Maru*, 4,800 tons.

When Gross returned to port, Lockwood was pleased. In a private note to Gross, he said, "Excellent, aggressive, and long headed patrol." Postwar records credited Gross with what he claimed: four ships, 23,361 tons. In addition, Lockwood gave Gross half credit with Burrows for the last ship sunk. This gave Gross a total of four and a half confirmed ships for 25,793 tons, one of the best

patrols of the war. Burrows received credit for one and
a half ships for 8,322 tons, both due to Gross's contact
report.

Lockwood, Christie and Fife had resisted the wolf-pack
concept for a number of reasons. Directing wolf packs,
either from home base or in the operating area, required
much radio chatter which could be picked up by the
enemy, disclosing the presence of the pack. Because of
this, the German submarine force had suffered heavy
losses in the Atlantic. Moreover, there was the ever-
present danger that in the confusion of battle, one sub
might sink another, a fate so appalling few liked to con-
template it. But in the fall of 1943, Lockwood organized,
trained and sent formal wolf packs on patrol.

The first formal Pearl Harbor wolf pack was commanded by Swede Momsen. His group consisted of three
boats: *Shad,* recently arrived from a long tour in Scotland, commanded by Edgar John MacGregor III; a brand-
new boat, *Cero,* in charge of the old hand, Dave White,
helped by his exec, Dave McClintock, who had been with
White on *Plunger;* and *Grayback,* returned from overhaul
at Mare Island with a new skipper, John Anderson Moore.

Although Johnny Moore lacked experience in fleet
boats, he was obviously headed for outstanding performance. An athlete at the Naval Academy (boxing and
soccer), he had made a fine record in R and S boats. His
classmate Hank Munson said later, "Professionally, Johnny
was tops and we placed him second to nobody in the
class"; MacGregor in *Shad* recalled that Moore was a "go-
getter" with a "vivacious personality." During refit, *Grayback* had been fitted with a 5-inch gun, one of the first
boats in the Pearl Harbor command to receive one. Mac-
Gregor recalled that Moore was very excited about the
big gun and talked enthusiastically about how he planned
to use it.

Momsen, who had never made a war patrol, chose to
fly his flag with the most experienced skipper, Dave White.
Before setting off, the three skippers and their execs
game-boarded tactics with Momsen on the black and
white tile dance floor of the sub base officers' club. Momsen also took the boats to sea, practicing against friendly
convoys operating between California and Pearl Harbor.

The three boats communicated with one another in code by means of a short-range radio known as the TBS (talk between ships).

In evolving wolf-pack tactics, caution was the watchword. The skippers were told not to use the radio often, lest Japanese antisubmarine warfare forces home in on the transmissions. The three boats would not attack a convoy simultaneously, lest they hit each other. One boat would attack first, then drop behind the convoy to reload and serve as a "trailer" to pick up damaged ships. The other two boats would take station on the starboard and port flanks of the convoy, attacking alternately in the hope that one attack would turn the convoy toward the other.

Momsen took his pack to the East China Sea near Okinawa to interdict the flow of traffic between Honshu and Formosa Strait. Although he received a steady—and useful—flow of Ultras, the pack was never able to solve communications and navigational problems sufficiently to make a well-coordinated attack. In effect, the pack was a "joint search" unit rather than a "joint attack" unit.

On October 12, Dave White in *Cero* attacked a three-ship convoy escorted by destroyers, damaging one freighter. The following day, Moore in *Grayback* picked up a convoy escorted by two light cruisers. He couldn't get into position on the cruisers, but that night he sank a 7,000-ton transport. About two days later, MacGregor in *Shad*, acting on an Ultra dispatch, intercepted an enemy task force composed of three or four heavy cruisers and possibly an escort carrier. MacGregor fired five torpedoes at the cruisers and counted three hits. A second attack was fouled when destroyers hove around and delivered a severe depth-charging. After dark, MacGregor surfaced and got off a contact report, but by then the pack was scattered, chasing other contacts. The next day, Moore in *Grayback* sank another 7,000-ton transport.

Five days later, the pack received word of an escorted four-ship troop convoy. In a nearer approximation of a wolf-pack attack, Moore in *Grayback* and MacGregor in *Shad* both attacked the same set of ships. Each put torpedoes into a big transport, *Fuji Maru*, 9,138 tons, and later were given one-half credit each for sinking her.

When the boats returned to Pearl Harbor, Lockwood called this pioneering wolf pack a complete success and awarded Swede Momsen a Navy Cross. The citation credited the pack with sinking five ships for 38,000 tons and damage to eight ships for 63,000 tons. In fact, only three ships had been sunk for 23,500 tons, two and a half for 19,000 tons by Moore in *Grayback* and one half for 4,500 tons by MacGregor in *Shad*.

The officers involved in the first pack had mixed feelings. Momsen believed the pack would be more effective if controlled from shore, à la Doenitz. MacGregor thought the whole thing a waste of time and effort and believed boats would do better operating alone. Everybody criticized the poor communications, which had, in effect, rendered the pack inoperable as a coordinated attack unit. On return to port, *Shad* was sent back for overhaul that would keep her out of combat for the next eight months. MacGregor, who had made a total of five patrols, went to the Submarine School as an instructor.

Later, Johnny Moore conducted a brilliant second patrol in the East China Sea. On the night of December 18, he picked up a four-ship convoy with three escorts. Sinking one of the freighters by periscope attack, he surfaced to chase the others. One of the escorts, *Numakaze*, a 1,300-ton destroyer, had lagged behind to trap *Grayback*. When Moore surfaced, the destroyer attacked, charging in from the stern. Moore dived and let go four stern tubes. *Numakaze* sank so quickly she was unable to get off a radio report. Two nights later, Moore picked up another convoy of six ships. He fired a spread of nine torpedoes into the formation, sinking one freighter and damaging others. Escorts drove *Grayback* under, but three hours later Moore surfaced and sank another ship. The following night, he made an attack that failed.

Having exhausted all his torpedoes in five days, Moore returned to port after a round trip of thirty-three days. On the way, he sank a trawler with his 5-inch deck gun. Total confirmed score: four ships, including the destroyer, for 10,000 tons. In two patrols, Moore achieved a confirmed score of six and one-half ships for almost 30,000 tons.

In October Lockwood organized a second wolf pack under Freddy Warder and sent it to the Marianas, to help shut off the flow of Japanese shipping during the invasion of Tarawa. The three boats were Sam Dealey's *Harder*, Chuck Triebel's *Snook*, and *Pargo*, commanded by Ian Crawford Eddy.

The codebreakers supplied Warder (who rode Eddy's *Pargo*) with good information on Japanese convoy movements, but communications between the submarines of the pack was poor and the "joint attacks" were not carried out as conceived on paper. On November 12, Sam Dealey picked up a freighter with two small escorts. He made a day periscope attack, firing three torpedoes; the freighter disintegrated. About the same time, Eddy on *Pargo*, making an approach on the same target from a different angle, was surprised to see it blow up in his face. Later that night, Dealey surfaced and sank one of the small escorts with gunfire. On *Snook*, Triebel noted in his log, "Surprised by *Harder*'s message that they had sunk two ships."

For the next week, the pack had no contacts. On November 19, Sam Dealey picked up another convoy: three big freighters with three escorts. He radioed a contact report to Triebel and Eddy. Triebel acknowledged, but there was no word from Eddy. Triebel wrote, "Received enemy's true bearing from *Harder* which was worthless as we did not know *Harder*'s movement during last three hours."

While Triebel flailed around trying to find the convoy, Dealey moved in to attack, with his exec, John Maurer, manning the periscope. Dealey fired ten torpedoes at the three ships, obtaining seven hits. One ship sank, one was badly damaged, and the third ran off. Triebel could hear the shooting and wrote, "Heard depth charges or torpedoes all morning. This was the most frustrated I have ever felt. On the surface at full speed, hearing explosions, and we couldn't make contact."

After firing his ten torpedoes, Sam Dealey was attacked by the three escorts. They drove him deep and dropped sixty-four depth charges. He waited them out until dark and then surfaced to chase the undamaged freighter. Finding it at ten o'clock, he fired four more torpedoes. All missed. He fired three more for two hits. The ship appeared to be sinking.

Dealey closed to 600 yards to give his crew a look through the periscope. What they saw were Japanese working frantically to save their ship, so Dealey set up and fired another torpedo. It ran erratically. He fired another, and it, too, was erratic, as was a third. The fourth, also erratic, circled back toward *Harder,* forcing the boat to go deep. Dealey battle-surfaced to polish off the ship, but return fire drove him off. Later, he wrote, "It was a bitter disappointment not to finish this ship off, but he was a worthy opponent. He won our grudging admiration for his fight, efficiency and unwillingness to give up." Later, when bad weather came up, Dealey decided neither of the damaged ships could survive.

Triebel wrote, "Received *Harder*'s message of torpedo expenditure. Had no idea from it who he had shot or where or when. We had evidently missed the convoy if the *Harder* hadn't sunk it. . . . Sighted *Pargo* and closed for visual rendezvous. Found out a little of what had been going on."

Sam Dealey, out of torpedoes, left the pack. When he returned to port, he claimed five ships sunk (including the small trawler) for 24,800 tons. Postwar records denied Dealey the small freighter he claimed sinking on November 12, but confirmed all three ships of the convoy he attacked on November 19 and 20—for 15,273 tons.

Early in the patrol, the *Harder*'s number four (main) engine, an H.O.R., had broken down completely. Dealey kept the other three in commission by babying them and cannibalizing spare parts from the fourth. When he reached Pearl Harbor, where Lockwood awarded him his third Navy Cross, he was ordered back to Mare Island to re-engine *Harder.* There, Jack Maurer got off to go to his own command and Tiny Lynch moved up to exec.

After Dealey had shoved off, Freddy Warder in *Pargo* was left with only two submarines. They patrolled in company (about 20 to 30 miles apart, searching) for a week without sighting anything worthwhile. Then, on the night of November 28, Eddy and Warder picked up another convoy. Eddy flashed word to Triebel, who was about 40 miles away. Triebel homed in on *Pargo*'s radar emissions. "I believed they knew where the convoy was and [I] didn't want to get left chasing my own shadow 10 miles on a flank again," Triebel wrote.

Without conferring by radio or other means, both submarines maneuvered to attack the four big freighters. Just as Triebel was about to fire his bow tubes, he saw an explosion on the freighter at which he was aiming. He let go six torpedoes. One hit the ship Eddy had already hit, another hit a second ship. At about this same moment, *Pargo*'s radar emission disappeared. For a while, Triebel believed that one of his torpedoes might have hit *Pargo*. But he went on firing—four stern tubes, six more bow tubes, two stern tubes at an escort, four more at a freighter, more stern tubes—until he ran out of torpedoes. Meanwhile, *Pargo*'s radar emissions reappeared, and Triebel breathed easier.

Having shot all his torpedoes, Triebel broke off and returned to port, Warder and Eddy following close behind. Triebel was credited with sinking two ships and damaging two. Eddy was credited with sinking two ships and damaging two. In addition, they both shared one-half credit for damaging the ship both hit. Postwar analysis gave Triebel credit for sinking two ships for 8,500 tons, Eddy two ships for 7,900 tons.

In all, Lockwood credited this second wolf pack with sinking nine ships for 58,000 tons. This was reduced in postwar analysis to seven ships for 31,500 tons. However, the experience soured Dealey, Triebel, and others on the wolf-pack concept. It was obvious that better communications would have to be devised before wolf packs could be effective. Warder suggested, if there were to be future wolf packs, that the pack commander was superfluous and command should be given to the senior skipper.

Following this patrol, Eddy's *Pargo*, another H.O.R. boat, followed *Harder* to Mare Island for new engines.

A third wolf pack set off in December. It was composed of Pete Galantin's *Halibut*; *Haddock*, commanded by John Roach, who had relieved Roy Davenport; and Charles Frederick Brindupke's *Tullibee*. Following Freddy Warder's suggestion that wolf packs be commanded not by a division commander but by the senior skipper of the group, Brindupke took tactical command of the unit. The pack was assigned to the Marianas to intercept men-of-war running between Truk and Japan.

First contact with the enemy was made on January 2 by Brindupke in *Tullibee*, who sighted an I-class submarine off Guam in dawn light. Although there was a floatplane flying nearby, Brindupke remained on the surface, firing four torpedoes from 3,000 yards. The Jap sub evidently saw the torepdoes and evaded. Brindupke dived and went deep. The floatplane attacked *Tullibee,* dropping six bombs.

Having obtained word of an approaching enemy task force, Brindupke ordered his pack to form a scouting line. On January 7 Galantin in *Halibut* saw a heavy cruiser escorted by two destroyers but he was unable to gain attack position. Four days later Galantin saw the tops of one or several battleships, sent off a contact report to the other boats, and chased but couldn't overtake. Neither of the other boats could close. On January 14 Galantin spotted a destroyer, closed, and fired four torpedoes at shallow depth settings. Two, or possibly three, prematured.

After a couple of weeks of this, the three boats rendezvoused one night to plan tactics. Galantin and Roach left *Halibut* and *Haddock* in rubber boats and went on board *Tullibee,* the first time any submarine skipper had ever left his boat at sea. In *Tullibee*'s wardroom, they worked over charts and search plans and exchanged ideas. *Halibut,* which was running low on fuel, tried to refuel from *Tullibee* with a makeshift hose, but the experiment was a failure.

Once again, the boats deployed. On January 19, running on the surface, Beetle Roach in *Haddock* picked up an enemy task force through the high periscope (a periscope watch while on the surface), range 20,000 yards. Roach had no time to get off a contact report. He stayed up for several moments, then dived on the track, watching through the periscope. The force turned out to be a large carrier (identified as *Shokaku*) and a small carrier, escorted by a cruiser leading the formation and several destroyers on the flanks.

The Japanese ships came on swiftly. Roach set up on the large carrier. When the range had closed to 2,100 yards, he fired six torpedoes set for shallow depth; then he took *Haddock* deep. He heard two explosions, then more, followed by "tremendous milling around" of the destroyers. Roach remained deep and made no second attack.

Roach had hit not *Shokaku* but the smaller carrier *Unyo,* which had been hit by David Lee Whelchel in *Steelhead* and Philip Ross in *Halibut* earlier in the year. *Unyo,* badly damaged, limped into Saipan. Following this, all three boats set up watch outside the harbor at Saipan. On January 23, Galantin (who could see *Unyo* clearly through his periscope) tried to get into position at the harbor entrance for a shot, but *Halibut* was driven off by a destroyer. On January 26, Brindupke, standing watch, reported *Unyo* still in the harbor. Two days later he took another look and *Unyo* was gone; evidently she had slipped away during the night.

After that, the wolf pack broke up and returned to base, Brindupke sinking a 500-ton net tender, the only bag for the three boats.

15

SUMMARY: 1943

The second year of the submarine war against Japan was a far better year in every respect than 1942. The three commanders, Lockwood, Christie, and Fife, deployed their submarines more imaginatively. Where in 1942 Pearl Harbor sent only 15 percent of its boats to Empire and East China Sea waters, in 1943 Lockwood sent 50 percent to those waters and for the first time began to exploit the bottleneck in Luzon Strait. Christie and Fife gave up the unrewarding "port watching" and deployed most of their boats seaward, along known shipping lanes. Radar, better Ultra reports, improved Mark XIV torpedo performance, more experienced skippers and crews—all helped.

Twenty months into the war, the force commanders had at last commenced experiments with wolf-packing. However, the three wolf packs sent from Pearl Harbor in the fall of 1943 were more "search" than "attack" units, and it was clear that if wolf-packing was to produce any significant increase in sinkings, much improvement of tactics and gear was needed. Generally, the skippers objected to wolf-packing, especially to having a senior division commander on board making the decisions and trying to coordinate the tactics. All lived in dread that wolf-packing might sooner or later result in the sinking of one friendly submarine by another. But it had begun.

During the year, the three commands conducted about 350 war patrols in the Pacific, about the same number as 1941–42. The three commands claimed and were credited with sinking 443 Japanese men-of-war and merchant ships for 2.9 million tons. According to postwar records, a closer figure would be about 335 ships for 1.5 million tons, still an increase in tonnage of over 100 percent over 1941–42, when 180 ships for 725,000 tons were sunk.

The 1943 sinkings seriously impeded Japanese shipping services. Imports of bulk commodities for 1943 showed a sharp drop, from 19.4 million tons in 1942 to 16.4 million tons in 1943. Japanese ship-building—in all categories except tankers—could no longer keep pace with the losses. At the beginning of 1943, Japan had 5.2 million tons of shipping, excluding tankers. At the end of 1943, the figure stood at 4.1 million, a net loss of about 1.1 million tons of non-tanker shipping.

In terms of tankers alone, the picture was different. Japan began the year with 686,000 tons. During the year, she built more or converted regular ships to tankers. In spite of losing 150,000 tons in tankers to submarines in 1943, she ended the year with a net *increase* in tanker tonnage of 177,000 tons—to 863,000.

During 1943, as the submarine offensive became more effective, Japanese countermeasures grew tougher. The United States lost more than twice as many boats in the Pacific as in 1942: fifteen. Fife lost four, Christie four, and Lockwood seven. Fife lost *Argonaut, Amberjack, Grampus,* and *Triton.* Christie lost *Grenadier, Grayling, Cisco,* and *Capelin.* Lockwood lost *S-44* in Alaska; *Pickerel, Runner,* and *Pompano* off northeast Honshu; *Wahoo* in La Pérouse Strait; and *Corvina* and *Sculpin.* Only three —*Grenadier, S-44,* and *Sculpin*—had survivors (the majority of them sent to work in the mines at Ashio).

As in 1942, enormous effort went into the pursuit of Japanese capital ships with the help of glamorous Ultra reports. These reports (plus lucky finds) resulted in about sixty major ship contacts (compared to only twenty-three in 1942), about ten contacts on battleships and forty-five on aircraft carriers. Two of the battleship contacts were developed into attacks—by Dave Whelchel in *Steelhead* and Gene McKinney in *Skate.* Whelchel missed; McKinney probably slightly damaged *Yamato.*

The approximately forty-five carrier contacts were developed into about thirty attacks. Fourteen of these attacks resulted in possible (but credited) damage to the carrier attacked, notably Roy Benson's attack on *Hiyo* off Tokyo Bay, John Roach's attack on *Unyo* off Saipan, Pete Galantin's attack on a carrier off Bungo Suido, and

Herb Andrews's attack on a carrier off Palau. The great majority of the attacks produced nothing but frayed nerves. One small carrier, *Chuyo,* was sunk by Bob Ward in *Sailfish. Chuyo* was the only major Japanese man-of-war sunk in 1943 by U.S. submarines.

The Japanese submarine war against Allied forces, which had cost the United States the aircraft carriers *Yorktown* and *Wasp* plus severe damage to *Saratoga* and the battleship *North Carolina* in 1942, took a curious—even inexplicable—turn in 1943. For the most part, Japanese submarines were withdrawn from offensive patrolling and assigned to resupply (or evacuation) missions for forces left behind in the Japanese retreat. In 1943, Japanese submarines sank only three worthwhile U.S. Navy vessels: the jeep carrier *Liscome Bay,* the submarine *Corvina,* and a destroyer, *Henley.* Again in 1943, thanks in large part to Ultra, the Japanese submarine losses were heavy: twenty-two in 1943 compared to twenty-three in 1942. Two of these were sunk by U.S. submarines: *I-24* by Albert Hobbs Clark, returning *Trout* from Fremantle to Pearl Harbor, and *I-182* by Walter Gale Ebert in *Scamp.*

The "skipper problem" continued unabated all through the year 1943. Too many were still turning in zero patrols because they lacked aggressiveness. But mainly because of the acute shortage, fewer skippers were relieved for non-productivity: about 25 out of 178, or 14 percent, compared to 30 percent in 1942. To help fill the gap, Lockwood had dipped first to the classes of 1933 and 1934, then to 1935. He was reluctant to dip further, or to appoint experienced and highly qualified reservists to command, for fear of increasing his loss rate.

The Mark XIV torpedo was declared "fixed" in September 1943; the Mark VI magnetic exploder was deactivated by Lockwood in June and by Christie later in the year. As yet it was too early to judge improved results from a statistical standpoint. In fact, the statistics were muddy. In 1942, Pacific submarines on about 350 war patrols had fired 1,442 torpedoes to sink 180 confirmed ships—an average of 8 torpedoes per sinking. In 1943 on about the same number of patrols, Pacific submarines fired 3,937 torpedoes to sink 335 ships—an average of 11.7 torpedoes per sinking (3.7 *more* torpedoes to sink a ship in 1943 than 1942). One factor that distorted the statistics

was that in 1943, Pacific submarines were firing many
more torpedoes at *larger* targets (carriers, tankers), and
though JANAC did not try to confirm damage figures, the
three commands claimed much higher damage figures in
1943, probably with ample justification. In any case, the
three commands reported a higher percentage of *hits* from
experienced skippers using the Mark XIV torpedo.

In general, then, the year 1943 was the year the submarine force, after much trial and error, learned how to
fight a submarine war and got the equipment to do it. The
top men in command—Lockwood, Christie, Fife—had
now gained much experience on the job and knew what
could and could not be done. Dick Voge had brought his
superlative analytical talents to bear on operational problems and devised new strategies and tactics, including—at
last—the wolf pack. The younger skippers moving up to
command were, for the most part, experienced in combat.
The flow of Ultras on Japanese convoys (as well as on fleet
units) was much improved and used to better advantage by
the skippers. By the end of the year, the torpedo shortage
had at last been overcome, and the boats put to sea with a
full load of armament (Mark XIV and XVIII) that on
the whole worked as it was supposed to. Week by week
the number of now-radar-equipped submarines operating
from the three commands increased significantly, and the
crews of most of the boats going on patrol were well
trained. The morale in all three commands was superlative; Mush Morton, Slade Cutter, Dusty Dornin, Benny
Bass, Sam Dealey, and others had seen to that. Submariners
believed, with some justification, that they were beginning
to make a substantial contribution to the defeat of Japan.

In one sense it could be said that the U.S. submarine
war against Japan did not truly begin until the opening
days of 1944. What had come before had been a learning
period, a time of testing, of weeding out, of fixing defects
in weapons, strategy, and tactics, of waiting for sufficient
numbers of submarines and workable torpedoes. Now that
all was set, the contribution of the submarine force would
be more than substantial: it would be decisive.

16

STOPPING THE REINFORCEMENTS

In January, 1944, Nimitz launched phase two of the Central Pacific drive with the invasion of the Marshalls—Majuro, Kwajalein, and Eniwetok. These invasions were followed up with devastating carrier air strikes on the Japanese bastions at Truk, Saipan-Guam, and the distant Palaus. Lockwood's submarines supported all these massive Fleet actions, reconnoitoring, lifeguarding and sinking ships that fled the air strikes. But his main effort was still mounted against Japanese shipping, especially convoys bringing reinforcements to Guam and Saipan, scheduled for invasion in June.

Dusty Dornin and Ned Beach, returning *Trigger* from overhaul at Pearl Harbor, patrolled in the waters between Truk and the Marianas. For the first time, Dusty Dornin found poor hunting. Three weeks dragged by before he made his first contact, and then he botched the attack. The target, discovered on the morning of January 27, was a small RO-class Japanese submarine cruising the surface en route from Guam to Truk. Dornin submerged and moved in close, planning to shoot from 800 yards. However, when Beach raised the periscope for the final look, he found to his consternation that the target had discovered *Trigger* and had zigged directly toward him! The Japanese sub crossed *Trigger*'s bow, then swung stern tubes to bear. Dornin went deep, holding his breath and waiting for the impact of Japanese torpedoes. Inexplicably, the sub did not fire. Later Dornin surfaced to chase, but the sub got away.

Four days later business picked up. *Trigger* found a

convoy, and Dornin swung in for a night surface attack.
Radar showed three big ships and three escorts. Beach
remained on the bridge, feeding bearings through the TBT
(Target Bearing Transmitter, a pair of binoculars in a
swinging mount designed especially for night surface attacks); Dornin was in the conning tower, overseeing the
attack, checking the TDC and radar plan position indicator (PPI) scope. As the attack developed, *Trigger* would
have to fire across the bows of an escorting destroyer at
extremely close range. Dornin decided to shoot six torpedoes, three by radar at the biggest ship and three by TBT
at the destroyer, now broadside to at 700 yards' range, in
a single salvo. On the bridge, Beach saw the three fired at
the destroyer spin off erratically just as she finally saw
the surfaced submarine and turned to attack. Beach called
for flank speed and full rudder, steadied with *Trigger*'s
stern on the swinging destroyer, and fired four stern
tubes. The destroyer, believing *Trigger* had submerged and
possibly confused by the cloud of sudden exhaust smoke
from her straining diesels, paused to drop depth charges,
and the submarine hauled clear from a near thing.

All torpedoes fired from the stern tubes missed, but
one of the initial salvo of three passed through the entire
formation and hit one of the other escorts, *Nasami,* a small
minelayer, which blew up and sank in minutes. Dornin
then ordered a fast end around on the convoy. In a second attack, he again fired at the biggest ship. The ship
blew up and went down. Dawn came before Dornin could
mount a third attack.

Dornin and Beach returned from this patrol crestfallen.
For the first time in many months, *Trigger* returned with
torpedoes in her tubes and racks. However, when they
reached Pearl Harbor, they received a tremendous welcome from Lockwood. The codebreakers had discovered
from Japanese battle-damage reports that the big ship
Dornin had sunk in the convoy was a real prize, the 12,000-
ton submarine tender *Yasukuni Maru*. Recently over-
hauled, she was en route to Truk to replace the light
cruiser *Katori*, then serving as submarine tender and
needed elsewhere. The incoming tender had been loaded
with valuable submarine stores and spare parts and the
cream of the Japanese navy sub repairmen. There were

only forty-three survivors. (Lockwood also believed that his counterpart, Vice Admiral Takeo Takagi, commanding the main Japanese submarine force, known as the Sixth Fleet, was on board, but he was mistaken. Takagi was in Truk, flying his flag on a sister ship of *Yasukuni Maru*, *Heian Maru*.) This was Dornin's final patrol.

Slade Cutter, making his second war patrol in command of *Seahorse*, patrolled off the Palaus. On this trip Cutter took pains to develop the talents of his bright young TDC operator, William Alexander Budding, Jr., then twenty-two.

On the way to the Palaus, while passing near the area where Dornin and Beach were patrolling north of Truk, Cutter picked up a contact—one ship with four escorts. With Budding on the TDC doing "an excellent job," Cutter closed on the surface at night. He maneuvered around the escorts and delivered four electric torpedoes. Two hit, and the freighter went down. (Lending further credence to the untrue submarine legend that Cutter and Dornin constantly poached on one another's area for the fun of it.)

Continuing onward, Cutter took station on the Palaus-Wewak route. He received an Ultra on a convoy and on the afternoon of January 21 picked it up by periscope: two fat freighters "heavily loaded, their decks piled with cargo," and three escorts. After dark, Cutter got into position and attacked. He set up on one freighter and fired three torpedoes from a range of 2,800 yards, obtaining hits in *both* vessels. One sank; one settled low in the water. "The Japs were no more surprised than we," Cutter wrote, "as we entertained no hope whatever of hitting second ship with first salvo. Both targets stopped and commenced firing their deck guns in every direction."

Cutter decided to reattack the settling ship and fired two more torpedoes from a range of 3,120 yards. No hits. Perplexed, Cutter huddled with Budding, then fired two more at 2,600 yards. Again no hits. Another huddle with the fire-control party. The guess was that the TBT on the bridge was either out altogether or putting out erroneous information. They were right and fixed it. "Regretting the waste of precious torpedoes," Cutter turned his stern to the target and fired two more from 2,250 yards. Later, he wrote:

At exactly the correct time (to the second) the first torpedo struck just abaft the stack. The target blew up and burst into flame. With the target brilliantly illuminated, the second torpedo hit forward of the bridge and the ship immediately sank. After she went down explosions were seen on the surface of the water, obviously gasoline drums exploding. During our retirement and for over an hour, the surface of the water where the target had sunk was a mass of burning gasoline. All hands were given an opportunity to witness the spectacular show and enjoy the unique experience of "below-decks-men" actually seeing the results of their work.

After sinking these two ships, Cutter moved *Seahorse* to Palau. On January 28 he spotted three freighters coming out, closely escorted. Cutter tracked this convoy for thirty-two hours before the escorts grew lax and gave him an opening. He fired three torpedoes at one of the freighters, obtaining three hits. The first two set the ship on fire; the third blew her stern off. It sank stern first, vertically.

Harassed by escorts and aircraft, Cutter continued to pursue this convoy for the next forty-eight hours. Shortly after midnight on February 1, he got into position and fired four stern tubes at a second freighter. All missed. He came around and fired two bow tubes. No hits. With only two torpedoes remaining in his stern tubes, Cutter fired them both in a quick setup from an unfavorable position. He thought he missed and went deep to avoid a charging escort. While depth charges exploded around *Seahorse,* Cutter heard his torpedoes hit the target, followed by many light explosions. "They sounded like strings of Chinese firecrackers," Cutter wrote, "and indicated either ammunition or gasoline drums going off." Later he surfaced and observed, "Scene of sinking a mass of gasoline flames with drums still exploding on the surface." In all, the convoy chase had lasted eighty hours, one of the longest and most tenacious on record.

Postwar records credited Cutter with sinking five ships on this patrol. Total score for two patrols: ten confirmed ships sunk.

A new boat joined those patrolling off Truk. This was *Tang,* commanded by Dick O'Kane. O'Kane and Morton had been quite a team. How would O'Kane do alone?

Tang came to her area by way of Wake, lifeguarding the air strikes on January 30 and February 5. On the morning of February 17, following the air strike on Truk, O'Kane picked up a fleeing convoy. During the approach, he was driven down but evaded, reapproached, and fired four stern tubes sinking the big freighter *Gyoten Maru,* 6,800 tons. He trailed the convoy but was not able to get off another shot. After that, *Tang* moved up to Saipan to stand by for the carrier air strike.

On the night of February 22, O'Kane found a westbound five-ship convoy: three freighters and two escorts. Going in and out of rainsqualls which made the targets hard to distinguish on radar, O'Kane eased in on the surface to 1,500 yards. With *Tang* "dead in the water, and holding her breath," he fired four torpedoes at a freighter. The ship, 3,600-ton *Fukuyama Maru,* blew up and sank instantly. O'Kane turned back for a second attack on the convoy. Setting up again at close range, he found another target and fired four torpedoes.

The first two were beautiful hits in her stern and just aft of the stack [he wrote], but the detonation of the third torpedo hit forward of his bridge was terrific. The enemy ship was twisted, lifted from the water as you would flip a spoon on end and then commenced belching flame as she sank. The Tang *was shaken far worse than by any depth charge we could remember, but a quick check, as our jaws came off our chests, showed no damage.*

The ship was *Yamashimo Maru,* 6,800 tons.

Two days later, O'Kane picked up another westbound convoy: freighter, tanker, and destroyer. He tracked it during the day, running in and out of rainsqualls, and then moved in to attack after dark, firing four torpedoes at the freighter. "The ship went to pieces," O'Kane wrote, "and amidst beautiful fireworks sank before we had completed our turn to evade. The tanker opened fire fore and aft immediately, while the destroyer . . . closed the scene rapidly, spraying shells in every direction."

While the destroyer nuzzled close to the tanker, O'Kane

tracked and got into position for a dawn periscope attack. He looked at both ships from close range, noting every detail, including an estimated 150 lookouts on one side of the tanker. Then, from the point-blank range of 500 yards, he fired four torpedoes at the tanker. "The first three hit as aimed," he wrote, "directly under the stack, at the forward end of his after superstructure and under his bridge. The explosions were wonderful, throwing Japs and other debris above the belching smoke. He sank by the stern in four minutes." This ship was identified in postwar Japanese records not as a tanker but as a freighter, *Echizen Maru*, 2,500 tons.

The next day O'Kane found a third convoy and tracked it, waiting for darkness. Then he surfaced and picked his target carefully, firing his last four torpedoes. He believed he had missed. However, postwar records credited him with sinking *Choko Maru* on that day, a freighter of 1,794 tons. With all torpedoes expended, O'Kane returned to Pearl Harbor.

Following this first sensational patrol, there was no longer any question about how Dick O'Kane would do on his own. He had sunk five ships for 21,400 tons.

Several boats patrolled near the Palaus during the carrier air strike. One was *Tunny*, commanded by John Scott. On March 22, he found a convoy and attacked, damaging a freighter. The following night, Scott picked up a Japanese submarine, *I-42*, en route from Palau to Rabaul with supplies. Scott fired four torpedoes from a range of 1,500 yards, then dived to avoid possible counterattack. As *Tunny* went under, Scott and his men heard and felt a violent explosion that lighted the interior of the conning tower. For a brief moment, Scott, fearing the sub had fired at *Tunny*, was not sure "who hit who." He went deep; his sonarman reported breaking-up noises. For Scott, this was the most nerve-racking attack on any of his five patrols to date. He remained submerged all the next day and passed out a ration of whiskey for the crew.

While the U.S. carriers approached the Palaus, Scott took up station near the main pass leading from the islands. At noon on March 29, the day before the carrier planes were scheduled to attack, Scott saw a group of "motley" freighters leaving the Palaus. He violated Lockwood's bird-in-hand policy and let them go by, hoping for bigger game: *Musashi,* for example.

Scott's gamble paid off. That same night he saw a curious-looking vessel coming out of the pass with destroyer escorts. At first Scott thought the mass was a floating drydock; then, on closer inspection, a *Kongo*-class battleship. In fact, it was the 63,000-ton *Musashi.* Scott, who had made the classic attack on three aircraft carriers at Truk in April 1943, made a second one: he outwitted the destroyers, closed to 2,000 yards, and fired a salvo of six torpedoes.

One of the destroyer escorts spotted the torpedoes and flashed a warning. While Scott went deep, *Musashi* turned to avoid. One of the torpedoes hit anyway, blowing off part of the bow and killing seven men, but the damage was not serious. By the time the carrier planes hit the Palaus the following day, *Musashi* was gone.

While *Tunny* was standing by on the surface 30 miles off the Palaus, a U.S. torpedo bomber attacked her, dropping a 2,000-pound bomb a few yards off the forward engine room that inflicted serious damage. Scott submerged to make emergency repairs, then surfaced to get off an angry report of the incident to Lockwood. Returning to lifeguard station, Scott found two Japanese aviators floating in the water. One came on board; the other refused. With the remaining torpedoes in the after torpedo room damaged by the U.S. Navy bomb, Scott left station, going to Brisbane for refit.

In squally weather, Charles Brindupke in *Tullibee* made contact with one group of fleeing ships—a convoy consisting of a large troop transport and cargo ship, two medium-sized freighters, two escorts, and a large destroyer. Brindupke set upon the large transport, making several approaches through the rain.

The escorts picked him up and dropped fifteen to twenty depth charges to scare him off, but Brindupke did not scare easily. He maneuvered through the escorts, closed to 3,000 yards, and fired two bow tubes. A couple of minutes later, a violent explosion rocked *Tullibee.* Gunner's mate C. W. Kuykendall, who was on the bridge when the explosion occurred, was thrown into the water, along with some other men. *Tullibee* was nowhere to be seen. Following the explosion she sank immediately, a victim, Kuykendall believed, of a circular run of one of the torpedoes whose contact exploder, unfortunately, worked as designed.

For about ten minutes, Kuykendall heard voices in the water, then nothing. All night long he swam in the ocean. At ten o'clock the next morning a Japanese escort vessel found him. After firing at him briefly with a machine gun, the crew of the escort picked him up. Kuykendall was told that the transport Brindupke fired at was hit by the other torpedo.

Kuykendall suffered the fate of the survivors of Fitzgerald's *Grenadier* and Connaway's *Sculpin*: he was interrogated, beaten, taken to the Naval Interrogation Camp in Ofuna, Japan, and then put to work in the Ashio copper mines. He was the only survivor of *Tullibee*.

Six hundred miles to eastward of the Palaus, Sam Dealey and his exec, Tiny Lynch, patrolled off Woleai in *Harder*, returning with new engines. On April 1, the withdrawing U.S. task force hit Woleai but found few good targets. During the strike, an aviator went down near the tiny island west of Woleai. Sam Dealey moved *Harder* in for a rescue.

By the time *Harder* got to the reported position, the aviator, Ensign John R. Galvin, was already stranded high and dry on the beach. Dealey lay to alongside a reef. His third officer, Samuel Moore Logan, and two volunteers jumped in the water with a rubber raft, secured to *Harder* by a line. They fought their way through the surf and coral to the island and picked up Ensign Galvin. As they were attempting to get back to *Harder*, a navy floatplane landed to help. It ran over the line and parted it. Another *Harder* volunteer jumped in the water and swam another line through the surf and coral to the beach. While navy planes circled overhead, providing protection, and Japanese snipers fired away from the foliage, *Harder*'s men pulled the raft and the five men aboard. This rescue was later hailed as one of the boldest on record.

Dealey lay off Woleai for two weeks more. On April 13, a patrol plane spotted *Harder*, forcing her under. Not long afterward, a destroyer that had arrived after the carrier strike, came looking for *Harder*. Dealey decided to attack and closed to 3,200 yards. The destroyer picked up *Harder* on sonar and charged. Dealey let her get within 900 yards and then fired four torpedoes. Later, Dealey noted in his report, "Expended four torpedoes and one Jap destroyer." The ship was *Ikazuchi*, 2,000 tons. She sank within four minutes. Her armed depth charges exploded among her survivors.

Three days later, Dealey spotted a freighter with two destroyer escorts coming out of Woleai. Aircraft circled overhead. Dealey tracked, waiting for dark. Then he surfaced and attacked the formation, sinking his eleventh confirmed ship in four patrols, the freighter *Matsue Maru*, 7,000 tons. Returning to the island, Dealey bombarded it with his new 4-inch gun and then set off for Fremantle.

The sister ships *Dace* and *Darter* patrolled near Davao Gulf. On April 4, Bladen Dulany Claggett in *Dace* saw an aircraft carrier leaving the gulf but was unable to close for an attack. Early in the morning of April 6, *Dace* and *Darter* picked up a grand sight: three heavy cruisers and four destroyers. Claggett went in, firing two torpedoes at one cruiser, two at another, and one at the third. All missed, and he was unable to make another attack. Later he wrote, "Made a mistake, I guess, shooting at three different targets but what a jackpot if we'd collected!"

Shirley Stovall in *Darter* picked up the same set of targets, but by that time they were making 22 knots and Stovall could not overtake.

Another Brisbane boat, *Scamp*, got on the scent. *Scamp* had a new skipper, John Christie Hollingsworth. *Scamp* was nearby when Claggett and Stovall picked up the enemy cruisers. Hollingsworth chased to no avail. The next day, while submerged off the mouth of Davao, Hollingsworth picked up a force of six cruisers standing out of the bay and dived for an approach. The sea was glassy calm. While running in, *Scamp* was detected and the destroyer escorts dropped twenty-two depth charges. Hollingsworth remained deep until early afternoon. Then, finding the horizon clear, he surfaced to get off a contact report. While he was so engaged, a Japanese floatplane came directly out of the sun. Hollingsworth dived. Then all hell broke loose inside *Scamp*.

When *Scamp* was passing 40 feet, a bomb landed near

her port side. "Terrific explosion jarred boat," Hollings-worth wrote later. She assumed a steep up-angle yet slipped backward to 320 feet. From every compartment of the boat, Hollingsworth received grim news of fire, smoke, damage. To take the up-angle off, Hollingsworth ordered every available man to the forward torpedo room.

For a time *Scamp* bobbed up and down like a yo-yo. Finally, Hollingsworth got her under control. He lay quiet the rest of the day, surfacing after dark to send a distress call. Claggett in *Dace* was ordered to provide assistance. Claggett escorted *Scamp* back to Milne Bay. From there, Hollingsworth took the boat back to Mare Island for a major overhaul.

After receiving a report, Christie noted in his diary, "A marvelous performance of duty saved the ship from: (1) diving to crushing depth, (2) surfacing under the guns of the enemy. I am sure . . . that the enemy was certain he had made a kill. Hats off to Hollingsworth and his stout crew."

Tommy Dykers in *Jack*, also with new engines, went to Fremantle by way of Manila. *Jack* was caught by a Japanese plane which dropped three bombs, two of them close. In mid-February, when he reached the South China Sea on a line between Camranh Bay and Manila, Dykers received an Ultra on a convoy of tankers loaded with avia-tion gasoline. At three o'clock in the morning on Febru-ary 19, he made contact with this convoy: five large tankers and three escorts in two columns.

Dykers proceeded to conduct one of the most brilliant —and effective—attacks of the war. First he fired three torpedoes at one tanker. Two hit. Dykers wrote, "In about two seconds she exploded with gasoline because flames shot hundreds of feet in the air and the whole area of the sea around the ship was instantly a seething mass of white hot flame."

With daylight coming on, Dykers made an end around and submerged twenty-one miles ahead of the convoy. The ships reached him about dusk, and he fired four torpedoes at two tankers. "Both of them exploded immediately and were completely enveloped in flames."

After dark, Dykers surfaced and fired three torpedoes

at another target. All missed. The target fired back with a 5-inch gun, and one shell hit close, shaking *Jack*. Dykers reloaded, swung around, and fired four more torpedoes for three hits on one target that also "exploded and was completely enveloped in tremendous flames instantly." With fourteen torpedoes, four out of the five tankers had been sunk.

For the next ten days Dykers cruised about but could find no other targets. On February 28 he received another Ultra, reporting a *Nachi*-class cruiser coming his way. Dykers picked it up—as it traveled alone at 25 knots—the next day, shortly after lunch. Either *Jack* or the cruiser was slightly off course; Dykers was unable to get closer than 9,000 yards. "This one was a tough one to lose," he wrote.

Next night, Dykers made contact with another convoy, a tanker and three freighters with two escorts. Dykers had only seven torpedoes, four aft and three forward. He decided to fire the aft tubes first. That plan didn't work out, so he fired the three bow tubes at a freighter. Dykers saw two hits, and the target "exploded violently." Then he fired his last four at another freighter, observing two hits. An escort counterattacked, driving Dykers off, but he believed he had sunk two ships.

All torpedoes expended, Dykers set course for Fremantle. On the way, he sighted another convoy—a freighter and tanker with two escorts—which ran right over him, forcing Dykers to go deep to avoid detection. He wrote, "We sit on station for days with twenty-four torpedoes and see nothing and as soon as we expend them we run into one we can't get out of the way of."

When Dykers reached Fremantle, Christie was prepared. "As soon as the lines went over," Dykers recalled, "he came aboard and gave me a Navy Cross." In a glowing endorsement to Dykers's report, Christie credited him with sinking seven ships—five tankers and two freighters—for 53,486 tons. Postwar analysis reduced this to four ships—all tankers sunk during the February 19 attack—for 20,441 tons.

Later, at headquarters, Christie showed Dykers the text of an Ultra intercept reporting the effect of his attack on Tokyo. The paraphrased text, which Dykers copied, read:

While returning to Japan, a convoy of six tankers was attacked by enemy submarine on February 20th in the waters northwest of the Philippines and five tankers were sunk. Compared to our past losses, the losses sustained by our tankers since the beginning of the year have almost doubled. The present situation is such that the majority of tankers returning to Japan are being lost.

Chuck Triebel in *Snook,* making his fifth patrol, returned to the East China Sea, with reservist Vard Stockton as his exec. On this trip Triebel decided to give Stockton more responsibility.

On the way to station, south of Honshu, while running on the surface at night, Triebel picked up a target. It was a dark, rainy night, visibility zero. Triebel fired six torpedoes into the void. Two hit, and the ship went down. "There were three more violent explosions aboard before he sank," Triebel reported. It was *Magane Maru,* 3,120 tons.

Arriving on station, Triebel found another convoy on February 8. After a long chase, *Snook* caught up. Triebel gave the attack to Stockton and took over as diving officer. Stockton fired four torpedoes at two ships. One, *Lima Maru,* 6,989 tons, went down. Escorts charged and *Snook* went deep to evade.

On February 10 Triebel fired four torpedoes at a passing destroyer. All missed. Four days later he found a freighter, *Nittoku Maru,* sailing alone, not zigzagging. Triebel fired three torpedoes. The ship went down. The following morning he sank his fourth ship, *Hoshi Maru II,* 875 tons.

On February 19 Triebel received an Ultra from Lockwood on an aircraft carrier. Triebel moved in to intercept. About noon, February 20, he sighted the carrier and two destroyer escorts making 19 knots. However, *Snook* was 9,000 yards off the track and going the wrong way. Triebel bent on flank speed but could get no closer than 7,000 yards. A plane from the carrier came back to circle *Snook.* When it left, Triebel surfaced and got off a report to Lockwood. Just as the message cleared, another plane came over, driving him down. Later that evening Triebel set course for Midway.

En route, Triebel was directed to intercept a convoy

headed south from Tokyo toward the Marianas. Benny Bass, who was making his sixth fine patrol as skipper of old *Plunger* in the same area, also received an Ultra from Lockwood on the convoy. Bass had sunk two freighters and, running low on fuel, was making his way back to Pearl Harbor. He had only one torpedo remaining on board.

Triebel, Bass, and the convoy all converged in mid-ocean early on the morning of February 23. Bass, unaware that Triebel was in the vicinity, headed southward on the surface to the point where he figured he would intercept the convoy. Triebel, who had submerged, watched *Plunger* go by close aboard. Then—partly as a joke—Triebel popped to the surface about 1,000 yards off *Plunger*'s port quarter.

"He scared me to death," said Bass later. "I was surprised, shocked. . . . I didn't know what to do. Some joke!"

Triebel maneuvered close to *Plunger* and talked to Bass by megaphone. "I just wanted to let him know I was there," Triebel said later with a straight face.

As the two skippers were exchanging information, radar picked up the convoy. Moments later, one of Bass's men saw smoke through the high periscope. Bass went north; Triebel went south.

It was a large convoy, six ships with many small escorts and one old coal-burning destroyer. Bass moved in with his one stern torpedo, picked out the biggest ship he could find, and fired. In one of the best shots of the war, he sank the cargo ship *Kimishima Maru,* 5,200 tons. The escorts jumped on *Plunger* and held her down for hours.

Watching from a distance, Triebel later wrote, "Observed one hit on ship in enemy convoy. . . . Later heard numerous explosions and observed two large distinctively separated smoke columns indicating two ships were hit."

Triebel was not able to reach firing position during the day. After dark, however, he surfaced and chased. He caught up and fired five torpedoes at two ships. He wrote, "Observed two good hits two minutes later. Eight minutes after firing felt a terrific explosion which shook the boat . . . target radar pip had just disappeared . . . evaded to the north for an hour and then set course for Midway." It was *Koyo Maru,* 5,471 tons.

On return to Pearl Harbor, both Triebel and Bass received high praise for these patrols. Triebel had sunk five confirmed ships for 21,046 tons; Bass three for 9,600 tons. Both men stepped down from command. In his six patrols on *Plunger*, Bass had sunk nine ships for about 38,000 tons, a remarkable achievement considering *Plunger*'s age and infirmities.

A new boat, *Sandlance*, commanded by Malcolm Everett Garrison, made the polar circuit. Garrison had helped fit out and commission *Trout*. In May 1943 he had reported to Portsmouth to put *Sandlance* in commission. Caught up in the backwaters of Portsmouth, Garrison had never made a real war patrol.

Garrison traveled far north to Kamchatka. The weather was bitterly cold, and the seas were full of floating ice. Garrison struck an ice floe with his periscope and it jammed in the fully elevated position, a serious handicap. Later he wiped off a sonar head in shallow water while attempting to look in a harbor.

Garrison picked up a ship which, he said later, "I positively identified as the *Florida Maru*." He fired and the ship sank while Garrison took photographs through the periscope. It was not *Florida Maru* but *Bella Russa*, a Soviet ship. It had no markings and was "not within the safe conduct lane" given the Russians. With that, Garrison joined the exclusive club of Russian-ship sinkers, founded by Eugene Sands in *Sawfish* and Moon Chapple in *Permit*.

During the days following, Garrison found many targets. He sank two freighters in the far north: *Kaiko Maru*, 3,548 tons, and *Akashisan Maru*, 4,541 tons. In addition, he wasted five torpedoes on what he concluded later was a shallow-draft decoy vessel. With only six torpedoes remaining, Garrison dropped southward to patrol off Honshu.

On March 12, Voge notified Garrison of a big convoy that had left Tokyo crammed with men and supplies to reinforce the Marianas. Garrison found the convoy in moonlight on the night of March 13, right on schedule. It consisted of five big freighters and several smaller ships, escorted by several destroyers and the 3,300-ton light cruiser *Tatsuta*. Regretting the wastage of five torpedoes against the decoy, Garrison prepared to attack with his remaining six.

Coming in submerged with the jammed periscope, Garrison chose the cruiser and one big freighter, planning to fire two stern torpedoes at each and then swing around and fire his last two bow torpedoes at another freighter. He executed his plan with cool precision. Two torpedoes hit *Tatsuta*, which sank immediately. The other two hit *Kokuyo Maru*, a 4,667-ton cargo vessel. The two bow torpedoes hit another freighter for damage.

In the confusion, the escorts could not at first find *Sandlance*. Garrison remained at periscope depth for a while, surveying his work with satisfaction. Then two escorts charged, and Garrison took *Sandlance*, a thick-skinned boat, to 550 feet. For the next eighteen hours, the destroyers zipped back and forth, dropping a total of 105 depth charges. But the charges were set to go off for 250 feet, 300 feet above *Sandlance*, and no damage was done. With all torpedoes expended, Garrison returned to Pearl Harbor from his first patrol. He had sunk a light cruiser, three Japanese freighters, and one Russian ship. Damage to the Japanese: four confirmed ships for 16,000 tons.

On his next patrol, Garrison went to Fremantle by way of the Marianas. Between May 3 and May 11, he sank three confirmed ships. On May 17 he joined forces to attack a convoy with John Scott in *Tunny*, coming up from Milne Bay. Garrison sank two more ships, one for 3,834 and one for 2,633 tons. John Scott sank one for 5,000 tons.

At about this time *Gudgeon* was lost. Scott in *Tunny* and Garrison in *Sandlance* were looking for a convoy near Saipan, and *Gudgeon* was in the area, presumably looking for the same convoy. Scott and Garrison may have heard the fatal attack on *Gudgeon;* Garrison reported "about forty depth charges eight to ten miles away." Since no other submarine reported being under attack at that time and place, Lockwood and Voge presumed the attack Garrison heard was on *Gudgeon*. Nothing was ever heard from her again. She was skippered by Robert Alexander Bonin, class of 1936, making his first patrol as skipper.

Scott remained in the Marianas. Garrison, who had shot off all his torpedoes, proceeded to Fremantle, arriving thirty-five days after leaving port. Total for the patrol:

five ships for 18,328 tons. In two brief patrols, Garrison had sunk nine ships—and he submitted two of the briefest patrol reports on record (five or six pages), describing the action.

In March Lockwood organized another wolf pack. It consisted of *Parche, Bang,* and *Tinosa. Parche,* commanded by Red Ramage from *Trout,* was a new boat. *Bang,* also new, was commanded by a new skipper, Anton Renki Gallaher, who came from command of *R-13* in the Atlantic but had never served in a fleet boat. *Tinosa* had been brought back from Fremantle by Donald Frederick Weiss, who—in a brilliantly daring action—had sunk four confirmed ships for 15,600 tons on the way.

The pack was led by George Edmund Peterson. Peterson had spent most of the war in the Atlantic, serving with the boats operating out of Scotland, and had never made a Pacific war patrol. Before setting off, the pack developed new and simplified techniques to facilitate communications.

The three boats took up station in Luzon Strait in mid-April, and for the next two weeks they milled about without any contacts. Red Ramage was so bored he filled his patrol report with humorous entries, such as the one on April 18: "Picked up sky lookout—bird—which took station on Number One Periscope going round and round and up and down, hanging on with dogged determination over four hours. Genus: unknown. Sex: undetermined. Habits: not altogether proper."

In the late afternoon of April 29, J. W. Champ, a keen-eyed quartermaster on *Bang,* alternating periscope watch with the officer of the deck, picked up smoke on the horizon. The smoke developed into a huge southbound convoy: fifteen to twenty ships and numerous destroyer escorts. Gallaher surfaced and got off contact reports—repeated every hour—to *Parche* and *Tinosa,* some 60 to 70 miles northwest of the convoy. *Tinosa* receipted after one hour, *Parche* after three hours.

Gallaher submerged again for a night periscope attack, selecting a tanker and two freighters for his initial ten-torpedo salvo. He was all set to fire when one of the destroyers, looking as big as a heavy cruiser to Gallaher, got in the way. In a change of tactics, Gallaher fired four torpedoes at the destroyer and two at the tanker. He missed the destroyer, which turned out of the way, but one or two torpedoes hit a freighter behind it. Another destroyer charged *Bang*, and Gallaher went deep to evade.

An hour or so later, after the escort broke off, Gallaher surfaced to chase. He caught up with the convoy in an hour, threaded through the escorts, and set up on a big freighter, firing six torpedoes. All missed. He swung around and fired his four stern tubes. There was confusion in the fire-control party; all four stern tubes also missed. Gallaher began reloading his tubes and making an end around.

Shortly after five o'clock in the morning, April 30, he caught up again and fired his four remaining bow tubes at a big freighter. Gallaher wrote, "The first explosion caused a tremendous flash. . . . The concussion was so great on the bridge that it felt as if there had been a bodily push away from the target. The second hit caused a ripple of flame. . . . Target sank amid a cloud of dense smoke." The escorts charged again and drove *Bang* down for eleven hours.

In these attacks, Gallaher had fired twenty torpedoes. He sank two confirmed ships.

All the while, *Tinosa* and *Parche* were hurrying down from the northwest at full speed, trying to find the convoy. At 4:20 A.M., Ramage saw flames on the horizon, the result of Gallaher's earlier attacks. About the time Gallaher made his dawn attack, Ramage picked up the convoy on radar. He counted ten large ships. Ramage and Weiss ran around the convoy to get ahead for a day periscope attack; Gallaher, with only four torpedoes left, was ordered to trail and sink any stragglers.

Ramage and Weiss dived in front of the convoy and waited. At about nine o'clock in the morning, it came into Weiss's range. He saw a "dream setup": five overlapping ships. He fired all six bow tubes, hearing and feeling four hits. With destroyers charging, Weiss went deep and remained there, losing contact. An hour later, Ramage set up and fired four torpedoes—two each at two freighters. All missed. Aircraft and destroyers charged *Parche*, and Ramage went deep for the rest of the day, also losing contact. The convoy ran into Lingayen Gulf, and none of the three boats could make another attack on it. Neither

Weiss nor Ramage received credit in postwar records for a sinking on this day.

Three days passed. About daylight on May 3, Weiss in *Tinosa* picked up another convoy and flashed the word. It consisted of twelve ships. The pack tracked it submerged during the day and surfaced after dark to chase. The boats caught up about midnight. Weiss attacked first, firing six torpedoes at a tanker and freighter. He saw two hits on the tanker and hits on the freighter, but destroyers drove him under before he could make a follow-up attack. Ramage attacked next, firing six bow tubes—four at one freighter and two at another. He saw three hits in the first ship, which "appeared to blow up" and sink immediately, and two hits on the second, which began settling in the water. He swung around and fired his four stern tubes at another freighter, observing two hits.

Gallaher on *Bang*, meanwhile, set up on another target with his last four stern torpedoes. When he fired, he believed he obtained two hits on a freighter and one hit on a destroyer. Both, he reported, "sank."

Weiss in *Tinosa* surfaced and prepared to attack again. He fired six torpedoes at a big freighter, obtaining three hits which seemed to disintegrate the target, and then fired four more for misses. He submerged for a daylight attack on another ship, firing his last four torpedoes—all misses. During the day the remnants of the convoy eluded *Parche*, the only boat of the three with any torpedoes left. In this combined attack the three boats sank five ships, almost half the convoy.

After *Tinosa* and *Bang* reported all torpedoes expended, the pack commander, Peterson, ordered them to return to base. Ramage hung around a few more days but found no further opportunity to shoot. In total, Pack Number Four sank seven confirmed ships for about 35,300 tons. Gallaher was credited with three freighters for 10,700 tons, Ramage two for 11,700 tons, and Weiss two for 12,900 tons.

Slade Cutter took *Seahorse* to the Marianas for his third patrol. On March 31, he rendezvoused with *Stingray* in the northern Marianas. *Stringray* was now commanded by Sam Loomis. Loomis had got on the trail of a convoy and sunk a 4,000-ton freighter the previous day. The two classmates (they had been to the same secondary schools and roomed together at the Naval Academy) exchanged information; then Cutter headed south, in pursuit of a convoy thought to be headed for Saipan. He took station at the normal channel, but the convoy gave him the slip and went into Saipan by a new route.

Another convoy soon came along. Cutter found it on April 8 and attacked, firing three torpedoes each at two freighters. He sank two ships: *Aratama Maru*, a 6,784-ton converted submarine tender, and *Kizugawa Maru*, a 1,915-ton freighter. Both were loaded with troops and supplies for the defense of the Marianas.

Meanwhile, *Trigger*, with a new skipper, Fritz Harlfinger, set off for patrol at Palau. His exec was the seemingly indefatigable Ned Beach, who had made all eight of *Trigger*'s patrols. Lockwood detoured *Trigger* to the Marianas to lend Cutter a hand.

On April 8, while Cutter was sinking his two ships, Harlfinger found one of the largest convoys anyone in the submarine force had ever seen. Manning the periscope, Ned Beach counted four columns of ships—tankers, freighters, transports, and auxiliaries—with about five ships in each column surrounded by ten or more escorts. *Trigger*'s fire-control party set up to fire a ten-torpedo salvo at a tanker and two other targets.

After Harlfinger had fired four torpedoes, a destroyer charged in, firing machine guns at the periscope. It was so close that it blanked out Beach's vision. Harlfinger ordered a deep dive, but nobody in the conning tower believed *Trigger* would make it in time; the destroyer was too close. Beach thought, "How long does it take a depth charge to sink fifty feet?"

Apparently it had all happened too fast for the depth-charge team on the destroyer. The first explosion the men in *Trigger*'s conning tower heard were "four solid torpedo hits" which were, Beach believed, two in the tanker and two in a freighter. By then *Trigger* had reached 300 feet.

A nightmare followed. The destroyer dropped twenty-five depth charges. They were, Beach wrote, "absolute beauties. . . . How *Trigger* managed to hold together we'll never know." Lights went out. Cork insulation flew. Switches came undone. Valves leaked. The hull buckled in and out.

Then, as Beach remembered later, six of the escorts

formed a ring around *Trigger,* keeping the submarine at the center. Every half hour or so, one charged in to pummel *Trigger* with a new series of charges. The attack went on for eighteen hours. Water leaked up to the level of the floor plates in the forward torpedo room. The temperature in the boat rose to 135 degrees. It was, Beach reported, a "long and horrible day," the worst beating *Trigger* had ever received, and one of the worst on record.

During the late afternoon, Harlfinger and Beach decided to surface and fight their way clear. They would make ready all torpedoes and man the deck gun. However, around sunset the escorts became lax, and *Trigger* slipped out of the deadly circle. That night, Harlfinger surfaced and set a course for the Palaus.

On the following day, April 9, Slade Cutter intercepted this same large convoy as it neared Saipan. It was, Cutter estimated, a fifteen-to-twenty ship convoy, the "largest we have ever seen." Cutter set up and fired four torpedoes from a range of 1,800 yards. "There were four ships overlapping in the field of the periscope with no open water between them," Cutter reported. However, just as Cutter fired, the targets zigged and all four torpedoes missed. One of the four made a circular run and, Cutter reported, "passed close aboard several times." Cutter fired two more at a freighter and obtained two hits. He lost depth control and went deep, just as two destroyers swung over dropping depth charges. Cutter went deeper.

Later that night, when Cutter came up, he found the freighter he hit still afloat, guarded by two destroyers. "Most discouraging," Cutter wrote. He moved in for another attack, but planes drove him under. Postwar records showed that the ship, *Bisaku Maru,* a 4,467-ton freighter, sank anyway.

On April 20, while Cutter was patrolling submerged off Saipan, he suddenly sighted a small RO-class Japanese submarine. Setting up fast, he fired two torpedoes from 1,800 yards. Again he lost depth control and went unavoidably deep. He reported one very loud explosion, "the loudest we have ever heard or felt." Cutter believed, "It must have been helped by an explosion in the target." The submarine was *RO-45.*

A week later, April 27, Cutter picked up yet another convoy about forty-five miles west of Saipan. It consisted of four freighters, a destroyer, and three smaller escorts. He attacked, firing four torpedoes at a freighter. Three hit, and down went 5,244-ton *Akigawa Maru*. Cutter's score: five ships (including *RO-45*) for 19,500 tons. In three patrols, Cutter had sunk fifteen ships—five on each time out.

Arriving at Palau on April 14, *Trigger* rendezvoused with Dick O'Kane in *Tang*. Following the air strike on the Palaus, O'Kane had had a discouraging two weeks. The seas were empty of targets. He gave *Trigger* some spare parts to repair her damage and headed eastward toward Truk.

Patrolling off the Palaus, Harlfinger and Beach picked up a six-ship convoy on the night of April 26. Harlfinger attacked, firing six torpedoes at overlapping targets and obtaining four hits. He believed he had sunk two freighters and an escort. He chased the remaining three, attacking again, believing he sank two more and damaged the other. Harlfinger received credit for sinking five ships for 33,200 tons, but postwar records reduced that to one ship sunk off the Palaus, the large 11,700-ton transport *Miike Maru*.

When *Trigger* returned from patrol, she was found to be so weakened by her encounter with the escorts off the Marianas that she required a lengthy overhaul.

17

THE DESTROYER KILLER

In 1944, as Nimitz advanced across the Pacific, Mac-Arthur, in Australia, launched the reconquest of New Guinea in a series of amphibious leaps along the north coast. The Australian-based submarine force, now commanded in its entirety by Ralph Christie (James Fife went to duty in the U.S.) numbering thirty-odd boats, did not operate in direct support of these amphibious and fleet actions. Basing from Fremantle, Brisbane, Darwin and advanced tenders in Milne Bay (and later Manus Harbor and Mios Woendi), Christie's boats concentrated on enemy shipping and kept a sharp eye out for Japanese naval forces, which had congregated in southern waters to be closer to the oil supply.

Walt Griffith in *Bowfin* made a double-barreled patrol. On the first half, he patrolled the South China Sea. In a furious few days of action, Griffith fired off most of his torpedoes, sinking one confirmed freighter for 4,408 tons and damaging several other ships.

After a mere fourteen days, Griffith was back in Darwin to obtain a load of torpedoes and more fuel. In addition, he received some mines and orders to plant them off the coast of Borneo. Ralph Christie, still eager to make a brief submarine war patrol, decided to go with Griffith on this second leg. Not wanting to risk another turn-down, he did not ask permission of his boss.

Christie flew to Darwin on January 29 and joined *Bowfin*. The mines had been loaded on board. In addition, Griffith carried sixteen torpedoes. The boat got under way immediately. Christie established his quarters in the wardroom, sleeping in a pull-down bunk over the ward-room table. He was quite pleased with himself. "If I came back," he wrote later, "I would be congratulated. If I did not, well . . ."

On the evening of the second night out, Griffith found a 4,300-ton merchant ship en route from Ambon to Timor, bringing food and supplies to the Japanese garrison. While Christie stood on the bridge looking on from a "box seat," Griffith swung and fired two torpedoes. Both hit, Christie reported later, and "sank the enemy ship in less than one minute." There was, he reported, "no applause—just silence—and everybody went about his own business." Postwar records failed to credit Griffith with sinking a ship on this day and at this place.

On the way to Borneo to lay the minefield, Griffith received an important Ultra. A Japanese seaplane tender, the 17,000-ton *Kamoi*, was en route to Makassar City. Griffith found her in the shallow waters of Salajar Strait the next night and trailed. She had three small escorts and air cover. Griffith could not achieve a firing position that night. He tracked her all the following day on the surface, diving eight times to avoid detection by Japanese aircraft. During the afternoon, Rear Admiral Christie stood watch as officer of the deck so the officers could rest up for the long night ahead.

That night about eleven o'clock, Griffith maneuvered around the escorts and attacked, firing six bow tubes. Owing to a fire-control error, all missed. The torpedoes alerted the escorts. They thrashed about, dropping depth charges at random to scare Griffith away. *Kamoi* began twisting and turning with radical zigs and zags to complicate Griffith's problem.

Griffith remained on the surface, maneuvering slowly for a second attack. Christie, who was on the bridge watching, became uneasy. "We were very close to him," Christie wrote. "Too close, within machine gun range. I thought we would dive, but [Griffith] chose to hold the initiative by remaining on the surface. . . . I thought surely he must see us. . . . I was most uncomfortable. . . . The enemy could easily have sunk us with gunfire or at least swept our bridge with machinegun fire."

Griffith swung around and fired two stern tubes from a range of about 1,000 yards. Christie heard the first torpedo leave the tube. He wrote, "I could see the luminous wake and WHAM! an enormous detonation which shook us up as though our own ship had been hit. We got two hits smack under his bridge this time. Debris was thrown skyward in a background of fire and smoke. I was slammed against the bridge railing by the force of the explosion and broke my binocular strap and lost my cap."

About then, the target responded with searchlights and gunfire. To Christie, the light seemed like a "million flashbulbs." After it came whizzing shells: 4-inch, 40-mm., and 20-mm. Griffith raced away from the target and then cleared the bridge of all personnel except himself. Admiral Christie lunged for the hatch like any lookout. "I don't think I hit a rung of the ladder to the conning tower."

There was one torpedo remaining aft. Griffith was determined to put it in *Kamoi*. He outran the guns, then swung around in the darkness, avoiding the searchlights. He set up and fired. Christie, taking station in the forward torpedo room, believed he heard a hit, but it was drowned out by the diving alarm. Griffith took *Bowfin* to 442 feet to evade. No depth charges followed. For that, Christie was grateful.

Kamoi did not sink. Christie learned from Ultra reports that, following the attack, the Japanese beached her. Later, they towed her into Surabaya for temporary repairs. Months later, according to Christie, she was towed to Singapore for major repairs.

Following this action, Griffith took *Bowfin* to the approaches to Balikpapan, where he planted the small minefield. On the way home, he shot up two sampans "loaded with cement." Then he dropped Christie at Exmouth Gulf, where a plane was waiting to fly him back to Fremantle. Christie arrived back at his office nine days after departing, the second oldest officer (after John Brown at Pearl Harbor) and first force commander—and admiral—in the history of the U.S. Navy to make a submarine war patrol. In this two-part patrol, Griffith had fired a total of thirty-five torpedoes, achieving sixteen hits.

After a brief refit, Griffith went out again for his third patrol, another double-barrel. This time he carried a special load of the "modified" exploders. They did not work very well. During his thirty-three days at sea, Griffith attacked seven ships, firing forty-one torpedoes. Of these, *eight* of the first twenty-four prematured; fourteen hit, sinking three big freighters for 15,000 tons; others caused damage to two ships. During the patrol, Griffith took *Bowfin* into narrow, shallow, and restricted waters, received six close depth-charge attacks and three close bombs from aircraft, and was twice shot at by shore guns.

When Griffith came in from this patrol, Christie decided he should return to the States for new construction and rest.

Gordon Selby, taking *Puffer* out for his second patrol, hunted north of Singapore. Shortly after sunset on the night of February 20, Selby found a ten-ship convoy made up of large ships, southbound. "Three of the first four ships sighted," he wrote later, "were very large, their superstructures having the triangular appearance of battleships and cruisers. . . . The night was too dark and the horizon too hazy to make out any definite type characteristics on the larger ships but the overall silhouettes were those of men-of-war and not freighters, tankers or transports."

Unaware at first that he had intercepted fast-moving combatant ships, Selby underestimated the convoy's speed. He gave chase, but the formation soon pulled out of range. These ships were probably units of the Japanese main fleet, en route to Singapore from Truk or Japan to be closer to the oil supply.

In midafternoon on February 22, Selby picked up another convoy. This one was northbound and consisted of several medium or small freighters. Selby began chasing, looking for deeper water to make his attack. Meanwhile, high-periscope lookouts reported two more ships; Selby moved his periscope around and saw what appeared to be a large camouflaged transport with one escort, zigzagging.

Turning to attack, Selby fired two torpedoes at the transport and two at the escort. One torpedo hit the transport, throwing up a column of smoke and debris. Closing in, Selby saw lifeboats being lowered into the water. Selby

fired two more torpedoes into the transport. Both hit. As
the ship began to sink slowly by the stern, Selby took
periscope pictures.

The ship, which soon slid beneath the waves, was later
identified from Selby's excellent photographs as an ocean
liner, *Teiko Maru*, 15,100 tons—which, as the French
liner *D'Artagnan*, had been captured in the early days
of the war. She was the third largest Japanese merchant ship sunk to that time, after Post's 17,526-ton liner
Kamakura Maru and Tom Wogan's 16,975-ton liner
Tatsuta Maru.

The rest of this patrol was frustrating. Selby found two
more convoys, one of which he attempted to attack on
three separate occasions but failed for one reason or another. "Except for *Teiko*, I was not too happy with our
third patrol," Selby said later. "I should have had a big
haul—too cautious I guess." When he returned to Fremantle, Selby received a "rude shock." After three days
of "letting off steam," he went down to the docks and saw
what appeared to be *Teiko Maru* moored in a slip. It turned out
to be her sister ship, *Porthos*, still in Allied hands.

Willard Laughon, making his second patrol as skipper of
Rasher, got under way from Fremantle February 19, a
day after James White Davis left for his third patrol in
Raton. Just north of Lombok Strait, Laughon received
an Ultra on a convoy going from Surabaya to Ambon.
Davis received the same report and joined with Laughon
in a coordinated search. On February 25 the two boats
rendezvoused and agreed on a battle plan. One and a half
hours later, they found the convoy: two freighters with
two escorts.

Laughon attacked first, just after dark, firing four torpedoes at one freighter from 1,000 yards and another four
torpedoes at the second from 1,300 yards. He obtained
three hits in each target, and both sank. They were *Tango
Maru*, 6,200 tons, and *Ryusei Maru*, 4,800 tons. Laughon
then noted in his report, "Told *Raton* that there were
no more targets and that we were clearing the area and
apologized for hogging the show."

Laughon took *Rasher* north through Molucca Passage
to the Celebes Sea. On March 3, he picked up a big convoy: six freighters, three escorts. After a hard chase,

during which his SJ radar went out of commission, he attacked at night, firing three torpedoes at one ship, three at another. Escorts drove him under, preventing another attack. One of the freighters, *Nittai Maru,* 6,400 tons, went down.

On the night of March 4, Laughon chased and attacked another convoy, firing two torpedoes at one ship and four at another. All missed or ran under. He swung, maneuvered, and fired his last four at another ship. It was a bad setup; all missed. Laughon returned to Darwin to take on another load of torpedoes and resume the patrol.

Davis in *Raton* went on to Indochina, where he joined in a loosely coordinated search with Brooks Jared Harral in *Ray* (who had laid a minefield off Saigon), *Bluefish* (now commanded by Charles Mitchell Henderson), and Selby in *Puffer.* On March 3, Christie sent all four boats an Ultra on a tanker convoy. Henderson in *Bluefish* sank one tanker for 10,500 tons, but the other three boats did not fare so well. Neither Davis nor Harral sank a confirmed ship on their patrols.

The Japanese organized a convoy at Shanghai for the purpose of lifting two divisions of reinforcements to New Guinea. The convoy, commanded by Rear Admiral Sadamichi Kajioka, who had captured Wake and led the Port Moresby invasion forces during the Battle of the Coral Sea, headed for Manila. Kajioka's flagship was a coal-burning minelayer, *Shirataka,* which gave off heavy smoke. The convoy left Shanghai on April 17, its progress followed closely by the codebreakers.

Two of Christie's boats were patrolling near Manila as the convoy approached: Tommy Dykers's *Jack* and Jim Dempsey's *Cod.* On the morning of April 26, *Jack* intercepted the convoy off the northwest coast of Luzon. As Dykers was taking up position, he spotted a Japanese submarine and evaded at high speed. A few minutes later, a plane came over and dropped a bomb. Dykers was certain the Japanese would route the convoy around him, but they didn't; at noon, Dykers picked up the heavy smoke of the flagship *Shirataka* again and trailed. An hour before sunset he surfaced to make an end around, but a plane came over and drove him down.

After dark, Dykers again surfaced and tracked the convoy, waiting for moonset. When it came, he moved in to attack. The escorts were more alert than usual, and Dykers, trying one side and then the other, couldn't find a hole. Finally he decided to shoot spreads of low-speed torpedoes under the escorts at the mass of overlapping targets in the convoy. In three separate attacks, he fired off nineteen torpedoes. They appeared to hit, and Dykers believed he had sunk one or more, but Christie only credited Dykers with damage to five ships.

In the postwar accounting, however, it was discovered that Dykers had hit and sunk a very valuable target, the 5,425-ton freighter *Yoshida Maru I,* packed with an army regiment of 3,000 men. She sank quickly, and all the troops, including the regimental commander, drowned. After that disaster, the convoy put into Manila, where it received more escorts before setting off again.

Jim Dempsey in *Cod* was unable to attack this convoy, but he made his presence felt later; on May 10, he attacked a convoy off the west coast of Luzon, sinking an old 820-ton destroyer and a big 7,200-ton freighter and damaging two other ships. Upon return to Fremantle, Dempsey stepped down as commander of *Cod.* Jim Dempsey had made a record ten Pacific war patrols as commanding officer, three on *S-37,* four on *Spearfish,* and three on *Cod.*

Herb Andrews in *Gurnard,* one of the last of the re-engined H.O.R. boats to shift from Pearl Harbor to Fremantle, went by way of Manila. By then, Admiral Kajioka's convoy was under way from Manila, bound for New Guinea, now reinforced by more destroyers. Christie put Andrews on the track.

Andrews intercepted on May 6 in the Celebes Sea. He submerged and began a slow, cautious approach to avoid detection by aircraft. Four hours later, the convoy bore down on him: eight transports in three columns with many escorts.

Andrews let a destroyer escort go by, then fired a salvo of six bow tubes at two of the transports in the near column. One torpedo of his first salvo hit his first target, but the second salvo missed the second target and traveled on to the far column, hitting another transport. Andrews swung around and fired his stern tubes, which hit the second target. An escort charged up, and Andrews went deep as about a hundred depth charges rained down, none close. Two hours later, Andrews came up cautiously, raising the periscope to find three sinking ships and a massive rescue operation in progress. He cruised around for a while, taking photographs through the periscope, and later that night he fired at one of the cripples which was still afloat.

In all, Andrews had sunk three big ships crammed with soldiers and equipment: the transports *Aden Maru*, 5,824 tons, and *Taijima Maru*, 6,995 tons, and a cargo ship, *Tenshinzan Maru*, 6,886 tons. Andrews was told later that about 6,000 Japanese troops drowned that day. It is possible but not probable. The historian Holmes reported after the war that the rescue operations had been unusually efficient, with the Japanese even lashing field guns to floating rafts.

Since leaving Shanghai, the convoy had lost four valuable ships: one to Tommy Dykers on *Jack* and now three to Herb Andrews on *Gurnard*. What remained of the force went not to New Guinea, as planned, but to Halmahera, where efforts were made to transship them to New Guinea by barge. These efforts either failed or came too late. Between them, Dykers and Andrews stopped the better part of two army divisions from reaching New Guinea.

Frank Walker, exec to Hank Munson on *Crevalle*, moved up to command when Munson stepped down. On his first time out as skipper, Walker patrolled off the west coast of Borneo. On April 25 he sank a small 1,000-ton freighter, but the next two weeks were a time of utter frustration. On April 26 he tried to attack an eight-ship convoy, but a destroyer beat him off. On May 3 he picked up two ships with one escort, tracked them in driving rain, and attacked after dark, firing eight torpedoes. (Walker believed he sank one ship, but postwar records failed to confirm it.) On May 4 he found a six-ship convoy, but it went into shallow water before he could attack.

On May 6—the day Herb Andrews sank three ships from the troop convoy—Walker's luck changed. He picked up an eleven-ship convoy with several destroyer escorts. With these ships was *Nisshin Maru*, 16,801 tons, a huge tanker (once a whale factory) similar to *Tonnan Maru III*, which Dan Daspit had tried to sink off Truk. Maneuvering in shallow water, less than 200 feet, Walker expertly out-guessed swarms of escorts and cirling planes and fired three torpedoes at *Nisshin Maru*. Two hit, and the great ship blew up and sank.

The escorts counterattacked violently, dropping sixty-one close depth charges and aerial bombs. Walker took *Crevalle* to the bottom—only 174 feet—and lay still. A little later, there was a terrifying scraping sound along the outer hull. The Japanese, Walker believed, were trying to snare *Crevalle* with grappling hooks. This was more than anybody could stand. Walker got off the bottom and cleared the area safely.

After that, Walker was ordered to a special mission: proceed northward to Negros Island to evacuate refugees. He took aboard a total of forty-one, including thirty-five women and children. Four of the men were survivors of the Bataan Death March who had escaped into the Philippine jungles. On the way home with his passengers, Walker picked up a six-ship convoy with five escorts. He went to battle stations to attack, but before he could get off any torpedoes a destroyer attacked *Crevalle*, dropping eight depth charges right on top of the boat. It was the worst working over *Crevalle* had ever received and a near thing. The damage was heavy and the passengers were terrified. Afterward, Walker set course for Darwin.

The Japanese fleet, which had been based in Singapore, moved to a forward base at Tawi Tawi, to prepare for a showdown battle with the U.S. Pacific Fleet, then staging to invade the Marianas. Christie's submarines converged on Tawi Tawi to report on fleet movements and to sink whatever they could.

Sam Dealey in *Harder*, going on his fifth patrol, was ordered to Tawi Tawi. Christie's operations officer, Murray Jones Tichenor, who had never made a war patrol, went along for the ride. In addition to a regular patrol, Dealey was asked to try to pick up the guerrillas on north-east Borneo. Dealey agreed to the special mission—re-luctantly.

On the night of June 6, while going into Sibutu Passage just south of Tawi Tawi on his way to pick up the guerrillas, Dealey ran into a convoy of three empty tankers and two destroyers headed for Tarakan for a refill. One of the destroyers picked up *Harder* and charged. Dealey let it get within 1,100 yards, then fired three torpedoes. *Minatsuki* blew up and sank immediately.

Dealey chased the convoy, making an end around. He submerged to radar depth and prepared to attack. A second destroyer peeled off and charged at *Harder*. Dealey let it get within 1,200 yards before firing six bow tubes. All missed. Dealey went to 300 feet to evade. One of his diving plane operators, a new man, misread his instruments and took *Harder* to 400 feet by mistake. As a result, Dealey lost another opportunity to attack the convoy.

Dealey turned back for Sibutu Passage, submerging for the transit shortly after 8 A.M. on June 7. At 11:43, he sighted another destroyer. Dealey let it get within the point-blank range of 650 yards and then fired three torpedoes at five-second intervals. All three torpedoes hit *Hayanami*.

Dealey went ahead full with hard right rudder to get out of the path of the destroyer. He later wrote, "At a range of 300 yards we were racked by a terrific explosion believed to have been the destroyer's magazine. Less than one minute after the first hit and nine minutes after it was sighted, the destroyer sank tail first."

A sister ship of the *Hayanami* came over and dropped seventeen depth charges in the next two hours. Shortly after 3 P.M., Dealey returned to periscope depth and found two more destroyers. They went away, but he found another, about 5:30, and then a line of eight. Feeling he had worn out his welcome, Dealey withdrew to pick up the guerrillas.

On the night of June 8, Dealey nosed *Harder* near the appointed rendezvous and sent two small boats ashore into the gloom. The boats picked up the guerrilla force and returned to *Harder*. Dealey cleared the area and went through Sibutu Passage to see what he could turn up at Tawi Tawi.

The following night he found two more destroyers. He submerged for an approach, firing four torpedoes at overlapping targets. Two of the four hit *Tanikaze*, which blew up and sank. Dealey thought one of his other torpedoes hit the other destroyer, but he must have been mistaken. There is no record of a second Japanese destroyer being lost on June 9 off Tawi Tawi.

The battleships *Yamato* and *Musashi* got underway at Tawi Tawi on the evening of June 10. Sam Dealey in *Harder* was patrolling off Tawi Tawi that evening. At about 5 P.M., he sighted *Yamato* and *Musashi* coming out of the anchorage. While Dealey maneuvered *Harder* for an approach, a Japanese pilot spotted his periscope and dropped a smoke bomb and a destroyer peeled off and headed for *Harder*. Dealey let him close to 1,200 yards, fired three torpedoes down the throat, and then went deep.

Going down, Dealey was positive that at least two of the torpedoes hit; he heard explosions far louder than depth charges. Passing 80 feet, he later wrote that "all hell broke loose. It was not from his depth charges—for if they had been dropped, this report would not have been completed —but a deafening series of progressive rumblings that seemed to almost blend with each other. Either his boilers or his magazine, or both, had exploded and it's a lucky thing that ship explosions are vented upward and not down."

Dealey took *Harder* to 400 feet to evade. The escorts —and land-based aircraft—delivered a violent counterattack that kept him down until after dark. Dealey wrote in his log, "It is considered amazing that [*Harder*] could have gone through such a terrific pounding and jolting around with such minor damage. Our fervent thanks go out to the workmen and designers at the Electric Boat Company for building such a fine ship." In the postwar records, there was no evidence that a Japanese destroyer was lost this day off Tawi Tawi. The noise Dealey heard might well have been close aerial bombs or depth charges.

After dark, Dealey surfaced and got off a contact report on the departure of *Yamato* and *Musashi*. He remained off Tawi Tawi for another day, watching the anchorage and reporting the ships he saw. On the evening of June 12, Christie ordered him to patrol northward along the Sulu Archipelago. Going north, Dealey rendezvoused with Chester Nimitz in *Haddo*, who was having a frustrating patrol. So far, Nimitz had found nothing to shoot at except a couple of mangy sampans, sunk by deck gun. Dealey continued on to Zamboanga, then to Davao, then back south through Molucca Passage to Darwin.

When Dealey reached Darwin, Christie was ecstatic. He credited him with sinking five destroyers, and the endorsements called the patrol "epoch-making" and "magnificent." Since Dealey had sunk a destroyer on his previous patrol off Woleai, his total was thought to be six. For this reason, he was nicknamed "The Destroyer Killer."

18

THE BATTLE OF
THE PHILIPPINE SEA

The stage was now set for a climactic naval battle in the Pacific. When Nimitz invaded the Marianas, the Japanese fleet at Tawi Tawi would steam out to administer what was hoped would be a "devastating blow" to the U.S. Fleet, and stop the invasion of the Marianas, the key to the control of the western Pacific Ocean. Lockwood's and Christie's submarines would play a major role in the coming battle.

While Nimitz's armada was assembling for the Marianas invasion in May, Lockwood sent a last wave of submarines into the Marianas to interdict Japanese attempts to reinforce the islands. John Coye in *Silversides* sank six ships, a remarkable score. In addition, Lockwood sent a three-boat wolf pack: *Pilotfish*, commanded by Robert Hamilton ("Boney") Close, *Pintado*, commanded by Chick Clarey and *Shark II* commanded by Edward Noe Blakely. The pack was commanded by Leon Nelson ("Chief") Blair in *Pintado*. It was called "Blair's Blasters."

When the pack reached the Marianas on May 31, John Coye in *Silversides* was trailing—and giving contact reports on—an outbound convoy. Blair's Blasters were ordered to close Coye's convoy and take over.

When the pack made contact, they found three freighters and two escorts. Blakely in *Shark* and Coye in *Silversides* wound up on one side of the convoy. Blakely held back so that Coye could go in and fire his last two torpedoes. Both missed. By allowing Coye to go in, Blakely deprived himself of a chance to attack. On the

276

other side of the convoy, Clarey in *Pintado* tried to get in but was chased off by gunfire from one of the escorts. He trailed and then mounted a second attempt near daybreak, firing six torpedoes. All six hit *Toho Maru*, 4,700 tons. The ship, Clarey wrote, "disintegrated before my eyes and sank immediately."

Meanwhile, Coye, having sunk six ships, set off for Pearl Harbor and found a second convoy—inbound—of five ships and several escorts. Boney Close in *Pilotfish* gave up trying to attack Convoy Number One in favor of Convoy Number Two. In the late afternoon of June 1, Close reported he had the convoy in sight. Blair, knowing an outbound convoy to be less valuable than an inbound one with reinforcements, ordered all boats to break off from the first and concentrate on the second. Boney Close trailed but was not able to get in an attack. Nor were the other boats. Convoy Number Two, which was carrying half of the Japanese 43rd Division, reached Saipan without damage.

In the meantime Close found yet another convoy, Number Three. It was outbound. On the evening of June 2, Blakely in *Shark* also made contact with this convoy. He set up and fired four torpedoes at a freighter, and all four hit. Down went *Chiyo Maru*, 4,700 tons. Clarey in *Pintado* tried to get in from the other side but was driven down by an escort and received a stiff depth-charging. Close was also unable to attack.

During the early hours of June 3, while chasing Convoy Number Three for another attack, Blakely found a fourth convoy, also inbound. It consisted of about seven big freighters and four or five escorts. Again, knowing that an inbound convoy was a more significant target than an outbound one, Blair ordered his three boats to close Convoy Number Four.

It took the boats twenty-four hours to get into shooting position. Late on the afternoon of June 4, *Shark* made the first attack. Blakely took the boat submerged into the middle of the convoy, watched an escort pass about 180 yards down his side, then set up on a freighter at 1,500 yards. "In the few brief looks taken on this target," Blakely reported, "it was noted that the topside, forecastle in particular, was heaped high with military packs and what appeared to be landing force equipment, the topside was jammed with personnel, apparently troops." As he learned later, Convoy Number Four was carrying the other half of the 43rd Division.

Blakely fired four torpedoes. All hit. During the attack, he lost depth control and went deep. An escort charged over, dropping four depth charges very close. *Shark* remained deep while the escorts unleashed another fortynine charges in the next two hours, none close. After dark, Blakely surfaced to chase. Neither Clarey in *Pintado* nor Close in *Pilotfish* was able to get in an attack. After dark, they too surfaced to chase.

Next day, it was Blakely who again got in the lucky position. Late in the afternoon of June 5, he made a submerged attack, firing six torpedoes at two freighters. Three torpedoes hit each target. Blakely paused a moment to swing the periscope on an escort, then back to the first freighter. "There was nothing left except his masts in a swirl of water sticking out," Blakely wrote. "It was unbelievable to me that a ship could sink so fast." Blakely had sunk two ships in this attack: *Tamahime Maru,* 3,000 tons, and *Takaika Maru,* 7,000 tons. He then went deep and received another drubbing, one which damaged his port shaft.

That night, all three submarines again surfaced to chase. Shortly after midnight, Clarey got into position and fired four torpedoes at overlapping targets. All four slammed into *Kashimasan Maru,* 2,800 tons, which was loaded with gasoline and burned far into the night before sinking. The escorts drove Clarey down before he could confirm that she sank or mount a second attack. He came up shortly and began an end around to get ahead of the convoy for a daylight periscope attack.

The opportunity came just before noon. Clarey got inside the escorts and fired six torpedoes at two overlapping targets. He heard six hits and then looked through the periscope. He wrote:

What was left of the near ship was burning furiously; she had broken in two and her bow and stern both projected up in the air as she sank. The second target was partially obscured by fire from the first ship. I could see that her stern was all under water and she had listed over to port

*about 40 degrees. She was enveloped in the most tremen-
dous fire I have ever seen.*

Five escorts closed on Clarey and drove him under,
dropping fifty depth charges. Postwar assessment gave him
only one of the ships, *Harve Maru,* 5,600 tons.

After this attack, Blair ordered the boats to break off
and regroup. When the score was tallied up in the postwar Japanese records, it was found that, in the four convoys, Clarey and Blakely had sunk a total of seven ships
for about 35,000 tons: one each out of outbound convoys
One and Three and Blakely three and Clarey two out of
the important inbound Convoy Four. In all this action,
Boney Close in *Pilotfish* had not shot a single torpedo.
His patrol was declared "nonsuccessful."

The virtual destruction of the inbound Convoy Four—
five out of seven ships sunk—made the invasion of Saipan
and Guam an easier task for the U.S. Navy. Most of the
Japanese troops were rescued, but their equipment had
been lost and the troops did not arrive in time to be integrated into the defense plan.

With the invasion forces bearing down on the Marianas,
Lockwood ordered Blair's Blasters out of the area. Blakely
in *Shark* went back to base for battle-damage repairs;
John Scott in *Tunny,* still in the area, joined Clarey and
Close; and Blair took the pack west toward Luzon Strait
to watch for major Japanese fleet units.

Lockwood and Christie deployed the bulk of their submarines in support of the Marianas invasion. Some were
placed in strategic areas to help keep tabs on the Japanese
fleet, others lifeguarded or lay in wait at likely places to
intercept enemy traffic.

Soon after the Japanese heard that U.S. carrier forces,
commanded by Admiral Raymond Spruance, were attacking Guam and Saipan, the Japanese fleet, commanded by
Admiral Jisaburo Ozawa, steamed out of Tawi Tawi, with
destroyers and two heavy cruisers in the van. Marshall
Harlan ("Cy") Austin in *Redfin* saw them come out. He
went to battle stations, but the cruisers commenced zigzagging radically; he tried to follow and attack but could

not close the range. Two hours later, Austin saw most of the main body of the fleet come out: at least six carriers, four battleships, five heavy cruisers, one light cruiser, and destroyers. He tried to attack a battleship, but the earlier chase of the cruisers had pulled him out of position and again he was not able to close the range. That night at eight, however, he got off a vital radio report announcing that the Japanese fleet was on the move.

Austin trailed the fleet, but it soon outran him, so he turned northeast to take station in the western end of Surigao Strait, hoping to catch cripples returning to Tawi Tawi from the battle.

Admiral Ozawa took his fleet through Sibutu Passage, northward into the Sulu Sea. He stopped at Guimaras on June 14 to refuel. At 8 A.M. on June 15, he got under way again, crossed the small Visayan Sea, then headed for San Bernardino Strait, lying between the southern tip of Luzon and Samar. Meanwhile, a supply force set out from Davao, and *Musashi* and *Yamato* plus supporting vessels left from Batjan. Both the latter sailed to the east of Mindanao, directly into the Philippine Sea. The plan was that all three forces would rendezvous in the middle of the Philippine Sea on June 16.

At 4:22 on the afternoon of June 15, while patrolling submerged in San Bernardino Strait, Robert Risser in *Flying Fish* picked up Ozawa's fleet, hugging the coastline 11 miles away. Risser could see three carriers, three battleships, and several cruisers and destroyers. It was a beautiful group of targets, but Risser had orders to report first, then attack. He watched the ships go by; then, after dark —at 7:25 P.M.—he surfaced and commenced transmitting and trailing. Risser's valuable report was received, although he didn't know it. After this, Risser, low on fuel, was ordered to Brisbane for refit.

Slade Cutter, who had taken *Seahorse* to Brisbane following his tough third patrol in the Marianas, got under way on June 3. He topped off his fuel tanks in the Admiralties and proceeded northwestward toward Surigao Strait to join Thomas Benjamin Oakley, Jr., in *Growler*, who had moved to that station after lifeguard duty in the Marianas. These boats were to guard the east entrance of the strait in case Ozawa's fleet—or parts of it—came out that way.

At 6:45 P.M. on June 15, the same day and almost the same hour that Risser picked up the Ozawa force in San Bernardino Strait, Cutter saw smoke on the horizon about 200 miles due east of Surigao Strait. At first it appeared to be coming from "four large unidentified men-of-war."

Cutter immediately commenced tracking at maximum speed, setting up to attack, and obtaining the enemy course, speed, and zigzag plan. He had closed to 19,000 yards when one of his main motors began sparking badly, forcing him to reduce speed to 14½ knots. *Seahorse* gradually fell behind the formation. At 3 A.M. the following day, he got off a vital contact report to Lockwood.

AT 1330 ZEBRA [Japanese] TASK FORCE IN POSITION 10–11 NORTH, 129–35 EAST. BASE COURSE 045, SPEED OF ADVANCE 16.5. SIGHT CONTACT AT DUSK DISCLOSED PLENTY OF BATTLESHIPS. SEAHORSE WAS ASTERN AND COULD NOT RUN AROUND DUE TO SPEED RESTRICTIONS CAUSED BY MAIN MOTOR BRUSHES. RADAR INDICATES SIX SHIPS RANGES 28,000 TO 39,000 YARDS. CRUISERS AND DESTROYERS PROBABLY COULD NOT BE DETECTED AT THESE RANGES WITH OUR RADAR. POSSIBLE CARRIER PLANE FORCED US DOWN THIS MORNING. SEAHORSE TRAILING.

The unit Cutter found was a force, built around the super-battleships *Musashi* and *Yamato*. The force soon outdistanced Cutter. He got off a final contact report which stated in part:

SEAHORSE LOST CONTACT 15 HOURS ZEBRA FIFTEEN [3 P.M. June 15, local time] DUE TO MOTOR FAILURE. REGRET UNABLE TO CLOSE TO AMPLIFY PREVIOUS REPORT. SIGHTED TOPS OF FOUR UNIDENTIFIED LARGE MEN-OF-WAR AND SIX OTHER SOURCES OF SMOKE AT DUSK FIFTEENTH.

By the time these reports from Risser and Cutter were received, U.S. troops were storming ashore against heavy opposition at Saipan. The invasion of Guam was set for June 18. However, it was now clear to Admiral Spruance that Admiral Ozawa was on the way to fight with all he

had. Spruance postponed the invasion of Guam and redeployed Task Force 58 to meet the oncoming threat from
the west.

A brand-new Pearl Harbor submarine, *Cavalla*, with a
new skipper, Herman Kossler, who had been exec to
Burt Klakring for *Guardfish*'s first five patrols, left Midway
on June 4 to relieve Risser at San Bernardino Strait. On
the way to station June 9, *Cavalla*, under way on the surface, collided with a whale, which broached in a pool of
blood. Kossler was concerned that the collision might
have bent one of his shafts or a screw. However, he felt
no vibrations or other defects and continued on his way.

On June 15, after Lockwood received the contact reports from Risser and Cutter, he shifted *Cavalla* and William Deragon's *Pipefish* to advance scout stations along
the probable track of the main body. The two boats rendezvoused about 8 A.M. June 16, directly on the "estimated
track" and about 360 miles due east of San Bernardino
Strait. According to the arrangement made between them,
Kossler would patrol 5 miles north of the estimated track
and Deragon 5 miles south. The two boats searched all day
without finding anything. At about 8 P.M., Kossler got off a
negative search report and informed Lockwood that he was
proceeding to San Bernardino Strait to relieve Risser.

Three hours later, at 11:03 P.M., Kossler picked up a
contact on radar. It was four ships. This was not the main
body—which had veered southeastward off the estimated
track—but a supply force which had continued due east
from San Bernardino. Kossler made an end around and
dived about 3:40 A.M. He went in to attack, setting up
stern tubes on one of the tankers. As he was about to fire,
one of the destroyers charged at *Cavalla*, forcing Kossler
to break off the attack and go deep to avoid a collision.
Kossler later estimated that the destroyer came over *Cavalla*'s engine room as he was passing 75 feet.

When he came up again about 5 A.M. Kossler could
not see the convoy. He decided not to chase, reasoning
that his relief of Risser took priority. He had already expended much fuel and a full day looking for Ozawa; to
chase the tanker convoy would take at least another day
and more fuel. Kossler radioed Lockwood his decision.

When Lockwood received the message, he was of a different mind. Risser had already reported the fleet coming out; his relief was not urgent. Obviously these tankers had come to the area to refuel Ozawa's fleet. If Kossler trailed the tankers, they might lead him to the carriers and battleships. If they were sunk, Ozawa's fleet could not refuel and would be left sitting ducks. At 7:04 A.M. on June 17, Lockwood radioed Kossler: "CAVALLA IS [TO TAKE] ACTION. COMSUBPAC ALSO SENDS TO MUSKALLUNGE, SEAHORSE AND PIPEFISH FOR INFO. . . . DESTRUCTION THESE TANKERS OF GREAT IMPORTANCE. TRAIL, ATTACK, REPORT."

Kossler spent thirteen seemingly fruitless hours running down the track of the tankers. However, at about eight that night, June 17, he ran into a Japanese task force. At about 20,000 yards, his radar showed seven good-sized pips, which Kossler presumed to be a carrier, battleships, and cruisers. He submerged and ran in.

Believing it more important first to report this force, then attack if possible, for the next hour or so Kossler remained submerged, letting the task force pass by. At 10:45 P.M. he surfaced and got off a contact report—"fifteen or more large combatant ships"—to Lockwood and attempted to trail. Upon receiving this information, Lockwood told Kossler—and all other submarines—to shoot first and report later. To Kossler he said: HANG ON AND TRAIL AS LONG AS POSSIBLE REGARDLESS OF FUEL EXPENDITURE. . . . THEY MAY SLOW TO FUEL FROM YOUR PREVIOUSLY REPORTED TANKERS AND YOU MAY HAVE A CHANCE TO GET IN AN ATTACK. But by then Kossler had lost track of the force.

The contact report from Kossler puzzled Admiral Spruance. From the time of Risser's report to the time of Kossler's report, Admiral Ozawa had advanced only 500 miles for a very low average speed of about 8.8 knots. Moreover, Kossler had only reported "fifteen or more" large ships, and Spruance believed Ozawa capable of sending over forty. Spruance was suspicious. The idea took root that Ozawa had split his force and would attempt to flank Task Force 58 and break up the landing on the beaches at Saipan. But Ozawa had not split his forces. He was killing time. Tokyo had got him under way a day too early. He was waiting for land-based aircraft to congregate in the Marianas to help him attack.

Based on Kossler's several reports, it appeared to Lockwood that the four submarines—*Albacore, Bang, Finback,* and *Stingray*—in the "square" scouting line west of the Marianas were too far north. At eight on the morning of June 18, he ordered all four to shift position 100 miles southward. During the morning hours, the four boats carried out these orders.

All day on June 18 the two carrier forces lay back, trying to find one another with search aircraft. None of the U.S. planes found the Japanese forces. Ozawa's planes found Spruance's forces, about 250 miles southwest of the Marianas, and he decided that the next day—June 19 —he would launch the "decisive" battle.

Spruance was still concerned that Ozawa might have split his forces to make an end run against the amphibious forces at Saipan. Another submarine report seemed to lend credence to that theory. At about eight on the night of June 18, Sam Loomis in *Stingray,* one of the "square" submarines, tried to get off a routine report on a minor fire in his radio antenna. The Japanese jammed his transmission, making it unreadable. Spruance thought Loomis might have found the Japanese and his radio transmission was a contact report. If so, it put the Japanese much farther *east* than anyone had guessed, possibly making the end run Spruance feared. Accordingly, Spruance took up an easterly course—back toward Saipan and away from Ozawa—during the night.

Shortly after Spruance gave these orders, Ozawa broke radio silence. He called headquarters on Guam to make arrangements for land-based air support for the morrow's attack and to tell Guam to be prepared to service carrier planes that might land there to refuel and rearm after hitting the enemy. Spruance's radio intelligence specialists DF-ed these transmissions, obtaining an accurate fix. The fix placed Ozawa's forces much farther *west* of *Stingray's* position. But Spruance did not trust DF-ing and preferred to be guided by *Stingray's* unreadable message.

About this time James Langford Jordan in *Finback,* patrolling the northwest corner of the square, saw two searchlight beams on the southern horizon. Jordan charged south toward the beams at full speed but could not get close enough to pick up whatever it was on his SJ radar. Six hours later—11 P.M.—Jordan reported what he had seen to Lockwood. Another three hours went by before the message reached Spruance. Jordan had probably detected the main body, but his six-hour delay in getting off the report and the further three-hour delay in relaying the message to Spruance—a total lapse of nine hours—had rendered the contact meaningless.

When dawn broke on the morning of June 19, Ozawa had 430 aircraft on his nine carriers. He launched these against Task Force 58 in four major raids, all the while expecting massive raids from his land-based aircraft on Guam. Unknown to Ozawa, none of the four raids went well. His planes were pounced upon by U.S. carrier aircraft or chewed to pieces by barrages of antiaircraft fire. On that day, which would become famous as "The Great Marianas Turkey Shoot," Ozawa lost about 330 planes without sinking a single U.S. ship. Nor did he receive much support from land-based aircraft, most of which had already been destroyed by U.S. carrier raids.

At about eight on the morning of June 19, as Ozawa was preparing Raid One, James William Blanchard in *Albacore*, working the southwest corner of the square, raised his periscope. Thanks to Lockwood's decision the day before to shift the square 100 miles south, Blanchard found himself right in the midst of Ozawa's main carrier group.

Blanchard let one carrier go by and selected a second one for his target. The initial range was 9,000 yards. A destroyer loomed in his crosshairs. Blanchard coolly changed course to allow the destroyer to pass ahead. The range to the carrier closed to 5,300 yards. As Blanchard went in, he took another periscope look. It was immediately apparent that something had gone wrong with the TDC. Cussing his luck, Blanchard fired six bow tubes by "seaman's eye."

At least three destroyers immediately charged *Albacore*. Blanchard went deep. Going down he heard—and felt—one solid torpedo explosion which timed perfectly for the run of his number-six torpedo. About that time, twenty-five depth charges rained down, many so close that cork flew off the overhead. Then Blanchard heard "a distant and persistent explosion of great force." Then another.

One of Blanchard's torpedoes had hit the carrier. It

was Ozawa's flagship, *Taiho,* 31,000 tons, newest and largest in the Japanese fleet. The explosion jammed the forward aircraft elevator; its pit filled with gasoline, water, and fuel. However, no fire erupted and the flight deck was unharmed. Blanchard believed that he had got a second hit as well, but he was mistaken. A Japanese pilot, who had just taken off from *Taiho* for Raid Two, launched at 8:56, heroically dived his plane at one of Blanchard's torpedoes, exploding it—and himself—100 yards short of the carrier.

The one torpedo hit on *Taiho* caused little concern on board. Ozawa still "radiated confidence and satisfaction" and by 11:30 had launched raids Three and Four. Meanwhile, a novice took over the damage-control work. He thought the best way to handle the gasoline fumes was to open up the ship's ventilation system and let them disperse. When he did, the fumes spread all through the ship. Unknown to anybody on board, *Taiho* became a floating time bomb.

About 3:30 that afternoon, *Taiho* was jolted by a severe explosion. A senior staff officer on the bridge saw the flight deck heave up. The sides blew out. *Taiho* dropped out of formation and began to settle in the water, clearly doomed. Though Admiral Ozawa wanted to go down with the ship, his staff prevailed on him to survive and to shift his quarters to the cruiser *Haguro.* Taking the Emperor's portrait, Ozawa transferred to *Haguro* by destroyer. After he left, *Taiho* was torn by a second thunderous explosion and sank stern first, carrying down 1,650 officers and men. But neither Blanchard nor Lockwood knew for many weeks that this prize had sunk.

Less than three hours after Blanchard shot at *Taiho,* Herman Kossler in *Cavalla,* who had been chasing one Japanese group or another for about sixty hours, raised his periscope. "The picture was too good to be true," he later wrote. There was the heavy carrier *Shokaku,* veteran of Pearl Harbor, the Battle of the Coral Sea, and many other engagements, with a "bedspring" radar antenna on her foremast and a large Japanese ensign. The carrier was launching and recovering aircraft.

Kossler closed and fired six torpedoes, range 1,200

yards. Then he went deep. He heard three solid hits and figured the other three missed. Eight depth charges fell near *Cavalla*. During the next three hours, over a hundred more were dropped, fifty-six of them "fairly close." Kossler went very deep and evaded.

In fact, four of Kossler's torpedoes hit *Shokaku*, setting off unmanageable internal explosions and flames. *Shokaku* fell out of formation. Her bow settled. Water flooded into the hangar space through an elevator. Shortly after three o'clock in the afternoon, she turned over and plunged beneath the waves.

Kossler returned a hero from this, his first war patrol. Lockwood knew from the codebreakers that *Shokaku* had sunk.

During the night of June 19, Admiral Ozawa on *Haguro* retired his forces and regrouped for refueling on the following day and then shifted his flag to *Zuikaku*. Even though he had lost two carriers to U.S. submarines, most of his planes had failed to return, and he had had no help from land-based aircraft, he was not dispirited. He believed that many of the aircraft which failed to return had gone on to bases in the Marianas and would be ready for battle again soon. Ozawa prepared for a second strike on June 21 which would truly annihilate the U.S. Pacific Fleet.

That night at 9:21, James Jordan in *Finback*, patrolling the northwest corner of the square, again sighted searchlights on the horizon. These must have come from Ozawa's force, which passed close to *Finback*'s area. Again Jordan charged in, and this time he made radar contact. He had closed to 14,000 yards when four destroyers came up astern, seemingly attacking *Finback*. Jordan submerged. Later he said, "The destroyers passed over us without attacking, followed closely by the major ships, which numbered more than twenty-five."

Three hours later, Jordan surfaced with all these ships still in sight. He trailed and tried to get off a contact report, but the radio transmitter was out of commission. Jordan said later, "We continued to track on the surface, hoping the transmitter could be quickly repaired, but were again forced down by one or more high-speed ships.

The pattern continued all night. Each time we surfaced we were forced to dive by returning aircraft or surface ship, although none stayed to attack us."

Jordan's radio transmitter remained out of commission for several days. Later, when *Finback* returned from patrol, Jordan's squadron commander wrote in despair, *"Finback*'s inability to transmit information on contact with enemy force on June 19 was one of the costly misfortunes of the war." The episode left Jordan in a deep depression, and when he returned to port, he requested immediate relief.

That same night, Admiral Spruance made a move that was strangely reminiscent of his move in the Battle of Midway: he again let the surviving and badly mauled Japanese fleet slip away. At Midway he may have been unlucky; this time it was, beyond doubt, a tactical error. He lost contact with Ozawa's forces, now maintaining strict radio silence. Nobody sent out night search planes to find it. While Ozawa retired to the northwest to rendezvous with his tankers, Spruance steamed east. Hour by hour the distance between the two forces grew greater.

Had Spruance followed up more aggressively and obtained a position report on Ozawa, U.S. submarines might have inflicted even more damage on the Japanese. Lockwood had three boats to the north of the battle scene ideally positioned to intercept: the wolf pack Blair's Blasters, composed of *Pilotfish*, *Pintado*, and *Tunny*. If Spruance had determined earlier that Ozawa was retiring northwestward toward Okinawa, these three boats could have intercepted. Having no positive information on Ozawa's movements, Lockwood kept the pack in place to the north, hoping Ozawa would head for Japan, passing through the pack's area. In addition, he moved *Archerfish* west from the Bonins to cover a northward retreat to Japan.

On June 20, Spruance belatedly headed west, launching the hunt for Ozawa. That afternoon, at about four, a search plane from *Enterprise* found Ozawa 275 miles away. It was the first time in the whole battle that a U.S. carrier plane had even *seen* the Japanese surface forces. Although it was late in the day and the Japanese lay almost at the extreme range of U.S. aircraft, Spruance gave the go-ahead for an all-out attack.

The planes reached the Japanese shortly before sunset. In a confused but lucky fight, they sank the carrier *Hiyo* (which Roy Benson had damaged off Tokyo Bay in June 1943) and two fleet tankers, *Genyo* and *Seiyo Maru*. They inflicted heavy damage on the battleship *Haruna* and the cruiser *Maya* and light damage on Ozawa's new flagship *Zuikaku* and the carriers *Junyo*, *Ryuho*, and *Chiyoda*. In addition, they shot down another twenty-two Japanese planes, leaving Ozawa with only about thirty-five operational aircraft.

Following this attack, Ozawa realized he was in no position to make a second strike against Spruance. He retired to Okinawa at best speed, and offered his resignation, which was not accepted. Spruance ordered up a stern chase, but Ozawa, who had a good head start, outran him.

After stopping at Okinawa to refuel, Ozawa returned his fleet to the Inland Sea. Lockwood had four submarines patrolling off southern Honshu near the entrances to the Inland Sea: *Batfish*, *Grouper*, *Whale*, and *Pampanito*. None made contact with Ozawa's forces. In this greatest carrier air battle in history, later to be known officially as the Battle of the Philippine Sea, Ozawa had lost three of his nine carriers: *Shokaku*, *Taiho*, and *Hiyo*—two to submarines.

The invasion of Guam now proceeded as planned. The victory turned out to be even more decisive than Nimitz had foreseen. The battle not only cost Admiral Toyoda three aircraft carriers but also most of his carrier air wings, a blow from which the Japanese naval air arm never really recovered. The remaining carriers were relegated to the role of divisionary forces for the future, and Japan began training pilots for its kamikaze corps: flying bombs, piloted by humans who would achieve everlasting fame by diving their craft into U.S. warships.

In Tokyo, the loss of the Marianas brought shock on an unprecedented scale. "Saipan was really understood to be a matter of life and death," said Vice Admiral Paul H. Wenneker, German naval attaché to Tokyo. Said Marine General Holland M. Smith, "Its loss caused a greater dismay than all her previous defeats put together." And Admiral King noted, "Saipan was the decisive battle of the war."

On July 18, the day the loss of Saipan was announced to the Japanese people, Prime Minister Tojo and his entire cabinet resigned. General Kuniaki Koiso formed a new cabinet. "And, although Koiso took office with a promise to prosecute the war vigorously and issued a defiant statement," Samuel Eliot Morison later wrote, "everybody who understood Japanese double-talk knew that a change in ministry meant an admission of defeat and a desire for peace. Yet nobody in Japanese military or political circles would accept the onus of proposing peace, so the Pacific war dragged on for another twelve months."

19

A VIRTUAL BLOCKADE

After the Battle of the Philippine Sea—during the summer of 1944—Lockwood and Christie flooded enemy waters with submarines, operating alone or in wolf packs. These boats were spectacularly successful, inflicting enormous damage on Japanese maritime forces. It amounted to a virtual blockade of Japan and her remaining possessions, decisively restricting the importation of vital war-making matériels and oil.

A Lockwood pack went on the polar circuit. It was a twosome made up of *Herring*, commanded by another Naval Academy football star, David Zabriskie, Jr., and *Barb*, now commanded by Eugene Bennett Fluckey.

Fluckey had been caught up in backwater assignments since the beginning of the war. After making five patrols out of Panama on the ancient *Bonita*, he had returned to the States for a postgraduate course in naval engineering. During *Barb*'s seventh war patrol (the second in the Pacific), Fluckey had made a PCO cruise.

While Fluckey was preparing to get under way from Midway, Lockwood flew out for an inspection. Fluckey said later, "I had never known the man but I did know he was a tough one and he wanted good skippers and good producers. I liked his methods. . . . If you produced, he supported you and gave you everything he could possibly give you. If you failed, he would give you another opportunity, but if you came back the second time with an empty bag, you usually were forced out of command."

For a brief moment, Fluckey feared he might be forced out of command before he set sail. "As he walked down the dock with my crew at quarters," Fluckey said later, "I had my heart in my throat for fear that he was coming aboard to tell me he didn't think I had enough experience and that he was going to remove me from command until I had proven myself. On his arrival on board, after saying hello, I immediately took an aggressive attitude and said, 'Admiral Lockwood, how many ships would you like us to bring back in our bag this time?' He looked at me with a smile and replied, 'How many do you think you can sink?' and I said, 'Would five be enough?' Lockwood said, 'I think five would be enough.' Then I said, 'What types do you want?' Lockwood said, 'Forget the types, you just get five. Now get out there and give 'em hell.' "

The two boats proceeded north. On the way, Lockwood sent them an Ultra about a three-ship convoy departing Matsuwa To in the Kuriles. Fluckey, the senior skipper, laid out the intercept plan: *Herring* close in, *Barb* to seaward. The convoy came out right on schedule. Zabriskie set up and sank an escort, then a 2,000-ton freighter. The remaining ships scattered and ran—directly toward Fluckey in *Barb*. Fluckey moved fast and fired three torpedoes; a freighter blew up and sank while he took pictures. It was *Koto Maru,* 1,000 tons.

After that, Fluckey surfaced to chase. He caught up with *Madras Maru,* 3,800 tons, and fired three stern tubes. This ship also blew up and sank. Fluckey then returned to the scene of his first sinking to capture a survivor for intelligence purposes.

He wrote, "It was a gruesome picture . . . an unholy sight . . . it was getting dark, the atmosphere was much like one you'd expect from Frankenstein. The people were screaming and groaning in the water. There were several survivors on rafts. The water at that time was very cold, about 27 degrees. These people were gradually freezing and dying. We took the most lively looking specimen aboard."

Meanwhile David Zabriskie closed in on Matsuwa and found and sank two ships at anchor in the harbor, *Iwaki Maru,* 3,100 tons, and *Hiburi Maru,* a transport of 4,400 tons.

Immediately after his torpedoes exploded, the shore batteries on Matsuwa opened fire on *Herring.* The Japanese evidently scored two direct hits on *Herring*'s conning tower, destroying the boat. The Japanese reported "bubbles covered an area about 5 meters wide and heavy oil covered an area of approximately 15 miles." Nothing further was ever heard from Zabriskie.

On his first patrol, Zabriskie had not sunk a confirmed ship and had been roasted for inadequacies in the fire-control party. On this, his second, he sank four confirmed ships for almost 10,000 tons within a two-day span and gave Fluckey an opportunity to sink two other ships fleeing his attack.

Fluckey wrote later that his POW turned out to be a "traitor to his country." Using sign language, he poured out valuable intelligence on Japanese ships and minefields. Fluckey radioed some of this—information on minefields off Hokkaido and northeast Honshu—to Lockwood.

Now alone, Fluckey shifted northwest to the Sea of Okhotsk, cutting among icebergs, bedeviled by mirages. He found some trawlers out sealing and sank them with his deck gun. On the night of June 11, he picked up two more ships and sank both with torpedoes; they were *Toten Maru,* 3,800 tons, and *Chihaya Maru,* 1,100 tons. Two nights later, Fluckey found another ship with a small escort. He fired two torpedoes and sank the large transport *Takashima Maru,* 5,600 tons. After that Fluckey returned to Matsuwa, poking *Barb*'s nose into the anchorage there and at other islands, threading through dozens of sampans. Twice Fluckey got caught in Japanese fishing nets. The first time he backed down submerged and got out. The second time, *Barb* was hooked solidly and Fluckey had to surface to cut himself loose.

When Fluckey returned to base, he was showered with congratulations. Later he said, "Admiral Lockwood reminded me that, by God, I was the only skipper during the war that told him exactly how many ships I was going to sink and then went out and did it."

Lockwood improvised a wolf pack for Luzon Strait composed of boats that had been deployed for the battle. These were Slade Cutter's *Seahorse,* Anton Gallaher's *Bang,* and Ben Oakley's *Growler.* The three boats met in the strait on June 25. Gallaher was senior, so he took command. Cutter and Oakley went on board *Bang* to plan tactics.

Shortly after midnight on June 27, Cutter picked up a ten-ship convoy: five big ships, five escorts. In keeping with pack policy, he prepared a contact alert but deferred sending it in the belief that both *Growler* and *Bang* were too far away to help. Cutter dived for a submerged attack, firing six torpedoes at a tanker and two freighters. He believed he got five out of six hits—three in the tanker, one each in two freighters. He wrote, "First hit in tanker at point of aim, forward of bridge. It was a beautiful hit, producing a huge sheet of flame and setting the ship on fire." Cutter was positive that the tanker and a freighter sank, but postwar records credited him only with the tanker, *Medan Maru,* 5,000 tons.

Gallaher in *Bang* was not as far away as Cutter thought. He saw the tanker burning on the horizon and closed in. But he was too late. The following night, Cutter and Gallaher rendezvoused again. Later, Cutter wrote, *"Bang* told us that they had seen the fire from our tanker last night and believed that they could have gotten in had we notified them early enough. If that is so, we made a grave error in judgment, and deeply regret the decision to maintain radio silence. We apologize to *Bang* for what they may consider a lack of cooperation on the part of *Seahorse."*

The next day, *Growler,* by now seriously low on fuel, departed for Midway, leaving Cutter and Gallaher as a two-boat pack. Oakley's fuel problem was so acute he was forced to proceed on only one engine. Nevertheless, on the day he left he found a cargo ship with four escorts and managed to track and attack. He sank *Katori Maru,* 2,000 tons, early on the morning of June 29. The ship was evidently carrying gasoline. It blew up with an awesome explosion, "like a 4th of July flowerpot."

Cutter and Gallaher went on patrolling the strait. Near dawn on June 29, Gallaher picked up another convoy. He made a long end around in daylight, getting off a contact report to Cutter. But *Seahorse* did not receive the report. About 3 P.M. Gallaher attacked the convoy submerged, firing ten torpedoes at three ships. Gallaher believed he had sunk one or two of the ships, but postwar records failed to confirm his estimate.

That night, Cutter noted in his report, "Received the rebroadcast of *Bang*'s dispatch reporting her brilliant attack this afternoon. Our radio had been manned continuously, but the contact reports the *Bang* sent out were not received. Cannot understand this as we were hearing Jap stations clearly on the assigned frequency. We were particularly happy to hear of *Bang*'s good fortune in view of what happened the night before last."

On the night of July 3, Cutter picked up another convoy and flashed an alert to Gallaher. Then he closed in and fired at two freighters loaded with troops and equipment. He hit both. They each gave off many secondary explosions, probably caused by exploding gasoline drums. An escort charged in, forcing *Seahorse* deep. Forty minutes later, Cutter returned to periscope depth to find one ship sunk and the other severely damaged and lying to.

Meanwhile, Gallaher in *Bang,* receiving the contact report from Cutter, moved in to attack. He tried to torpedo the cripple, but a destroyer got in the way. Gallaher fired three torpedoes down the throat at the destroyer and went deep. At the last minute, the destroyer turned and avoided. Then it attacked *Bang,* dropping twenty depth charges.

After daylight, both Cutter and Gallaher made end arounds, gaining position ahead of the convoy. About noon, Cutter, who had ignored aircraft flying over him all morning, submerged ahead of the convoy to attack. He let the ships come close, so close that one passed directly over *Seahorse*. Cutter came up to periscope depth for a look at her stern. He wrote, "Troops were packed tight on the fantail and sitting up on the canvas-covered deck cargo. Every bit of deck space appeared to be utilized. . . . It was a fascinating picture."

Cutter fired at two of the freighters; he hit one and missed the other. Gallaher, harassed by aircraft and escorts, was not able to make an attack. Later he was commended for drawing off some of the escorts, enabling Cutter to make his attacks without excessive interference.

Following this attack, Cutter departed for Pearl Harbor, leaving Gallaher alone. Cutter had sunk four ships for about 11,000 tons. His total score in four patrols: nineteen ships. In his endorsement to Cutter's patrol report, Lockwood stated, "This was the fourth successive brilliantly conducted war patrol for *Seahorse*." He presented Cutter with his fourth Navy Cross.

When Cutter returned to Midway for refit, he was

exhausted and asked for two weeks' leave to return to the States to see his wife and young daughter. After Cutter had been home for a while, he received unexpected orders to new construction—*Requin*, which his wife was to sponsor at commissioning. Cutter did not make another war patrol.

Like the late Mush Morton, Slade Cutter had been an inspiration to the submarine force, a skipper's skipper and Lockwood's pride and joy. Like Burlingame and Triebel, Cutter was sometimes a terror while unwinding on the beach. But at sea he was awesomely cool and able, and possessed of an uncanny ability to find Japanese ships. (Lockwood wrote, in jest, that he believed that, if asked, Cutter could even find Japanese ships in Pearl Harbor.) In the postwar accounting, his nineteen confirmed ships sunk put him in a tie for second place with Mush Morton for the greatest number of ships sunk by a U.S. skipper. For years afterward, whenever submariners gathered to recount the war and spin yarns, the name of Slade Deville Cutter—football star, heavyweight boxer, and submariner extraordinary—would soon surface.

Three other wolf packs patrolled Luzon Strait during this period. Between them they sank twelve ships, by postwar accounting.

One of them began as a four-boat pack: *Apogon*, commanded by Walter Paul Schoeni; a new boat, *Piranha*, commanded by Harold Eustace Ruble; *Thresher*, commanded by Duncan Calvin MacMillan; and *Guardfish*, back from a long overhaul and still commanded by Bud Ward. The pack commander was William Vincent ("Mickey") O'Regan, who called his pack the "Mickey Finns." O'Regan rode in *Guardfish*.

Late in the evening of July 11, the Mickey Finns moved in on a convoy. Harold Ruble in *Piranha* sank one ship for 6,500 tons, but Schoeni's boat, making a submerged attack, was rammed: the leading freighter in the center column hit *Apogon* on the starboard side, bending the periscopes and shears 45 degrees, tearing off the number-one periscope, and flooding the conning tower. Seven depth charges rained down. Schoeni managed to hold everything together, and *Apogon* escaped to go to overhaul.

Schoeni, congratulated for saving his boat, went to shore duty.

Now short one boat, O'Regan received an Ultra on July 15 on an important southbound convoy. The pack changed course to intercept—all but *Piranha*, which didn't receive the message. Ironically it was *Piranha*, off course, that found the convoy at 4 A.M. and flashed the word. While *Guardfish* and *Thresher* were coming up, Ruble sank another ship.

That night—July 16—Ward in *Guardfish* closed the convoy for a night surface attack. He counted ten ships and several escorts. He fired six torpedoes at five overlapping ships, including a tanker. As he later described it, "The tanker was loaded with gas and blew up immediately, sending flames thousands of feet high. The large freighter was also loaded with combustibles, commencing to burn aft, and later blew up. The third ship in line, a freighter, broke in two in the middle and sank, and the fourth ship in line went down bow first. The scene was lit up as bright as day by the explosions and burning ships."

Ward then maneuvered around for a stern shot, firing three torpedoes at a freighter. One torpedo missed, two hit. Ward wrote, "Target leaned over on its starboard side and disappeared from sight and SJ [radar] screen." Finding another target, Ward "became impatient" and fired two torpedoes which missed. He turned around and fired two more at the same target. Both hit. Ward believed the ship sank, but he claimed only damage. He hauled clear to reload and rest, noting, "Everyone in the control party was beginning to show fatigue after six hours at battle stations under constant tensions. . . . Commanding Officer had had no rest for over fifty hours."

In action no less furious, MacMillan in *Thresher* attacked the convoy from another quarter, firing off twenty-three torpedoes. He believed he had sunk four ships and two destroyers, but postwar records credited him with only two ships: *Sainei Maru*, 5,000 tons, and *Shozan Maru*, 2,800 tons. Ward believed he had sunk five ships during his series of attacks, but postwar analysis gave him credit for three: *Jinzan Maru*, 5,200 tons; *Mantai Maru*, 5,900 tons; and *Hiyama Maru*, 2,800 tons. There was no record of a tanker sunk on this night at this place.

When Ward came back up at 6 P.M. on July 18, having rested himself and his crew, he found that a gale had kicked up huge seas. But he had surfaced in the middle of a massive convoy: two aircraft carriers (type unknown), two large tankers, one transport, one seaplane tender, and a naval auxiliary—all southbound. Ward fired three bow tubes at the naval auxiliary, range 1,370 yards. He swung to set up on a tanker, but it was coming in to ram, so Ward had to go deep to avoid and lost contact.

At dawn the following morning, July 19, he found yet another convoy. He submerged and fired four torpedoes at a target. One of them made a circular run around *Guardfish;* two hit. "Target broke in half immediately," he reported later. In these two attacks, according to postwar records, Ward sank only one ship, *Teiryu Maru,* 6,500 tons.

Following Bub Ward's attack, the Mickey Finns, out of torpedoes, left the area and returned to Midway. In all, the pack had sunk eight confirmed ships for about 40,000 tons, making it the best wolf-pack performance to date. Bub Ward, who had fired twenty torpedoes in the space of fifty-six hours, sank half: four ships for 20,400 tons.

A second pack operating in the strait arrived to attack Ward's convoy of the nineteenth. It consisted of three boats: John Jay Flachsenhar's *Rock,* Alan Boyd Banister's *Sawfish,* and Roger Keithly's *Tilefish.* (Gallaher in *Bang* had come down from Formosa to join the pack for about nine days and had returned to base independently.) The pack, "Wilkin's Wildcats," was commanded by Warren Dudley Wilkin, in *Tilefish.* All three boats closed and inflicted damage, but postwar records credited no ships sunk.

More significant action came a week later, when they were alerted by Ultra to an important contact. A Japanese submarine, *I-29,* was returning from a sea voyage to Germany, bringing a "precious cargo" (as historian Holmes later put it) of "German technical material." *Tilefish, Rock,* and *Sawfish* formed an ambush. The prize fell to Banister in *Sawfish.* When a submarine came along, right on schedule, Banister fired four torpedoes, three of which hit. Keithly in *Tilefish* was beginning an approach when he saw the explosion.

There was no immediate rejoicing in Pearl Harbor when Banister reported sinking what he assumed to be *I-29*. Nothing had been heard from Ruble's *Piranha* since the Mickey Finns had cleared the area, and Lockwood and Voge were convinced that, by a tragic error, Banister had actually sunk *Piranha*. It wasn't till a few days later that Ruble spoke up with a radio dispatch and Lockwood breathed easier.

The third wolf pack in the Luzon Strait in July was commanded by Lewis Smith Parks, riding Red Ramage's *Parche*. Besides *Parche*, the pack was made up of David Whelchel's *Steelhead* and a new boat, *Hammerhead*, commanded by John Croysdale Martin. "Parks' Pirates," as the pack was called, had spent much of its patrol in frustration since leaving Midway on June 17. En route, Red Ramage had bagged just one small patrol craft with *Parche*'s deck gun. In the strait on July 5, when Ramage was moving in to attack what appeared to be two cruisers and a destroyer, he had to take his boat deep when one of the cruisers opened fire and he lost contact. After many days of bad weather and no targets, Parks received a report from Ward, on the Mickey Finns' boat *Guardfish*, of the massive convoy Ward had discovered on July 18, when he'd surfaced in its midst. Parks' Pirates never made contact with it. On the way to intercept, Parks and Ramage came upon an unescorted aircraft carrier—"the perfect dream come true" —only to have this vulnerable target zig and escape them.

It was only after eleven empty days that Parks' Pirates made their next convoy contact, and again bad luck plagued them. In the early hours of July 30, Martin in *Hammerhead* picked up a big convoy—twelve to fifteen freighters and tankers and many escorts—and flashed the alert. While Martin trailed, Red Ramage and Dave Whelchel moved in. With daylight fast approaching, Martin attacked, firing ten torpedoes at two big ships. He believed he sank one and damaged another, but postwar records showed no sinking at this time and place. Martin then attempted to trail the convoy submerged, but it got away. That night, running low on fuel, he surfaced and set course for Fremantle.

The contact reports that Martin flashed to Parks and

Ramage were confused, erroneous, and niggardly. While Martin attacked, both Ramage and Whelchel thrashed around the dark seas, unable to make contact. They were somewhat puzzled, then angry. Ramage wrote bitterly, "As the sun came up, it finally dawned on us that we were the victims of another snipe hunt. That was bad enough but we never expected to be left holding the well known burlap bag by one of our own teammates."

During the day, July 30, Whelchel and Ramage kept up the hunt, both harassed by planes. At 10:30 A.M., Whelchel spotted smoke and sent off a contact report. At about noon, Ramage saw the smoke, trailed, then lost it. After dark, Whelchel, who was still in contact, vectored Ramage into position. At 2:40 A.M. on the morning of July 31, Ramage made radar contact and went to battle stations.

Meanwhile, Whelchel attacked. At 3:32 A.M. he fired ten torpedoes at a tanker and two freighters. He observed a hit in the first freighter and black smoke near the waterline of the tanker. He missed the second freighter. He pulled off and began reloading his torpedo tubes.

The next forty-eight minutes were among the wildest of the submarine war. Ramage cleared the bridge of all personnel except himself and steamed right into the convoy on the surface, maneuvering among the ships and firing nineteen torpedoes. Japanese ships fired back with deck guns and tried to ram. With consummate seamanship and coolness under fire, Ramage dodged and twisted, returning torpedo fire for gunfire.

After Ramage hauled clear, Whelchel came in again. At 4:49, he fired four stern tubes at a freighter. He heard two explosions and saw a flash under the stacks. At 5:16, he fired four bow tubes at another freighter, observing two hits amidships. Escorts charged, forcing Whelchel under. He received a bone-jarring depth-charging.

Both boats remained submerged the following day, and that night Parks gave orders to leave the area. When the pack returned to Pearl Harbor, Lockwood credited Ramage with sinking five ships for 34,000 tons, Whelchel two ships for 14,000 tons. In the postwar reckoning, Ramage received confirmation for sinking two ships for 14,700 tons, Whelchel two for 15,400. In addition, each skipper received half credit for sinking the 9,000-ton transport *Yoshino Maru*. Total for both: five ships, 39,000 tons.

The attack mounted on the convoy by Red Ramage was the talk of the submarine force. In terms of close-in, furious torpedo shooting, there had never been anything like it. Although the score was no record, Lockwood's staff believed Ramage deserved more than a Navy Cross. Accordingly, the recommendation went forward that Ramage be awarded the Medal of Honor. The recommendation was subsequently approved and Ramage became the third —and at the time the only living—submariner, after Howard Gilmore and John Cromwell, to receive this recognition.

Three boats went to the East China Sea. They were not a formal wolf pack, since they operated in separate—but adjacent—areas, but they mapped out a semicoordinated attack plan. The boats were Dick O'Kane's *Tang,* Donald Weiss's *Tinosa,* and a new boat, *Sealion II,* commanded by Eli Reich.

Weiss in *Tinosa* went to the area by way of the Bonins. On the night of June 15 he sighted a five-ship convoy: two tankers, a small transport, and two destroyer escorts. He tracked and dived for a daylight attack, firing six torpedoes at the two tankers. All missed and the destroyers charged in, forcing Weiss deep. He was not able to make another attack.

On the night of June 18, Weiss battle-surfaced on a fishing sampan, riddling the craft with small-arms fire and getting an occasional hit with the deck gun. When the sampan stubbornly refused to sink, Weiss decided on more drastic action. Later he wrote, "Tommy guns, hand grenades, rags and fuel oil were mustered topside. Moving close aboard the sailer, rag firebrands and about a half a dozen buckets of fuel oil were tossed on board. . . . The target quickly became a raging mass of flame."

On the night of June 24, the three boats rendezvoused about 120 miles southwest of Nagasaki. Since Donald Weiss was the senior skipper, O'Kane and Reich sent their execs to *Tinosa* for a strategy meeting.

The next night O'Kane picked up a large convoy heading into Nagasaki. He flashed the word to *Tinosa* and *Sealion,* but neither boat was able to close, so O'Kane had this one all to himself. It consisted of six large ships with an enormous number of escorts, probably sixteen. O'Kane came in on the surface, firing six torpedoes at a freighter and tanker. Later, he wrote, "Observed two beautiful hits in the stern and amidships of the freighter. . . . The explosions appeared to blow the ship's sides out and he commenced sinking rapidly. . . . Our fourth and fifth torpedoes hit under the stack and just forward of the superstructure of the tanker. His whole after end blazed up until extinguished as he went down by the stern." Escorts drove *Tang* under.

O'Kane claimed two sinkings for that night and Lockwood so credited him, but O'Kane's torpedoes evidently did far more damage than he thought. Postwar Japanese records revealed that four ships of the convoy went down: two transports and two freighters, totaling 16,000 tons. If the records are accurate, it means that O'Kane sank four ships with six torpedoes, making this the single best attack of the war. If his report that he saw two torpedo hits in both the freighter and tanker is correct, then the other two torpedoes got one ship each.

After that, the three boats moved northward, taking station off the southwest coast of Korea in the shallow waters of the Yellow Sea. On June 26, O'Kane picked up a lone freighter and fired four torpedoes. All missed. On June 28, Eli Reich in *Sealion* sank a 2,400-ton ship near the minefields in Korea Strait. The next day, O'Kane picked up another single, fired two torpedoes, and missed again. He attacked this ship a second time, firing a single torpedo. Down went *Nikkin Maru*, a 5,700-ton freighter. On July 1, O'Kane sank a small freighter and a small tanker.

Two days later, O'Kane and Reich rendezvoused again to compare notes. (Weiss in *Tinosa* had moved south.) Reich decided to have a look near Shanghai; O'Kane would stay off the coast of Korea. The following day, July 4, O'Kane sank two large freighters: 6,886-ton *Asukazan Maru* and 7,000-ton *Yamaika Maru*, from which he took a prisoner. On July 6, he fired his last torpedoes at a 1,500-ton freighter. It sank immediately.

While O'Kane and Reich were conferring on July 3, Weiss found a convoy and sank two ships: *Kosan Maru*, 2,700 tons, and *Kamo Maru*, 8,000 tons. Reich also found other ships. On July 6, off Shanghai, he sank a 2,000-ton freighter; moving up into the shallows of the Yellow

Sea on July 11, he sank two more ships, one for 2,400 tons and one for 1,000 tons.

One by one the three boats left the area and returned to base. When *Tang* reached Midway, Lockwood credited O'Kane with sinking eight ships for 56,000 tons. In the postwar accounting, the number of sinkings was readjusted upward to ten and the tonnage cut to 39,100. In terms of confirmed ships sunk, this was the best war patrol by any submarine in the war. For it, O'Kane received his third Navy Cross.

Eli Reich in *Sealion II* turned in an excellent maiden patrol; he had sunk four confirmed ships for 7,800 tons. Weiss sank two confirmed ships. After this patrol, he took *Tinosa* back for an overhaul. In three patrols on *Tinosa,* Weiss had sunk eight confirmed ships for 40,000 tons.

Altogether, the three-boat foray into the East China Sea cost the Japanese sixteen confirmed ships for 58,000 tons.

Ralph Christie's first formal wolf pack put to sea in June shortly after the Battle of the Philippine Sea. It consisted of three boats: Reuben Whitaker's *Flasher,* Frank Walker's *Crevalle,* and *Angler,* now commanded by Franklin Grant Hess. Whitaker, the senior skipper, commanded the pack. To avoid a concentration in Lombok Strait, the boats left for patrol in the South China Sea independently.

Whitaker went up through Lombok Strait into the Java Sea. He traveled along the southern coast of Borneo, going through Karimata Strait, until he reached the equator, directly on the Surabaya–Singapore traffic lanes. Shortly after sunset on June 28, he picked up a thirteen-ship convoy bound for Singapore. Because the water was shallow and pitted with uncharted shoals and reefs, Whitaker elected to attack on the surface. He fired six torpedoes at two freighters, obtaining hits in both. "The first target," he later wrote, "with three hits, was seen to break in two and sink almost immediately." It was *Nippo Maru,* a 6,000-ton freighter. Whitaker believed the second also went down, but postwar records failed to bear him out.

While waiting for the other members of his pack to arrive, Whitaker took up station north of Camranh Bay. On the night of July 7, he saw a freighter with one escort. He sank the freighter, *Koto Maru*, 3,500 tons, with four stern tubes. The escorts zipped back and forth menacingly but never did find *Flasher*.

On July 13, *Angler* and *Crevalle* arrived and the pack was officially formed up. For five days, the boats rotated between the middle of the South China Sea and the Indochina coast, finding nothing. Whitaker, somewhat discouraged, got off a message to Christie stating that in view of the lack of traffic he doubted the need for three submarines to patrol the area; then he ordered a routine surface patrol on July 19 in the middle of the South China Sea.

At 10:46 that morning, Whitaker's officer of the deck saw a ship approaching through the haze and dived immediately. When Whitaker got a look through the periscope, his heart skipped a beat; the target he saw was a Japanese light cruiser escorted by a single destroyer, approaching at 18 knots. Whitaker set up quickly. Twenty-four minutes after diving, he fired four stern tubes at the cruiser. The destroyer was a mere 500 yards distant, headed dead on. "Don't think he saw us," Whitaker recorded, "but he sure looks mean."

Whitaker went deep, hearing two torpedoes hit. The destroyer dropped fifteen depth charges, but Whitaker outwitted him and eased away. An hour and twenty minutes after shooting, Whitaker came to periscope depth for a look. He saw the cruiser stopped dead in the water, down by the stern with a port list. At 1:26 P.M., Whitaker moved in for another attack, firing four bow tubes. The destroyer charged again, forcing Whitaker deep. Something went wrong with the attack. "I didn't see how we could miss," Whitaker wrote, "but we did." Whitaker took *Flasher* deep. The destroyer dropped thirteen more charges, none close.

While down, Whitaker was forced to reload, a time-consuming process, since it had to be carried out with absolute silence. When he came up again at 4:08, the destroyer was there but the cruiser was gone. Whitaker did not know whether the cruiser had sunk or had crept off toward Saigon. Assuming the latter, Whitaker surfaced after dark and alerted *Angler* and *Crevalle* to watch for a damaged cruiser heading for Saigon. For the next twenty-four hours, Whitaker jockeyed the boats around, looking for the cruiser. It was all wasted effort. Whitaker's first salvo had been successful, and the light cruiser *Oi,* 5,700 tons, had gone down while he was reloading.

Christie next ordered the pack to move up the South China Sea to a position off the west coast of Luzon, north of Manila. About dawn on July 25, Hess in *Angler* picked up a large northbound convoy and flashed the word. An hour later, Whitaker found it and got off a contact report but was driven down by an airplane. An hour and a half later, the entire convoy passed directly over Whitaker. He raised his periscope to find one escort passing over his after torpedo room, 100 feet away from the periscope. In his look, Whitaker counted fourteen large ships plus half a dozen escorts.

At that time, Whitaker had only six torpedoes. Since both *Crevalle* and *Angler* had a full load, Whitaker believed it would be better if Walker and Hess attacked first; then he could pick off what was left. He let the convoy go by and trailed. At 12:22, Walker in *Crevalle* submerged in a driving downpour, made a snap setup, and fired four stern tubes at one of the largest freighters. At the moment of firing, Walker sighted an escort carrier which was evidently providing the convoy air protection. After the torpedoes left the tubes, he lost depth control, almost broached, then went deep. Escorts found him and dropped fifty-two depth charges.

After dark, Whitaker surfaced, regained contact with the convoy, and flashed a report to his packmates. At 2:11 on the following morning, July 26, he attacked, firing his last six torpedoes at two ships, obtaining two hits in one freighter and one in another. He was feeling pretty good about that, he reported later, but then "our feeling of security" came to an abrupt end. One of his torpedoes had run through the near formation and hit a tanker beyond. Whitaker wrote that

the whole scene was lighted up as bright as daylight by the explosion of a tanker in the center column. One of our torpedoes which had missed the second target hit this large tanker about amidships. The ocean appeared full of ships and we were in an uncomfortable position. We cleared the bridge immediately and started down. By the time we hit fifty feet we could hear shells landing all around where we had been. We felt that we must have been seen and went to three hundred feet, turning at high speed and expecting an immediate depth charge attack. Although many high speed screws passed over us, and although escorts were pinging in our vicinity for a long time, it appears that they still thought we were on the surface as they dropped no depth charges. We were giving out a tremendous cloud of smoke when we submerged, and I believe that they were firing at our smoke thinking that we were still on the surface. We took a southerly course to clear the vicinity in order to surface and trail.

The tanker, which blew up and sank, was *Otoriyama Maru,* 5,280 tons.

After Whitaker withdrew, Frank Walker moved in for a second attack, firing nine torpedoes at two freighters just before dawn. He believed he hit and sank both targets, but postwar records failed to credit him. Escorts drove *Crevalle* deep. When Walker came up again, he saw a ship Whitaker had damaged. He fired four torpedoes, obtaining four hits. The ship, *Tosan Maru,* an 8,700-ton transport, sank quickly, while Walker snapped pictures of it through the periscope. Escorts again drove Walker deep, delivering many depth charges.

That night, when all the boats surfaced, Whitaker reported he was out of torpeodes and returning to Fremantle. The next-senior skipper, Frank Walker, took command of the pack. Two days later, Walker and Hess picked up another convoy: eight ships, four escorts. Walker fired his last six torpedoes, sinking the 6,600-ton transport *Hakubasan Maru.* Hess made two attacks but failed to achieve any sinkings.

This first formal Fremantle pack had done well. Whitaker had sunk four and a half confirmed ships for almost 25,000 tons (sharing credit with Walker for *Tosan Maru*); Walker had sunk one and a half ships for almost 11,000 tons. (Hess had sunk no confirmed ships.) The pack as a whole got six ships for about 36,000 tons.

Ralph Christie decided to make a second war patrol. Looking at the schedules, he saw that Enrique D'Hamel Haskins in *Guitarro* would be arriving in Darwin about June 19 from Pearl Harbor. Christie decided that Haskins could refuel and get a new load of torpedoes at Darwin and take him out for a "three-week patrol."

On June 21, Christie flew up to Darwin. Upon arrival, however, he discovered that *Guitarro* had engine problems that required immediate repairs in Fremantle. What to do? There was one possible answer. That same day, Sam Dealey in *Harder* arrived in Darwin from his epic destroyer-killing patrol off Tawi Tawi. His crew was worn out from this arduous cruise. Yet when Christie asked, Dealey agreed to make a brief extension. Thereafter, the forepart of the patrol would be known unofficially as 5A and the extension as 5B.

According to some accounts, the extension did not sit well with the crew. Lockwood later wrote that the news caused "bitter disappointment," and he quoted one of *Harder*'s radio technicians: "After blowing up the last destroyer on June 10, everyone was overjoyed, figuring on a short patrol and then back to Rest Camp in Perth. Unfortunately we pulled into Darwin and Admiral Christie wanted to go out with us. The crew was pretty sore."

In effect, Christie changed places with his operations officer, Murray Tichenor, who had gone along for the ride on 5A. Dealey got under way that same day, June 21. Christie wrote later, "The primary purpose of this short patrol was to intercept and sink what we called the 'Nickel Ship,' which left from Pomalaa in the Gulf of Boni, Celebes, about once a month. This was the sole source of nickel for the Japanese. We generally knew when it was leaving."

On the way to the Gulf of Boni, *Harder* received an Ultra. A damaged Japanese cruiser with two escorts, returning from the Battle of the Philippine Sea en route to Surabaya or Singapore, would pass their way, probably through Salajar Strait, south of Celebes. Dealey took up station 5 miles east of the strait.

On the morning of June 27, Dealey, expecting the cruiser any moment, dived at dawn. Christie, who was standing junior-officer-of-the-deck watch, manned the periscope. At 7:30 A.M., Christie sighted the cruiser and two destroyer escorts, right on schedule. However, as happened so many times with Ultra intercepts, *Harder*—or the cruiser—was slightly off course. The range was 9,000 yards. Dealey rang up flank speed, but he could get no closer than 5,600 yards.

After the cruiser and destroyers disappeared over the horizon, Christie turned to Dealey and said only half jokingly, "Why didn't you expose your conning tower and lure the destroyers in and sink them?"

Later, in private, Dealey asked Christie, "Admiral, were you serious about luring them in?"

Christie, who had unbounded faith in Dealey, replied, smiling, "Well, Sam, you're the Destroyer Killer." He explained later, "I was neither criticizing nor directing . . . the way we felt about Sam and *Harder*, the risk was not great."

Christie and Dealey then turned their attention to the Nickel Ship, going north into the Gulf of Boni to patrol off Pomalaa. Christie said later, "We could see the Nickel Ship being loaded under lights at night. However, we couldn't do anything then because there was a breakwater between *Harder* and the target. The only thing to do was withdraw to Salajar Strait and wait for it to come out."

On June 30, *Harder* submerged at the east entrance of Salajar Strait, waiting. About 7:15 that morning, the periscope watch picked up a ship coming eastward through the strait. Dealey and Christie had a look. The ship was close to shore, merging with the backdrop, making it difficult to identify. Both men agreed it was small, a tugboat, fishing trawler, or small freighter.

Dealey thought whatever it was might be worth attacking, either by torpedo or deck gun. Christie agreed. Dealey ordered the gun crew to stand by below, then surfaced and ran in at 17 knots. On the way in, a lookout spotted an aircraft. Dealey dived for twenty-four minutes. Seeing no further sign of the aircraft, he surfaced to resume the chase.

When they came to within 5 miles of the target, Christie and Dealey received a jolt. There were now two ships: the small one they had been chasing and the Nickel Ship. Both were westbound, the smaller ship trailing. Belatedly, it dawned on Christie and Dealey that the "trawler" was in fact a small escort vessel which had come to meet the Nickel Ship. Moreover, there were two aircraft circling overhead. They banked and headed for *Harder*.

Dealey dived. The planes dropped three small bombs,

none close. Afterward, the men in the after section of the ship reported they could hear something rolling around on the deck topside. An unexploded bomb? Dealey put the rudder hard over and rang up full speed. The rolling noise stopped. "Whether the sound was caused by an imagination or by a dud," Dealey wrote, "it now ceased."

The escort churned over to help the aircraft. For the next two and a half hours, depth charges fell at a distance. This was not a real attack, Dealey thought, but rather a harassing action to keep them from getting at the Nickel Ship. The tactic worked. The escort and the planes kept Dealey down all day, and the ship got away.

Christie and Dealey were chagrined. They had been faked out. Had Dealey ignored the escort, he might easily have maneuvered around it to sink the Nickel Ship. It was, Christie wrote later, "one of the very rare instances in which Sam was fooled." Dealey wrote, "We had been maneuvered into trying to stop the ball carrier on an end run while he made an off-tackle play."

Having missed both these Ultra contacts, Dealey set course for Darwin. On the night of July 1, while passing close to Timor Island on the surface, the sky around *Harder* was suddenly illuminated "bright as day." The officer of the deck, scared out of his wits, dived *Harder* instantly. A Royal Australian Air Force Catalina patrol plane pilot had picked them up on radar and dropped a magnesium flare to see what he had found. Fortunately he dropped no bombs. An angry Sam Dealey kept *Harder* submerged four hours. Then he continued on to Darwin without incident, arriving July 3.

On the way to Darwin, Christie and Dealey had a long discussion about what to do with Sam Dealey and *Harder*. Dealey had made his five patrols. It was time for him to step aside. As Christie saw it, Sam's exec, Tiny Lynch, should take command of *Harder;* Sam should return to the States for thirty days' leave, after which he could go to new construction or back to Christie's staff to serve as Tichenor's assistant, or possibly to command a division if BuPers was ready to give the class of 1930 that responsibility.

Sam had other ideas. He agreed that Lynch should take command of *Harder* but thought that Lynch, who had also made five patrols, ought to have shore leave before taking on the heavy responsibilities of command. There were eighteen or twenty men scheduled to leave *Harder* after the fifth patrol; it was not fair to have Lynch assume command and train a new crew all at once. Dealey wanted to take *Harder* on one more patrol, shape up the new men, and then turn over the boat to Lynch.

Christie replied, "Sam, let's don't try to decide all this now. When you get to Fremantle, I want you to be my guest at Bend of the Road, if you want. It will be quiet and you can think it all out."

Dealey agreed.

After a two-week vacation at "Bend of the Road" Dealey had decided he was sufficiently rested to make another patrol in *Harder,* while Tiny Lynch, who was to assume command of *Harder* on the next patrol, stayed for a longer rest.

This decision did not sit well with Lynch, who believed that Sam Dealey was mentally exhausted and that Lynch, not Dealey, should take the boat out. "Sam was showing unmistakable signs of strain," Lynch said later. "He was becoming quite casual about Japanese antisubmarine measures. Once, on the previous patrol, I found Sam in a sort of state of mild shock, unable to make a decision." Dealey's former roommate at the Academy later reported receiving a letter from Dealey written from "Bend of the Road" that, he believed, showed signs of extreme fatigue; the letter was incoherent and the penmanship almost unreadable.

Christie himself was not fully convinced that Dealey should go out again. He said, "Sam, I give great weight to whatever you say, but I want you to know that I stand ready to send you to the States for thirty days' leave. Whatever job you want, I'll try to get it for you." Christie remembers that Dealey said, "I've got to make this patrol."

Christie's operations officer, Murray Tichenor, later wrote, "I believe that when he came in from his fifth patrol, Sam was quite tired and Admiral Christie seriously considered taking him off. However, Dealey had marvelous recuperative powers and bounced back to real health and fighting spirit in a very few days."

Dealey was to command a three-boat pack. In addition to *Harder* there would be Chester Nimitz's *Haddo,* and *Hake,* commanded by a new skipper, Frank Edward Haylor. Dealey and Haylor got under way on August 5; Nimitz departed three days later. The boats were to rendezvous near Subic Bay and concentrate on the traffic south of Luzon Strait.

Just before they left Fremantle, William Thomas Kinsella, a new skipper on *Ray*, patrolling off southwest Borneo, had received an Ultra on an important northbound convoy and had moved in to intercept. Kinsella already had had a busy patrol; he had fired twenty-two torpedoes at a single tanker (*Jambi Maru*, 5,250 tons) before she finally sank. After sinking three ships of this convoy—a troop transport, a freighter, and a tanker—he had only four torpedoes left of his second load, so he sent out a call for help. By that time he had tracked the convoy up the western coast of Borneo, past the entrance to Balabac Strait, and north to Mindoro, where he watched it go into Palaun Bay.

Sam Dealey and Chester Nimitz answered the call first, arriving alongside *Ray* about eight on the night of August 20. In addition, Enrique Haskins in *Guitarro* and Maurice Shea in *Raton*, patrolling off Manila, came southward to join the group. There were now five submarines lying in wait for the convoy holed up inside the harbor: *Harder, Haddo, Ray, Guitarro,* and *Raton*. Sam Dealey, the senior skipper, deployed the boats for action.

The convoy came out at 5:45 the following morning. Kinsella was in the most favorable position to attack. He fired his last four torpedoes at a 7,000-ton transport, *Taketoyo Maru*, which sank immediately. Kinsella went deep, withdrew, and returned *Ray* to Fremantle, having sunk five confirmed ships on his double-barreled first patrol.

Kinsella's attack evoked a tremendous counterattack by the escorts. Chester Nimitz wrote, "Depth-charging was started on all sides and it kept up, almost without interruption, until 0616. I have never heard such a din, nor would I have believed it possible for the whole Jap fleet to unload so many charges so rapidly. . . . I had to shout to make myself heard in *Haddo*'s conning tower."

When Kinsella sank his ship, others in the column veered off, presenting a perfect target for Nimitz. He fired six bow tubes at two targets, sinking his first ships, two large transports: *Kinryo Maru*, 4,400 tons, and *Norfolk*

Maru, 6,600 tons. Haskins in *Guitarro* sank the 4,400-ton transport *Naniwa Maru.* Neither Dealey nor Shea could get into position to attack, but in one morning the five submarines had sunk four more ships from the convoy for 22,400 tons. After this action, Haskins and Shea separated from the Dealey pack and went south to the Sulu Sea.

Dealey and Nimitz moved northward to the mouth of Manila Bay, arriving the same evening, August 21. Shortly after midnight, they picked up three small pips on radar heading into the bay. Nimitz sent Dealey a message stating the targets were too small to bother with. Dealey responded succinctly: NOT CONVINCED.

The three vessels were small 900-ton frigates, escorts from the battered convoy HI-71. Dealey directed an attack. About 4 A.M. he fired a bow salvo at two, stopping *Matsuwa* and *Hiburi.* Nimitz stopped the third, *Sado.* At dawn's first light, Dealey fired again at *Matsuwa,* sinking it. Nimitz attacked the two remaining frigates, sinking *Sado* but missing *Hiburi.* Dealey fired again and sank *Hiburi.*

The two boats moved northward along the west coast of Luzon with plans to rendezvous with the third boat of the pack, Haylor's *Hake,* which had come a roundabout way and had missed all the action so far. That night, August 22, Nimitz picked up a destroyer and attacked. The destroyer saw *Haddo* and turned to counterattack, forcing Nimitz to fire four down-the-throat shots which missed. Near daybreak the following day, Nimitz picked up a tanker escorted by another destroyer. He fired four torpedoes at the destroyer, blowing off her bow. He fired another but missed. Two trawlers and another destroyer came out to tow the crippled ship into Dasol Bay, south of Lingayen on the gulf. But unknown to Nimitz the destroyer (*Asakaze,* 1,500 tons) slid beneath the sea before they could help. Having shot off all his torpedoes, Nimitz set course for the new advance base at Mios Woendi to refuel and reload.

Dealey in *Harder* and Frank Haylor in *Hake,* meanwhile, rendezvoused off Dasol Bay. Believing *Asakaze* had been towed inside and that the Japanese might tow her down to Manila.the following day, Dealey decided he and

Haylor should lie in wait. Dealey graciously offered Haylor first crack.

At 5:54 the following morning, August 24, Haylor picked up propeller screws on sonar. Two ships were emerging from Dasol Bay, a destroyer and a minesweeper. The destroyer was an old tub, *Phra Ruang,* which belonged to the Thailand navy. Haylor maneuvered to attack, but the Thai destroyer turned off and went back inside the bay. The minesweeper continued on, pinging. Haylor did not like the setup, so he broke off the attack and began evading. At 6:47, he saw *Harder's* periscope.

Later he wrote, "I believe that at 0710, the minesweeper actually had two targets, Sam and myself, and was probably somewhat confused. But at any rate, at 0728, we heard a string of fifteen depth charge explosions. . . . We remained in the vicinity the rest of the day. . . . We surfaced at 2010 and attempted to contact *Harder,* as previously arranged, with no success."

For the next two weeks, Haylor continued to try to contact Dealey. There was no reply. Gradually, Haylor let himself think the unthinkable: Sam Dealey, destroyer killer, had been killed by the minesweeper attack on the morning of August 24.

On September 10, Chester Nimitz returned for rendezvous. Haylor still hoped that Dealey had been forced to return to base and that Nimitz had word of him, but after talking it over by megaphone Nimitz concluded that Dealey had been lost. He sent a shattering message to Christie: I MUST HAVE TO THINK HE IS GONE.

Dealey was awarded the Medal of Honor posthumously.

20

DRAWING THE NOOSE

By the end of summer, 1944, Lockwood and Christie had more than one hundred fleet boats operating in enemy waters. They now based from tenders near the front lines, in the Marianas and Mios Woendi, vastly cutting down travel time to the combat zone, though, of course, the main bases at Pearl Harbor, Brisbane, Fremantle and Midway were still utilized for major upkeep and repairs. The large number of boats now available for patrol and the shorter travel time enabled Lockwood and Christie to draw the noose around Japan's neck even tighter.

Chick Clarey in *Pintado* and an old hand John Lee (ex-*Grayling*) in a new boat, *Croaker*, were sent to the East China Sea as a loosely coordinated twosome, and together they sank five ships for 38,500 tons.

On the way to station, Lockwood sent them an Ultra on a convoy southbound from Japan to the Bonins. Clarey and Lee made the intercept near Lot's Wife, but neither was able to achieve attack position, so after trailing and sending off contact reports to the boats in the Bonins, they took station along the approaches to Nagasaki.

On August 4 Clarey saw a light cruiser that appeared to be going in and out of Nagasaki on training cruises. He lay in wait, hoping it would come out the following day or the next, while Lee in *Croaker* patrolled nearby.

On August 6 Clarey picked up a large southbound convoy. He attacked, firing six torpedoes—three each at two ships—and thought both sank, but postwar records credited only one, a 5,400-ton freighter. Shortly after this attack, *Pintado* suffered a freak accident: while reloading a torpedo, the forward torpedo room gang accidentally tripped the starting switch, flooding the compartment with steam and gas.

This was a grave matter. Clarey ordered all air lines and doors to the compartment shut. In order to get the men out, he was forced to surface in broad daylight, immediately following his attack on the convoy, within sight of the Japanese mainland. Clarey's exec ran forward on the deck and battered open the forward torpedo room hatch with a maul. In this manner, the compartment was evacuated. Meanwhile, Clarey ordered the main induction and conning tower hatch shut and "took a suction" through the boat to get rid of the gases. "Papers, dust, curtains and loose rags sailed towards the engine rooms in the hurricane winds," he reported later.

The next day at about eleven o'clock in the morning, John Lee in *Croaker* spotted the light cruiser coming out of Nagasaki for another training cruise. It was zigzagging. Lee let it close to 1,300 yards and then fired four stern tubes. Some hit and, Lee reported, "flames and water rose to the mast top." Soon the ship began to settle by the stern. While Lee took color movies through the periscope eyepiece, he heard a "tremendous explosion," followed by breaking-up noises. *Nagara,* 5,700 tons, went to the bottom. In the next week, Lee sank two more ships for 8,200 tons.

On August 21, Clarey received an Ultra reporting a convoy in the middle of the East China Sea. It showed up right on schedule: a whale-ship tanker, half a dozen other tankers and freighters, and many escorts. Clarey picked the whale factory for his main target and fired ten torpedoes. Several hit the target, and several went on to hit another tanker. The whale factory blew up and caught fire, an "incredible sight," Clarey reported. She was *Tonan Maru II,* 19,262 tons, the largest merchant ship sunk thus far by U.S. submarines. By a curious coincidence, Clarey had helped "sink" this ship once before; when he was exec of Bole's *Amberjack* they had caught *Tonan Maru II* in Kavieng Harbor, October 10, 1942, but she had been salvaged to fight on.

Patrol scores in Empire waters had been declining during the summer of 1944. Dick O'Kane suspected the reason might be that Japanese merchant ships were running

very close to the beach in shoal water. He postulated that
this might be an advantage for the submarine; running
close to the beach cramped zigzagging, forcing ships to
steer a more or less straight course.

When he took *Tang* to Empire waters, therefore, he
patrolled only a mile and a half (3,000 yards) off the
shore of Nagoya, in less than 250 feet of water. He
proved his point.

On August 10 he found an old tanker, hugging the
beach. He fired three torpedoes. All missed. Seeing aircraft, O'Kane turned away to evade, bouncing off an uncharted upturn on the bottom. The following day, O'Kane
picked up two freighters, escorted by a gunboat. He crept
into position 1,800 yards away and fired six torpedoes,
three at each freighter. One freighter, *Roko Maru*, 3,328
tons, "disintegrated with the explosion." The other was
damaged. The gunboat jumped on *Tang*, dropping twenty-
two close depth charges, trying to force O'Kane toward
the beach. O'Kane evaded to seaward and deep water.

A week went by with no targets in sight. Then on August 20 O'Kane found a freighter coming out of the mist
with two small escorts. He closed to 900 yards and fired
two torpedoes. The first missed astern and exploded on the
beach. The second "left the tube with a clonk but did not
run," O'Kane reported later. The next day, O'Kane found
another freighter "unbelievably close to the beach" with
two small escorts. O'Kane eased into 200 feet of water
and fired three electrics. All missed and exploded on the
beach.

The next night, O'Kane found one of the escorts anchored in a cove. O'Kane stuck *Tang*'s nose in the cove
and fired one electric torpedo. The torpedo ran erratically
and sank, hitting bottom, where it blew up "with a loud
rumble." O'Kane fired two more electrics, one at a time.
The first evidently ran under; the second missed astern.
O'Kane—now whispering orders from the bridge—closed
to 900 yards and fired another electric. Forty seconds later
the escort blew up. "The explosion," O'Kane reported
later, "was the most spectacular we've ever seen, topped
by a pillar of fire and more explosions about five hundred
feet in the air. There was absolutely nothing left of the
gunboat." O'Kane estimated her at 1,500 tons, but she

must have been under 500 because the sinking was not listed in postwar Japanese records.

The next day, hugging the beach, O'Kane found two more freighters. He couldn't get into position to attack them, but a few hours later he found a ship, well escorted by surface ships and aircraft, standing out to sea. "The decks on his long superstructure," O'Kane reported, "were lined with men in white uniforms, as was his upper bridge." This indicated a navy auxiliary. He closed to point-blank range of 800 yards and fired three torpedoes. "The first and third torpedoes hit beautifully in his short well deck forward and the after part of his long superstructure, giving him a 20 degree down-angle which he maintained as he went under with naval ensign flying." It was a navy transport, *Tsukushi Maru*, 8,135 tons.

In the following days, O'Kane (with three torpedoes left) kept close to the beach, searching. On August 25 he closed to 600 yards of the beach and fired his three torpedoes at a tanker, heavily escorted. O'Kane believed that two hit the tanker and sank it and one "blew hell out of the leading escort," but neither ship was listed in postwar accounts.

O'Kane returned to Pearl Harbor after a mere thirty-four days at sea. He was credited with six ships sunk for 31,000 tons, a total trimmed by postwar records to two ships for 11,500 tons. Squadron Commander Charles Frederick Erck commented, "As the wide open sea areas diminish by reason of further U.S. Naval conquest, it is incumbent upon all submariners to develop the tactic of attack and evasion in shoal water. The tactics used in this patrol point the way."

Not many would follow.

A Lockwood pack under Donc Donaho (who took temporary command of *Picuda*) patrolled Luzon Strait also and turned in a smashing success. This was Donaho's seventh war patrol. The other boats were new ones: *Spadefish*, commanded by Gordon Waite Underwood, who had made two patrols in Scott's *Tunny* as PCO and exec, and *Redfish*, commanded by Sandy McGregor, who had commanded *Pike* on her last two patrols.

The pack, known as "Donc's Devils," departed Pearl

Harbor on July 23, reaching station August 11 in stormy seas. Sandy McGregor thought it was a typhoon. He estimated the winds at 100 knots. The heavy seas jarred loose many plates in the superstructure of *Redfish*.

On the evening of August 17, when the seas had abated, McGregor picked up a very large southbound convoy. He did not know it, but this was a special convoy, HI-71, consisting of about a dozen big tankers and freighters, escorted by the small carrier *Taiyo* (*Otaka*) often shot at by U.S. submarines. McGregor passed the word to his packmates and attacked.

By about 5:00 A.M. on the morning of August 18, McGregor was in position. He fired four torpedoes at a big unidentified ship; then he saw *Taiyo* (*Otaka*). He shifted targets quickly—perhaps too quickly—and prepared to fire two torpedoes at the carrier. He got the first one off, but then the solution light on the TDC went out, forcing him to withhold fire. With daylight fast approaching, McGregor submerged. Four hours later, he saw a tanker riding high. He surfaced and chased it in a driving rain, firing two torpedoes that missed. Then he lost the target and hauled clear.

"Decided it was time to think things over," he wrote later, "and find out where we went wrong. Already muffed the ball twice."

Meanwhile, all submarines in the vicinity were converging on HI-71 to capitalize on McGregor's contact report. One of Christie's skippers, Hank Munson, who relieved Willard Laughon in *Rasher*—south of the boundary—picked up the alert and in turn alerted his packmate Charles Henderson in *Bluefish*, plus Maurice Shea commanding *Raton* in the adjacent area. Because he had not been able to obtain a good navigational fix for several days, McGregor's position report was inaccurate. Donaho in *Picuda* and Underwood in *Spadefish* tore around for many hours, unable to make contact.

Munson in *Rasher* moved northward in a blinding rain. At 8 P.M. on August 18, Munson ran right into the southbound HI-71. He counted about twenty ships and fifteen escorts. The dark, rainy night was "absolutely ideal for night attack," he wrote.

At 9:22 P.M., Munson commenced firing four torpedoes. After two had left the tubes, he ordered cease fire, thinking that the gyros were not matching properly. He drew off and ran along the starboard flank of the convoy to make another attack. As he was steadying down, he saw that both torpedoes had hit the target. It was apparently a tanker. It blew up with "an appalling explosion" that sent a column of flame 1,000 feet into the sky. Later Munson wrote:

The entire sky was a bright red momentarily and the target and the whole convoy was seen for an instant. Part of the ship blew off and landed about 500 yards from the remainder of the tanker and both parts burned fiercely for about twenty minutes and then disappeared from sight in one grand final explosion. The near escort decided something was wrong, he fired his guns at all points of the compass, reversed course and fiercely depth charged something or other two miles astern of us. Pandemonium reigned in the convoy, lights flashed on and off, side lights turned on, depth charges fell in every direction, gun fire broke out all over and some badly aimed 40mm tracer passed astern of us about 100 yards wrong in deflection and way over. Two ships appeared to indulge in a spirited gun duel for a few moments. We proceeded up the starboard side of the convoy about 4000 yards off reloading and enjoying the spectacle.

The ship Munson hit was not a tanker but the escort carrier *Taiyo (Otaka)*. While she was sinking, Munson went in for a second attack, firing ten torpedoes at two big freighters. He saw and heard three hits in the bow tube target. He believed one of the bow torpedoes ran on and hit another ship in the far column. Two of the stern tubes slammed into the other target. Munson believed one of the stern torpedoes also ran on and hit a ship in the far column. He then hauled clear to reload, broadcasting for help.

Following the reload (he had only six torpedoes left, four forward, two aft), Munson came in for another attack. He fired all six torpedoes at two targets and believed he hit both.

After Munson finished this attack and was out of torpedoes, he received orders to go on to Pearl Harbor. When he arrived there, he was credited with sinking four ships that rainy night, plus one sunk earlier, on August 6, for a total of five for 45,700 tons. In addition, he was credited with damaging four ships for 22,000 tons. Later, when it was discovered that he had sunk not a tanker but *Taiyo* (*Otaka*), the tonnage figure was revised upward to 55,700 tons. Postwar Japanese records credited five ships for 52,600 tons, making this patrol, in terms of confirmed tonnage sunk, the best of the war to date.

All the while, two other submarines were nibbling at the convoy. Henderson in *Bluefish*, who came up too late to make a coordinated attack with Munson, found two tankers. He attacked, believing he sank both, but postwar records credited him with only one, *Hayasui*, 6,500 tons.

Shortly after midnight on August 19, Gordon Underwood in *Spadefish*, who was stern-chasing the convoy, found several large ships, evidently some that had reversed course and fled northward after Munson attacked. Underwood fired four torpedoes—his first as commanding officer—from a range of 3,000 yards. All missed. He went deep, then came up again, to receive a report of Munson's attack on the convoy. "This explained the mystery," Underwood later wrote, "of unescorted ships running all around the ocean."

At 3:33, Underwood picked another target and fired six bow tubes. He reported, "Loud explosion from target. Radar pip died down and disappeared. No doubt about this fellow." He surfaced and ran through the place where the ship had been, reporting "wreckage and oil slick of our target." The ship Underwood had sunk was the large transport *Tamatsu Maru*, 9,500 tons.

Munson, Henderson, and Underwood had riddled convoy HI-71. Munson sank three big freighters plus *Taiyo* (*Otaka*); Henderson sank one tanker; Underwood sank one 9,500-ton troopship. Total: six ships. There are no existing records about what went down with these ships. Whatever it was—troops, ammunition, supplies, guns, gasoline—it would not be in the Philippines to face MacArthur's armies when he landed.

Donc's Devils continued on patrol. On August 22 Underwood picked up another convoy, two large empty tankers with escorts. Underwood fired three torpedoes at each, sinking *Hakko Maru II*, 10,000 tons. The second tanker, severely damaged, ran into Pasaleng Bay on the coast of Luzon, where a destroyer was patrolling. Underwood coolly took *Spadefish* into the glassy waters at the entrance of the bay, intent on sinking the destroyer and firing again at the beached tanker. For three uneasy hours he played cat and mouse with the destroyer, trying to get into position to fire electrics from his stern tubes. Finally, at 10:15 A.M., he shot four. All missed. Later in the afternoon, Underwood again tried to penetrate the bay submerged, but the destroyer began dropping depth charges and Underwood prudently hauled clear. Donaho called for a rendezvous of his three boats and ordered Underwood to put into Saipan, get a new load of torpedoes from *Holland*, and then return to station.

On August 25, Donaho in *Picuda* picked up a ten-ship convoy hugging the coast of Luzon. He slipped past five escorts, got in close, and sank the 2,000-ton transport *Kotoku Maru*. A destroyer charged. Donaho turned and fired down the throat, sinking 1,200-ton *Yunagi*. Hearing all this racket, Sandy McGregor in *Redfish* picked up the convoy, maneuvered between it and the beach—some 3,000 yards distant—and fired four torpedoes at a freighter. This time, McGregor did not muff the ball; as he went deep he heard three hits, then breaking-up noises. The ship he sank was the 6,000-ton *Batopaha Maru*. Escorts delivered forty-three depth charges, none close.

After this attack, Donaho and McGregor followed Underwood into Saipan to refuel and get a fresh load of torpedoes. By September 5, they were en route back to the area.

Slightly ahead of his packmates, Underwood arrived back at Luzon Strait on September 5. Three days later, he picked up another convoy: eight big ships, three escorts. In a flawless series of attacks, Underwood fired twenty torpedoes and sank four ships for 12,000 tons. He followed the rest of the convoy to a harbor and then sent a call for help to Donaho and McGregor, who were coming back into the area. After Donaho and McGregor arrived on station, Underwood was ordered back to Pearl Harbor.

Donaho and McGregor went back to work. On September 12 McGregor picked up a small ship and fired three torpedoes, but they all ran under. On September 16 Donaho found an eight-ship convoy from which he sank one ship, the 6,000-ton *Tokushima Maru*. Part of the convoy came McGregor's way. He sank *Ogura Maru II*, a 7,300-ton tanker. On September 21, Donaho and McGregor attacked another convoy. Donaho sank a 2,000-ton freighter, McGregor an 8,500-ton transport.

Donc's Devils turned out to be one of the most successful double-barrel packs of the war. In the two forays, Donaho, McGregor, and Underwood sank thirteen confirmed ships for almost 65,000 tons. Underwood got six for 31,500 tons, Donaho four for 11,270 (including the destroyer *Yunagi*), McGregor three for 21,800. The advance base at Saipan, which enabled all three boats to refuel and reload, had already paid for itself.

Lockwood sent two more packs to Luzon Strait. The first was commanded by his flag secretary, Edwin Robinson Swinburne, class of 1925, who had never made a war patrol. Known as "Ed's Eradicators," it consisted of Gene Fluckey's *Barb* (flag); a new boat with a new skipper, *Queenfish*, commanded by Charles Elliott Loughlin, an All-American basketball player who had been stuck in Panama commanding the old *S-14;* and an old boat with a new skipper, *Tunny*, commanded by George Ellis Pierce (brother of Jack Pierce, lost on *Argonaut*), who had made a PCO run in *Steelhead*.

Ed's Eradicators went to Luzon Strait by way of the Bonins. On August 18 they encountered Gordon Selby in *Puffer*, returning to Pearl Harbor. At first Fluckey thought he was a Japanese submarine, and the pack evaded at high speed. Three days later the pack passed Hank Munson in *Rasher*, also returning to Pearl Harbor. On August 24, the pack arrived on station.

The second pack departed Midway on August 17. It consisted of three boats: Ben Oakley's *Growler*, Paul Summers's *Pampanito*, and Eli Reich's *Sealion*. Ben Oakley, the senior skipper, named his pack "Ben's Busters." They reached Luzon Strait on August 29.

A day later, both packs received an Ultra on a southbound convoy, and all six boats rushed to intercept. Elliott Loughlin in *Queenfish*, who had never fired a torpedo in anger, made the first attack at 2:23 A.M., shooting three torpedoes at a freighter and three at a tanker. The tanker blew up and sank. Eli Reich in *Sealion,* who was watching, wrote that it "burned with an immense flame and heavy black smoke—silhouettes of ships could be seen against the backdrop of the burning ship." It was *Chiyoda Maru,* 4,700 tons.

With that, the convoy scattered in all directions. Ben Oakley in *Growler* fired his stern tubes at a destroyer for damage. Eli Reich in *Sealion* fired ten torpedoes at a tanker and a freighter for damage. Then Reich fired three at a freighter and three at what he believed to be a destroyer. He hit both, sinking the minelayer *Shirataka,* 1,300 tons. Later he fired three more torpedoes at a patrol craft. All missed. Gene Fluckey in *Barb* fired three stern tubes at a freighter and tanker, sinking the freighter, *Okuni Maru,* 5,600 tons. (He believed he sank another freighter with three torpedoes, but it was not confirmed in postwar records.) All that night and the next day, depth charges and aerial bombs rained down on the submarines.

The convoy turned around and headed back to Formosa. Whatever it was carrying never reached the Philippines. In the confusion of this six-boat attack against a multiplicity of scattering targets, the postwar accounting may not have been accurate; it credited three ships: Reich's minelayer, one of Fluckey's freighters, and Loughlin's tanker. Afterward, the two packs regrouped and went to separate areas.

Ed's Eradicators—*Barb, Tunny,* and *Queenfish*—patrolled the strait near the northwest coast of Luzon. Radar-equipped antisubmarine aircraft attacked the group relentlessly. Shortly after dark on the evening of September 1, the planes caught *Tunny* and delivered a devastating bombing attack. Fluckey in *Barb* submerged about 4 miles away and watched. The bombs dished in *Tunny's* hull. Pierce was granted permission to withdraw and go home for repairs.

About noon on September 8, Loughlin in *Queenfish* picked up a convoy and trailed. After dark, he surfaced and flashed word to Swinburne and Fluckey in *Barb* and then made an end around, submerging in bright moonlight. At about 2 A.M. September 9, the convoy came right over Loughlin. He fired ten torpedoes at four targets, sinking the 7,000-ton transport *Toyooka Maru* and

the 3,000-ton transport *Manshu Maru*. Fluckey in *Barb*
fired three torpedoes at what he believed to be a destroyer. One made a circular run over *Barb;* the other two
missed. Aircraft, dropping close bombs, prevented
Fluckey from firing any more torpedoes.

The other pack, Ben's Busters—*Growler, Pampanito,*
and *Sealion* (after a quick dash to Saipan for more torpedoes)—moved 300 miles to the west and lay in wait
along the Singapore–Formosa convoy routes. On September 6, an important convoy consisting of six ships and
five escorts had departed Singapore for the Empire. There
were 1,350 British and Australian POWs crammed in the
hold of one ship, *Rakuyo Maru,* and 750 in another.
These POWs, survivors of a large group of slave laborers
who had built a railroad for the Japanese in Malaya,
were being shipped to Japan to work in the factories and
mines. Three ships from Manila joined the convoy, making
a total of twelve big ships plus escorts.

Dick Voge had information on this convoy from the
codebreakers, but not on the POWs aboard. He gave
Oakley the position reports. On the night of September
11–12, the Busters made contact. Oakley opened the attack
by sinking the lead escort, a frigate, *Hirado,* 860 tons. He
then pulled around and sank the destroyer *Shikinami,*
2,000 tons. Eli Reich in *Sealion* followed up, firing six torpedoes at a big transport and a tanker. The transport was
Rakuyo Maru, 9,400 tons. His torpedoes hit her and the
tanker and another transport *Nankai Maru,* 8,400 tons.
Both transports sank. Although many Japanese were rescued from the two transports, the POWs on *Rakuyo Maru*
were left to fend for themselves. They went into the water;
some found small life rafts.

The convoy turned west to flee toward Hainan, 200
miles away. The three boats followed. Oakley in *Growler*
fired off all his torpedoes and then broke off to go down
to Fremantle. Reich, the next-senior officer, took charge of
the pack. Summers in *Pampanito,* who had not yet been
able to attack, trailed the convoy westward. Reich, driven
down by escorts, lost contact. When he surfaced, he
wrongly assumed the convoy would continue its general
route toward Formosa and planned an interception course
to the north.

Summers trailed the convoy to the coast of Hainan and then attacked, firing nine torpedoes at three targets after dark and sinking a 5,000-ton tanker and a big transport, *Kachidoki Maru*, 10,500 tons. The remnants of the convoy evidently rounded the north coast of Hainan and scurried into Hainan Strait.

All the next day, September 13, Reich headed westerly in an effort to correct his mistake. Near midnight he found Summers's tanker, which was still on fire. He continued north to parallel the east entrance of Hainan Strait, where he patrolled all the following day. The convoy did not come out. Early on the morning of September 15, Reich rendezvoused with Summers and laid out a search plan that would take them east, back to Luzon Strait.

That afternoon about four o'clock, Summers, who was patrolling to the south of Reich, re-entered the area where the pack had first attacked the convoy. For miles the water was filled with debris and dead bodies held afloat by oily life jackets. Then Summers began finding live survivors—the British and Australians left behind by the Japanese. They had now been in the water four days and three nights. Those still alive, Summers reported later, were "a pitiful sight none of us would ever forget." He sent a call for help to Reich, who came barreling south at full speed.

Summers maneuvered *Pampanito* from raft to raft, gingerly taking on board survivors. He picked up seventy-three men. When Reich came on the scene, he rescued another fifty-four. By ten that night, no more could be safely taken aboard either submarine. Reich got off a report to Lockwood, then ordered both boats to head for Saipan. "It was heartbreaking to leave so many dying men behind," Reich wrote. On the way, four of his passengers died and were buried at sea.

Upon receiving Reich's report, Lockwood ordered the two boats remaining in Ed's Eradicators—Fluckey's *Barb* and Loughlin's *Queenfish*—to head immediately to the scene and rescue as many survivors as they could find. The scene was 450 miles away. The two boats rang up flank speed and proceeded southward at 19 knots. At midday they passed Reich in *Sealion* heading north. The seas were rising, the barometer falling.

At about 9:40 P.M. September 16, when they were

within 150 miles of the scene, Loughlin in *Queenfish* picked up a northbound convoy. A few moments later, Fluckey found it too. The pack commander, Ed Swinburne, ordered an attack; the POW survivors would have to wait. Loughlin shot first, firing his last four torpedoes for damage. Twenty minutes later, Fluckey moved in, maneuvering through escorts at very close range. He could see "several large, deeply laden tankers." Then he saw something else in the darkness, the target of a lifetime:

> *Ye Gods, a flat top! This was the large pip about 300 yds to port and just ahead of the very large after tanker in the starboard column. Range 4900 yards. Went ahead standard to close for a good shot.*

2328   *Working for an overlap. This is undoubtedly the prettiest target I've ever seen.*

2331   *At 2000 yds slowed to 10 kts. We have a perfect overlap of the tanker and just beyond, the flat top. About 1000 feet of target.*

2332   *Commenced firing all bow tubes, point of aim bow of tanker, range 1820 yards. First torpedo broached badly. Other torpedoes normal. As soon as all fish fired went ahead emergency with full right rudder to put the stern tubes into the carrier. Can't make it without being rammed by escort.*

2333   *Dived. Rigged for depth charge, going deep.*

2334–16   *First hit in tanker.*

2334–24   *Second hit in tanker.*

2334–53   *First hit in carrier.*

2335–01   *Second hit in carrier.*

2335–10   *Third hit in carrier.*

2337   *Breaking up noises, very heavy underwater explosions, whistlings, cracklings. One ship sunk. Random depth charges started.*

In retrospect, Fluckey was critical of his attack. He said, "Being so excited, I fired a continuous salvo with my point of aim on the bow of the tanker, so that three torpedoes were to hit the tanker and three [were] to hit the carrier . . . if I had been in my normal senses . . . I would have fired all six at the carrier. That is what I should have done."

The carrier Fluckey hit was *Unyo*, 20,000 tons, an escort type that had often been a target for U.S. submarines. This time she blew up and sank. At the same time, the tanker went down. It was *Azusa*, 11,000 tons. In one famous salvo—nobody had ever sunk two huge ships with one shot—Fluckey had sunk two ships for 31,000 tons.

Fluckey had three torpedoes left and was sorely tempted to try to sink another ship, but he broke off and continued on the rescue mission. He and Loughlin reached the scene about dawn the following morning. By then the survivors had been in the water six days and five nights. The seas were steadily rising. Fluckey and Loughlin searched all that day and the next. In all, Fluckey picked up fourteen men, Loughlin eighteen. On the evening of September 18, with a typhoon coming on, they gave up the search and headed for Saipan.

Both these packs were extremely successful, demonstrating what aggressive, well-coordinated packs in Luzon Strait could do. Ed's Eradicators—*Barb, Queenfish, Tunny*—had sunk six ships for 51,600 tons: Fluckey three for 36,800, including *Unyo*, and Loughlin three for 14,800 tons. Ben's Busters—*Growler, Pampanito, Sealion*—had sunk seven ships for 37,500 tons: Reich three for 19,100 tons, Summers two for 15,600 tons, and Oakley two for 2,800 tons, including the destroyer. Total for both packs: thirteen ships for 89,100 tons.

21

THE BATTLE
OF LEYTE GULF

The Allied juggernaut in the Pacific moved relentlessly westward. On September 15, Nimitz's forces invaded the Palaus and on that same day, MacArthur's forces invaded Morotai to the south. A little over a month later, October 20, MacArthur's forces landed on Leyte in the Philippines. Here, the Japanese put up a do-or-die fight. The remnants of the Japanese Navy gathered once again to do battle, hoping to eject the invaders from the Leyte beaches, and to inflict crippling damage on the U.S. Fleet.

Christie deployed a dozen submarines to intercept and report on Japanese fleet movements. Claggett's *Dace* and McClintock's *Darter* took station at the south end of Palawan Passage and the west entrance of Balabac Strait. Flachsenhar's *Rock* and a new boat, *Blackfin*, commanded by a new skipper, George Hays Laird, Jr., en route from Pearl Harbor to Fremantle, took stations to the west of *Darter* and *Dace*, forming a line across the South China Sea. Another new boat, *Bergall*, en route from Pearl Harbor to Fremantle under skipper John Milton Hyde, who had been Chet Smith's exec on *Swordfish* and who had been patrolling off Indochina (where he sank a 4,200-ton ship on October 13), joined *Blackfin* and *Rock*. Moon Chapple in *Bream*, Enrique Haskins in *Guitarro*, Frank Hess in *Angler*, Lawrence Lott Edge in *Bonefish*, and James Alvin Adkins in *Cod* patrolled the area extending from the north end of Palawan Passage to Manila. Albert Lilly Becker's *Cobia*, en route from Pearl Harbor to Fremantle, patrolled Sibutu Passage. John Kerr

("Jake") Fyfe in *Batfish,* en route from Fremantle to Pearl Harbor, patrolled Makassar Strait, along with Joseph Paul Fitz-Patrick in *Paddle.*

For security reasons, none of these skippers had been forewarned about the Leyte invasion. Late on the night of October 20, after the first U.S. troops started going ashore, they heard about it from news broadcasts on the ships' radios. After that, all skippers understood the reason for their deployment and went on the alert for movements of the Japanese fleet toward Leyte.

McClintock in *Darter* was first to make contact. On the night of October 20, the Japanese Third Force—a troop ferry unit led by the heavy cruiser *Aoba* and light cruiser *Kinu*—got under way from Brunei Bay for Manila, where it would join forces with the transport destroyers to carry out the mission of lifting troops from Mindanao to Leyte. It came up to the west of Palawan Passage, making 23 knots. Shortly before midnight, McClintock intercepted. He chased at flank speed, sending off contact reports to Christie and to Claggett in *Dace,* trying to coach Claggett into intercept position. Neither *Dace* nor *Darter* could get close enough to attack, but the boats up the line near Mindoro picked up the contact report, or received it by relay from Christie, and set a sharp watch.

The Japanese force was lucky—for a while. It got by Hess in *Angler* near the north end of Palawan Passage and Haskins in *Guitarro* in the southern region of Mindoro Strait. However, at 2:40 A.M. on the morning of October 23, Moon Chapple, who was slightly north of Haskins, picked it up on radar. Chapple chased the force for forty minutes, identifying it as two cruisers, "very large." At 3:24, he commenced firing six torpedoes at one of the cruisers. The escorts charged and Chapple went deep. Chapple hit *Aoba* with two torpedoes. She did not sink, but she was so badly damaged she had to be towed into Manila.

Early that same morning, Claggett and McClintock picked up the main Japanese fleet coming north through Palawan Passage. It was moving slowly, seemingly oblivious to submarines, the destroyers not even pinging. McClintock in *Darter,* the pack commander, sent off a contact report to Christie. Claggett kept radio silence. McClintock maneuvered the two boats into a favorable attack position. At 5:09, McClintock in *Darter* submerged. Seven minutes later, Claggett in *Dace* submerged. By the dawn light, both skippers examined this awesome sight, preparing to fire.

McClintock let the ships come within 1,000 yards. The tension in *Darter*'s conning tower was almost unbearable. The TDC operator, Eugene ("Dennis") Wilkinson, a reservist, who in postwar years would be the first skipper of the nuclear-powered submarine, *Nautilus,* kept shouting, "Give me a range! Give me a range! I want you to shoot. You can't shoot without a range!"

Each time McClintock shifted his crosshairs from ship to ship, his exec, Ernest Louis ("Ernie") Schwab, Jr., would ask, "What's there?" McClintock replied calmly, "Battleship. . . . Cruiser. . . . Battleships. . . . Cruisers."

At 5:32 A.M., McClintock fired six torpedoes at one of the cruisers. Then he swung around and fired all four stern tubes at another cruiser. While he was firing his stern tubes, the bow tubes hit the first cruiser. Later, McClintock wrote:

Whipped periscope back to the first target to see the sight of a lifetime: (Cruiser was so close that all of her could not be seen at once with periscope in high power). She was a mass of billowing black smoke from number one turret to the stern. No superstructure could be seen. Bright orange flames shot out from the side along the main deck from the bow to the after turret. Cruiser was already going down by the bow, which was dipping under. #1 turret was at water level. She was definitely finished. Five hits had her sinking and in flames. It is estimated that there were few if any survivors.

A few minutes later McClintock heard four hits in his second target. Then he went deep. He could hear breaking-up noises and depth charges and many ships roaring overhead. Curiously, the destroyers dropped no depth charges. Over on *Dace*, Claggett, awaiting his chance, wrote:

0532 *Heard five torpedo explosions.* DARTER *must be getting in.*

0534 *Four more torpedo hits.* DARTER *is really having a field day. Can see great pall of smoke completely*

*enveloping spot where ship was at last look. Do not
know whether he has sunk but it looks good. Ship
to left is also smoking badly. Looks like a great day
for the* DARTER. *Can see two destroyers making
smoke headed for scene. There is much signalling,
shooting of Very stars, etc. It is a great show. The
big ships seem to be milling around; I hope they don't
scatter too far for me to get in. Light is still pretty
bad but I have counted eight large ships, battleships
or cruisers, plus two destroyers. Two of these large
ships have been hit so far.*

Claggett was low on torpedoes. He had none aft. As the
fleet bore down on him, he picked his targets carefully.
The tension in his conning tower was no less than Mc-
Clintock's. His exec, Rafael Celestino ("Ralph") Benitez,
read off the ranges and bearings. Two heavy cruisers came
into his crosshairs, but Claggett saw something bigger
behind them, probably a battleship. Later he wrote, "Famous statement: 'Will let them go by—they're only heavy
cruisers.'" Then:

0552 *The two cruisers passed ahead at about 1,500 yards.
They were overlapping; appeared to be running
screen for my target, presenting a beautiful target—
a submarine should have 24 torpedo tubes. Had a
beautiful view of them and identified them positively
as* ATAGO *or* NACHI *class. My target can be seen better
now, and appears to be a* KONGO *class battleship. He
looks larger than the two cruisers that have just
passed ahead—he has two stacks, and superstructure
appears much heavier. Have not checked the identi-
fication as well as I should as I have been busy
getting complete composition of force which I consider essential for contact report. Sound also reports
target screws as heavier and slower than those of
cruisers.*

Two minutes later, Claggett fired all six bow tubes at
his "battleship." He heard four solid hits. Then:

0601 *Heard two tremendous explosions both on sound and
through the hull. These explosions were apparently*

magazines as I have never heard anything like it. The soundmen reported that it sounded as if the bottom of the ocean was blowing up. They were obviously shallow as there was neither any shaking of the boat nor water swishing through the superstructure. Nothing could cause this much noise except magazines exploding.

0603   *Heard tremendous breaking-up noises. This was the most gruesome sound I have ever heard. I was at first convinced that it was being furnished by the* DACE, *and called for a check of all compartments and was much relieved to receive reports that everything was all right. Noise was coming from northeast— the direction of the target, and it sounded as if she was coming down on top of us. I have never heard anything like it. Comment from Diving officer: 'We better get the hell out of here.' After about five minutes of these tremendous breaking-up noises, continued to have smaller ones and much crackling noises for next twenty minutes. These noises could be heard on sound and throughout boat. I am convinced that this ship sank; nothing else can explain these noises.*

Since both boats remained submerged for several hours, neither skipper was certain what damage he had inflicted on the Japanese force. Postwar records cleared it up. In his ten-torpedo salvo, McClintock had hit and sunk Vice Admiral Kurita's flagship, the heavy cruiser *Atago,* and severely damaged a second cruiser, *Takao.* Claggett had not hit a battleship but rather the heavy cruiser *Maya. Atago* sank in nineteen minutes, *Maya* in four.

The loss of the flagship *Atago* caused much confusion in the Japanese high command. The destroyer *Kishinami* came close aboard to take off Kurita, but the admiral had to jump in the water and swim for his life. While he was being rescued and dried out, Rear Admiral Matome Ugaki in *Yamato* took tactical command. Three hundred and sixty officers and men were lost on *Atago.*

Counting Chapple's *Aoba,* U.S. submarines had sunk or knocked out four heavy Japanese cruisers, all within the space of about two and a half hours.

A couple of hours later, McClintock returned to periscope depth and saw the damaged cruiser *Takao* lying motionless in the water. For most of the day, McClintock tried to get in for another shot, but Japanese destroyers hovered close by, blocking him, and aircraft circled over the cruiser. Claggett found *Takao* at about three o'clock that afternoon but decided his chances of getting in were "slim." McClintock decided to wait until nightfall and then coordinate with Claggett in a night surface attack. Meanwhile, *Takao* got her damage under control and set off for Brunei Bay, making 6 to 10 knots.

After dark, McClintock rendezvoused with Claggett and laid out a plan of attack on *Takao*. It would take McClintock near an area of water filled with rocks and shoals, appropriately named Dangerous Ground. McClintock had not been able to get an accurate navigational fix for about twenty-four hours and during that day had been pushed along by uncertain currents in Palawan Passage. However, his mind was more intent on getting *Takao* than precise navigational fixes. He gave Claggett his orders and both boats commenced an end around at 17 knots.

The main force, meanwhile, was steaming north. Hess in *Angler,* Haskins in *Guitarro,* and Moon Chapple in *Bream* were in position to intercept. Chapple somehow failed to get the word, but Hess and Haskins picked up the main force about 8:30 P.M. Hess was closer. He bent on all possible speed and got off contact reports to Christie and Haskins. During the stern chase, Hess ran across a convoy and was tempted to break off and attack it. However, he wisely decided it was more important to trail the main body of the Japanese fleet and see exactly where it was going. By this time, Haskins in *Guitarro* was on the trail, too. Both boats tracked the fleet as it turned eastward toward Leyte. The Japanese jammed Hess's radio, but Haskins got off an accurate report to an Australian radio station, which rebroadcast it to Halsey and Kinkaid in the early morning hours of October 24. Unable to overtake and attack, Hess and Haskins returned to patrol stations off Mindoro and the northern end of Palawan Passage. U.S. carrier planes picked up the trail of the fleet the following morning.

*   *   *

Back at the south end of Palawan Passage, meanwhile, McClintock and Claggett were wolf-packing the damaged *Takao*. At five minutes past midnight, October 25, *Darter* ran aground with such a crash that for a moment McClintock, who was on the bridge, believed he had been torpedoed.

The exec, Ernie Schwab, who was navigating in the conning tower, rushed to the bridge. "What was that?" he said.

"We're aground," McClintock said grimly.

Schwab disappeared back in the conning tower to consult a chart. He returned to the bridge a moment later and said, "Captain, we can't be aground. The nearest land is nineteen miles away."

Darter stayed aground while McClintock tried every way possible to get his ship off the reef. He ordered all excess weight jettisoned: ammunition, food, fuel oil, fresh water. Then at high tide, 1:40 A.M., he backed the engines full and sallied ship—had the crew run back and forth to set up a rocking motion. Nothing worked. *Darter* was stuck high and dry.

When he saw it was hopeless, McClintock reluctantly radioed Claggett in *Dace*. He was reluctant, he said later, because he knew Claggett would give up trying to sink *Takao* and come to his rescue. After that, McClintock gave orders for his crew to destroy the sonar and TDC and begin destruction of classified papers and other gear.

One of the Japanese destroyers escorting *Takao*, apparently having heard *Darter* crunch aground, came close but then turned away. Belowdecks, as crewmen fed the mountain of confidential papers on the fires, *Darter* filled with smoke, causing much gagging and temporary discomfort.

Hearing the news of *Dace*'s sister ship, Claggett immediately broke off his attack on *Takao* to rescue the crew of *Darter*. It may have been a rash decision. Claggett still had four torpedoes. He could have shot them at *Takao* and then rescued the *Darter* crew later in the night. But Christie approved of Claggett's decision. Had Claggett attacked *Takao*, he might have been held down by the destroyers until daylight. McClintock and his crew would have been picked up by the Japanese and may have been executed for the damage they had inflicted on the fleet.

McClintock continued destroying papers and machinery and then transferred his crew to *Dace* by rubber boat, a slow, tricky operation that went on for two and a half hours. He then set demolition charges and left the ship, carrying a wardroom ashtray for a souvenir. Claggett hauled clear at full speed. The charges exploded. But in place of a deafening explosion, there was only a dull pop. Something had gone wrong.

What to do? McClintock and Claggett decided there was only one answer: torpedo *Darter*. During the next hour or so, Claggett fired four torpedoes, one at a time. All hit the reef on which *Darter* had grounded and blew up without inflicting any damage on *Darter*. The two skippers then decided to destroy *Darter* with *Dace*'s deck gun. The crew pumped twenty-one shells into *Darter*, doing some damage but not destroying her; then a Japanese plane came over and forced Claggett to break off this effort. Fortunately, the Japanese plane attempted to bomb *Darter*, not *Dace*, though unsuccessfully.

During the day, Claggett hung around, intending to put another demolition party on board *Darter* that night. A Japanese destroyer came alongside *Darter* and probably sent a boarding party on her. That night, when Claggett got within 2,000 yards of *Darter*, his sonarman picked up echo ranging. Since there was nothing on radar, Claggett and McClintock assumed the ranging to be a Japanese submarine and hauled clear again, this time setting course for Fremantle. It took eleven days to get there. With eighty-five officers and men from *Darter* on board, plus her own eighty, *Dace* soon ran low on food. By the time the boat reached Fremantle, the men were subsisting on nothing but mushroom soup and peanut butter sandwiches.

Christie made two more efforts to destroy *Darter*. He ordered John Flachsenhar in *Rock* to try torpedoes again. Flachsenhar came down and fired ten torpedoes at *Darter*, but these too apparently blew up on the reef without inflicting serious damage. Finally, Christie called in George Arthur Sharp in *Nautilus*, then in the Philippines on a special mission. With her big six-inch guns, *Nautilus* pumped fifty-five shells into *Darter*. She didn't blow up as hoped, but she was so badly holed that she was not worth trying to salvage and remained on that reef for years afterward. Her crew was transferred as a unit to new construction: *Menhaden,* in Manitowoc.

Takao limped into Brunei Bay. From there she made Singapore, where she remained for the rest of the war, unable to find parts to repair a smashed engine.

The main Japanese fleet, as planned, split into two groups. Kurita's First Force steamed eastward from Mindoro for San Bernardino Strait; Nishimura's Second Force steamed through Balabac Strait eastward for Surigao Strait. Meanwhile, Admiral Ozawa was approaching Luzon from the northeast with a carrier force to "lure" Halsey away from the landing beaches. Admiral Shima's small cruiser force had been lost in the vast shuffle of Japanese forces. More or less on his own, he decided to follow Admiral Nishimura through Surigao Strait.

What took place over the next forty-eight hours—to be known as the Battle of Leyte Gulf—was the greatest naval engagement in the history of the world. In the first exchange, October 24, U.S. aircraft hit both Kurita's First Force and Nishimura's Second Force while Japanese land-based planes struck at the conglomeration of ships near the Leyte beaches. The United States sank the super-battleship *Musashi,* damaged two battleships and two cruisers from Kurita's force, and damaged a battleship and destroyer from Nishimura's force. The badly mauled Kurita First Force reversed course, requesting land-based air support, then came about and charged again for San Bernardino Strait. Nishimura's Second Force continued on, reducing speed to allow for Kurita's double turnabout. Admiral Shima's cruiser force, not yet integrated into the battle plan, followed behind Nishimura's force.

Meanwhile, Admiral Ozawa was approaching from the north. On the afternoon of October 24, about the time Kurita was doubling back, planes from Halsey's carrier force found Ozawa. Halsey then made a decision that would keep naval strategists busy arguing for decades. Concluding that Kurita and Nishimura had been decisively attacked and presented no real threat to the landing forces, Halsey turned his carrier force north to attack Ozawa. He took the bait, just as the Japanese had hoped. San Bernardino Strait was unguarded; there was not even a submarine there.

Left by Halsey to his own resources, Admiral Kinkaid deployed his forces to stop the pincers aimed at him. To oppose Nishimura's Second Force, followed by Shima's cruiser force, Kinkaid deployed PT boats, six old battleships (some of which had been raised from the Pearl Harbor mud), six cruisers, and thirty-odd destroyers. These met and annihilated Nishimura's force, sinking everything except one destroyer, *Shigure*. Shima came up after this battle, wondering what was going on. His light cruiser, *Abukuma*, was damaged by torpedo boats and later abandoned. His heavy cruiser, *Nachi*, collided with one of Nishimura's crippled heavy cruisers, *Mogami*. Shima then withdrew with all he had left.

Kurita's First Force, meanwhile, pushed eastward through San Bernardino Strait. To oppose this mighty fleet, Kinkaid had little more than his dozen jeep carriers, which were slow and thin-skinned. These naval forces met on the morning of October 25. The jeep carrier pilots fought gallantly, sinking three heavy cruisers, all the while sending urgent calls for help to Halsey. Kurita badly damaged the light carrier *Princeton* (later abandoned and sunk by U.S. forces), and sank the jeep carrier *Gambier Bay*, two destroyers, and a destroyer escort. With victory almost in his grasp, Kurita made a decision as controversial as Halsey's: he ordered his fleet to withdraw. This decision, he explained later, was based on misinformation and an incomplete grasp of the situation. Kurita believed that Halsey was coming up with a powerful carrier force, that land-based U.S. aircraft were gathering to assault his fleet, and that even if he did proceed to the landing beaches the landing ships would have fled by the time he got there. He retired through San Bernardino Strait, where he was further hounded by U.S. planes, which damaged *Yamato* and other vessels. He returned to Brunei Bay, evading submarines in Palawan Passage by going to the west of Dangerous Ground.

That same morning, October 25, Halsey's massive fast carrier force engaged Ozawa's decoy force and devastated it, sinking all four carriers—*Zuikaku*, *Zuiho*, *Chitose*, and *Chiyoda*—and three destroyers. The hybrid carrier-battleships, *Ise* and *Hyuga*, three light cruisers (including *Tama*, badly damaged), and five destroyers escaped and retreated northward. Halsey might well have annihilated this force, too, but he turned back to support Leyte, unaware that Kurita had already retreated through San Bernardino Strait.

While this battle was in progress, two packs *SUB* arrived in Luzon Strait, one commanded by Chick Clarey in *Pintado*, (*Pintado*, *Jallao*, and *Atule*) and one commanded by Roach in *Haddock* (*Haddock*, *Halibut*, and *Tuna*). Lockwood directed them to form a scouting line to intercept retiring Japanese cripples from the battle between Ozawa and Halsey.

By chance, Pete Galantin in *Halibut* was closest to the scene. At five o'clock on the evening of October 25, he heard U.S. carrier pilots on radio directing the follow-up (and unsuccessful) attacks on the carrier-battleships *Ise* and *Hyuga* and their escorts, including the cruiser *Oyodo*. Then he saw smoke and antiaircraft fire on the horizon.

At 5:42, Galantin saw something else: pagoda masts of a battleship coming his way. This was probably *Ise*. Galantin got off a contact report to his packmates and then submerged to attack. At 6:43 he fired six bow tubes at *Ise* from very long range, 3,400 yards. There was a destroyer coming right at him so he elected not to fire his stern tubes —a decision he later regretted—and went deep. He heard what he believed were hits in *Ise* and believed he sank her. Actually, however, he hit not *Ise* but the destroyer *Akitsuki*, 2,000 tons, one of the escorts which wandered into the torpedo track. *Akitsuki* sank.

At about 8 P.M., Galantin surfaced. To the northward, he saw signal lights, which he believed to be the escorts of the "late" battleship. To the southward he could see gunfire flashes on the horizon. He took off northward after the "escorts" (actually his original target, *Ise*). While pursuing, he received a contact report from a packmate, Edward Frank Steffanides, Jr. in *Tuna*. Thinking *Tuna*'s targets better than the "escorts" he was chasing, Galantin broke off the chase and headed for *Tuna*'s position.

Actually *Tuna* had probably sighted *Ise* and *Hyuga*; Beetle Roach in *Haddock* also picked them up and chased. At about 11 P.M., Galantin found them again. The Japanese force was making 19 knots. There was no way any of the three boats could overtake and gain a firing position, so they flashed word to Clarey's pack, which had taken position farther north.

Clarey was then busy with another target. At about 8 P.M., one of his boats, *Jallao*, commanded by Joseph Bryan Icenhower making his maiden patrol as skipper, had picked up the damaged light cruiser *Tama* and flashed word to Clarey. Clarey directed his own boat, *Pintado*, and the third boat of the pack, John Maurer's *Atule*, into intercept position and gave the honors to Icenhower. Shortly after eleven o'clock, Icenhower fired seven torpedoes at *Tama*, obtaining three hits. *Tama* sank almost instantly, while Clarey, who was 15,000 yards away, watched on his bridge. When Icenhower surfaced, he learned that on his first shots of the war he had sunk a light cruiser.

During this time, John Coye's pack (*Silversides*, *Trigger*, and *Salmon*) had been moving down to backstop the scouting line. On the morning of October 26, Harlfinger in *Trigger* intercepted *Ise*, *Hyuga*, and escorts. He was slightly out of position to attack, blaming this on Galantin's contact report, which had not, Harlfinger noted, contained *Halibut's* position. Coye in *Silversides* chased on the surface in broad daylight, with land in sight 15 miles away. Harley Kent Nauman in *Salmon* joined the chase, but he sighted a Japanese periscope and turned away. Lockwood ordered all three boats of this pack to pursue the force northward at high speed.

Vernon Lowrance in *Sea Dog* lay along the track. On the evening of October 28, at about 9:20, he picked up the force at 10 miles. He submerged ahead to radar depth and fired six electrics at *Ise*, but at the last minute the ship zigzagged and all the torpedoes missed. By that time, the Japanese force was making 22 knots. There was no way Lowrance could end-around. He chased—making a contact report—but lost the force at 15 miles. "It was a heartbreaker," he said.

Orme Campbell Robbins in *Sterlet* lay to the north of *Sea Dog*. Robbins had sunk a big 10,000-ton tanker on the day of the battle and then joined forces with John Lee in *Croaker*, returning from the East China Sea. Robbins received Lowrance's contact report, then "went to full power to intercept." Wogan in *Besugo* and *Ronquil* dropped down from Bungo and Kii Suido to intercept. The three boats —*Sterlet*, *Besugo*, and *Ronquil*—formed an informal pack, Wogan leading.

At 4:15 on the morning of October 29, Robbins made contact with the two ships and destroyer escorts, range 12 miles. Robbins reported later he went to "full emergency power," meanwhile alerting the other boats. He closed to 6 miles but then, as dawn began to break, gave up the chase. *Besugo* and *Ronquil* also made radar and visual contact with the force, but they were not able to gain firing position either.

Allied troops continued to storm the beaches on Leyte. For a while it looked easy. On the first day, in a carefully staged ceremony, General MacArthur waded ashore from a landing craft in knee-deep water and said, "People of the Philippines, *I have returned*." After that, the fighting—and the weather—grew worse. In spite of repeated carrier strikes against the Visayas and Luzon, the Japanese managed to reinforce the 22,000 troops on Leyte with another 45,000. The land fighting dragged on for weeks. Before it was done, 68,000 Japanese were killed. The U.S. sustained 15,500 casualties, about 3,500 killed.

From a naval standpoint, the real significance of Leyte was not the land fighting and what was gained there but the four sea battles fought in support of the landings. The U.S. Navy had demolished much of the remaining striking seapower of the Japanese: the superbattleship *Musashi*, four aircraft carriers (*Zuikaku*, *Zuiho*, *Chitose*, and *Chiyoda*), and numerous other vessels. U.S. submarines had made a substantial contribution during the fight, sinking two heavy cruisers (*Atago* and *Maya*), one previously damaged light cruiser (*Tama*), and a destroyer (*Akitsuki*) and inflicting serious damage to the heavy cruisers *Aoba* and *Takao*. After Leyte, the Japanese navy was reduced to a few major units that never again fought as an integrated force.

22

CLOSING DAYS

During the closing days of 1944, the primary task of
U.S. submarines was to stop the flow of reinforcements
and war matériel to the Philippines. This was a combined
effort by Lockwood and Christie. Lockwood's boats patrolled in northern waters; Christie's in the south, with a
slight overlap in Luzon Strait. Information on enemy
movements was freely exchanged between the two commands, who were now fighting in relatively confined waters
with a single purpose. Christie's boats found poor hunting.
Lockwood's scored heavily.

Dick O'Kane in *Tang* patrolled alone in Formosa Strait.
In the early hours of October 23 he found a ten-ship convoy near the China coast, five freighters and five escorts.
O'Kane maneuvered inside the escorts and joined the convoy, firing nine torpedoes from point-blank range at what
he believed to be three small overlapping tankers. The
convoy scattered in confusion, one freighter ramming a
transport. Postwar records credit O'Kane with sinking
three small freighters that night: *Toun Maru*, 2,000 tons;
Wakatake Maru, 2,000 tons; and *Tatsuju Maru*, 2,000 tons.
It is possible—even probable—that all three ships were
carrying aviation gasoline for Japanese aircraft in the
Philippines and that in the resulting explosions and confusion O'Kane mistook them for tankers. Counting two
ships O'Kane had sunk on October 10 and October 11, his
score for the patrol now stood at five ships.

The following evening, October 24–25, O'Kane found
another convoy. He again maneuvered *Tang* inside the
escorts to point-blank range and fired ten torpedoes, sinking two big, heavily laden freighters, *Kogen Maru*, 6,600

tons, and *Matsumoto Maru*, 7,000 tons, and damaging
at least one other. With only two torpedoes remaining,
O'Kane hauled out to catch his breath and check the torpedoes. Then he bored in again to polish off the cripple.

O'Kane set up and fired these last two torpedoes. The
first ran true; the second broached and began a circular
run, turning back toward *Tang*. Later, O'Kane wrote:

*Rang up emergency speed. Completed part of a fishtail
maneuver in a futile attempt to clear the turning circle of
this erratic circular run. The torpedo was observed
through about 180° of its turn due to the phosphores-
cence of its wake. It struck abreast the after torpedo room
with a violent explosion about 20 seconds after firing. The
tops were blown off the only regular ballast tanks aft and
the after three compartments flooded instantly. The* TANG
*sank by the stern much as you would drop a pendulum
suspended in a horizontal position. There was insufficient
time even to carry out the last order to close the hatch.*

O'Kane and eight other men on the bridge were hurled
into the water. One other officer in the conning tower
escaped to join them. During the night these ten men tried
to hang together, but one by one they slipped away and
drowned. By dawn, only O'Kane and three others were
left.

Belowdecks, *Tang* was a shambles. Thirty men survived
the blast, many with serious injuries. Some in the control
room flooded the forward ballast tanks, bringing *Tang* to
rest, more or less level, at 180 feet. The thirty survivors
gathered in the forward torpedo room with the intent
of getting out through the escape trunk. An attempt
was made to burn the confidential papers, but the smoke
drove the men forward. Fire broke out in the forward battery compartment, further complicating the problem.

Commencing at about 6 A.M., four parties, comprising a
total of about thirteen men, began the escape procedure
they had learned in sub school, using the escape trunk
and Momsen Lungs—the only known case in the war
where the Momsen Lung provided escape. Only five men
survived the ascent or subsequent exposure in the water.
In all, eight men, including O'Kane, his chief boatswain,
W. R. Leibold, two officers, H. J. Flanagan and L. Savad-

kin, and three other enlisted men survived. They were
picked up by a Japanese patrol boat and severely beaten.
O'Kane said later, "When we realized that our clubbings
and kickings were being administered by the burned, muti-
lated survivors of our own handiwork, we found we could
take it with less prejudice." O'Kane and the other seven
served out the remainder of the war in a POW camp.

After the war, when O'Kane submitted a patrol report
from memory, Lockwood credited him with sinking thirteen ships for 107,324 tons: five tankers, four transports,
three freighters, and one destroyer. According to these
figures, this was by far the best war patrol of the war,
and for it O'Kane was awarded a Medal of Honor. Japanese records reduced the total to seven ships for 21,772
tons.

In just over four war patrols, Dick O'Kane sank twenty-
four confirmed ships for 93,824 tons, which made him
the leading skipper of the submarine war in terms of ships
sunk. (Slade Cutter and Mush Morton tied for second
place with nineteen ships each.) In addition to the Medal
of Honor, O'Kane received three Navy Crosses and three
Silver Stars and a Legion of Merit.

The Blakely (*Shark*) and Banister (*Sawfish*) wolf packs
patrolled due south of *Tang* in Formosa Strait. The seven
boats in these two units (*Shark II, Icefish, Drum, Snook,
Sawfish, Blackfish, and Seadragon*) picked up several Ma-
nila-bound convoys during the period October 23–26.
Some of these ships were northbound, some southbound.
Some may have been the same ships attacked by O'Kane.

During the nights of October 23 and 24, the two packs
sank a total of ten confirmed ships. Banister in *Sawfish*
got the first, *Kimikawa Maru*, a 6,900-ton converted seaplane tender. George Henry Browne in *Snook* got the next,
a 5,900-ton transport. Before the day was over, Browne
sank two more, a 3,900-ton tanker and a 6,900-ton freighter. Maurice Herbert Rindskopf in *Drum* got a 4,700-ton
freighter. James Henry Ashley in old *Seadragon* got three:
a 6,500-ton transport, a 7,400-ton transport, and a 1,900-
ton freighter.

Unknown to any skipper in either pack, one of the
ships in the vicinity of the combined attack that day was
an old freighter transporting 1,800 U.S. POWs from Ma-

nila to Japan. It is believed that Ed Blakely in *Shark* made contact with this vessel and then attacked. The ship was torpedoed, and all but five of the POWs were lost. These five somehow got to China and made contact with friendly forces, reporting the tragedy. Counting the work of *Paddle* on September 7 and *Sealion*, *Growler*, and *Pampanito* on September 12, this new loss meant that U.S. submarines had accidentally killed or drowned well over 4,000 Allied POWs within a period of six weeks. Perhaps more went unrecorded.

Blakely reported to Ashley in *Seadragon* that he was making this attack. That was the last word ever heard from Blakely. Japanese records revealed that on October 24 a submarine was attacked in Blakely's vicinity and that "bubbles, and heavy oil, clothes, cork, etc." came to the surface. Lockwood and Voge believed this was *Shark*. Since Lockwood's boats had been ordered to search for POWs after sinking an Empire-bound ship, Blakely may have been engaged in a rescue mission when he was attacked.

Two days after *Shark* was lost, Banister's pack got into another convoy. Rindskopf in *Drum* sank two ships, both large freighters of 6,900 tons. Dick Peterson in *Icefish* sank a freighter of 4,200 tons. After that, the Banister pack withdrew from the strait and returned to port.

In the seventy-two-hour period from October 23 to October 26, O'Kane and the Blakely-Banister wolf packs sank a total of seventeen Japanese ships. Many of these had been transporting reinforcements to the Philippines.

Two Lockwood packs patrolled the shallow waters of the Yellow Sea. The first was commanded by Gordon Underwood in *Spadefish*, leading Edward Ellis Shelby in *Sunfish* and a new skipper, Robert Hugh Caldwell, Jr., in *Peto*. The second was commanded by Elliott Loughlin in *Queenfish*, leading Gene Fluckey in *Barb* and Evan Tyler ("Ty") Shepard in *Picuda*. These two packs, operating mostly between Shanghai and southwest Korea, exchanged information and attacked the same convoys.

First contact was made by Elliott Loughlin in *Queenfish* on the night of November 8: two ships, three escorts. Loughlin fired six torpedoes at the two ships—freighters of 1,000 and 2,000 tons—and sank both. In the early hours of the morning, he found another three-ship convoy and fired another six torpedoes at a tanker and freighter, sinking the freighter, 2,100 tons, following which he was forced down by escorts.

While this was going on, his packmate Gene Fluckey in *Barb* happened on a large unescorted ship and attacked, firing three torpedoes and obtaining two hits. The ship did not sink. Fluckey came in for another attack, firing a single torpedo which broached and "ran off into the night." He fired another; it, too, missed. Fluckey then submerged and closed to point-blank range of 500 yards and fired one more. This torpedo hit. *Gokoku Maru*, a fine ship of 10,400 tons, rolled over and sank stern first.

On Armistice Day, November 11, Loughlin picked up a large convoy of a dozen freighters with six escorts. He fired four torpedoes from an unfavorable position, obtaining one hit on one freighter before escorts drove him deep and delivered an expert working-over with fifty depth charges. Later, Loughlin surfaced and flashed news of the convoy to his packmates. Fluckey in *Barb* got the word and shortly after midnight, in heavy seas, fired eight torpedoes at four ships. Some of these hit, but many of the torpedoes were thrown off course. Fluckey's crew conducted a difficult reload; then he attacked submerged, firing three torpedoes at a freighter from about 500 yards. He hit *Naruo Maru*, 4,800 tons. Later, Fluckey wrote, "First torpedo hit in forward hold and target blew up in my face, literally disintegrating. This explosion was terrific. . . . Parts of the target commenced falling on top of us, drumming on the superstructure."

Underwood's pack, patrolling to the east of the convoy, picked up Loughlin's original contact. Underwood was at that moment engaged in a lifeguard mission, but he directed Caldwell in *Peto* to intercept the convoy. Caldwell saw Fluckey's target blow up and then he attacked, firing ten torpedoes at three targets. He heard hits in all three ships, but postwar records credited only one sunk, *Tatsuaki Maru*, 2,700 tons.

About the same time, an important convoy left Manchuria, transporting the Japanese 23rd Infantry Division to the Philippines; it was the jeep carrier *Jinyo* (*Shinyo*), carrying a load of aircraft to Manila, plus freighters and tankers, all heavily escorted by about six destroyers.

Lockwood received word of this convoy from the code-breakers and flashed Ultras to his two packs. All six submarines went on sharp alert for this prize.

Loughlin in *Queenfish* made the first contact on November 15. The convoy was swarming with aircraft and escorts. Submerged, Loughlin closed what he believed to be the carrier to 1,500 yards and fired four stern tubes. As destroyers drove him deep, he believed he heard two hits in the carrier, but what Loughlin had hit—and sunk—was an aircraft ferry, *Akitsu Maru*, 9,200 tons.

That night, 30 miles away, Fluckey in *Barb* found *Jinyo* (*Shinyo*) and her destroyer escorts. She looked huge to Fluckey, who identified her as a *Shokaku*-class carrier. He got as close as he could on the surface—3,500 yards—and fired five torpedoes. He believed he got one hit but there was no record of it. Fluckey chased but could not catch up. He found a freighter, fired his last two torpedoes, and then headed for home.

The other two boats of the pack, Loughlin's *Queenfish* and Shepard's *Picuda*, pursued the convoy, edging down into Underwood's territory, where the two packs merged. On the evening of November 17, Shepard attacked, sinking a troop transport, *Mayasan Maru*, 9,400 tons, and damaging a tanker. That same night, one of Underwood's boats, Shelby's *Sunfish*, found *Jinyo* (*Shinyo*) and chased, giving contact reports. Shelby could not get into position to fire, and he broke off to go after the freighters. That evening and the next morning, he sank a 7,000-ton freighter and the 5,400-ton troop transport *Seisho Maru*. Another of Underwood's boats, Caldwell's *Peto*, attacked the convoy and sank two freighters, one 7,000 tons and one 2,800 tons.

The big prize fell to Gordon Underwood in *Spadefish*, who on November 14 had sunk a 5,400-ton freighter independently of all this. Hearing Shelby's contact report on the night of November 17, Underwood moved into the probable course of *Jinyo* (*Shinyo*). He picked her up about 9 P.M., went in, and fired six torpedoes at her and four at a tanker. Later he wrote:

The carrier burst into flames and started settling by the stern. The fire could be seen spreading the length of the

*ship below the flight deck. . . . The carrier was loaded with
planes that could be seen rolling off the deck as the ship
settled aft and took a starboard list. When last seen, the
bow was sticking up in the air, still burning. The stern was
on the bottom in 23 fathoms of water.*

Underwood had evidently missed the tanker. After reloading, he came in for a second attack. His helmsman
misinterpreted an order and slowed *Spadefish* to 8 knots.
An escort 1,000 yards away turned toward *Spadefish*,
firing 20- and 40-mm. guns. Underwood avoided these
shells, lined up on another escort, and fired four torpedoes, sinking a subchaser.

In all, these two packs sank eight ships of this convoy,
including Underwood's *Jinyo (Shinyo)*; Loughlin's aircraft
ferry, *Akitsu Maru;* and Shepard's large troop transport,
Mayasan Maru. There are no precise records as to how
many Japanese troops of the 23rd Division were drowned
or knocked out of action, but the figure must have been
high. In addition, ammunition, supplies, field guns, and
other equipment, including many airplanes, failed to reach
the Philippines. All this made MacArthur's job in the
coming weeks easier.

The packs sank four more ships. On November 23,
Shepard in *Picuda* got a 7,000-ton freighter and a 5,300-
ton transport. On November 29, Underwood sank a 4,000-
ton freighter. The next day, Shelby in *Sunfish* sank a
3,700-ton transport. All boats except *Sunfish* then returned
to port.

In terms of confirmed sinkings these two packs, Underwood's and Loughlin's, were among the most successful of
the war. Their grand total: nineteen ships for about
110,000 tons.

Four Pearl Harbor boats patrolled the southern waters
of the East China Sea. These were a three-boat pack commanded by Sandy McGregor in *Redfish*, leading Anton
Gallaher in *Bang* and Lawrence Virginius Julihn in *Shad*,
and a fourth boat patrolling alone, *Sealion II*, commanded
by Eli Reich.

Reich entered the East China Sea via Tokara Strait and
proceeded more or less toward Shanghai. On November

15 he picked up Loughlin's report of the Shanghai-bound convoy but decided that *Sealion* was "out in left field" and broke off the chase. Off Shanghai, Reich had two torpedo malfunctions. First, during a drill, his men accidentally fired one tube with the outer door closed; the torpedo smashed through, breaking the outer door and putting the tube out of commission. A day or so later, he had a battery explosion in another tube and was forced to surface in a fleet of junks in order to back down at flank speed and eject the damaged torpedo. After that, Reich left the Shanghai area and went south toward Formosa Strait.

On November 21, Reich was at the northern mouth of Formosa Strait. Shortly after midnight he picked up three huge pips at a range of 20 miles. It was a dark moonless night, with bad visibility. Closing at flank speed, Reich saw that he had two battleships escorted by two destroyers, one ahead of the battleships, one astern. The battleships were *Kongo* and *Haruna*, en route from Brunei Bay to Japan. (*Kongo* had supported the carrier attack on Pearl Harbor and then fought in many Pacific engagements, most recently as a part of Kurita's fleet at Leyte.) Reich decided to attack on the surface. He got off a contact report and then bent on flank speed to overtake.

Three hours went by before Reich could turn in to attack. From the long range of 3,000 yards, he fired six slow electric torpedoes at the first battleship, then three stern tubes at the second. Reich saw and heard three hits on the first battleship; his stern tubes were intercepted by one of the destroyer escorts, *Urakaze*, which blew up and sank. When Reich realized what had happened, he was "chagrined," he reported.

The battleships continued on at 16 knots. Reich again bent on flank speed, trying to catch up and turn in. During the long tedious chase, the torpedomen reloaded the nine usable tubes. Green water crashed over *Sealion*'s bridge as Reich ordered maximum power and more. Then, luck! One battleship with two destroyers began dropping astern, making only 11 knots. This was *Kongo*, badly damaged by Reich's first salvo. Reich easily overtook this group and got ready to attack *Kongo* again. But before he could fire another shot, as he wrote in his report:

0524 *Tremendous explosion dead ahead—sky brilliantly illuminated, it looked like a sunset at midnight. Radar reports battleship pip getting smaller—that it has disappeared—leaving only the two smaller pips of the destroyers. Destroyers seen to be milling around vicinity of target. Battleship sunk—the sun set.*

0525 *Total darkness again.*

Reich was stunned. He had done what no other submarine skipper had done, sunk a battleship—and he had done it with three electric torpedoes, fired from extreme range.

Reich tried to chase the other battleship, *Haruna*, but the seas were too heavy. He sent out another contact report and then turned off, returning to the scene of his battle for evidence of the kill or a prisoner. He found a large oil slick and circling planes.

McGregor's pack—*Redfish, Bang,* and *Shad*—had entered the East China Sea near northern Formosa and spent the next two weeks coping with a series of problems: a huge storm that battered the boats for five days, appendicitis attacks on two of the boats (though no surgery was improvised this time), and zero rewards in their efforts to find worthwhile targets. Finally, on the day after Reich—only 150 miles away—had sunk the battleship *Kongo*, the pack found a seven-ship convoy. McGregor ordered his three boats to attack.

In a furious three-hour battle, Gallaher in *Bang* fired off all twenty-four of his torpedoes. He believed he sank four ships for 18,000 tons, but postwar analysis gave him credit for sinking only two, one freighter of 2,800 tons and one of 2,400 tons. McGregor in *Redfish* fired twenty torpedoes. Thirteen missed. Seven hit, sinking, he believed, two ships; however, postwar records credited him with only one, a 2,300-ton freighter. Julihn in *Shad* fouled up his attack, firing many torpedoes (some by accident) but sinking nothing.

After this battle, McGregor ordered his pack to Saipan to reload torpedoes and conduct a second leg of the patrol. Leaving the area, Gallaher found a small fishing sampan. Later he wrote:

*Surfaced. Thought perhaps sampan had picked up some
survivors from the previous night's attack. Set sampan on
fire with 20mm. and a .30 cal. Crew consisted of three
men, two boys and a woman. All but the woman jumped
overboard. Picked up two of the men and a boy. All
seemed to be unintelligent fishermen so brought them
back close aboard their burning sampan, and let them go
back aboard to put the fire out if they could. Continued
search for convoy survivors on the surface.*

The evening after the McGregor pack left station, November 23, Lockwood sent Reich an important Ultra:
another Japanese battleship force was coming down Formosa Strait en route from Japan. It was probably *Ise*
and *Hyuga* taking reinforcements to the Paracel Islands
for transshipment to the Philippines. Reich maneuvered
Sealion to the probable course and waited seventy-two
hours. On November 26, at about 8 P.M., his radar picked
up the force at the phenomenal range of 35 miles. At first,
Reich believed his pip must be land, but it was a battleship
(*Ise?*) and four destroyers.

Reich began maneuvering to attack. For a while, he
doubted that he could gain a favorable position. However, the formation turned toward him, and he dived and
set up to fire. Rechecking, Reich realized that the formation would pass at extreme range, 4,500 yards. That was
the limit of the electric torpedo, but he fired six anyhow.
All missed. Escorts drove him to the bottom in 270 feet
of water and dropped two close charges. Then the formation went off.

Shortly after midnight, November 27, Reich came to
the surface again. His radar picked up another Japanese
task force, range 35 miles: another battleship (*Hyuga?*).
However, *Ise* evidently warned *Hyuga*. The ships detoured around Reich, and he was not able to make an
attack. After he sent off contact reports on both formations, Lockwood ordered Reich to Guam.

On November 24 and 27, over a hundred B-29 Super-
fortresses based at the newly completed airfield in the
Marianas made their first two bombing runs over the
Japanese mainland. Patrolling off Tokyo Bay, Frederick
Arthur Gunn, commanding *Scabbardfish*, and Joseph

Francis Enright, commanding *Archerfish*, were ordered to lifeguard for these attacks. As it turned out, neither was called upon for rescues, and both boats were subsequently released to conduct regular antishipping patrols in the immediate area off Tokyo Bay. Gunn on *Scabbardfish* sank a Japanese submarine, *I-365*, 1,500 tons, almost immediately. For Enright there was bigger game.

Enright had made his first patrol on *Dace* and then asked to be relieved because he had no confidence in himself. He had come to *Archerfish* after nearly a year of shore duty. Now, on the night of November 28, Enright made contact with *Shinano*, brand new sister ship of *Yamato* and *Musashi*, which had been converted to an aircraft carrier while still being built. Her conversion being almost finished, she had been hurriedly commissioned on November 18, with Captain Toshio Abe in command, and was getting her finishing touches in Tokyo Bay when the B-29 raids began. Though these initial raids did relatively little damage, they made the Japanese uneasy. On November 28 *Shinano* got under way under orders from Imperial Naval Headquarters that she be moved out of the bay to the relatively safer waters of the Inland Sea. Four destroyers escorted her.

Structurally, *Shinano* was finished, but many details, such as fire pumps, were not yet complete. There were 1,900 people on board, some of them crew, others yard workers who would finish the ship, which at 60,000 tons would be the largest warship in the world (slightly larger than *Yamato*). Many of the crew were green; they had never been to sea. There had been no training.

That night, Joe Enright in *Archerfish* patrolled the outer entrances to Tokyo Bay. At 8:48, his radar operator reported a pip at 24,700 yards. Fifty-two minutes later, Enright knew he had an aircraft carrier, headed south, speed 20 knots. He laid a course to intercept and called for flank speed. "From here on," Enright wrote later, "it was a mad race for a possible firing position. His speed was about one knot in excess of our best, but his zig plan allowed us to pull ahead very slowly."

Enright thought he was losing the race and sent off two contact reports to Lockwood, so that he could alert submarines to the south. But then at 3 A.M.—about six hours after the chase began—the carrier changed course and headed right for *Archerfish*. Enright submerged ahead. The huge ship came onward while Enright's crew made everything ready.

At 3:16, Enright began firing his bow tubes from a range of about 1,500 yards. Sigmund Albert ("Bobo") Bobczynski, his exec, was watching the TDC, holding his breath. After four torpedoes had left the tubes, he shouted, "Check fire! New setup. Switch to stern tubes." Then Enright fired two stern tubes.

Forty-seven seconds after the first torpedo was fired, Enright, manning the periscope, saw and heard a hit in the carrier's stern. "Large ball of fire climbed his side," Enright noted. Ten seconds later, he saw a second hit, 50 yards forward of the first.

There was a destroyer only 500 yards on *Archerfish*'s quarter. Enright went deep. On the way down, he said later, he heard four more properly timed hits, indicating all six of his torpedoes had hit *Shinano*. Sonar reported breaking-up noises. The escorts dropped fourteen depth charges, the nearest, Enright reported, 300 yards distant. When that noise died away, the sonarman reported more breaking-up noises. The heavy screw noise of the carrier could not be heard.

At 6:10, Enright returned to the surface for a look through the periscope. "Nothing in sight," he reported. He was certain that the carrier went down on the spot.

After the war, the records revealed that *Shinano* took four hits. Captain Abe was not overly concerned; the sister ship, *Musashi*, had taken nineteen torpedoes and many bombs before sinking at Leyte. He continued on his course at 18 knots. His inexperienced damage-control parties tried to stop the flow of water, but they fought a losing battle. It was discovered that *Shinano* did not have all her watertight doors, and some that were in place leaked. Captain Abe could have grounded *Shinano* in shallow water and saved her, but he continued on. By dawn, it was evident to all that she was sinking. At 10:18, Abe ordered abandon ship. Half an hour later, the world's largest warship slid beneath the waves, taking down Abe and 500 men.

Enright remained on station another two weeks, lifeguarding B-29 raids. He received two calls for help but could never find the downed pilots. On December 9, another off day, he fired four torpedoes at two small patrol boats and missed. He returned *Archerfish* to Guam December 15, claiming to have sunk a *Hayatake*-class carrier of 28,000 tons.

Some people were naturally skeptical. The codebreakers believed they had identified all the remaining Japanese carriers and knew where they were. But Enright's division commander, Burt Klakring, submitted a drawing of the carrier composed by Enright, and Babe Brown, acting in Lockwood's absence, credited him with sinking a 28,000-ton carrier. It was not until after the war that the whole story of *Shinano*, converted in secret and unknown to the codebreakers, came out. Then the tonnage was upped to 71,000 and Enright received a Navy Cross.

The unlikely Joe Enright, a cautious and uncertain skipper, had by the luck of the draw sunk the largest warship in history and the largest ship ever sunk by a submarine. Although in the postwar accounting the tonnage was reduced to 59,000, from a tonnage standpoint Enright's first patrol on *Archerfish* was still the best of the war.

About December 7 Lockwood received word from the codebreakers that an important task force would arrive in the Nagasaki area. Lockwood concentrated a pack—*Sea Owl*, *Piranha*, and *Sea Poacher*—plus Sandy McGregor in *Redfish*, Shelby in *Sunfish*, Clyde Benjamin Stevens, Jr. in *Plaice*, and Ralph Emerson Styles in *Sea Devil*, near the island of Danjo Gunto. Carter Bennett in *Sea Owl* commanded the pack.

On the night of December 8, Sandy McGregor made contact with the enemy force on radar at 15 miles. It consisted of the light carrier *Junyo* and several destroyers. He sent off a contact report to all submarines and began tracking.

About 9:30 that night, Styles in *Sea Devil* made contact with the task force, range 8 miles. Styles approached submerged to radar depth and fired four torpedoes at the largest target—*Junyo*, range 4,300 yards. He was lucky. Two torpedoes hit the carrier. He raised his radio antenna and got off a contact report.

Clyde Stevens in *Plaice* picked up the task force shortly after midnight, range 12 miles. As he was closing to attack, he heard torpedo explosions—*Sea Devil*'s attack.

Stevens picked the closest target, a destroyer, and fired three torpedoes. Then "the big boy" popped out of the mist. Stevens had no chance to fire at the carrier, but he shot another three torpedoes at another destroyer. He heard hits in the first destroyer and believed it sank, but postwar records did not bear out the claim.

On the other side of the formation, Sandy McGregor in *Redfish* moved in close to the carrier and fired six steam torpedoes at a range of 2,900 yards. One made an erratic circular run, forcing McGregor to maneuver wildly to avoid it, but the other five ran true. McGregor "heard and saw one terrific hit in carrier." He reloaded his forward tubes, came in for another attack, and fired six more torpedoes. One prematured, but others hit. *Junyo* limped into Nagasaki so badly damaged she was out of the war for the duration.

McGregor in *Redfish* rendezvoused with Lawrence Julihn in *Shad* about December 12, and the two boats snooped around Shanghai and then dropped down toward the mouth of Formosa Strait. On about December 16, McGregor received an Ultra from Lockwood stating that "an important enemy task force" was proceeding south.

McGregor took up position "along track that Jap task forces use between Empire and Formosa and/or Philippines." He was not altogether confident of his location; the weather had been bad for several days. A day passed, and then another, with no sign of the Japanese task force. (Later McGregor said, "They were late because they had trouble getting out of the shipyard.")

At 4:27 on the afternoon of December 19, while submerged, McGregor picked up the enemy force. It was a brand-new carrier, *Unryu*, with three destroyer escorts, one ahead and one on either beam. McGregor closed to point-blank range (1,470 yards) and fired four torpedoes. One hit, causing *Unryu* to stop. She took a strong starboard list and McGregor saw a fire break out aft. When *Unryu* trained her guns on *Redfish*'s periscope and commenced firing, McGregor responded by firing his four stern tubes, which missed.

While his torpedo crews reloaded one torpedo aft, McGregor fearlessly kept his periscope eye on the damaged carrier. The destroyers zipped about wildly, dropping depth charges. When the torpedo was in the tube, Mc-Gregor closed to 1,100 yards and fired. As he wrote later, "Torpedo hit carrier at point of aim. The sharp crack of the torpedo explosion was followed instantly by thundering explosions apparently from magazine or gasoline stowage, probably the latter. Huge clouds of smoke, flame, and debris burst into the air completely enveloping the carrier. . . . He has sunk!" The escorts came after *Redfish* in a fury, and McGregor hastily ordered 200 feet. As he recorded the results of their attack:

On passing 150 feet all Hell broke loose when seven well placed depth charges exploded alongside starboard bow. The closest one of these charges is believed to have exploded a little above keel depth and gave the sensation of pushing the bow sideways to port. At this time the following casualties were reported: Steering gear jammed on hard left and hydraulic leak in after room manifold, bow planes jammed on 20 degrees rise, and hydraulic oil leak in pump room and loss of all hydraulic power, all sound gear out of commission, pressure hull cracked in forward torpedo room with gear out of commission, pressure hull cracked in forward torpedo room with water leaking through #1 M.B.T. riser [main ballast tank pipe] and #1 Sanitary Tank discharge valve numerous air leaks throughout boat and a torpedo making a hot run in #8 torpedo tube. One man was injured when a W.T. [watertight] door jolted loose and hit him in the head practically severing one ear.

McGregor crept away from the scene of the battle as quietly as possible. *Redfish* was returned to the States for rebuilding. In his four war patrols—two on *Pike*, two on *Redfish*—Sandy McGregor had shot at three aircraft carriers, severely damaging two and sinking one.

Enemy ships in Christie's southern waters were scarce. Eliot Hinman ("Swede") Bryant led a wolf pack using Francis Worth Scanland's *Hawkbill* for his flagship. The pack consisted of *Hawkbill;* Reuben Whitaker's famous *Flasher,* now commanded by George Grider, moving up from serving as exec in *Hawkbill;* and Henry Dixon Sturr's

Becuna. The pack patrolled west of Mindoro during the invasion to stop the approach of Japanese fleet units, should they elect to sortie from Singapore.

On December 4, Scanland picked up a westbound convoy about 200 miles west of Mindoro. Grider in *Flasher* was 15 miles off his proper position and, by chance, right on the track of the convoy. When it came in sight, Grider was apprehensive. Later he wrote, "I stood in the quiet conning tower, feeling the rush of blood to my skin, knowing the test I had dreamed and wondered and worried about since my earliest days at the Naval Academy was upon me at last. My day of command in combat had arrived. What would I do with it?"

Grider prepared to attack, submerging and maneuvering for favorable position. Then it began to rain. Grider felt heartsick. Sound reported high-speed screws coming close, obviously an escort. Grider swung the periscope, searching, worrying that he would bungle his first attack. Then he saw the destroyer.

Grider fired four torpedoes and felt two hits. Later he wrote that "as I swung the scope to look, a feeling of exaltation like nothing I had ever experienced before swept over me. By heaven, I had paid my way as a skipper now, no matter what happened." The destroyer began to smoke heavily. Its screws stopped; the ship fell off to the left, settling aft and listing.

Through the mist, Grider saw a large tanker. Setting up quickly, he fired two torpedoes, then checked fire when he saw the tanker turning. He turned his attention back to the damaged destroyer. Then he saw another destroyer or patrol boat boiling in and he went deep.

As *Flasher* was going down, Grider heard two timed hits in the tanker. The exec, Philip Thompson Glennon said, almost in disbelief, "My God. We hit him!" When *Flasher* reached 250 feet, the depth charges began to explode. In all, there were sixteen, mostly close.

About an hour and a half later, Grider returned to periscope depth. He found the tanker burning furiously and settling aft. In addition—unbelievably—he saw another destroyer motionless on the water. Grider was wary. Why was this destroyer making himself a perfect target? He fired four torpedoes: three at the stopped destroyer, one at the tanker just beyond. Three torpedoes hit the destroyer.

Grider went deep again to avoid depth charges from the other escorts. When he returned to the surface, he could see the tanker, still burning. Then he saw Sturr's *Becuna*. Grider surfaced. Both boats approached the burning tanker cautiously. It was abandoned. Sturr went on his way; Grider held back to deliver the coup de grace, one more stern torpedo. The tanker sank quickly.

In this, his first attack of the war, Grider claimed he sank two destroyers and one large tanker. Postwar records bore him out. With only eleven torpedoes he had sunk the destroyers *Kishinami* and *Iwanami*, both 2,100 tons, and *Hakko Maru*, 10,000 tons.

On December 19, Otis Robert Cole, Jr. in *Dace* picked up a five-ship convoy with three escorts coming out of Camranh Bay, headed north. He made a submerged approach in the heavy seas, but the weather defeated him. A Japanese plane or escort detected *Dace* and dropped bombs or depth charges, forcing Cole to break off the attack. In her evasion, *Dace* hit bottom, and the strong current carried her bumping, scraping, and clanking along the seabed.

Grider picked up Cole's contact report and tried to move north to intercept. "It was impossible to make over seven knots into the sea," Grider reported, "and the current was setting south at four knots." Making northward progress of only 3 knots, *Flasher* gave up the chase after half an hour. That night, she exchanged places with *Dace*, guarding the Camranh Bay entrance.

On December 21 the weather moderated slightly. Shortly after 9 A.M., Grider spotted a convoy: five fat tankers, three small escorts, and a destroyer bringing up the rear. The destroyer passed by at 2,000 yards but Grider withheld fire, believing that his torpedoes would broach in the heavy seas. After the convoy passed by, Grider surfaced and headed north in pursuit. The best speed Grider could make in the heavy seas was 12½ knots. He was fighting a 3-knot southerly current, so his true speed was 9½ knots. The convoy was making 8½ knots. Grider's speed advantage: 1 knot.

Grider chased north all day and into the night. The

convoy pulled out of reach, Grider reported; "Our spirits began to droop." But he decided to go on another three hours, hoping he would regain contact; the seas had calmed down and he could make better speed. At 1 A.M. on December 22, as Grider was preparing to break off and return to Camranh Bay, Phil Glennon saw the convoy on radar.

In one of the most daring attacks of the war, Grider eased *Flasher* into shallow water between the convoy and shore. He fired three bow tubes that hit two tankers. One blew up and "illuminated the area like a night football game." Grider swung and fired four stern tubes at a third tanker. All hit and the tanker blew up. "The flames from the second and third targets flowed together," Grider wrote in his report, "and made a really impressive fire." Moments later the first target blew up and "added his light to the flames. The entire sea aft was covered with billowing red fire which burned for about forty minutes." None of the escorts attacked *Flasher*. The tankers sunk by Grider in this brilliant attack were *Omurosan Maru*, 9,200 tons; *Otowasan Maru*, 9,200 tons; and *Arita Maru*, 10,238 tons.

When Grider reported the results to Christie, the latter replied: WONDERFUL CHRISTMAS PRESENT GRIDER. CONGRATULATIONS TO YOU ALL. COME ON HOME. . . .

On this, Grider's first patrol, he had sunk a total of six ships, two destroyers and four large tankers. He was credited with six ships for 41,700 tons, upped postwar to 42,800 tons. In terms of confirmed tonnage sunk, it was the third best patrol of the war, after Enright in *Archerfish*'s fifth patrol and Hank Munson in *Rasher*'s fifth. In terms of tanker tonnage, it was the best of the war.

23

SUMMARY: 1944

The third year of the submarine war against Japan was devastatingly effective. During the year, and allowing for losses, the force level increased another thirty-three boats. These additions, plus the use of advance bases in Milne Bay, Manus, Mios Woendi, Majuro, Saipan, and Guam, enabled the three commanders to mount a total of 520 war patrols (some double-barreled), compared to about 350 in 1941–42 and 1943. The commands claimed sinking 849½ men-of-war and merchant ships for about 5.1 million tons. The postwar records credited 603 ships for about 2.7 million tons. This was more shipping and tonnage than in 1941, 1942, and 1943 combined (515 ships for 2.2 million tons).

The 1944 sinkings drastically impeded Japanese shipping services. Imports of bulk commodities fell from 16.4 million tons in 1943 to a disastrous 10 million tons. At the beginning of 1944 the Japanese had 4.1 million tons of merchant shipping afloat, excluding tankers. At the end of 1944 this figure had declined to about 2 million tons, excluding tankers. As for tanker tonnage, the Japanese began the year with 863,000 tons, built 204 tankers for 624,000 tons, and ended the year with 869,000 tons. Including tankers and merchant ships, the net loss in 1944 was over 2 million tons.

The flow of oil from the southern regions to Japan was almost completely stopped after the invasion of Mindoro. In September 1944 (in spite of all the losses), about 700,000 tons of Japanese tanker tonnage was engaged in transporting oil from the south to the home islands. By the end of the year this figure had been reduced to about 200,000 tons. Reserve stocks were so low that Japanese leaders launched experiments in making oil from potatoes.

U.S. submarines took a heavy toll of Japanese men-of-war. During the year there were about one hundred contacts on major Japanese fleet units. These developed roughly into ten attacks against battleships, twenty-five attacks against aircraft carriers, fifteen attacks against heavy cruisers, and twenty attacks against light cruisers. U.S. submarines sank one battleship, seven aircraft carriers, two heavy cruisers, seven light cruisers, about thirty destroyers, and seven submarines. In addition, they severely damaged the carrier *Junyo* and four heavy cruisers: *Myoko, Aoba, Takao,* and *Kumano.*

The major sinkings were:

Carriers and Battleships

Shokaku (30,000 tons)	June 19	*Cavalla* (Kossler)
Taiho (31,000 tons)	June 19	*Albacore* (Blanchard)
Taiyo (*Otaka*) (20,000 tons)	August 18	*Rasher* (Munson)
Unyo (20,000 tons)	September 16	*Barb* (Fluckey)
Jinyo (*Shinyo*) (21,000 tons)	November 17	*Spadefish* (Underwood)
Kongo (31,000 tons)	November 21	*Sealion II* (Reich)
Shinano (59,000 tons)	November 29	*Archerfish* (Enright)
Unryu (18,500 tons)	December 19	*Redfish* (McGregor)

Cruisers

Agano (7,000 tons)	February 16	*Skate* (Gruner)
Tatsuta (3,300 tons)	March 13	*Sandlance* (Garrison)
Yubari (3,500 tons)	April 27	*Bluegill* (Barr)
Oi (5,700 tons)	July 19	*Flasher* (Whitaker)
Nagara (5,700 tons)	August 7	*Croaker* (Lee)
Natori (5,700 tons)	August 18	*Hardhead* (McMaster)
Maya (12,200 tons)	October 23	*Dace* (Claggett)
Atago (12,000 tons)	October 23	*Darter* (McClintock)
Tama (5,200 tons)*	October 25	*Jallao* (Icenhower)

U.S. submarine losses continued to mount. Lockwood lost thirteen fleet boats: *Scorpion, Grayback, Trout, Tullibee, Gudgeon, Herring, Golet, Shark II, Tang, Escolar, Albacore, Scamp,* and *Swordfish*; and Christie lost six: *Robalo, Flier, Harder, Seawolf, Darter,* and *Growler* for a total of nineteen, compared to seven in 1942 and fifteen in 1943. In addition, *S-28,* commanded by a reservist, J. G. Campbell, was lost in a training accident at Pearl Harbor. Forty-nine men died on *S-28.*

*Previously damaged by naval aircraft.

During 1944 lifeguarding became big business for the submarine force; Pacific submarines rescued 117 navy and air corps airmen. Dick O'Kane in *Tang* was the leading rescuer, having picked up 22 airmen in a daring cruise off Truk.

During the year, twenty-three older submarines were retired from combat or readied for retirement and three (*Barbero, Halibut* and *Redfish*) were retired because of battle damage. Most of the famous old boats went to training duties.

Japanese submarines, many detailed to resupply missions, continued to be ineffective and to suffer heavy losses. Japanese submarines deployed to stop the invasions of the Marshalls, Marianas, Palaus and Philippines achieved almost nothing. During the year, the Japanese submarine force lost fifty-six boats—seven to U.S. submarines.

The "skipper problem" in the U.S. submarine force remained constant. There was always a shortage and always nonproductivity. During the year, perhaps 35 of about 250 skippers were relieved for nonproductivity. This was 14 percent, compared to 30 percent in 1942 and about 14 percent in 1943. Both Lockwood and Christie were forced to dip down to the class of 1938 for new skippers and even to use three reserve officers, who had been steadfastly denied command during three years of war. The impetus came from Admiral Nimitz: foreseeing a large postwar navy which would have to be manned for the most part by reservists. Four more reservists were named to command in 1945, making a total of seven reserve officers who commanded fleet boats on war patrol in World War II.

During the 520 war patrols in 1944, Pacific submarines fired a total of 6,092 torpedoes. This was more than all the boats had fired in 1942 and 1943 put together (5,379). In spite of improved torpedo performance on both the Mark XIV steam and Mark XVIII electric, statistically it took an average 10 torpedoes to sink a ship—compared to 8 in 1942 and 11.7 in 1943. One reason was that many skippers, no longer under orders to conserve torpedoes, fired full salvos. Another was that submarines, generally, encountered many more big targets (and convoys) deserving of full salvos. Again, skippers reported many more

hits for damage. Had the torpedo warheads been larger
—as large as Japanese submarine torpedo warheads—
many more ships would have gone to the bottom.

For all practical purposes, the U.S. submarine war
against Japanese shipping ended in December 1944. The
enemy ships that were left were forced to operate in the
confined waters of the Sea of Japan or the Yellow Sea,
running very close to shore and holing up in harbors at
night, making it almost impossible for submarines to get
at them.

24

MOPPING UP ENEMY WATERS

By the beginning of 1945, Japan was reeling in defeat. Her Navy had been reduced to a few scattered units, never again to fight as an organized force. She had almost no oil for these ships or aviation gasoline. Production of new weapons had fallen off drastically for want of raw materials and electrical power. Yet the Japanese war lords hung on—fanatically—and it was necessary for the Allies to mount three more major bloody invasions: Luzon, Iwo Jima and Okinawa, plus many smaller operations in by-passed areas and the southern Philippines.

After the invasion of Luzon in January, ship traffic between Japan and the southern regions virtually ceased, except for a few vessels hugging the China coast. The Australian-based submarines, now commanded by James Fife (Christie returned to duty in the States) concentrated on a few targets in the Singapore–Java area and new territory, the Gulf of Siam. In March, Fife moved the Australian-based submarine headquarters forward to Subic Bay on the west coast of Luzon. All the while, Lockwood's boats patrolled the Formosa Straits, East China Sea and Empire waters. Here, too, targets were scarce; a sinking in 1945 became almost a rare event.

Gene Fluckey in *Barb*, Elliott Loughlin in *Queenfish*, and Ty Shepard in *Picuda* teamed up again to make a three-boat pack. They were assigned to Formosa Strait.

The pack left from Guam, sweeping northward toward the Bonins before turning west. On January 1, Shepard and Loughlin came across a patrol craft and attacked with their deck guns. Then Fluckey came up behind and

sent a boarding party on the riddled craft to pick up
charts and codebooks. Unknown to Fluckey, there were
some Japanese hiding belowdecks. After the boarding party returned to *Barb,* Fluckey ordered his gun crew to sink
the boat. Later Fluckey wrote, "When the diesel tanks
caught fire, the eight or nine Japs came running out . . .
on deck. They stopped for a minute and our 4-inch crew,
being very blood-thirsty at that time, landed a shot right
in their midst which blew them all apart."

The pack took station in Formosa Strait in shallow water, close to the spot where Dick O'Kane in *Tang* had gone
down. Early on the morning of January 7, Fluckey picked
up a seven-ship convoy and broadcast a contact report.
Then he made an end around in broad daylight, submerging ahead of the convoy. When the convoy came along
an hour later, visibility was bad and Fluckey had a hard
time getting set on a target. He picked a big tanker, but it
zigged away just as he got ready to fire. A destroyer came
by but Fluckey withheld his fire, writing later, "I have now
developed enough self-control to resist the temptation to
let three torpedoes fly at an escort unless conditions are
right. The latter the result of twelve torpedoes I have
wasted in the last three patrols."

The convoy got by Fluckey. At 9:41 A.M. he surfaced
to make another end around. While this was in progress,
Shepard in *Picuda,* who had received Fluckey's contact
report and submerged in good position, fired four torpedoes at a 10,000-ton tanker, *Munakata Maru.* Some hit
and the tanker was severely damaged, but the attack
alerted the convoy, which scattered and scurried into Formosa before Fluckey or Loughlin in *Queenfish* (too far
away) could attack. All in all, it was a less than satisfactory beginning. "Some consolation in *Picuda* making
the grade," Fluckey wrote.

The pack regrouped close to the China coast. The next
day, January 8, at about one in the afternoon, Fluckey
picked up another big convoy and flashed the word. Again
he made an end around on the surface, submerging ahead
of the convoy. It came along on track and Fluckey
planned his attack to drive the ships away from the coast
and toward his packmates. He began to fire, shooting three
torpedoes at one freighter and three at another. While
swinging around for a stern shot, there was an awesome

explosion that forced *Barb* down sideways. Fluckey had hit an ammunition ship. Loughlin saw it blow up and "completely disintegrate in a sheet of fire, explosions and bursting shells." Fluckey went "deep" to 140 feet to reload. After dark, he surfaced.

About that time, Loughlin in *Queenfish* attacked, firing ten torpedoes: four at one ship, three each at two others. All torpedoes missed. "It seemed incredible," Loughlin wrote in his report, "but no explosions were seen or heard." Loughlin pulled off to reload.

Then it was Shepard's turn. Like Loughlin, he fired ten torpedoes in one great salvo: four at a tanker, three each at two freighters. Shepard got hits in at least two of his targets, maybe three. He pulled off to reload and Fluckey moved in for his second attack.

Fluckey fired six more torpedoes, three each at two targets. One blew up with another awesome explosion. Fluckey wrote later, "Three hits timed and observed followed by a stupendous earth-shaking eruption. This far surpassed Hollywood and is one of the biggest explosions of the war. . . . A high vacuum resulted in the boat. Personnel in the control room said they felt as if they were being sucked up the hatch." Loughlin saw this explosion, too.

Queenfish moved in for another attack. Loughlin picked out a tanker and fired four bow tubes. Two hit. A destroyer charged *Queenfish* and Loughlin fired two stern torpedoes down the throat. Both missed, forcing him to make evasion maneuvers. Meanwhile, Shepard in *Picuda* conducted a second attack.

No one is really certain who sank what in these series of attacks, but in the postwar accounting Fluckey was credited with sinking three ships: *Shinyo Maru,* a 5,892-ton freighter; *Anyo Maru,* a 9,256-ton transport; and *Sanyo Maru,* a 2,854-ton tanker. In addition, he shared one third credit with Loughlin and Shepard for sinking *Hokishima Maru,* another 2,854-ton tanker. The pack also inflicted severe damage on two freighters, *Meiho Maru* and *Hisagawa Maru,* and a 6,516-ton tanker, *Manju Maru.* Whatever the convoy was carrying never reached the Philippines.

In subsequent days, the boats of the pack operated more or less independently. On January 18, Loughlin picked up a small convoy near the China coast and fired eight torpedoes at several ships, but all of them missed. He returned to Pearl Harbor. Shepard in *Picuda* attacked a small convoy on January 29, firing his last torpedoes at a transport and freighter. He hit both, and the transport *Clyde Maru*, 5,500 tons, sank.

Gene Fluckey still had twelve torpedoes left. Although he hunted relentlessly, he could find no targets. Based on information from coast watchers in China and the China Air Force, he reasoned that the convoys were hugging the coast very close and holing up in harbors at night. When he received word on a northbound convoy, Fluckey closed the coast, mingled with some fishing craft, and confirmed his belief: radar showed a mass of ships anchored in Namkwan Harbor.

Fluckey decided the best way to get at these ships was simply to proceed up the long, ill-charted, and perhaps mine-infested channel into the harbor and shoot. He put his exec on the bridge to conn the ship and took station in the conning tower at the radar set. On the long and scary trip in, the fathometer registered 36 feet of water, sometimes less.

Once inside the harbor, Fluckey decided he would fire eight torpedoes, leaving four in case he had to shoot his way out through the escorts. He fired four bow tubes, range to targets 3,200 yards, swung around, and fired four stern tubes, range 3,000 yards. Ordering flank speed, he took station on the bridge. All over the harbor, he saw ships blowing up and firing guns. He believed he had sunk at least four, but postwar records credited him only one, *Taikyo Maru*, 5,244 tons. Threading her way through the junks and sampans to deep open water, *Barb* was not even scratched.

Fluckey fired his last four torpedoes at a freighter, but they all missed. After that he returned to Pearl Harbor, where he was received with a red carpet. His endorsements were ecstatic. One stated, *"Barb* is one of the finest fighting submarines this war has ever known." Fluckey was credited with sinking eight big ships for 60,000 tons and damaging four for 25,000 tons, making his total bag (sunk and damaged) 85,000 tons. The sinkings were reduced in postwar records to a total of four and one third for 24,197 tons.

For this outstanding performance, Gene Fluckey was awarded the Medal of Honor.

A wolf pack led by Joe Enright in *Archerfish* took station in Luzon Strait. The other boats were *Batfish*, commanded by Jake Fyfe, and *Blackfish*, commanded by Robert Frederick Sellers.

About the time this pack reached Luzon Strait, the codebreakers picked up information that the Japanese intended to evacuate some pilots from Luzon to Formosa by submarine. The four boats detailed to this mission were *RO-46*, *RO-112*, *RO-113*, and *RO-115*. The routes and sailing dates were relayed to Enright, who deployed his pack in a probable intercept position in the strait. The pack was joined by another made up of *Plaice*, *Scabbardfish*, and *Sea Poacher*.

The scouting line waited patiently. On the night of February 9, at about 10:15, Jake Fyfe in *Batfish* picked up radar emissions on a device known as the APR. A little later, he got radar contact at 6 miles. Believing this to be one of the Japanese submarines southbound from Formosa, he closed to 1,850 yards and fired three torpedoes. All missed. The Japanese skipper evidently did not see the torpedoes; he continued on course. When only 1,000 yards away, Fyfe fired three more torpedoes. One ran hot in the tube, but the second hit the sub, causing a "brilliant red explosion that lit up the whole sky." This was *RO-115*.

The following morning Fyfe intended to remain on the surface for a daylight search, but friendly aircraft (perhaps also looking for the Japanese submarines) drove him under. At about 10 A.M., when Fyfe came up to have a look through his periscope, the friendly planes attacked *Batfish*, firing an aerial torpedo. Fyfe went deep in a hurry. The torpedo passed over *Batfish*. "A tender moment," Fyfe wrote later, "and a very unfriendly act."

Plaice, *Scabbardfish*, and *Sea Poacher* left the scouting line to patrol elsewhere. *Batfish*, *Archerfish*, and *Blackfish* remained in position. On the evening of February 11, shortly after surfacing to charge batteries, Fyfe again picked up radar emissions on his APR. Then he saw a Japanese submarine, range 1,200 yards. As Fyfe was setting up to fire, the submarine dived. Fyfe thought that was that, but the sub surfaced again half an hour later, giving off radar emissions. Fyfe made an end around and at about ten o'clock fired four torpedoes from the point-blank range of 880 yards. Fyfe later wrote, "The target literally blew apart and sank almost immediately." This was *RO-112*, southbound from Formosa.

The next night, shortly after midnight, Fyfe again picked up Japanese radar emissions on APR. At 2:15, he made contact on his own radar, range 5 miles. Fyfe moved in but the sub dived. An hour later, Fyfe picked the target up on radar again and attacked, firing three torpedoes from 1,500 yards. One hit, and the submarine blew up in a "large yellow ball of fire." This was *RO-113*, southbound from Formosa.

On the following evening, February 14, Joe Enright in *Archerfish* believed he picked up yet another Japanese submarine. Firing two salvos of four torpedoes, he saw a "large white flash" that illuminated the target and believed he sank a submarine. Lockwood credited him with the sinking, but postwar records did not bear it out. After this attack, the pack returned to Saipan and Guam.

Joe Willingham, on the first patrol of *Tautog,* had sunk two Japanese submarines and nearly sunk two or three more, but no other skipper had ever actually sunk three on one patrol, let alone three in three days. Lockwood, sparing no praise, called Fyfe's performance "brilliant." The Japanese gave up trying to evacuate the aviators by submarine. Counting *RO-49,* sunk by Frank Latta in *Lagarto* on February 24, the Japanese lost four boats to U.S. submarines in February.

In March a new boat, *Tirante,* commanded by George Levick Street III, arrived at Saipan for her first war patrol. Street's exec was Ned Beach, who had made ten previous patrols on *Trigger;* Street had made nine previous war patrols on *Gar.* The two men got along famously, Street later describing Beach as "one of the outstanding young submariners of all times."

Lockwood sent *Tirante* to the East China Sea. Street began by patrolling the approaches of Nagasaki (in the area where John Lee in *Croaker* had sunk the light cruiser *Nagara*) and on March 25 sank a small tanker, *Fuji Maru.* Three days later, he sank a small freighter, *Nase*

Maru. During the next few days, while U.S. troops went ashore at Okinawa, Street stood guard at the western exit of the Inland Sea in case major Japanese fleet units should come out. During this time, he battle-surfaced and sank a lugger and missed an amphibious vessel with three electric torpedoes.

After being released from reconnaissance duty, Street moved north to patrol off the south coast of Korea. Soon after reaching these waters, Street battle-surfaced on a schooner. A boarding party captured three Koreans, one of whom escaped by diving over the side. On April 7 Street attacked a small single freighter, firing two electric torpedoes and observing the thunderous double explosion through the periscope. He surfaced immediately and surveyed the wreckage, saw two survivors clinging to debris, and by hand signals vectored a nearby native Korean craft to rescue them. This is another sinking that must have slipped through, for postwar records failed to confirm it.

Tirante had an extraordinarily powerful SJ radar, and her engineers had fixed the speed governors on her Fairbanks-Morse diesels so as to increase her maximum speed by about a knot. When Street learned from the *Threadfin* and *Hackleback* reports that *Yamato* had sortied from the Inland Sea, it seemed logical to him and Beach that she might round Kyushu, perhaps heading for the naval base at Sasebo, in *Tirante*'s area (since the only other way to get there, through Shimonoseki Strait, was now blocked by aircraft-laid mines). With her speed and radar both operating at maximum, *Tirante* ran a "retiring search curve" which completely blanketed all *Yamato*'s possible positions, had Sasebo been her destination. To Street and his eager crew, it seemed certain they would have a shot at her. They were of course disappointed, but there was other business coming their way.

Responding to an Ultra on April 9, *Tirante* attacked a small convoy. Street fired six electric torpedoes at two different ships. He missed one but the others hit *Nikko Maru,* a 5,500-ton transport which was jammed with troops and seamen returning from Shanghai. Escorts jumped *Tirante* and delivered a close attack. Street responded by firing one Cutie. It apparently hit the mark because there was a terrific overhead explosion and break-ing-up noises. The escort either was too small for the records or did not sink.

On the night of April 12 or 13 (as Beach later recalled) *Tirante* received an Ultra reporting that an important transport had holed up for the night in a small harbor on Quelpart Island (Cheju Do) about 100 miles due south of the southwestern tip of Korea. Street proceeded there, ar-riving the night of April 13. *Tirante* went to battle stations and, proceeding boldly on the surface past an escort, crossed into 60 feet of water. Then Street nosed *Tirante*'s bow into the harbor—à la Gene Fluckey.

Beach, manning the TBT binoculars on the bridge, picked up three targets anchored in the murk: the trans-port and two small frigate escorts. While Beach aimed from the bridge, Street in the conning tower made ready torpedo tubes and fired three steam torpedoes at the transport. Moments later, it blew up with an awesome explosion. Street ordered *Tirante* to head for deep water, changed his mind, paused, and fired three torpedoes at the two frigates. Both blew up and sank while *Tirante* was making flank speed out of the harbor. Confirmed re-sult: with six torpedoes, Street and Beach had sunk *Juzan Maru*, 4,000 tons, and two frigates of about 900 tons each.

With only one torpedo remaining, Street headed for the barn. On the way home, he found three Japanese airmen sitting on the overturned float of a seaplane. He captured two, but the third drowned himself. For all these exploits —including the sinking of six confirmed ships for 12,621 tons—George Street received the Medal of Honor and Ned Beach, one of a few execs so honored, a Navy Cross. Following this, Beach received orders to command his own boat.

In their endless search to find targets, Lockwood and Voge once again cast covetous eyes on the Sea of Japan. It had not been exploited since September 1943, when Mush Morton was lost in *Wahoo* trying to exit through La Pérouse Strait. Now, Lockwood and Voge believed, the Sea of Japan must be thick with ships, forced there by U.S. submarines and carrier task forces.

The big problem still was how to get in and out. The

east and west straits (separated by the island of Tsushima) were heavily mined. The narrow center exit, Tsugaru Strait, was also mined. The northern exit, La Pérouse, where Morton was lost, was believed to be heavily patrolled by aircraft and surface vessels. Lockwood doubted that a submarine could enter from La Pérouse (as the eight boats had done in the summer and fall of 1943) without being detected.

By now, Lockwood believed, a new piece of sonar gear, the FM, was sensitive enough to pick up mines. If the sets proved reliable enough, if a group of operators could be trained to use them properly, they might serve to guide a submarine through the minefields of Tsushima Strait into the Sea of Japan, and the boats could get out by making a dash through La Pérouse.

This scheme dominated Lockwood's waking hours for weeks. He appointed Barney Sieglaff to work on it full time; hence the plan was called Operation Barney. Lockwood himself worked on the FM sonar problems, urging the manufacturers who were hand-building the sets to hurry up and to make improvements. When boats arrived at Guam equipped with FM sonar, Lockwood took them to a dummy minefield and personally trained both operators and skippers in the use of the gear. He was an exacting taskmaster.

As a preliminary, Lockwood sent out two boats to probe minefields—that is, to check the FM against the real thing. The boats were *Tinosa*, commanded by Richard Clark Latham, and *Spadefish*, now commanded by William Joseph Germershausen. Latham was ordered to minefields in the East China Sea, Germershausen to the field at Tsushima Strait.

On the way out, Lockwood sent the two boats an Ultra to intercept a convoy southbound from Japan. Germershausen found it and sank a 2,300-ton freighter. Latham, trying to intercept, was driven down by a Japanese plane. On the way down, the bow planes failed to rig out. Latham went to 180 feet and remained there, trying to fix them. During that time, *Tinosa* was swept along by strong currents and grounded lightly on an island, damaging one of the outer torpedo doors. With all this trouble, *Tinosa* missed an opportunity to attack the convoy.

Latham then proceeded to his minefield plotting mission, determined to do it on the surface if necessary. The FM gear was operating "beautifully" at first, and Latham was getting a good minefield plot. But in the middle of the operation, the FM broke down—with mines all around. *Tinosa* was then in about 100 fathoms of water. Latham decided the best thing he could do until the FM gear was repaired was anchor, so he began walking the anchor out. He had 120 fathoms of anchor chain. At 89 fathoms, the chain broke—from the weight of the anchor and chain. However the FM gear was repaired and Latham slipped out to sea, finishing out the patrol with a cruise along the China coast.

Germershausen took *Spadefish* to the edge of the minefields at Tsushima Strait. His FM gear was not working properly either. He made three separate attempts to close —and chart mines—but all failed. Later, he wrote, "I must say mine-hunting was dull, unrewarding work that could not compare with the thrill of coming to grips with a big, fat enemy ship." Germershausen returned to regular patrol in the Yellow Sea, where he sank another freighter.

Next, Lockwood sent a pack of four FM-equipped boats to probe the minefields: *Bowfin*, commanded by Alexander Kelly Tyree; *Seahorse*, commanded by Harry Holt Greer, Jr.; *Bonefish*, commanded by Lawrence Edge; and *Crevalle*, commanded by Everett Hartwell Steinmetz. (On the way to her job, *Seahorse* was bombed and strafed by a B-24 Liberator, which fortunately did little damage.) At the Tsushima minefields, these boats did good work. The FM gear was more reliable, and the operators obtained more information on mine locations.

After completing these special tasks, the boat went on to normal patrol. Tyree in *Bowfin* sank two ships off northeast Honshu, one a transport and one a freighter. Greer in *Seahorse* sank a junk. Later the boat was attacked by two patrol boats that delivered a punishing depth-charge attack. The boat survived, but, her historian reported, "*Seahorse* was a shambles of broken glass, smashed instruments, cork and dirt, with hydraulic oil spilled over everything," and she was returned to Pearl Harbor for a complete overhaul. Her FM gear (still intact) was shifted to *Sea Dog*.

By May, Lockwood felt he had enough information—and the FM gear worked well enough—to send a submarine task group into the Sea of Japan. He asked Nimitz's permission to lead the group in person—his sixth request to make a war patrol. Nimitz, of course, denied the request.

To lead the expedition, Lockwood picked Earl Twining Hydeman, an older officer from the class of 1932 who had had relatively little combat experience. Hydeman had spent most of the war in New London and Washington. On his first patrol off Tokyo Bay, Hydeman had sunk a 6,850-ton freighter and rescued a fighter pilot from the carrier *Intrepid*.

In all, Lockwood assigned nine FM-equipped boats to make the foray. The group, code-named "Hell Cats," was divided into three wolf packs, as follows:

Hydeman's Hep Cats
Sea Dog (Earl T. Hydeman)
Crevalle (Everett H. Steinmetz)
Spadefish (William J. Germershausen)

Pierce's Pole Cats
Tunny (George E. Pierce)
Skate (Richard B. Lynch)
Bonefish (Lawrence L. Edge)

Risser's Bob Cats
Flying Fish (Robert D. Risser)
Bowfin (Alexander K. Tyree)
Tinosa (Richard C. Latham)

Before departure, each of the nine boats was equipped with external "clearing wires." These were steel cables strung from the bow to the tips of the bow planes and from the stern deck to the tips of the stern planes. The wires—in theory—would prevent a mine cable from hooking on bow or stern planes.

Hydeman and five other skippers left from Pearl Harbor on May 27 and May 29. *Tunny, Skate,* and *Bonefish* received last-minute additional FM training under Lockwood's supervision at Guam and then left from there on May 28.

On the way to the rendezvous at the south end of the strait, Dick Latham in *Tinosa* picked up ten airmen from a B-29. Later historian Holmes wrote, "When the aviators learned of *Tinosa*'s destination they were unanimous in their desire to be put safely back in their rubber boats." Lockwood arranged a rendezvous with *Scabbardfish*, returning from patrol, and Latham turned the pilots over to her.

South of Kyushu, the expedition commander, Earl Hydeman in *Sea Dog*, had a severe casualty: his radar went out of commission. He joined up with Steinmetz in *Crevalle* and Steinmetz provided "Seeing-Eye" services, leading *Sea Dog* toward the strait in bad weather by short-range radio.

The boats went through the field by packs. *Sea Dog*, *Crevalle*, and *Spadefish* went first on June 4. All stayed deep—below 150 feet—to avoid the mines. Some of the boats had the FM sound head mounted near the keel. These went through with a 6-degree up-angle, so the FM gear could "look" forward and pick up mines. Hydeman reported, "During this passage, no FM contacts were made which could possibly have been mines."

There were, however, many disquieting moments. A few hours after submerging, Hydeman heard "several distant explosions." An hour later he heard "nine distant explosions, heavy enough to shake us a bit," followed by six more. Germershausen in *Spadefish* and Steinmetz in *Crevalle* also heard these explosions. Germershausen later described them as "loud." He wrote, "From then on our spirits were considerably depressed. Had *Sea Dog* or *Crevalle* come to grief?" They had not. All three boats made it safely. The explosions remained a mystery.

After *Sea Dog* reached the Sea of Japan, as Hydeman wrote, "All hands breathed a little easier. The emotional strain, especially on the officers, was very heavy and its effects were now quite evident. Everybody was on their toes at all times however; officers and men performed their duties in a manner deserving of the highest praise."

The next day, June 5, Pierce took his pack through (*Tunny*, *Skate*, and *Bonefish*). Richard Barr ("Ozzie") Lynch on *Skate* had a spine-chilling experience. At about 9 A.M., his FM operator picked up the unmistakable bell-like tone of a mine line 400 yards ahead. The mines were closely set. Lynch dropped to 175 feet and proceeded. Then every man on the boat heard a noise none ever forgot: a mine cable scraped down the entire length of the boat. Lynch and his crew held their collective breath, praying that the cable would not snag the mine down to *Skate*. The clearing lines evidently worked.

After passing the second of four mine lines (that is, while in the middle of the field), Lynch, perhaps feeling *Skate* had developed some kind of mine immunity, decided to come up to periscope depth and get a fix on the location of the field. He rose slowly to 60 feet, poked up "the pole," and took bearings on landmarks on the shoreline. Then—having obtained this valuable information—Lynch went deep again and proceeded to underrun the last two lines.

The next day, June 6, Bob Risser led the Bob Cats (*Flying Fish, Bowfin,* and *Tinosa*) through the fields. *Tinosa,* too, had a close call. Richard Clark Latham ran right up on a mine, maneuvered to avoid it, and then stopped his screws. Later he wrote:

Tinosa stopped swinging right and started left again, but that mine was coming closer and closer abeam until it was too close any longer to show on the [FM] scope. Then there was a scraping, grinding noise as the mine cable slid down the starboard side. No one moved or spoke. Would it snag and drag the mine into us? We were at 120 feet keel depth and the mine was hopefully clear of us. God bless the fairing cables leading from the hull to the outboard forward edge of our stern planes! That mine cable slid on aft past the stern planes and our silent screw and off the end. How much it dragged down the mine or how close the mine came to us, we'll never know.

Tinosa went safely through two more lines of mines.

Once inside the sea, the nine boats deployed to patrol stations. (Like the boats on the first foray into the Sea of Japan in the summer of 1943, all had orders to withhold fire until sunset on the evening of June 9—to allow time for the boats going to the farthest point to get into position.) Hydeman led the Hep Cats far to the northeast, to patrol the western coast of Hokkaido and Honshu. Pierce led the Pole Cats to station along central and southern Honshu. Risser led the Bob Cats to the east coast of Korea, where the pack encountered dense fog. While waiting for Germershausen in *Spadefish* to reach his far north position off Hokkaido, the other Hell Cats passed many ships. They were all sitting ducks—unescorted, not zigzagging, burning running lights. Most of the skippers had itchy trigger fingers and were tempted to shoot before the deadline. After sighting his fifth Japanese ship, Steinmetz in *Crevalle* wrote, "Of all contacts this was the toughest to throw back in the pond. Was strongly tempted to swing left, shoot and then use as an excuse 'I was just cleaning my torpedoes and . . .!' "

The Hell Cats turned out to be one of the most successful submarine operations of the war. Hydeman in *Sea Dog* sank six ships in ten days. Germershausen in *Spadefish* sank five ships. Lynch in *Skate* sank four, including a submarine, *I-122*. Latham in *Tinosa* also sank four. Steinmetz in *Crevalle* sank three. Edge in *Bonefish*, Risser in *Flying Fish*, and Tyree in *Bowfin* each got two. Total: twenty-eight ships for 54,784 tons.

Only George Pierce in *Tunny* failed to sink a confirmed ship. It was not from lack of trying. Like the other skippers, Pierce practically put his boat's bow on the beaches of Japan, but he had bad luck; he saw only a few targets. He attacked two, firing seven torpedoes, but missed on both, and he had a "running gun battle" with two destroyers.

One boat was lost. After sinking one big ship, Lawrence Edge in *Bonefish* met with Pierce on June 18 and asked permission to penetrate Toyama Bay, a relatively shallow and confined body of water. As soon as he got in the bay, Edge sank another big ship, but he was spotted and pounced on by Japanese antisubmarine forces. They delivered a depth-charge attack which fatally holed the famous *Bonefish*. She was lost with all hands.

The pack made one serious error. On the night of June 13, Germershausen in *Spadefish*, patrolling to the northwest of La Pérouse Strait, picked up a freighter on radar. This was an area where Russian ships passed en route to and from Vladivostok, so Germershausen closed to 1,100 yards to look over his quarry. The ship had no lights burning and "was not following a designated Russian route." Germershausen fired two torpedoes and sank it. It was the Russian ship *Transbalt*, 11,000 tons.

The Russians protested almost immediately. Lockwood radioed the Hell Cats, DID ANYBODY SHOOT NORTHWEST

OF LA PEROUSE STRAIT? Germershausen, who by then suspected he had made a mistake, replied GUILTY.

Not wishing to disclose that U.S. submarines were again operating in the Sea of Japan, Nimitz or King blamed the incident on a Japanese submarine. But the Russians weren't fooled. Germershausen joked later, "They blamed it on a reactionary U.S. submarine skipper."

With this sinking (actually giving *Spadefish* a total of six ships sunk), Germershausen swelled the Russian-ship-sinking club membership to four, joining Eugene Sands (two Russian ships), Moon Chapple (one), and Malcolm Garrison (one).

After two weeks inside the Sea of Japan, the Hell Cats prepared to leave. This, they feared, would be the hardest part of all; surely the Japanese would be guarding the exits with everything they had. Hydeman decided the best way out was to exit through La Pérouse Strait at night on the surface, gun crews standing by. Should the group be attacked by Japanese destroyers, they could fight back with the combined firepower of nine 5-inch deck guns—a considerable array of armament.

In addition, Lockwood provided a diversionary act to trick the Japanese into believing the boats were going out through Tsushima Strait. Early on the morning of June 24, *Trutta*, now commanded by a reserve officer, Frank P. Hoskins, shelled the island of Hirado Shima on the east channel of Tsushima Strait in a "purposely conspicuous manner."

On the night of June 24, the boats rendezvoused just inside La Pérouse Strait—all but *Bonefish*. With eight submarines bunched together, Hydeman could not wait. He ordered the pack to enter the strait at 18 knots. Hydeman in *Sea Dog* led one column, but his radar failed again and *Crevalle* resumed her role as Seeing-Eye dog. A dense fog shrouded the boats as they barreled through the strait. There were two contacts—a lighted ship, probably Russian, and a Japanese minelayer that did not see them. By 5:20 A.M. on June 25, all eight boats had made it out without a shot being fired at them. No one could understand why it had been so easy.

Pierce in *Tunny* received permission from Hydeman to go into the Sea of Okhotsk to wait for—and radio—*Bonefish*. On the night of June 25, Pierce sent two messages to

Bonefish. When no reply was received, Pierce set course for Midway. He arrived on July 2, a day or two after the other boats. Then all went to Pearl Harbor for an epic party—and medals and praise from Lockwood.

Germershausen had some unfinished business regarding the Russian ship he sank. As he recalled it later, when he got into port, Lockwood said, "Go see Nimitz." Germershausen reported as ordered, expecting a royal chewing out or worse. "He asked what happened," Germershausen recalled. "I told him I didn't see any markings. All he said was, 'Glad you made it back safely, son.'"

After this "first wave," Lockwood sent seven other boats singly into the Sea of Japan: *Sennet, Piper, Pargo, Pogy, Jallao, Stickleback,* and *Torsk.* Charles Robert Clark, Jr., in *Sennet* went first and sank the most ships, four for 13,105 tons.

On August 6, the U.S. Air Force dropped an atomic bomb on Hiroshima, followed by another on Nagasaki, August 9. Emperor Hirohito advised his war cabinet to accept the unconditional surrender terms demanded by the Allies. At fifty-six minutes to midnight, August 14, Admiral Nimitz sent a message to all naval units in the Pacific:

CEASE OFFENSIVE OPERATIONS AGAINST JAPANESE FORCES. CONTINUE SEARCH AND PATROLS. MAINTAIN DEFENSIVE AND INTERNAL SECURITY MEASURES AT HIGHEST LEVEL AND BEWARE OF TREACHERY OR LAST MOMENT ATTACKS BY ENEMY FORCES OR INDIVIDUALS.

Victory flags

AFTERWORD

Following the surrender ceremonies in Tokyo Bay, September 2, 1945, most of the submarines in the Pacific returned almost immediately to the United States. They nested in seaports and were opened to the public. The skippers and crews were permitted—for the first time—to discuss their exploits freely with friends and newsmen. The books on submarine operations written during the war but held up by censorship were released. But in the flood of postwar news, the submarine service failed to get its story across—it remained a silent victory.

Meanwhile, Lockwood and his staff tabulated the final results for all submarine commands and submitted the figures to the Navy Department. Lockwood claimed that U.S. submarines had sunk about 4,000 Japanese vessels for about 10 million tons. His figures included one battleship, eight heavy and light aircraft carriers, and twenty heavy and light cruisers. Fifty-two submarines had been lost from all causes (including training) during the war, including forty-five fleet boats. Some 375 officers and 3,131 enlisted men had died out of about 16,000 who actually made war patrols. This was a casualty rate of almost 22 percent, the highest for any branch of the military.

The Joint Army-Navy Assessment Committee (JANAC) drastically trimmed Lockwood's sinking figures. By the (imperfect) reckoning of this group, the U.S. submarine force actually sank 1,314 enemy vessels for 5.3 million tons. The figures included one battleship, eight heavy and light carriers, and three heavy and eight light cruisers. The tonnage figure, 5.3 million, represented 55 percent of all Japanese vessels lost. The other 45 percent were lost to army and navy aircraft, mines, and other

380

causes. (In addition, JANAC gave submarines "probable" credit for another 78 vessels of 263,306 tons.)

The JANAC figures significantly altered the scores of many leading skippers. Medal-of-Honor winner Dick O'Kane, for example, had been credited with sinking thirty-one ships for 227,800 tons; JANAC reduced him to twenty-four ships for 93,824 but still left him the leading submarine ace of the war, in terms of ships sunk. By JANAC figures, Slade Cutter and Mush Morton tied for second place with nineteen confirmed ships each. Medal-of-Honor winner Gene Fluckey came in fourth with sixteen and a third ships for 95,360 tons. This was the highest tonnage sunk by any skipper. The most spectacular drop in standing was Roy Davenport's. Credited with seventeen ships sunk for 151,900 tons during the war, his score as confirmed by JANAC was only eight ships for 29,662 tons.

This downward readjustment caused an awkward moment for the navy. Most of the medals awarded submarine skippers during the war had been given out on the basis of ships or tonnage scores. Should they now be withdrawn? There was no way, and nobody was inclined to do it. Roy Davenport, for example, kept his five Navy Crosses, just as many air force and naval aviators kept medals awarded for claims that were undoubtedly exaggerated or were disclaimed by postwar accounting. The only complaint raised about medals was that there should have been more Medals of Honor awarded. Only six skippers had received them; many more were deserving, especially Slade Cutter and Mush Morton.

The loss of men in the Japanese merchant marine was heavy. Japan began the war with about 122,000 merchant marine personnel. About 116,000 of these became casualties: 27,000 killed, 89,000 wounded or "otherwise incapacitated." Of this total, the majority of the casualties —16,200 killed and about 53,400 wounded or "otherwise incapacitated"—were inflicted by submarine attack.

When confronted with the revised sinking figures according to JANAC, Lockwood laid most of the blame for the large discrepancy between claims and actuality on defective torpedoes. A total of 14,748 torpedoes had been fired. Had all these run, hit, and detonated as designed, the claims might well have been closer to the actuality, he maintained. Few could disagree. The torpedo scandal of the U.S. submarine force in World War II was one of the worst in the history of any kind of warfare.

Lockwood took pains to point out that the actual damage inflicted on the Japanese navy and merchant marine by U.S. submarines was, in reality, large compared with the effort expended. The U.S. submarine force, composed in total of about 50,000 officers and men (including back-up personnel and staffs), represented only about 1.6 percent of the total navy complement. In other words, a force representing less than 2 percent of the U.S. Navy accounted for 55 percent of Japan's maritime losses.

No matter how the figures were looked at, the damage inflicted by the U.S. submarine force on Japan was severe and contributed substantially to winning the war in the Pacific. As the report of the United States Strategic Bombing Survey stated, "The war against shipping was perhaps the most decisive single factor in the collapse of the Japanese economy and logistic support of Japanese military and naval power. Submarines accounted for the majority of vessel sinkings and the greater part of the reduction in tonnage."

INDEX

Abe, Toshio, 351, 352
Abukuma, 337
Aden Maru, 83
Adkins, James Alvin, 328
air power, 206, 243
Akagi, 42, 43, 49–50
Akashisan Maru, 256
Akitsu Maru, 346, 347
Akitsuki, 338, 340
Alaska, 116
Albacore, 88, 95, 285–86
Allen, Nelson John, 225
Allied POWs, 343–44
Allies, 133, 169, 206
Alston, Augustus Howard, Jr., 138–39
Amagiri, 160
Amberjack, 88–89, 147
Ambruster, Stephen Henry, 84, 122
Anderson, William Robert, 92–93, 137
Andrews, Charles Herbert, 184–187, 270–71
Angler, 303–5, 328, 333
Anyo Maru, 365
Aoba, 90, 329, 332, 340
Aparri, 14
Apogon, 296
Aratama Maru, 261
Archerfish, 288, 351–53, 367
Argonaut, 144–45
Arima Maru, 141
Arita Maru, 358
Asahi, 66
Asakaze, 312
Ashley, James Henry, Jr., 343, 344
Asukazan Maru, 302
Atago, 332

Atlanta, 96
atomic bombs, 378
Attu, 169, 171
Atule, 339
Austin, Marshall Harlan ("Cy"), 279–80
Australia, 41, 72
Aylward, Theodore Charles, 18, 33
Azer, John Behling, 112–13, 139
Azusa, 327

Bacon, Barton Elijah, Jr., 19, 33
Baker, Harold Edward, 61
Bang, 258–60, 293–95, 347, 349
Banister, Alan Boyd, 298–99, 343
Barb, 291–93, 322–27, 344–45, 363–66
Baskett, Thomas Slack, 74
Bass, Raymond Henry ("Benny"), 198, 200, 202, 204–5, 255–56
Bataan Death March, 272
Batfish, 328, 367
Batopaha Maru, 321
Beach, Edward Latimer ("Ned"), 115
    at Midway, 53
    and Morton, 157
    Navy Cross to, 370
    on *Tirante*, 368
    on *Trigger*, 174–76, 222, 243–244, 261–63
Becker, Albert Lilly, 328
Becuna, 356
Bella Russa, 256
Benitez, Rafael Celestino ("Ralph"), 331
Bennett, Carter Lowe, 107
"Ben's Busters," 322

383

Dr B

① Hearing Test

② Specialist —

Fall ?

✱ Rear ADM. U.S Sub. Commander – Pacific Region.

ABOUT THE AUTHOR

CLAY BLAIR, JR., was born in Lexington, Virginia, in 1925. He served in the U.S. Navy in World War II, volunteering for submarine service. He attended submarine school (including a cruise on an S-boat) and was attached to the tender *Sperry* for four months at the advance submarine base, Apra Harbor, Guam. In 1945 he made the last two long war patrols of *Guardfish*, the first off Honshu, February to April, the second off Honshu and Hokkaido during May and June. Rising to the rank of Quartermaster 2nd Class, he qualified in submarines and was decorated with the Submarine Combat Insignia and the Asiatic-Pacific Theater medal with three battle stars. After the war, Mr. Blair joined a submarine reserve unit, making a summer cruise in a newer fleet submarine.

As a Washington journalist for Time-Life and the *Saturday Evening Post* from 1950 to 1960, Mr. Blair followed submarine developments closely and came to know many wartime submarine skippers with whom he spent many hours "diving the boats" and analyzing the submarine war. He was the first journalist to go to sea on the new *Tang*-class submarine *Trigger*, the guided missile submarine *Barbero*, and the first to write about the nuclear-powered submarine *Nautilus*, and her "father," Captain Hyman G. Rickover. He led a successful journalistic crusade to retain Rickover in the navy and subsequently was one of the first journalists to make a sea voyage on *Nautilus*. In later years he inspected and wrote about nuclear-powered Polaris submarines and the nuclear-powered attack submarine *Guardfish*.

Mr. Blair has published three previous books on submarines: *The Atomic Submarine and Admiral Rickover*; *Nautilus 90 North*, the best-selling account of the *Nautilus* voyage beneath the Arctic ice cap, which was published in twenty-six countries; and *Pentagon Country*, a novel centering on the controversy over the navy's submarine weapons system of the near future, Trident.

He is also the author of *The Strange Case of James Earl Ray*, *The Board Room*, *The Archbishop*, *The Pentagon*, *Scubal* and *Silent Victory*.

BANTAM WAR BOOKS

Introducing a new series of carefully selected books that cover the full dramatic sweep of World War II heroism—viewed from all sides and in all branches of armed service, whether on land, sea or in the air. Most of the volumes are eye-witness accounts by men who fought in the conflict—true stories of brave men in action.

Each book in this series has a dramatic cover painting plus specially commissioned drawings, diagrams and maps to aid readers in a deeper understanding of the roles played by men and machines during the war.

FLY FOR YOUR LIFE by Larry Forrester
The glorious story of Robert Stanford Tuck, Britain's greatest air ace, credited with downing 29 enemy aircraft. Tuck was himself shot down 4 times and finally captured. However, he organized a fantastic escape that led him through Russia and back to England to marry the woman he loved.

THE FIRST AND THE LAST
by Adolf Galland
The top German air ace with over 70 kills, here is Galland's own story. He was commander of all fighter forces in the Luftwaffe, responsible only to Goëring and Hitler. A unique insight into the German side of the air war.

SAMURAI by Saburo Sakai with
Martin Caidin & Fred Saito
The true account of the legendary Japanese combat pilot. In his elusive Zero, Sakai was responsible for downing 64 Allied planes during the war. *SAMURAI* is a powerful portrait of a warrior fighting for his own cause. (May)

BRAZEN CHARIOTS by Robert Crisp

The vivid, stirring, day-by-day account of tank warfare in the African desert. Crisp was a British major, who in a lightweight Honey tank led the British forces into battle against the legendary Rommel on the sands of Egypt. (June)

REACH FOR THE SKY by Paul Brickhill

The inspiring true story of Douglas Bader. The famous RAF fighter pilot who had lost both legs, Bader returned to the service in World War II as a combat pilot and downed 22 planes in the Battle of Britain. Shot down, Bader survived the war in a German prison camp. (July)

COMPANY COMMANDER
by Charles B. MacDonald

The infantry classic of World War II. Twenty-two-year-old MacDonald, a U.S. infantry captain, led his men in combat through some of the toughest fighting in the war both in France and Germany. This book tells what it is really like to lead men into battle. (September)

Bantam War Books are available now unless otherwise noted. They may be obtained wherever paperbacks are sold.